When serial ▮▮▮▮▮▮ *captured and* ▮▮▮▮▮▮▮ *they said the horror was over. They said he would never kill again. Tell that to his latest victims. . . .*

Using the wrench, he bashed a hole in the thick ice several feet away. He dragged her body over to the hole and laid her next to it. He lifted her stiff body and lowered it into the icy water. She sank down partway into the water, then stopped. The arms wouldn't fit through the hole, so he unlocked the handcuffs and threw them aside. Then he pushed *it* through the ice and *it* sank down, the long hair bobbing for a moment before being consumed by the black, chilled water. He threw in her shoes and clothes, then picked up the handcuffs and put them in his back pocket.

He pulled out a Marlboro, lit it and began to walk back to the car. The snow had already covered the tracks they had made while walking out. No doubt the ice would freeze over again that night, eliminating all traces of his activity till the spring.

The Cabriolet started right up. *I love Volkswagens,* he thought . . .

THE STRANGER RETURNS

MICHAEL R. PERRY

POCKET STAR BOOKS

New York   London   Toronto   Sydney   Tokyo   Singapore

An *Original* Publication of POCKET BOOKS

A Pocket Star Book published by
POCKET BOOKS, a division of Simon & Schuster Inc.
1230 Avenue of the Americas, New York, NY 10020

ISBN: 0-671-73495-4

First Pocket Books printing October 1992

10 9 8 7 6 5 4 3 2 1

POCKET STAR BOOKS and colophon are registered
trademarks of Simon & Schuster Inc.

Cover art by Jane Sterrett

Printed in the U.S.A.

To members of *The Casa:*
Crager, Tom, Bob, Nicole & Gavin

THE STRANGER RETURNS

Some do the deed with many tears,
And some without a sigh:
For each man kills the thing he loves
Yet each man does not die.

OSCAR WILDE, "The Ballad of Reading Gaol"

January 1989

The mob of citizens waited impatiently in the cold just before dawn for news of a violent act they believed would give them some peace of mind. Groups of drunken students waved pickets with vengeful taunts like Fry Baby Fry and Back to Hell Where You Came From. A group of blue-collar workers sang an obscene variation of a popular tune, improvising verses as they warmed their hands over a fire burning in an oil drum. The drum had been stolen from the beach; the Coppertone ad changed from Tan Don't Burn to Ted Do Burn. A young girl toddled up to the drum and threw in a Ken doll dressed in prison blues; the crowd cheered as her proud father lifted her to his shoulders for all to admire. The only dissent came from a small cadre of nuns, holding signs proclaiming All Life Is Sacred, Only God Can Take a Life. They stood away from the main throng. Their faith in the almighty was not resolute enough to make them believe that the man for whom the vigil was kept would be spared.

The steel gray sun slipped over the wall of Florida State Prison's Q Wing and illuminated a solitary figure standing apart from both groups. Web Sloane had been in Florida one week. When he was younger, he would have condemned capital punishment. Then he could have successfully argued with the students in his classes against the violence of the state. Yet those times were a fading memory. He was a different man now, leading a different life.

He thought often of happier times but had finally recognized the futility of nostalgia and the stress of living in the past. Web knew he must get on with his life, and he intended to against every straining emotion in his body.

For twelve years, Web had been raising Joyce, his second daughter, by himself. Above all, he felt he owed her the chance to have a normal, happy childhood or at least as normal as possible. Joyce was extremely outgoing and personable when she wanted to be but could swing into a black mood in an instant, drawing up into herself, cutting off the world. Just fifteen, Joyce threatened to become as beautiful as his first daughter had been, with sweeping eyebrows and long, wavy chestnut hair. *Vicki's long brown hair, parted in the center, had attracted the killer. Part of his modus operandi. He always lured pretty, dark-haired girls . . . usually their hair was parted in the middle . . . always strangled them or beat them to death once he had his way . . .* Web wrenched his thoughts away from the images with near-physical effort.

He had come to the prison not from a desire for revenge, but from a need to bring closure to this horrifying episode in his life. In only a few minutes, the man who killed Vicki would himself be put to death. Web put on his hat to keep the sun out of his eyes. It would be only a little while now. After waiting twelve years on the slim chance that Vicki would come home, Web Sloane was very accustomed to waiting. He folded his arms and waited some more.

Nine days earlier Sloane had been washing Joyce's car when a Western Union truck pulled up. Web signed for a telegram sent by the Florida Board of Rehabilitation. It read:

Information concerning the disappearance of Victoria Anne Sloane has recently been made available in a videotaped interview with prisoner Theodore Robert Bundy. Please call Warden's Office for details.

Sloane called the number, spoke briefly to an officer Blount, and caught the next plane from Seattle to Miami. Two hours later he was registered in the run-down Good-Nite Motel close to the enormous prison complex. It was past midnight when Sergeant Dobson, a thin pale man with a terse manner, came to the hotel with a portable videotape player and a videotape. Dobson dutifully checked Web's identification and noted it on a pad of paper he kept in his jacket pocket. Web signed a long printed form without reading it.

Because the room lacked a television, Sloane and the police officer went to the reception desk, which had the only TV in the motel. Web felt uncomfortable about seeing the tape in a public place, but he had no choice. The office was thick with the clerk's cigar smoke, which dried Web's throat.

A single couch rested against a gray unwashed window, reeking from the dozens of drinks spilled on it over the years. The red carpet had been peeled up in one corner, exposing bare cement. The glass on the cigarette machine was broken. It looked as if it had been out of order for months. Outside the door a scrawny gray puppy, abandoned and covered with sores, emitted a mournful whine, then pressed its paws against the transparent lobby door, as if longing to find warmth and companionship. None was offered.

On the television mounted high above the lobby, in full view of the clerk, Sloane and the sergeant watched the blurry black and white videotape, a copy of a copy of a copy.

A flickering image of Bundy talked for a few minutes about inconsequential subjects—did the interviewer bring cigarettes, what book he was reading, how his Supreme Court appeal was going—and then without missing a beat said, "Let's look at some pictures."

Web's heart beat faster, and his face flushed. He breathed hard as the videotape played.

On the television, only the smiling, good-looking prisoner could be seen. He might as well have been talking about his favorite recipes, he seemed so relaxed. The interviewer, off-camera, held up pictures that were only visible in the bottom of the frame, blurred.

Bundy examined a picture, smiled, and said, "Yes. That one's from Salt Lake, right? I can confirm that one. Let's see the next picture . . . can't tell about that one."

The interviewer said something that couldn't be heard. Bundy laughed in response. Then he lit a cigarette and took a long drag.

"Let's see some more."

A pause. Off-camera, the sound of rustling paper.

"I can confirm. That one's from Seattle, right?"

He paused and listened to the interviewer say something.

"I don't know, what'll convince you? It definitely was one. I confirmed."

He paused and puffed on the Marlboro that the interviewer had given him.

"I can give you some more information. That one played saxophone. I kept the saxophone at home for several months before selling it. I don't remember what I did with her body . . . afterward."

Web turned off the television. Vicki had played saxophone in the school marching band. The girl Bundy referred to as *"that one"* had been Web's daughter.

The edges of Web Sloane's vision started to go black. Nothing in his life had ever produced such an immediate and profound physical effect. The room started to blur and it was sweltering hot; the clerk's cigar smoke sat in the back of his throat like a tongue depressor.

Web found himself outside the building in the parking lot, wretching. The repulsive dog approached, then dropped its bone to watch Web, as if sensing his emotions.

"That one" was Web's daughter Vicki.

Again, Web threw up.

Although he had always understood logically that Vicki must have been picked up by Bundy, the emotion of knowing for certain was more than he had ever anticipated.

He had always told himself she wouldn't be coming home, but now he knew. He had always thought Bundy had taken her, but now he knew. The difference between deducing, rationally accepting, and actually knowing was profound.

Now he knew what Bundy had done with his daughter, and he was disgusted. Now he knew Vicki's body had been dumped in some unholy place, alone. Now Web knew the doorbell would never ring one night with Vicki's surprise return.

Web had been hyperventilating. Sergeant Dobson, videotape in hand, stood a distance away and watched. Dobson was accustomed to delivering bad news and knew nothing he might say would help. Web got hold of himself, forcing himself to breathe regularly to keep from passing out.

"I'm okay," he told the cop.

"Do you have any family here?" asked Dobson.

"No."

"Let's get some coffee."

"No. I'll be okay." Web went back to his seedy, stuffy room in the hotel and lay awake listening to trucks pass in the distance and to the periodic yelps of the diseased mongrel outside his window. In his mind he played over and over again the few sentences the man on the videotape had said.

"That one's from Seattle."

"That one played saxophone."

Anger brought on by despair shot through Web's veins like venom. Many nights he had imagined scenarios where Vicki was really fine, living on her own somewhere else in the world. He had tried to imagine what she might look like now, what she might be doing, in case he saw her on the street. But now he realized it was all foolish. Vicki Sloane had died more than a decade earlier at the hands of a perverted killer.

Her remains probably would never be found. Web would stay in Florida another week until the execution in case the killer chose to remember where Vicki's bones languished. He considered begging the authorities to let him ask Bundy himself. But he knew if he ever met Bundy face-to-face, nothing and no one could keep him from trying to kill the man.

Web had thought that to know for certain would give him some peace of mind. But now Web clearly his daughter's suffering and death, images he had never allowed his mind's eye to picture during years of meticulous, methodical searching. Now Web Sloane was not sure if he would ever again know peace of mind.

". . . the serial sex slayer will be put to death in the electric chair within the hour," read the earnest late-night anchor. "Convicted of the murders of three women in Florida and suspected in the deaths of more than fifty others across the country, Theodore Robert Bundy will be executed today for the 1978 murder of a twelve-year-old girl . . ."

The guest in room 114 of the San Francisco Grove Hotel leaped out of the bathtub and pulled the plug on the television. The handsome man with the intense eyes poured the last few sips of Dom Perignon into a plastic hotel cup and knocked it back. The doorbell rang.

"Bring it in, please!"

The girl from room service was beautiful and innocent. She giggled and bounced on her heels as she held out the bottle; a sly grin graced her ripe full lips. "Got yer champagne, dude!"

The man wondered why kids in California sounded so different from those in other parts of the country. He wrapped a towel around himself, leaned out of the bathroom door, and held out a fifty-dollar bill. His eyes dilated as he looked at the girl.

"No way do I got that much change, man. It's after hours and I'm not even supposed to bring booze up after 2 A.M."

"Keep it."

"Thanks, man! Anything else I can do, just ring."

fight the temptation, be careful, careful

"Lock the door on your way out."

After hearing the door click, the lean muscular man went into the hotel room and listened to the girl's footsteps fade down the hall. *HE would have tried something funny with her. That was his way with the world. But now he's dead and I'm much smarter and I won't ever make such obvious mistakes.* He shook the champagne bottle and popped the cork.

Champagne sprayed the room, and the man held the bottle over his head like a World Series winner. The sticky wine spilled down his body.

He turned on the radio to a pop station and started doing a little dance. The towel fell to the floor.

Naked, manic, and covered with suds, he hoisted the bottle high into the air.

"The killer is dead!" he said to no one.

He danced a crazed jig and shook the bottle again, soaking the room. Then he threw the bottle across the room. It smashed the mirror. He laughed.

"The killer is dead!"

He caught a view of himself in the cracked glass and turned to face his reflection. He thought he looked pretty good, even nude and covered with bubbles. He moved right up to the mirror and ran his finger along the broken glass. *Everything he did was wrong and he got caught and now his debt is paid.*

"The killer is dead!"

Then he focused on the reflection of the sharklike black pupils set in his bright, piercing eyes, leaned into the mirror, and whispered.

"Long . . . live . . . the killer."

The next morning the graveyard shift clerk at the Grove Hotel lost his job. The guest in 114 had left without checking out, after breaking the lamps, the TV, and a mirror. The credit card the guest had used to register came up stolen. The night man's only excuse was, "He seemed like a decent guy. I thought he was just a businessman or something."

The long hallway was brightly lit and smelled of ammonia. The prisoner walked down the corridor in shackles, examining the few parts of the institution he hadn't seen before. *So this is death row,* he thought. *Looks just like the rest of the prison.* He stared into the television cameras blankly, refusing to snarl like the monster they all believed him to be or scream and cry like the coward they hoped he'd become. The 50 cc of Thorazine the doctor had injected helped the prisoner maintain a measured gait, and the seventy-odd pounds of chains he carried forced him into the plodding walk of the condemned.

The combination of lack of sleep and the drugs made time seem fragmented, like waking up from a drinking binge every few minutes. Now he was sitting down. Now he felt cold steel against his leg, against his back. Now he heard bits and pieces of a droning voice: "In fulfillment of the sentence handed down by the great state of Florida, you, Theodore Robert Bundy, shall have an electric current passed through your body until you are pronounced dead." Cold steel and a damp sponge touched his newly shaven head. A mask was fastened obscuring his face.

When the venetian blinds were opened, the mask prevented him from seeing the three dozen faces staring at him through the glass, like a monkey in the zoo. There was no letter from the governor. There were no more appeals to any

7

court. In another room a hooded female executioner, paid six hundred dollars for the morning's work, pushed a button. The prisoner's hands and teeth clenched as two thousand volts surged through his body. Breath exploded out of his lungs. *My ears are on fire my head is on fire must put it out,* he thought, and instinctively he tried to raise his arms; as in a dream, they wouldn't move. Urine steamed on the hot metal touching his leg. It seemed like the fire would consume everything, then all went black. An odor similar to that of roasting pork permeated the room as the prisoner's flesh literally cooked. A life had been terminated by the will of the People of the state of Florida.

Outside the prison, Web heard a crescendo of noise from the crowd. He moved closer to the prison wall. A voice from a public announcement system echoed against the high concrete walls, and the crowd hushed. "Theodore Robert Bundy," the loudspeaker announced, "was pronounced dead at 7:16 A.M. eastern daylight time."

Web just walked away. The football game style cheering sounded as if he were hearing it through cotton balls stuffed in his ears. He walked across the muddy field, down the straight, flat road leading away from the complex, and got into his car. The day was warming up.

Web had several hours before his plane left for Seattle. He went through a McDonald's drive-through and ordered an Egg McMuffin and a large coffee. The pimply Latino teenager who took his order asked him, "Didja hear about Ted? He's dead." Web slowly nodded. It seemed everyone in the world was following this story.

As he drove to the motel, the sun burst through the clouds, warming up the world. He sat on a rickety bench in front of the motel and began to eat his breakfast. The motel owner, screaming in Arabic, shooed the stray dog out of the motel. The mutt squealed as it was hit with a broom, then sat a respectful distance from Web, watching him eat.

Web took pity and shared half his sandwich with the animal. By night, the mutt had repulsed him, but now it only seemed lonely and forlorn.

"Good boy, there, eat it."

It took the food from his hand. In spite of its bad

condition, the animal seemed to have a good temperament and sat by Web, wagging its tail. Web hadn't allowed himself or his daughter Joyce to get a dog since Vicki's disappearance. Vicki had been a great lover of animals; pets always reminded him of her. But this dog was different. Or maybe, Web realized, somehow he himself was now different, now that Bundy was dead.

Several hours after the macabre news, playing fetch with the stray mongrel in the brown strip of grass adjacent to the motel, he had to admit to himself he did feel better because Bundy was dead. He would put this difficult episode behind him. He decided to adopt the dog, scabs and all. Web Sloane would start a new life with his daughter Joyce and never think of Ted Bundy again. He knew now he had the strength to do it.

2

April 1989

Sara Chandler couldn't think of a graceful way to excuse herself from the speech at the fund-raising dinner for the Bay Area Opera Lovers so she just stood up and left. She believed it was either the crab salad on crackers or the stuffy banquet room that caused the wave of dizziness to grip her, never considering the three Gibsons she had downed in quick succession. Sara didn't feel like saying good-bye to the only person who had talked to her, an old fart who kept trying to look down her expensive low-cut dress, so she made a hasty exit and quickly found the bathroom.

"Are you all right, Ma'am?" asked the British maid who passed out warm towels and combs in the rest room.

"It's just hot in there," said Sara, embarrassed that someone else was present.

"The air conditioner's broken. Here, drink this." The woman filled a glass with water and handed it to Sara.

"You seem awfully young for the opera crowd."

"I love opera," Sara lied.

Only twenty years old, she'd attended the fund-raiser because her uncle, who hadn't even bothered to show, paid for the two-hundred-dollar ticket. Sara believed that High Culture might help get her into the right circles. She drank the water, and it made her feel a little better.

"Do you have any Visine?"

"Yes ma'am," answered the maid, pulling a half-empty bottle from a glass shelf filled with toiletries.

"Thanks." Sara liked being called "ma'am."

She put a couple drops in each eye, but it only made them feel worse. As soon as she ran her fingers through her long brown hair, the maid was right there with a little box of brushes and combs.

After freshening herself up, Sara looked for a tip. She had a special glossy black purse that she had bought for one hundred twenty-nine dollars to match her dress, but all it contained was some makeup and her car keys.

"I forgot to bring any money," she said to the maid.

"Don't worry about it, honey! You don't need money for what you do." The maid was angry, but Sara didn't care.

She walked down the hallway and peered into the banquet room. Some famous diva was performing an unrecognizable aria for the dinner crowd. She quietly closed the door, thinking she'd wait till the song was over to reenter.

"It's unbelievable how hot it is in there," whispered a man's voice.

A smiling man was standing so close behind her she felt his breath on her neck. Startled, she whipped around, then saw that it was another opera patron: a trim, late thirty-something man in a tuxedo.

"I know!" she said excitedly, then lowered her voice to a whisper. "Is it like this every year?"

"The last couple years have been fine. I think it's just a problem with the hotel they're using this year."

They moved away from the door. Sara liked the smell of the man's cologne.

"My uncle said they've always held it here," she said.

"Is he inside?"

"No, he couldn't make it so I had to come by myself."

"That's too bad." The man kept smiling as his eyes glanced down the empty hallway.

"Tell you the truth, I don't know anything about opera. What's that she's singing?" Sara asked.

"Ah, that is from *Madame Butterfly*, one of my favorites."

"I've heard of that," Sara laughed.

A round of applause signaled that the performance was over. Sara cracked the door open, and the man jumped away from the door. She noticed that in spite of his tuxedo, he was wearing loafers. Odd. But he *was* cute.

"You coming back in?"

"No, I think I'll just wait a little. Too darn hot."

"Okay."

Sara returned to the table at the edge of the room and looked in the program to see how much longer it would be. There was at least another hour of entertainment, followed by the fund-raising auction. An older woman dripping with jewels seated next to her tried to make small talk.

"That was some performance!"

"Oh yes. I've always loved *Madame Butterfly*," said Sara, hoping to impress.

"No, no, she was singing the final aria from *Faust*. But it was beautiful."

After a speech from the president, Sara felt her bare back sticking to the chair from sweat. The chocolate mousse made her feel nauseated so she excused herself and left.

The cool night air in the parking lot revived her somewhat. Sara felt guilty leaving a two-hundred-dollar dinner but knew she could convince her uncle that she'd stayed until the end. She found her Cutlass, got in, and turned the ignition key.

Click.

"Goddammit." She thought she must have left the lights on but checked and they seemed to be off. She turned the key back and forth several times, but the engine obstinately refused to come to life.

"I can't believe it!"

A pair of headlights moved slowly closer across the parking lot, and Sara got out and waved. The car, a Volkswagen Cabriolet, pulled up right next to her car.

"Excuse me, do you have jumper cables?" she shouted.

The window on the Cabriolet came down, and she saw the friendly man she'd met in the hallway.

"Hi. I guess you decided to leave."

"Yeah, but my car won't start. You don't have jumper cables, do you?"

"I just happen to." He immediately produced a shiny new pair of jumpers from the passenger seat and got out.

"I could call AAA if you don't want to get all dirty in your tuxedo," she offered.

"No problem. By the way, my name's Alan DeVries."

"I'm Sara. Thanks for the help."

He immediately went to work, quickly finding the hood latch on her car and connecting the two car batteries. Then he started his own car.

"Okay, try starting it now," he yelled over the engine.

She turned the key. Again, nothing.

"It's not doing any good!" she shouted back.

He turned off his car and walked over to her window.

"It's probably a fuse," he offered.

"I'll just call AAA. If it doesn't start, they'll tow me," she said.

The man clasped his large hands tightly together and shook his head.

"Don't call them. It's just a fuse. I'm sure it's just a fuse." The knuckles of his clasped hands began to turn white.

He opened the door of her car and helped her out. "I know what I'm doing." He kneeled on the ground, reached up behind the accelerator pedal, and extracted a little glass vial with two metal ends.

"See? This is the ignition fuse. Forty cents to replace it and you're on your way." He shook it at her. "Give me the keys. Maybe we can just swap this with another fuse and you'll be driving off in one minute."

Sara obeyed, hoping that he was right. She was anxious to leave.

The man fiddled around on the car floor for a minute, then sat in the driver's seat and tried the key. *Click.* Nothing happened.

"You just need to get a fuse. Any service station will have one," he said.

He got out of the car and shut the door.

"I'm sure there's a good station right around here."

He closed both hoods then opened the passenger door of his Cabriolet.

"Come on."

"Are you sure it's okay? I don't want to waste your whole night fixing my car."

"I don't mind. I've got nothing pressing—I was supposed to be at the Opera Ball anyway," he said.

"That's very kind of you."

"I'll have you running in fifteen minutes. I promise." He smiled at her, a warm smile. She had been warned since childhood about getting in strangers' cars, but there was something compelling in his warm blue eyes, something that made her believe he really would fix her up faster than the Auto Club. Besides, he was an opera guy—cultured, maybe even rich. She got in his car.

The guard at the edge of the parking lot nodded at them as they left, then returned to his racing form.

"Good thing I was there when I was," offered DeVries.

"Yeah."

"It's amazing the kinds of things that can happen to a woman when she goes out by herself. You could have been stranded, or who knows what might have happened."

"Well, it's a pretty safe hotel."

"But I mean dressed the way you are, you know."

"Oh, this is nothing fancy. You should have seen some of the really rich women there," she giggled.

He ran a red light.

"There's a gas station," said Sara, pointing to a well-lit Shell station.

"That one's no good. I know a place just a little further that's much better. I know the mechanic."

"What's wrong with it?"

"It's a bad station. You don't know what could happen there, really!"

"What?"

"Think of it, a single girl going into a gas station in this part of town, uh, displaying her charms so openly." He raised his hands apologetically and laughed. "I just mean you're not very covered up, and a mechanic or some bad person not accustomed to seeing high-society women might

13

get the wrong idea and you could be in trouble." The man spoke very fast. He could hardly get the words out. He laughed again. "You know?"

"Oh."

Sara halfheartedly laughed, then straightened the strap on her dress. She kept an eye on the driver.

"I'll take care of you. We'll go to my mechanic and he'll give us a fuse and we'll be okay. I just don't want you to get hurt."

They approached another red light, and he didn't slow down.

"It's red!" she yelled.

He stomped on the brakes. There was a moment of silence at the empty intersection. Gently, Sara tried the door handle. It came off in her hand.

"Can I get out? Please?"

"No! Anything could happen. Don't you know? Don't you know what happens to a girl going out by herself? What are you thinking?"

The light turned green, but he didn't move the car forward. Sara looked for a way out. She rattled the window crank. It was stuck.

"Look. I don't know anything about you, just let me get out and I'll take care of my car by myself. Just please let me out," she said.

"How can I let you out in this part of town? Look at your dress. I can see right up your dress!"

He slapped his hand onto her thigh.

"Don't you know what men think when they see that?"

He yelled so furiously that bits of spittle hit her face.

Sara tried to force the window crank. It spun and spun, but nothing happened. She started to pound on the glass.

"Let me out! Please, please let me out!"

He pulled her away from the window and wrapped his arm tightly around her neck. He moved his face right next to hers and stared in her eyes. "Don't mess up my car. Get with the program, okay? Nothing's going to happen. Trust me on this." He groped inside her dress, laughing.

She could hardly breathe. The man pulled something from the glove compartment with his free hand. Sara felt an electric jolt go through her body, and then she blacked out.

When she regained consciousness, she looked around and saw she was in a deserted parking lot behind a closed store. She felt the cold steel of handcuffs around her wrists and panicked, kicking the man.

"Let me go! What are you going to do? Let me go!"

No one other than her abductor heard her cries. The man walked a few steps away to his car and emerged holding something about the size of a pack of cigarettes. As he approached she saw that it was a stun gun. A blue spark flew between two electrodes, producing an eerie buzzing sound.

"Don't make me use this," he said.

Sara kicked him in the knees. The next thing she felt was incapacitating pain rushing from the nape of her neck. She collapsed.

The man picked her up by her shoulders, kneeling behind her.

Oh my God Jesus please let it be over please. Tears ran down her cheeks as her bare knees scraped rhythmically on the rough pavement. She tried to think about something else, anything else, as the man grunted an animal growl. He momentarily stopped, and Sara felt pain spreading through her body. Her left knee had a deep cut in it. She was terrified.

"Please, please, stop, you're hurting me."

"Shut up!"

She knew he couldn't go on forever. She pictured the woman singing at the dinner, and the haunting melody of her aria ran through her mind. He let go of her right shoulder; it was bleeding from his grip. Then something closed around her neck. Her breath was cut off.

Sara blacked out.

When her bones were found eleven months later outside of Tico, California, there were not even enough fragments to make a positive identification. Most of her remains had been carried off by wild animals. Jane Doe 90-4, the fourth unidentified female corpse found in Vine County in 1990, was determined by the coroner to have most likely died from a massive cranial fracture caused by a blunt object.

What was left of Sara's skeleton was stored in a refrigerated drawer at the county sheriff's morgue next to the bones of Jane Doe 90-5, found at the same site. The only way the coroner knew there were two bodies, not one, was the extra metatarsus fragments—a surplus of foot bones—found at the site.

3

September 1990

Joyce Sloane took a meandering route on the walk home from her new high school, exploring Berkeley, getting a feel for the neighborhood where she'd be spending her senior year. Verdugo Street was only two blocks from home and yet contained some of the fanciest estates in the city. She spied a massive garden with yellow roses and hot pink geraniums and decided that she must have some for herself. Without breaking pace, she headed directly across the large lawn for the garden and casually selected a fine bouquet.

No doubt they have a professional gardener and probably don't even enjoy what they've got. These flowers won't even be missed, and I'll appreciate them a lot more than whoever lives here, Joyce thought. *Of course, if my Dad found out, he'd be pissed.* She was sure she'd escaped undetected. She watched the street till a white van passed by, then headed for home.

Flowers she swiped always smelled better than any others to Joyce, who, after reading Jack Kerouac for the first time that summer, had decided that she would be a bohemian, cutting a wide swath through life and savoring every experience. She half-skipped till she got to her own street, remembering she'd read somewhere that flowers belong to everyone.

When she turned the corner onto her suburban street, Joyce watched the same white van pass her again and park in her driveway. It had a satellite dish on its roof. A man in a dark blue suit got out and walked toward her. She held the flowers down by her side, fearful she'd been caught.

"Hi, you must be Joyce Sloane," said the man in the suit, using a slick, velvety voice. Hair spray had hardened his man-made blond hair into an immovable helmet, and he held out a hand like he'd known Joyce all her life.

"I don't think I know you," said Joyce, stopping in her tracks.

"You sure you don't know me? Think hard . . ." he said, grinning as if he believed she cared to figure out his name. Although Joyce hadn't returned his handshake, he kept his hand outstretched.

"Okay, you're Rumplestiltskin. If you'll excuse me, I'm on my way home."

She passed the man, who turned and walked beside her. "I'm Clinton Bernard!"

"Okay, you're Clinton Bernard. Congratulations," she said, speeding up. Only two more houses to go.

"Oh come on. Surely you've heard of my show 'Suspect at Large'?"

"Yeah, I heard it sucks. And you'll have to get your van out of our driveway."

The man blocked her path.

"Look, we're doing a TV special about families of tragedy on my show, and we want to talk to you and your dad."

She pushed him to the side.

"Sorry, Rumplestiltskin. If you'll excuse me, I've got to go inside and call the police. There's an *asshole* in my driveway."

"Come on . . ." said Clinton Bernard, then ran ahead of her, disappearing around the van.

As Joyce came around the van, she saw that Clinton Bernard was talking with two tanned men in black T-shirts and jeans, one fifty-ish, one twenty-ish, who were setting up a camera and video deck on her lawn. As they adjusted their tripod, they tore patches of turf out of the lawn. She knew her father would be pissed; he had just put in seventeen hundred dollars worth of new grass.

Joyce ducked around the camera crew and got to her front porch just as her father, Web Sloane, walked out, squinting at the bright sunlight.

"Dad, these guys think they're going to interview us for TV. I told them otherwise."

She knew how much he hated reporters. Web smiled at his daughter.

17

"Don't you think it's about time to water the lawn?" he asked her quietly.

"It's getting awfully dry," she said, grinning.

"Hey, guys—wait there a minute," said Web, waving. Clinton Bernard nodded his head theatrically, flashing a perfect smile and waving an "okay" sign with his thumb and index finger.

"Told you they'd come around," Clinton Bernard muttered to the camera crew.

Web opened a green box on the porch, turned a valve, then padlocked the box shut. Father and daughter ducked inside the house just as sprays of water began shooting up all over the lawn.

Through the glass they watched Clinton Bernard's hairdo melt as he ran toward the street, and the unwelcome camera crew scurried to protect their equipment from the water. The older technician yelled at the younger one, then grabbed the camera and held it over his head above the water. Just then, Mud, the gangling family dog, physically grown but still mentally a puppy, ran toward the camera crew, teeth bared for a fight. He leapt on the teetering cameraman, who promptly dropped the camera. Mud growled and snapped at the men as they picked up their gear. The cameraman swore at the dog, then got the gear to the van and packed it up quickly. As they pulled out of the driveway, Clinton Bernard raised his middle finger at them.

First Joyce, then Web began laughing uncontrollably.

"Those guys have been calling me for a week," said Web. "I told them no, no, no, and finally I had to tell them no."

"He came up at me on the sidewalk like a big poodle," said Joyce. She imitated his breathy synthetic voice. "Hullo there TV viewer, I'm Clinton Bernard, and I want to make you a stahr."

"Good riddance. Hey, those are nice flowers," said Web.

"Yeah, I got them from one of our neighbors," said Joyce.

"I told you you'd like Berkeley."

There was a scratching sound at the door.

They opened it and admitted the damp pooch. Web patted him on the head.

"Good Mud, good boy. We hate cameramen, don't we?"

Mud wagged his tail and danced a little ecstatic jig as Web scratched his ears. Web had never for a moment regretted bringing the dog back from Florida.

"What's for dinner, Daddy-O?"

"That darn maid didn't cook anything again," Web replied. They had no maid. "Let's try another of the take-out places."

Ever since moving to Berkeley, their porch had been littered with restaurant delivery menus representing cuisine from every corner of the globe. That night they enjoyed a Thai feast, sharing a liberal portion with Mud, and watched a Chevy Chase movie together. Life was good.

At 5:28 A.M. Web awoke to the shrill "whoop whoop" of a car alarm. He threw on a bathrobe and peered through the bedroom window at the street below. A garbage truck had shaken the motion detector on his neighbor's car. No crime was underway. But Web was constantly vigilant. The circumstances of his life would not permit him to behave otherwise.

In spite of the early hour he was wide awake. His lecture wasn't till 2 P.M. He slipped downstairs to the kitchen. An unopened box from Quality Paperback Book Club sat on his table. He'd forgotten to send in a form, and they had forwarded their main selection. He intended to return the books, but curiosity compelled him to open the package first, just in case it was something good.

Two books were inside: A coffee table book called *A Pictorial History of the English Garden* and a companion how-to volume, *The English Gardener in North America.* Soon he was engrossed in the color photos and the goofy Britishness of the prose. The how-to book featured photographs of a British man, about Web's age, wearing a vest and tie as he worked the soil. Although the man's face was essentially blank, to Web he appeared deeply satisfied. He reflected on how Joyce had enjoyed the flowers given to her by their neighbor.

An hour and a half later Web was standing outside the Builder's Emporium garden supply store when it opened at 7 A.M. By the time he left the store, he'd accumulated nearly three hundred dollars worth of supplies: bulbs, fertilizer, a wheelbarrow, shovels, knee pads, exotic flower tools, and five more how-to books.

Mud watched with great fascination as his owner unloaded the car, then dug up the earth in front of the house and placed bulbs in the ground, each hole's depth precisely measured with a metal ruler. Mud trotted back and forth wagging his tail, trying to get a view of what Web was doing before giving up to sit with his head between his paws, a few feet from his master.

Joyce emerged from the house, a book bag slung over her shoulder, dressed head-to-toe in black, as usual. She put her hands on her hips in a simulated state of shock.

"Hey, Daddy-O! You giving up teaching to become a gardener?"

Web stood up and brushed off his knees. "No, smart aleck. I just thought it would be nice to have some flower gardens. Don't you think so?"

"I think it'd be awesome. I just didn't know you were the 'working with the earth' type."

"By the way, which neighbor gave you those flowers yesterday? I'd like to ask them some questions about the climate and so forth."

Joyce threw her hands up in the air. "You know—I don't remember. It was during the walk home."

"Well, if you see them again, I'd love to meet them."

"Right on, Daddy-O. I gotta get going to school."

She kissed her father quickly on the cheek.

"If your gardening is anything like your cooking we're in real trouble." She laughed. "Bye!"

As Joyce disappeared around the corner, Web remembered something Alice, his late wife, had said seventeen years earlier. Alice was an avid indoor gardener. She'd placed dozens of macrame planters throughout their Seattle home; she had a knack for growing anything from a fern to an exotic orchid. One night in particular stood out:

Alice, very pregnant with Joyce, teetered on a small step ladder, applying liquid fertilizer to an ailing fern. Web walked to her side.

"You should get down, Alice. What if you fall? Maybe I should do your plants for a while, and you can lie down."

Alice laughed, her special chuckle reserved for Web. "I'll be fine. You know, I just thought of something." She climbed down and sat on the step ladder. "I think the qualities that make a good gardener also make a good parent. With plants, you can water them some, but not too much. You can give them food and put them in the light. But you can't pull them out of the ground with your hands. It's a mystery why flowers grow and bloom. You can only help make the conditions right for them to flourish; the rest is an act of faith. Don't you think the same is true of children?"

That night, seventeen years earlier, Web put his hand on Alice's belly and felt the kicking of a new life. Alice was right: The same traits that make a good gardener also make a good parent.

He wondered why he hadn't remembered those words for so long. He reflected on her words as he tamped down the dirt covering his tulip bulbs. Mud, the dog, strutted along proudly behind Web as he carried his new gardening tools into the garage. Then, Web showered and drove to work, thinking about his new flowers and hoping they would grow.

Midlecture, Web didn't notice a Hispanic woman enter his classroom halfway through a presentation on "The Ethics of Data." With the right combination of a difficult, fascinating subject and receptive students, he was unstoppable. Spinning an idea out before students, Web would occasionally find himself stretching the limits of his knowledge, making previously unseen connections and reaching an exhilarating intellectual high ground where everything made sense: a kind of "lecturer's high."

In the sanctity of the lecture hall, Web could temporarily forget his other shortcomings. That morning he'd had an argument with the personnel administration office. *"Where are your health insurance records from Washington? We've asked for them three times, and it's holding up your processing."* He thought that he'd sent them in; but then, details like that often escaped his attention. His focus was always on the bigger picture, and he was embarrassed by an inability to handle the practical details. It often got him into trouble.

U.C. Berkeley had given him an exceptionally sweet deal

to teach whatever he wanted and virtually to handpick students. He was especially fond of today's group and treated them like peers. When he needed to use a difficult equation, he didn't have to stop the mental flow to explain its ramifications. They inevitably understood. Berkeley treated him well, and even better, they had more than doubled the pay he'd gotten at Washington State.

University of Washington—where he had been revered by those few who understood his achievements and intensely disliked by the practical souls who ran the university. Push came to shove when he failed an entire class of eleven graduate business students forced to take his advanced course in statistics. He'd spent months answering peer review board questions and responding to petitions circulated by the Biz School Student Government, all of which he considered nonsense. He believed five words summed up the situation: They didn't do the work. Web eventually prevailed, but after that crisis his stature was under constant fire.

In spite of the many promises made by Berkeley, he knew that sooner or later he would run into problems. But now he was in his element—the lecture hall. Here, everything was perfect.

The class went five minutes past the hour, and when he saw the students become restless, Web excused them. He ceremoniously wiped off the boards and sat down to collect his composure as the students filed out. Lecturing was physically demanding, and the forty-nine-year-old man usually found himself out of breath and lightheaded after a class, as if he'd just run several miles.

When he stood up to collect his notes, the woman approached the podium. She obviously wasn't a student—near his age, she had no notebooks, and she wore an expensive red dress. There was confidence—or arrogance—in the way she carried herself. Even though she wore heels, her posture was perfect.

"Dr. Sloane?"

"Yes, how may I help you?"

The euphoria of lecturing quickly dissipated as he assessed the nature of this intruder into his sanctuary. His hackles were up and he knew why. No one, students or staff, called him "Dr. Sloane." He'd never gotten a Ph.D. If she was from "Suspect at Large," he'd consider calling campus police.

She hesitated a moment before speaking. "Dr. Sloane, I would like to talk to you in private if possible . . ."

"Are you a student? My office hours are on the course outline."

"No, it is another matter entirely. My name is Maria de Rivera."

She had a slight Spanish accent. He clenched his jaw and listened, waiting for the bomb to drop.

"I read about how you, eh, developed the computer system that caught Ted Bundy and that you think perhaps Bundy was involved with your daughter's disappearance . . ."

Sloane cut her off. In an icy tone he said, "And you're making a TV special, right? Number one, I *know* that Bundy killed Vicki. Number two, I'm never talking to another so-called journalist about it again. Now please leave my classroom."

"I did not say I am a journalist, Dr. Sloane." The woman threw her head back, offended.

"Yeah, I wouldn't call what you do journalism either. I've met too many people like you in the past ten years. Ms. de Rivera, I recommend you try to mine some other poor fool's personal tragedy." He scowled at her in a condescending manner.

Without warning she slapped him.

"Dr. Sloane, a friend said you would be the one person who would listen to me, but it is obvious that you are a hardened, bitter man. I am sorry I wasted my time coming here. Good day." Her accent heightened the consonants and made her words sound particularly damning. She grabbed her purse and walked out the door.

Sloane rubbed his cheek, bewildered by the woman. A couple of pieces of paper had fallen out of her purse. He picked them up.

They were flyers marked "Missing Person" with an 800 number. On the front were six photos of a girl. One was a graduation photo. The others were informal snapshots of the girl at a birthday party, skiing, posing with friends. Sloane examined them. She could have been anybody's daughter. On the reverse was a typewritten plea. He read it.

Tanya, please come home.

Tanya Samantha de Rivera, age 17, disappeared from her home near Tico, California, on the night of April 15, 1990. She was last seen wearing a red skirt and black sweater over a blue blouse. A $28,000 reward for any information leading to her return will be paid with absolutely no questions asked.

Tanya, if you are reading this, please come home. Your mother loves you. Your friends miss you. If you are in trouble, I want to help. We suffer every moment you are away and will do anything to help you come home.

I love you,
Mom

A chill slowly worked its way up Sloane's spine. The names, faces, and locations were different, but the situation was identical to what he had gone through a dozen years earlier: the indifference of the police, the anguish of searching for a missing child, the flyers, the desperate individuals trying to make sense out of what was essentially insane. He assumed that the reward money represented every cent Maria de Rivera had.

Web was embarrassed. He ran into the hallway. The woman was nowhere to be seen. He darted out the back door. Swarms of students moved between classes. He jogged toward the nearest parking lot, a couple hundred yards away, his shoes clacking on the pavement. He still held the flyer.

He saw a flash of red near the student union, a hundred yards away. He cut across the muddy field separating them. The woman was stapling flyers to a kiosk. As he watched, she suddenly put her hand up to her eyes as if willing herself to continue stapling. Web approached her, out of breath.

"Ms. de Rivera."

Slowly, she finished fastening a flyer to the board and

turned to face him. She tilted back her head, then gazed at him quizzically, angrily. She studied him for a long moment to decide what his feelings might be.

"Yes?" she said.

Web held out the flyer.

"I just read this." He stopped. "I'm sorry—I didn't understand."

She looked down at the flyer in his hand, and a sort of heaviness seemed to cocoon around her. Her slim, upright figure visibly slumped.

"Can I get you a cup of coffee?" he quickly asked.

"Yes, please," she said, once again drawing herself to her full height.

They sat at a table in a garden outside the student union, sipping cappucino from Styrofoam cups. There was more to her story than appeared in the flyer.

"My daughter Tanya disappeared in April. But a month before that, the bodies of two girls were found in some woods near Tico, sixteen miles from my home. I pray Tanya is safe, but I suspect there may be some connection."

"Why did you come to me?"

"No one else will listen, Dr. Sloane. The county sheriff would not even file a missing person report for two weeks after she was gone. He says Tanya ran away. The FBI says no federal crime has been committed; the state police took a written report that I am sure rests in a drawer in Sacramento. Everyone complains of lack of funds. What they really mean is they do not care."

"I'm not a doctor—call me Web, okay?"

She nodded.

"What agency is following your case, then?"

"Officially, the Vine County sheriff. In reality, no one. Tico, where the girls' bodies were found, is unincorporated but has a little task force working with me."

"That's it?"

"Yes. Four men in Tico and me. Until we can get more law enforcement help, that is all we have."

Web set down his coffee. He knew the desperation she felt.

"I don't know how I could help. I'm not the police, and I don't have any contacts in California. Until last summer, I lived in Seattle."

"You have been through it before, though. And you helped catch Ted Bundy," she said.

"I wrote some computer programs, but only because no one else could or cared to. It was his own stupidity that got Bundy caught. What I did only helped corroborate his actions for the courts."

"Could you come talk to us? Just one day. Tell us how to organize, what to look for. I really do not know where else to turn. The FBI and police are not doing anything."

Web had intended to decline politely, but it was hard to refuse this woman.

"I suppose I could review what you have and write a letter, but that's about all."

She gazed at him a long moment, perhaps bottling her growing anger.

"I understand," she said.

Web saw that she was disappointed. He remembered the frustration of the search: Many give sympathy, but few give assistance. He tried another tack.

"Tell me a little bit about your daughter."

"Like what?"

"Why are you so sure she didn't run away?"

"I am certain she did not run away. Are you going to treat me like a fool, the way the police do?"

"No, you're no fool. I just want to hear the details for myself."

Maria spoke in a hushed voice.

"Tanya was a good girl. *Una muchacha buena.* She played in a softball league, and everyone at her school liked her. That night, she did the dishes and then got on her bike to go study at her best friend's house."

"And?"

"At around eleven I called over there to ask her to come home. Sometimes they just get carried away, and it was a school night. Her parents said Tanya never came over that night. I knew right away something was wrong. I was angry with her for being late, but under the anger was fear. At about 1 A.M. I called the sheriff, who couldn't do anything. He said, 'She'll come home.'"

Web knew that attitude all too well.

"I gave him living hell, pardon me, and told him I would write a letter to everyone above him and to every newspaper in the state unless they sent out a car right then. I was up all night riding around with a deputy."

She balled her hand into a fist. "You know the rest. Tanya's still gone."

Maria appeared quite shaken, and her eyes brimmed with moisture.

"Will you please excuse me, Dr. . . . Web."

Web offered her a handkerchief. She accepted it, stood up, and went into the crowded student union.

Web knew she was a rare person. He had met dozens of parents searching for missing children in his life, and many of them had virtually disintegrated, throwing off the mask of civility that normal life permits, his wife included. Maria had a special dignity in the face of overwhelming circumstances. Grace, they called it. Her personal strength covered the vulnerability that he had witnessed only briefly when she was putting up a flyer and, again, when she excused herself.

She emerged from the student union rejuvenated. He reflected how women use makeup as a kind of protection against the adversities of life.

"Hello, Web."

"Are you okay?"

"I am fine, thank you. Now where were we?"

She was back to business-as-usual.

"I'll write you a letter. What has your task force done so far?" he asked.

"They are primarily concerned with the bodies found in Tico. I am concerned with finding Tanya. Our common ground is in working with groups who help with missing children. And we both want more action by the police. Will you talk to us?"

He was forced to refuse her a second time. He could *not* sabotage his new life with Joyce.

"No. I'm sorry, but I can't."

She pulled a large envelope out of her purse. It was heavy with papers.

"Here. This is what we have uncovered so far. It may be of use to you in composing your letter."

They stood up.

"Should I walk you to your car?"

"No, thank you, Mr. Sloane. I still have much work to do here."

She lifted her purse and disappeared into the throng of students. Web felt slightly guilty denying her, but his precious sense of balance was too hard to achieve. He couldn't decide which was more painful: getting involved or not getting involved. He decided to err in the direction of self-preservation.

That night Web examined the papers Maria de Rivera had given him. Joyce was at a movie, so he had the house to himself, several hours of uninterrupted concentration. He laid out all the available materials in his home office. The previous tenants had used the space as a downstairs bedroom, but Web had installed bookshelves and a mahogany desk. It was this room that had made him want the house: He could close the door and have total privacy or open it and see everyone who came and went. A window to the front yard let him see who was approaching his home before they saw him.

He had newspaper clippings, copies of police reports, photos of the site where the bodies had been found, and about a hundred pages of hand-typed reports gathered by the Tico Investigative Group, the ad-hoc committee to which Maria had referred. There were photos of several dozen missing girls besides Tanya.

The known facts were sketchy. The bones of one unknown female, age range eighteen to twenty-four, and a few other bones from a person presumed to be, but not definitely, female, age range fifteen to thirty years.

Tanya de Rivera had last been seen on April 15. She had no real motive for running away that Web could see, although official investigations tended to indicate "runaway," not "kidnapping." That's what they always assumed and they were usually right, but Web knew there were important exceptions.

The committee had gathered reports of missing girls within a fifty-mile radius from newspapers, the various police departments in the area, and persistent footwork. Sixty-one females from eighteen to thirty-five, including Tanya, had been reported missing since January first—but true to the norm, forty-eight of them had been located or had returned home. A "seventy-five percent success rate" sounds better to taxpayers who support police departments than "thirteen missing girls."

Information was Web's life. He knew that some of the thirteen missing girls would be found. But he also knew that among them might be victims of the same person who had left the bones in Tico. He examined the photos, mostly senior-class portraits and those taken at birthday parties, and searched through the stack of papers for additional information on each girl. There were short biographies for some, letters from parents for others. Some had a history abbreviated to one page, and some had bits of information scattered through various reports: high school grades, make of car, birthmarks, favorite color. The facts gathered were haphazard and disorganized. He had many questions that remained unanswered.

In the early seventies, before his elder daughter's disappearance, Sloane had been at the forefront of artificial intelligence research, working toward his Ph.D. by creating a computerized expert system for identification of insect species. When tragedy befell his family, he abandoned the doctorate and turned all his talents toward developing the Serial Killer Information Database, SKID, for Washington State Police. SKID had identified Bundy as a suspect long before traditional methods, but police had ignored the program's correlations until too late: Bundy escaped to Utah where he claimed yet more victims. Descendants of his software were in use by the FBI and many other state police forces.

In the intervening years his ingenious software, born of despair, had been turned into a bludgeon in the hands of law enforcement technocrats, who added hundreds of secondary and tertiary features that rendered SKID virtually useless. Web's second axiom, elaborated in his textbook *Extracting Meaning from Chaos*, was that having too much information was as bad as having too little. The folder before him might contain clues never to be discovered by the "professionals" in Washington and elsewhere.

He looked at an overdue paper he was supposed to review for the *Journal of Information Science,* but it couldn't hold his attention. Maria de Rivera needed his help. He turned on his personal computer and loaded the micro version of SKID. Painstakingly he spent the next several hours organizing known facts, speculation, and rumor gleaned from the pages before him. He began by entering the probable height of Jane Doe 90-22 and Jane Doe 90-23 determined by the coroner under "Victim Profile."

Several hours later Web knew at least what needed to be asked. Of the thirteen girls still missing, five of them yielded "hot" results in crucial categories: All five had little motivation to run away; they were similar in age to the victims found in Tico; they couldn't be disqualified from the "Obedient/Malleable (Victim) Personality Profile," although he'd still have to ask more questions; and four of the five had left cars behind—virtually unheard of in a runaway situation. The fifth, Tanya, didn't drive. He believed that the scenario he'd put together in just a few hours should be enough to get some additional law enforcement support. However, a simple letter could not explain what he'd discovered. Reluctantly he realized he should visit this group in person. He called Maria's number.

"Hello?"

Maria's voice was vulnerable and slightly startled. For an instant he imagined she was in bed. "Did I wake you up?"

"Mr. Sloane? No, I just got back a little while ago."

"I've reconsidered. I would be pleased to address your group."

On the other end of the phone line Maria grasped for words.

"Oh!—all right—I am very pleased to—thank you, Web. Thank you for doing this."

He arranged to address her group Saturday. It was a relief to be able to help her.

He turned off his computer. It was 11:30 P.M. Web went into the kitchen to see if his daughter Joyce had returned. She hadn't.

He sat in the living room by the door to wait for her return, reading a book called *Teenagers—For the Single Parent*. Web approached parenting like his beloved rock climbing: examine all possibilities for the next step and take the best one. Decide, then act. Even with the danger of falling, hanging off a sheer wall of rock was much less stressful than raising children.

In a trunk at his office were two or three hundred books on parenting, most of which he read once and dumped. The subjects included everything from "Dad & Daughter: The Single Father's Difficult Journey" to "Teaching Young Children about Death and Loss." He'd already gotten most of the "teenager" books, which seemed to advocate wildly different advice from one another. For every book advocating discipline, another suggested restraint; for every writer saying "Don't worry about declining grades," another said bad grades were signs of deeper trouble. The only subject on which every book agreed, and the one thing Web had never done, was to be sure to talk frankly about sex. He figured he'd get around to it eventually.

The book put him promptly to sleep. He awoke with a start when he heard footsteps on the staircase. He checked the clock. It was 1:22. Web jumped out of the La-Z-Boy and ran up the stairs. Joyce was just ducking into the bathroom. He smelled pot smoke on her hair and clenched his teeth.

"Hi, Dad," Joyce whispered.

"It's the middle of the night. Where have you been?"

"Just out. We met some kids at the movie and went over to their house. We watched Letterman."

Web folded his arms and stared into her eyes, trying to determine if she was telling the truth. "You have to let me know where you are."

"Dad, I'm almost eighteen years old."

"Were you smoking?"

"No! Her mother smokes, and it's a small apartment."

She didn't lie very well, but he didn't call her bluff either.

"Next time you don't call to say where you are, you're grounded. Okay, Joyce?"

"Okay," she said, in a tone of exasperated resignation. "Sorry."

Web unfolded his arms. "Joyce, I'm going out of town Saturday and won't be back probably till Sunday night. While I'm away, I don't want you staying out late."

"You got a girlfriend, Dad?"

His eyes widened. It was startling to hear Joyce ask him such a question. "What?"

"A woman called today. I left you a message. It's okay if she's your girlfriend—you could use a little action, Dad." She laughed. Joyce was expert at putting her father off balance.

"She's not my girlfriend! I'm giving a lecture up there, that's all." Web neglected to mention the bodies and the missing girl. He figured that Joyce didn't need to know.

"But Dad, I'm worried about you—who is this woman? What if she *wants* you? She sounded hot to me on the phone . . ."

Web felt the blood rise in his neck. He wasn't comfortable with his daughter's innuendo. "Joyce—enough.".

She made a face at him. He really does need a woman, she thought.

"I'm going to give you the number where I'll be, and I'll call to check up and see if you're okay."

"Roger ten-four, Robo-Dad. Robo-Daughter will obey without fail. Over and out." she said, in a machinelike monotone.

Then, laughing, she said "G'night."

Joyce went into the bathroom. Web returned to his office. He couldn't sleep and chose to use the insomnia to get some work done. He started to look at the paper he was supposed to review but put it down and flipped through Maria's files one more time.

The smell of jasmine came in on the night air, beckoning. Web donned a jacket and went outside for a walk. The air was crisp and still. As he strolled up the street, he noticed that the lights were out in every house. He was king of the neighborhood, traveling undetected through the boulevards of suburbia. The serene night air helped him focus his thoughts. His mind worked so hard he soon found himself at a vacant lot on a steep hill overlooking the city.

Web stopped and looked up at the night sky, then out at the quiet city below. A fog bank was stealthily creeping in, obscuring the street lights, darkening the world. Below the cloud millions of people were asleep, unaware of its presence. Alone on the hill, Web watched the fog thicken until the city disappeared beneath the mist. Then he turned and walked home.

4

Saturday morning Web packed a small suitcase and drove north on Highway 1. He drove past Tico before he realized he'd arrived; a rusted sign stating "Leaving Tico—Come Back Soon" alerted him to the fact. He made a U-turn and drove past two miles of grazing cattle and bean fields before reaching the four-way stop that was the heart of Tico. A three-story hotel, restored to look like a turn-of-the-century inn, dominated the town. Most of Tico could be seen from his vantage point: A grocery, two restaurants, several gift stores catering to the tourist trade, a car repair shop, and a Presbyterian church seemed to be all the town had to offer beyond several dozen small houses.

He entered the hotel lobby. No one sat behind the counter, so he rang the bell. A muscular man of about thirty-five with close-cropped hair emerged from the hallway.

"May I help you?"

"I'm Web Sloane. I'm meeting Maria de Rivera and some others here this afternoon."

"Do you have a reservation?" The desk man put on a pair of reading glasses and opened a leather-bound book.

"I'm not looking for a room. There's some sort of group here, I don't know what they're called, but it's about the police investigation."

There was a long pause. The desk man closed his book and set down his glasses.

"Reporter?"

"No. I'm an acquaintance of Maria de Rivera."

"I see. One moment."

He disappeared into the office again, gently closing the door behind him. Web glanced out the front window. He watched the man run across the street to a restaurant painted in the same old-fashioned style as the hotel. Moments later a balding blond man of about forty came out, untying his cook's smock as he crossed the street. He went to the side of the hotel.

A minute later the blond man emerged from the office, wearing a clip-on tie and jacket. He looked and acted all business. Thick lines encircled his eyes, as if he had lived hard at some point. *Or he is concealing something,* Web thought. He eyed the man suspiciously.

"Mr. Sloane, I'm Peter Rowan."

They shook hands.

"Nice to meet you."

Rowan led Web back to his office, a meticulously neat room dominated by a cherry desk facing two overstuffed chairs. "Rod Butler, a friend of mine who works at the county sheriff's office, gave me your name. I passed it on to Maria. Thanks for coming."

"What's the sheriff's office doing?"

"Unfortunately, not enough. There're only five homicide detectives in all of Vine County, and they're pretty overworked on cases with leads much stronger than the . . ."—he searched for the right word—". . . incident here."

"From what I see, they don't have much to go on."

"The police have no idea who murdered the girls and left their bodies outside of town. Myself and three other merchants in Tico formed a support group to aid them. Maria's searching for her daughter and is afraid that there is a connection, so she's also a member of our group. Mainly we want to get the FBI or state police interested and keep the case active until some resolution is achieved."

His reasons sounded a little shaky. In Web's experience, people other than families of victims wanted to stay as far as possible from a tragic occurrence.

"Why? Why are *you* getting involved?"

Rowan stood, slowly closed the office door, and sat back at his desk.

"Tico is my whole life. When Neil, my . . ."—he briefly hesitated—"partner, and I moved here from San Francisco in 1977, it was a dump. We built a restaurant and this hotel with a little money and a lot of hard work. Half our customers are senior citizens who retire to Tico to get away from the city, and the other half are tourists."

Web was unimpressed. "So?"

"Since the events in the spring, people have lost confidence. Homes are going up for sale. Reservations have been canceled. When we came, Neil and I started the volunteer fire department and paramedic team. We made it a real town. Retirees value that kind of thing. I want Tico to be known as a safe place. It's one of the only things we have to offer."

Web nodded. The hotelier appeared on the level. He assumed that the deep lines around Rowan's eyes must have come from exhaustion. Peter Rowan had taken personal responsibility for the well-being of an entire town.

They went upstairs to the second floor of the old hotel, where Maria and two other men waited by a door, the only one on the hall secured with a padlock. Peter produced a key and took off the lock.

"Thanks for coming, Web," said Maria. She wore tailored slacks and a coral sweater that showed off her slim, proud figure. The brilliant color warmed the tone of her olive complexion.

"This is Dick Gable, who owns the grocery, and Jacob Tiel, from the Presbyterian church."

They went into the hotel room, which had been converted into a kind of office. The bed had been replaced with a folding table surrounded by school chairs. There was a bulletin board crammed with news clippings, dozens of color-coded plastic trays overflowing with papers, a map with pins, three chalkboards covered with text, and a coffee maker. Web was reminded of similar rooms in Colorado, Utah, and Washington he'd seen during his search for Vicki.

The four others sat down silently, waiting for Web to address them.

"Take notes. You've done quite a bit of work so far, but there is still a lot to do. Who is in charge?"

Maria spoke. "I came to Tico and met Peter, and we sort of decided that we could help each other. Dick and Jacob have contributed a lions' share of the work, too, as well as lots of others."

"You need a leader. Someone who can be reached at any time. Breaks come when they come. It might be today, it might be in six months."

They looked around for an answer.

"Maria might be a good leader," offered Jacob, the minister.

"There can be no doubt. If she's in charge, she's in charge." Web's manner was matter-of-fact; there could be no gray areas.

"It's okay with me if it's okay with her," said Peter.

"Can you do it, Maria?" asked Web.

"Yes."

"Then it's done. Let's get her phone number."

All four scribbled the number on paper.

"What, exactly, are you looking for?"

Blank expressions.

"First, let's define what you're doing."

He wrote on a chalkboard as he talked.

"Number 1—find the person who left two bodies near here. Right?

"Number 2—find Mrs. de Rivera's daughter."

Jacob Tiel spoke. "We've come across many interesting occurrences that could help families of runaways. I think we should broaden our scope a little."

Rowan nodded in approval. Web put down the chalk, narrowed his eyes a little and spoke sternly.

"You can find suspicious coincidences anywhere you look. It's extremely important to separate the essential from the irrelevant. The two tasks on this board would be enough for twenty policemen working full-time. I suggest you keep your focus narrow."

Reverend Tiel sat back down. "I see your point."

"How are you organizing your facts?"

Maria answered.

"Just as you see. When some new subject comes up, we start a new basket and put all related information into it."

"That's it?"

"So far."

"Okay." He saw his work was cut out for him. "First, you've got to have access to a computer. In one night I probably assembled a clearer picture of what might be happening than you have since you began."

Sloane's impromptu seminar ran all afternoon, then late into the night. They only broke for a meal, which Peter's partner Neil brought over from the restaurant. By the end, they filled a second hotel room with the nonessential papers—what Web called junk—retaining and organizing what remained to be entered into the computer Maria had agreed to buy. Scribbled notes covered the chalkboards from top to bottom.

It was just after midnight when Web wrapped up. The committee was extraordinarily grateful for his advice; his experience and information gave them the push they needed to become highly effective.

"I'd like to see the place where the bodies were found," he said to Peter and Maria, as they walked down the stairs into the lobby.

"Maybe it'd be better to wait till morning," suggested Peter. "It's pretty far off the road."

"I'd rather see it tonight. I'm hoping to get an early start in the morning."

"I'll take him. It's on the way back to my house," said Maria.

"I was going to stay here at the hotel."

"Well, I have an extra room, and it is a lot more convenient for me not to come back to Tico tonight—if you do not mind," she said.

"Okay. Let me call my daughter before we leave. I need to give her your phone number."

Web entered the office and dialed home. The phone machine answered. Web left a message.

"Hi, Joyce, it's Dad. Hope everything's okay. Please call me as soon as you get this message—I want to be sure you're okay." He left Maria's number in Green Grove, then pressed two buttons causing the machine to play back the messages left by previous callers.

"Hello, prof, this is Ramiah Bose." The recorded voice of a student from his economics class. "I was calling . . ." Shrill feedback, then Joyce's voice. "Hello? I'm here. Just a second." End of message. He was relieved. Joyce had answered the phone earlier; therefore, she was home. She was probably just asleep.

Sloane rode with Maria rather than take both cars to her house.

"I need to be back in town early anyway," she said. "I'll give you a ride." She really wanted to talk to him during the drive. Both were a little tense with the macabre knowledge that they were visiting a grave site of sorts. Maria drove slowly on the dark winding road out of town.

"How can we get the sheriff more involved?" she asked.

"Agitate. Send them weekly updates of the work you're doing. Forward anything you learn to the FBI and state police, too. Write to your member of Congress."

"What about newspapers?"

Web sighed. "Tempting but ultimately bad. Headlines may get the attention of law enforcement, but it'll get you into more trouble. If there is a killer, he'll be reading the paper too. Copy cats start up—publicity brings them out of the woodwork. And false leads—four hundred and some odd people confessed to Ted Bundy's crimes."

"Do you think my daughter is safe?"

Web turned aside and bit his lip. It was the question he'd hoped she wouldn't ask. On the basis of what he had learned that week, it seemed to him likely that more bodies were to be found; if he gave her vague reassurances, she'd sense his pessimism.

"I can't say. You've just got to keep trying till you find out. When I was looking for my older daughter, I ran into a couple who feared the worst for their daughter. She turned up three years later in a religious cult in Oregon, confused and wearing a towel on her head, but very much alive. You never can tell. What the police say is true—most disappearances are runaways, nothing more."

They drove out of the orchards into an area thick with

evergreens. A sign indicated that they were entering Western Woods National Forest.

"You still want to see the place where the bones were found?" asked Maria.

"Yes. Do you mind?"

"It's kind of late," she said.

Web sighed. "I haven't seen my daughter much this weekend. I was hoping to get on the road early tomorrow morning. Is it close to the road?" he asked.

"Yes. If you think it will help, we can go there."

"I think it's important to take a look," said Web.

They drove silently up a winding gravel road that cut a steep path through the woods. She parked by a brown redwood shelter with maps of paths for day hikers and a water fountain. It was dark as a tomb.

"It is about a hundred yards back there." She pointed to the opposite side of the road to a steep tree-covered hill.

"Do you have a flashlight?"

"In the trunk. I have some tennis shoes, too. I'll go with you."

"That's not necessary."

"Please, I would rather not stay here alone."

Web nodded.

A path had been cut to the sight, probably by investigating police, he thought. As they climbed, Maria slipped. Web caught her arm, supporting her. It was a difficult walk, even through the path.

"Thanks," she said.

The flashlight illuminated the woods a few feet in front of them. They didn't talk, perhaps from fear of disturbing the dead. Maria took a step, and Web grabbed her shoulder. They stood silent, listening.

Twigs broke in the distance. Web's heart pounded. There was another presence in the woods. More twigs snapped, then dead silence.

"Deer," he whispered to Maria. Nonetheless, he trained the flashlight on the ground and picked up a thick, heavy tree branch.

"It's right up here. You can still see the police tape on the trees," Maria whispered.

Web lifted the end of a yellow plastic ribbon marked Police Line—Do Not Cross. It had been cut with a knife. Holes were burned into the tape with a cigarette. The stench of melted plastic was strong; the holes had been burned recently. He shined the flashlight on the plastic. The holes were in the shape of a pentagram.

Web tightened his grip on the log, ready to lash out, then took a few tentative steps forward.

They reached a clearing.

"This is the place," said Maria.

Web and Maria stood at the edge of the area where the trees had been cut down. Web shined the light back and forth on the ground. It could have been any patch of woods. Something shiny glinted in the light beam. *Metal? A knife?* he thought.

"Who's there?" yelled Web.

No answer.

He walked toward the shiny object, ready to strike with the log at any moment. As he got closer, he saw it was merely a pile of beer bottles.

"Hello?" Web yelled again. He heard the rustle of leaves a few feet away and took two cautious steps toward the sound. He stumbled and looked down to see a head of long hair. A human head.

"Oh, my God."

Then he looked again, illuminating the spot with his flashlight. A boy and girl, teenagers, were passed out together in a sleeping bag.

"Goddammit!" he grumbled.

Web poked the bag with his foot and held the stick high. "Wake up! C'mon, get up!"

The girl woke up first. She groggily opened her eyes. Seeing Web, she emitted a cry of fear.

"Don't kill me!" she said, drawing her hands over her face.

The boy glanced up, then turned over and vomited.

"What the hell are you doing here?" Web demanded.

"It was a dare, it wasn't my idea!"

"Stand up!"

They climbed sheepishly out of the sleeping bag.

"Please don't hurt us, please," said the boy, who had long wavy black hair. He wore nothing but a leather jacket and his underwear. The girl self-consciously adjusted her corset and black mesh skirt.

"Get dressed," Web demanded.

"Are you the police?" asked the boy.

"Get dressed. Where do you live?"

"Green Grove," said the boy, trying unsuccessfully to balance on one foot while pulling on his pants.

"Is this your idea of a joke? Do you know what happened here?" Web was yelling.

"I swear to God it was a dare," offered the girl.

"What're your names?"

"Lyle Tanner."

"Jeanne O'Brien."

"Jeanne O'Brien? Your dad runs the gas station?" Maria asked.

"Yeah."

"You should know better. C'mon, get dressed."

The boy had drunk too many beers and had trouble standing. The spandex pants appeared to be the right size for a nine-year-old.

"Can't get 'em on, man!"

The boy put one foot into a pants leg, then fell over. Web grabbed him by the shoulder and hauled him upright.

"Put the other foot in," said Web.

"Okay, okay, man," said the boy, sticking his foot in.

Web grabbed the waistband of the pants and lifted up hard. The pants clung to the boy's skin like spray paint. They were so tight, he could barely move. The boy grimaced but finally pulled them into place.

"What, do these belong to your little sister or something?" asked Web.

"Shut up, man. I can hardly get in 'em when I'm sober." The boy put on his boots and stood.

Web turned to the girl. "This was your idea of a hot date?"

"I don't know," she said sulking. "I swear it wasn't my idea."

"You kids get the hell out of here now," said Web.

"Okay."

The boy started to gather his things.

"They're too drunk to drive," said Maria.

"Let's take them, then."

The girl broke into tears. "My dad will kill me!"

"You'll live," said Web.

As Maria escorted the teenagers to her car, Web examined the area. No doubt cops had been over it with a fine tooth comb. He wasn't looking for evidence. Web just wanted to get a feel for why someone had chosen *this* spot to leave bodies. The murderer knew his trade. It was a carefully chosen dumping ground, not the sort of place a panicked lover might choose. Close to a road, yet relatively inaccessible because of the woods and the hill.

Walking back to the car, Web slipped on the steep incline. As he picked himself up, words flashed in his mind as clear as a baseball scoreboard:

You made them walk.

The bodies had once been inhabited by living girls. The "blunt object," so scientific sounding in the coroner's report and yet so brutal, had been wielded somewhere near here, where the bodies had been found. In these woods. Web could hear the screams in his mind, mixing in with the wind through the trees. Without specifying anything, the police reports suggested that the bodies had merely been dumped here. Web realized that those unknown girls had been forced to climb this hill, that this was the last walk they ever took, and that their dying cries had been heard only by the trees. *You made them walk up this hill, knowing full well what you would do to them.* Web gritted his teeth. The peculiar satisfaction he drew from his sudden insight was unsettling. The hunter within him had been awakened: a primitive facet of his personality that was at once forceful and uncannily perceptive, yet which could endanger the stability of his new life if given free reign.

Shaken, Web brushed himself off and half-slid, half-walked down to meet Maria at her car. The kids sat shame-faced in the back seat.

Dan O'Brien was watching the late show in his office at the Green Grove 25-Hour Gas Station when Maria and Web walked in and told him where his daughter had been. The gaunt man in a jumpsuit and John Deere gimme cap leaped up from his seat. "She was supposed to be at her sister's house!" he said, then stormed out to the car.

"You got a lot of explaining to do, Jeanne Marie O'Brien," he said, pulling her out by her arm. A car full of boys drove up to the other side of the pump.

"We're closed! Closed!" He flipped a switch and the Open sign changed to Closed. "Can't you read the darn sign?"

The boys drove away, yelling, "Good luck, Jeannie!" Dan followed his daughter into the office. Web and Maria unloaded the sleeping bags onto the sidewalk and stood with Lyle outside the window. On the other side of the glass Dan O'Brien talked nonstop at his daughter, who was sitting slumped in a chair. When Dan saw that Web and Maria were waiting outside, he leaned out the door.

"Thanks for bringing her around, Maria, but you don't have to wait. It's gonna take some time before I'm done yelling at her." He slammed the office door.

They left the worried teenage boy waiting by the gas pumps and drove in silence to Maria's house, a Cape Cod–style home on a large lot.

As soon as they were in the door, Web grinned and said, "I'm surprised he can get his pants on when he's sober."

Maria smiled and asked facetiously, "I wonder if Dan O'Brien's done yelling at Jeanne yet?"

"Is that what kids do on dates nowadays? Find unromantic spots? Next week they'll be making out at a toxic waste dump," Web quipped.

"It is not funny," said Maria, breaking into a new fit of laughter.

Then, suddenly, she grew quiet. "You'll stay in the downstairs room." She showed him to a door across the split-level living room. The house looked like it had been decorated by *Architectural Digest*.

"This is a beautiful home," said Web.

"I'm a realtor. My ex-husband was a builder. The house is sort of a showplace to let people know that a nice life can be had out here, off the beaten track." He set down his briefcase and bag.

"Would you like a drink before retiring?" she asked.

"I'd love one. It's been a long day."

"Scotch?"

"You read my mind. On ice, please."

She poured two long Scotches. They sat at the kitchen table.

"You teach math at Berkeley?" she asked cheerily.

"Graduate statistics. We're developing new methodologies for analysis of information. The new trend is toward 'fuzzy' data analysis, but I'm more of a classicist."

"Oh. Classicist. I see." She nodded, vaguely. "And what is fuzzy analysis?"

"It's a little hard to describe. Do you really want to know?"

"No, not really. Please don't be offended."

"Not offended one bit." Web spotted a phone. "Think it's too late to call my daughter?"

"It's 2:30 A.M."

"I'll call her in the morning."

"How old is she?"

"Seventeen."

"My daughter Tanya is seventeen, too. She'll be eighteen in two weeks." Her face drained of color. She put down her drink. The prospect of enduring Tanya's birthday without Tanya had suddenly hit her.

"I think about all the things I might have said that could have upset her. During our divorce she turned a little wild, drinking some, discovering boys . . ."

She stood up. "We only had one real bad fight, and that was during last Christmas vacation, months before she disappeared. Tanya came in one night late from a party. I said some things that were not very nice about the way she was dressed. She had on that Madonna underwear kind of thing that I do not think is right for a girl of her age. I called her some names. I probably shouldn't have."

"Every parent has those fights."

"I know, but I still think I went too far. I just did not want her to be like her dad—drunk and dishonest." Maria turned away from Web. "I just wanted her to be good!"

She walked into the living room, away from Web, to compose herself. Web looked around the kitchen—flyers and posters with pictures of Tanya were stacked up. Phone numbers for missing children organizations and police departments were on a sheet of paper stuck to the refrigerator. He wanted to go to bed.

Maria came back in.

"I'm sorry. There is no one who really can understand," she said.

"It's okay. I want to listen."

"Thanks. One more question. When you were looking for your daughter, how did you get to sleep? Before you knew what had happened?"

"That's easy to answer. I worked till I was exhausted. When I had an ounce of energy in me, I put it toward trying to find her. At night I combed through articles and reports, wrote letter after letter, crunched information, whatever I could do. I got in the habit of falling asleep at my desk."

"That's not much consolation."

"I guess not."

"But it sounds like the truth."

He finished his drink, and they said good night.

In the middle of the night Web awoke with a parched throat and got up to get a drink of water. Maria was asleep at the kitchen table. He turned out the lights for her and walked on tiptoe back to his room so as not to wake her up.

Web couldn't get back to sleep. The events of the day replayed in his mind. *Serial killer?* A thoroughly ridiculous notion. The events were spread out over more than a year. He could think of no way to convince another thoughtful person that the two bodies found on the hill had resulted from anything other than a garden-variety crime of passion. There was no conclusive evidence to demonstrate that Tanya de Rivera had not just run away. It was entirely reasonable to believe that the other missing girls would be found. And yet . . .

Web did not usually believe in hunches. But the sum of what he had seen seemed to fit into a familiar, ugly pattern. Years of training in skeptical thinking had taught him to choose the simplest explanation for any event. An extraordinary hypothesis required extraordinary proof. He had nothing beyond some bones in the woods and a few photos. Even though he could not confirm the presumption of a single killer methodically preying on young girls, nothing he had seen would contradict it either.

When he was a child, his grandmother claimed she could smell rain approaching. His early education had convinced him that she was merely superstitious. But later, studies demonstrated that some individuals could smell the negative ions in the air that arrive shortly before a storm. His grandmother had been right all along, regardless of whether he believed her. He had been blinded from the truth because there was no explanation for it.

The stakes were much higher now: The hunter within sensed that a killer was at large. Web smelled the rain approaching. He did not know why, but he could not deny it either.

When Web turned out at seven, Maria was already up, making coffee. They ate a quick breakfast of cold cereal, and then she drove him back to his car. The roads looked completely different in the daylight; lush green vegetation, little patches of fog in low spots, more like Seattle than Berkeley.

"You've been extremely helpful to us, Web."

"I'm glad I could help."

"Do you think you can come back and help us get set up on a computer?"

He'd known she would ask. The more he became involved, the more time he'd have to spend away from home, and the more unpleasant memories would be dredged up. He had planned to tell her of his late-night intuition, but in the light of day it sounded implausible at best.

"Maria, I can send you the software and a manual I wrote for it. It's supposed to be easy to use. I don't know how much I can help you. It's a question of my time, and . . ."

"You don't have to make excuses."

"It's not that I don't want to, but I have responsibilities to my job and daughter."

She stepped out of the car when they reached the hotel in Tico and watched him move his briefcase and bag into his trunk.

They both hesitated. Then Maria shook his hand warmly, taking it in both of hers.

"Thank you," she said.

Web got in his car.

Maria watched Web drive away. She didn't move until his car disappeared over the horizon.

5

Two miles out of Tico, Web pulled off at a gas station and dialed a number.

"Vine County sheriff," said a female dispatcher.

"May I speak to Sheriff Block?"

"One moment."

He got Muzak on hold. Funny thing for a police department to have.

"Block speaking."

He was in luck. He'd called on the off chance that someone working on the case might be there.

"Sheriff Block, this is Web Sloane. You don't know me, but I wanted to stop by and ask a couple of questions about the bodies found in Tico."

"You a reporter, Sloane? 'Cause I don't have nothin' to say to the press."

"I'm a friend of Maria de Rivera's and something of an investigative information specialist."

"What the hell is that?"

"Well, I developed some computer programs for the FBI."

"Swear you're not a reporter?"

"Yes."

"Well, I'll be here another couple hours. Why don't you come on by."

"I'll be there in about an hour. I'm just outside of Tico."

"Fine."

The sheriff hung up without saying good-bye.

He dialed home again and got the answering machine.

"Joyce, this is Dad. If you're there, pick up . . . I'll be home around eight o'clock." He hung up. Joyce must already be gone. He felt a twinge of fear at not hearing her voice, but she was seventeen, old enough to take care of herself.

Endocino was on the main road but in the opposite direction from home. Web surveyed the town on his drive in—little bed-and-breakfasts, lots of shops for tourists to buy sweaters, souvenirs, art, and New-Age crystals. He had no trouble finding the sheriff's station. The building was a converted vacation house, sitting on a bluff overlooking the ocean, near the center of the town.

He walked into the front hall, which had been converted into a waiting area by blocking it off with glass. He talked through the window to the dispatcher.

"I'm here to see Sheriff Block."

"He's not seeing visitors today."

"I just called."

A huge man, who might have been mistaken for a lumberjack by his faded jeans, plaid flannel shirt, and full beard, entered the room.

"You Sloane?"

"Yes. Hi. You're Sheriff Block?"

"It's Sunday so call me Bruce." Block squinted at Web. "Nope, you don't look like a reporter."

"I'm not."

"Then come on in and have a beer."

Web followed Block back into his office, which commanded a superior view of the ocean. A bank of fog was starting to roll over the water below them. Block opened a little dormitory fridge and pulled out two Budweisers, handing one to Web. He sat down and put his cowboy boots on his desk.

"It's my goddam day off, and I have to come in to type up a funding report that goes to the county. One-finger hunt and peck. Last Wednesday not one, but both my secretaries quit in a huff. So I'm entitled to a beer. What can I do you for?"

"I wanted to talk to you about the bodies found in Tico."

"Bodies in Tico? Shoot. I never heard of them."

"What?"

"I'm pulling your leg. Why do you think we're so over-worked? It seems as if ever since someone found a couple bones on a hill, my whole professional life has revolved around them. I got my undersheriff working on it full-time for another month at least."

"Well, I just wanted to share a couple things with you. First, I think that the victims died right on the hill, not someplace else."

"How come?"

"Because one person couldn't carry the bodies up that steep incline."

"How do you know it's this one person?"

"I'm just familiar with this sort of crime, and it's almost always one person."

"Friend of yours?" Block grinned.

"What? I just mean that if you study this kind of murder, you'll see that almost without exception it's carried out by a single person acting alone."

"Well, I think that's kind of assuming a lot. We don't know if we're looking for one guy or a football team. But I'll type myself a memo that says, 'Mr. Sloane who came in on Sunday thinks it's one guy who made his victims walk up a hill,' if it'll make you feel better."

Web began to see why the Tico committee didn't like the sheriff. He sipped on the beer.

"So why else did you come? You said you had two things to tell me, and it's Sunday and I want to go home. Maybe you also solved the crime and I can take a vacation?"

"I just wanted to say you should give the group in Tico a little more credit. They're doing some serious footwork."

"You mean that woman whose kid ran away?"

"We don't know that Tanya ran away. I think she was kidnapped."

"Anyone you know did it?"

"Sheriff Block, I'm trying to tell you that the girl's disappearance and the discovery of the bodies may be linked. You might have someone in your county who likes killing young girls. If you don't explore that possibility, then you're being irresponsible."

"So Mr. Sloane, tell me what I should be doing."

"First of all, I hope all this information is going into SKID. Do you get SKID?"

"The Serial Killer computer doodad? Yep. We got a Teletype and it gives us a couple hundred pages of nonsense every week. If I ever want to find out who's getting killed in Texas, I read it."

"You should be entering everything that's happening in Tico into the system."

"I have, sir. There. We enter every murder report into the system as a matter of course. That, plus a $1.50 will get us a beer."

"Okay. How about Maria de Rivera? She and several others have been following up leads and doing some serious footwork that you shouldn't ignore."

"By several others, you mean including Rowan?"

"Yes."

"Well, if I thought that girl had been kidnapped, that homo Rowan would be my number one suspect. He thinks he's the mayor and the grand pooh-bah for the whole county, and he's been causing nothing but trouble for my office. And it's an election year. So maybe if you knew a little more about my work, you wouldn't come in here telling me how to run my station."

Block downed his beer and reached back into the fridge for a second. Web sat silent in his chair.

"I been kidding you a little, Mr. Sloane, but the truth is we have no leads and we're still throwing a lot of manpower we don't got at this Tico thing. Come with me."

He led him through a door into a room with five desks.

"This is where my undersheriff sits, a very good man named Slavik. He's been doing nothing but overtime for three months. He reads the SKID shit, and he tells me it's worthless. So far he's interviewed just about everyone who got as much as a parking ticket in the county and hasn't come up with a thing."

"Oh." Web sized up Block. The man seemed like the type who would be good at solving any ordinary crime—car theft, holdups, any event that had a discernible motive. But investigating the irrational takes something more.

"See that filing cabinet? Packed with nothing but reports

about what we call 'dem bones.' So far we have people calling in to tell us it's satanic cults, wild hippies who live in the hills, and Charlie Manson sneaking out of prison at night. Slavik's followed up on every lead. So I'm not neglecting your buddies in Tico, but they're not the only people with theories about things."

Block belched, then chuckled.

"I've reviewed their material, and it seems pretty solid," said Web. "I think you ought to be getting some support from the FBI labs."

"With what money? FBI costs us unless they decide it's a federal crime, at which point I become *their* secretary, too," said Block, scowling.

"What about the state police?"

"Mr. Sloane, I know what I'm doing, and when I need the state police you can rest assured I'll call them."

"And Tico?" Web cracked his knuckles, irritated.

The sheriff softened and spoke sincerely. "I'll send Slavik out there next week. He'll get a full report." Block wasn't grinning any more. "Okay?"

"All right."

Block threw an empty bottle across the room, which landed with a loud clink in the trash can.

"So if you'll excuse me, Sloane, I got some reports to type."

"Right. Here's my card."

"Thanks."

Web had to be led through the maze of doors back to the front office. He didn't enjoy the beautiful sunset over the ocean on his drive home because he was worrying about the Vine County sheriff sitting on crucial material. *People find what they're looking for,* thought Web. And Block wasn't looking for a methodical, deliberate killer. Web had to find a way to lend credence to his hunch. Something that would convince another person.

It was after eight o'clock before Web got back to Berkeley. As he approached his house, he saw a flashing yellow light in the driveway. It was a tow truck. An invisible hand grabbed his stomach and pulled hard. In his brief absence his world had already begun to come unraveled. He stopped and ran over to the truck. The front left end of Joyce's Volvo was crumpled in. The headlight was smashed, and the left tire hung crooked. He leaned in the window of the tow truck.

"Joyce?"

She was in the passenger seat of the truck.

"Hi, Dad," was her sheepish response.

"Joyce, are you okay?"

"Yes, I'm totally fine."

"Put it down here."

The driver put down the car in the driveway. Joyce signed a credit card receipt, and the driver left. Joyce and Web walked silently into the kitchen. Mud jumped off the couch and circled nervously, tail between his legs.

"What happened, Joyce?"

"Well, last night one of your students called."

"I mean with the car."

"I'm getting to that!"

"Okay."

"So I said you weren't in, and he said he was going to invite you over and why don't I come?"

"So?"

"So I went."

"I said I wanted you to stay out of trouble."

"It wasn't trouble like a kid party; it was all adults. You know, college graduate students. Harmless."

He sighed, almost a grunt. Web didn't consider graduate students adults, and he certainly didn't think they were harmless.

"Who was the host?"

"Ramiah Bose, the guy who called."

"Why didn't you call me?"

"I did call you first thing this morning. I woulda called you last night, but I forgot to bring the number."

"So how'd it happen?"

"I was driving home and a guy came down the wrong way on a one-way street. He ran into me and sped away."

"So why are they towing it home now?"

"Well, I was just a couple blocks from Ramiah's house, so I went over there. He and his roommates and I went back to the car and pushed it to the side of the road, figuring we'd tow it today."

"How'd you get home last night?"

"I stayed there."

"What!"

"I said I stayed there."

"Joyce, I don't want you staying over at men's houses. You know that's against our rules."

"Dad, nothing happened."

"There was drinking there, am I right?"

"There might have been."

"I don't like you being at drinking parties."

"It wasn't a 'drinking party,'" she said sarcastically.

"You should socialize with kids your own age."

Joyce stood up and raised her voice to take the offensive, waving her finger at her father.

"Dad, I had lots of friends my own age in Seattle. And now you had to move to Berkeley, right in my senior year, and you didn't even ask me what I thought of it. So you can't complain about me going to a party to meet some people."

Web was shocked that Joyce was blaming him. He raised his voice to match hers.

"Look, Joyce, I had to take this job. It was a once-in-a-lifetime opportunity. It's paying for your car and for your college education next year."

"Daddy-O, I don't even think I want to go to college. I just wanted to stay in Seattle, and I think it's unfair that you didn't even ask me what I thought."

Suddenly he disliked being called Daddy-O.

"What the . . . when did you decide not to go to college? Don't you think you should have told me?"

"I've been thinking about things. Ramiah said he spent five years hitchhiking around India before college, and he's glad he did. He saw some of life, you know. And he's a good student, too. I think I . . ."

Web cut her off.

"I don't want you seeing him."

He stood up.

"And make no doubt about it, you're going to go to college next year, Vicki."

The name hung in the air between them.

"Vicki! You called me *Vicki!*"

She was hurt and angry; Web was just as shocked. What did he mean by saying such a thing?

"I'm not your perfect Vicki, Dad. I know I'm not perfect like she was and I never will be! I'm sorry, but maybe I don't want to go to college! Maybe I don't want to be perfect!"

"I didn't mean to call you that . . ."

Joyce ran up the stairs in tears. Mud, confounded by their fight, ran after her.

Web yelled up the stairs. "We'll talk more about this later!"

Her door slammed. Mud, disturbed, lay down outside her door, his tail drumming out a nervous tattoo on the carpet.

Web went out to examine the damage to the car. It looked like the frame was bent. Her almost-new car would never be the same. Somehow, he felt responsible.

6

The Devil cannot enter a home uninvited.

WELSH PROVERB

Mars Chittenden nibbled on a raspberry and avocado bagel as she cleaned out the display case at the Mars Bakery. Fall was slow for tourists in Endocino, California, but it seemed to her that the locals bought more goodies when the weather was chilly and the rains came. She peered out the front door to see if anyone was heading toward her small shop. The street was quiet. The sky was rapidly darkening, and the air smelled as if it might rain at any moment.

She counted her register. Two hundred sixty-five dollars so far, a pretty good day's take, and it was still a half hour till close. That included the ninety-five that Roslyn paid her once per week for supplying the local coffee shop with pastries, but even without Roslyn's payment the income represented a respectable day's earnings at the Mars Bakery. A few drops of rain began to rattle the tin roof.

Mars had started the shop four years earlier with the proceeds of her divorce settlement. Her original intention of adopting a "holistic and compassionate attitude toward life, love, and muffins," as was printed on the first menu, had never been completely abandoned, although her lofty aspirations had been refined somewhat through the difficulties of running a small business. Her youthful looks and inexperience didn't help her credibility at first. She still had the figure of a teenager, and her thick red hair was usually gathered into a ponytail. Some people were amazed to learn that she had a fifteen-year-old son. In spite of it all, she had earned respect in the community through hard work; she was proud that vendors happily extended credit, knowing she always paid.

She hummed to herself as the rain increased to a steady drumming on the roof and mentally went over what was left to do for the day. *Close out the register, clean out the dough machine, get whatever berries I need for the morning, pick up Farrell . . .* Her reverie was cut short by a panicked thought: The word *sunroof* flashed into her mind.

"Shit!" Mars yelled. She remembered that her fifteen-year-old son Farrell had opened the car sunroof on the way to school that morning, and now her little Toyota was probably getting soaked. She set her glasses down on the counter, grabbed her purse, and reached for the keys. They weren't there. She pulled out her change purse, a little note pad, her checkbook, a wad of Kleenex, a bottle of Advil, then dumped the purse on the floor. No keys. Then she realized where they were. She had unloaded two fifty-pound bags of flour that morning from the hatchback of her car and had probably set the keys down inside it.

Mars looked out the door. The rain had quickly increased to the point where the storm sewers gushed like river rapids. Her car seats were probably soaking up water and would stink all winter unless she did something fast. She made a run for it out the back door.

In just a few steps across the dirt parking lot Mars was already drenched. Her initial fear had been well founded; the sunroof was halfway open. She looked in the hatchback —there, tantalizingly close, were her keys. The door was locked. In short order she tried the passenger and driver side doors, and both those were locked, too. Mud splattered her shoes and slacks. The new purple silk blouse, a gift from her best friend Roslyn, would soon be ruined. Mars stood next to the car and stuck her arm into the partially open sunroof.

She couldn't quite reach the door lock, and the wet grime from her car got on her sleeve. Frustrated, she ran back into the bakery to look for something to cover the car until she could get another set of keys.

Inside, she dumped her shoes, realizing there was no sense in ruining those as well, and got a big industrial-sized trash bag. Mars also looked for something that she could use to pick the lock. She had no coat hangers, nothing handy to lift up a latch, so she grabbed the longest thing in her shop, a wooden bread paddle from the oven.

Dashing toward the back door, she slipped on the slick floor and fell, smacking her elbow on the ground. She took two deep breaths, stood up, and flexed her arm; it would grow a nice bruise. The rain smashed on the tin roof like steel drums from hell. Mars stepped back out the door.

Just as she got outside, a gray Volkswagen Cabriolet with the top down skidded up and stopped in her parking lot. A tall, dark-haired man jumped out and expertly pulled up the convertible top. His soaked clothes clung to his muscular frame. Mars had never seen the man before, but his looks and manner suggested he was different; not a local, definitely, but he didn't have traveling companions, like a tourist, and his clothes were more casual than a traveling businessman's.

Mars smiled sheepishly at the stranger and continued trying to break into her car. The pebbles in the mud hurt her stockinged feet. She half-climbed up the side of the car and stuck the bread paddle through the sunroof. The blunt paddle wouldn't pull the lock. It was futile.

"Wouldn't you know it? Rain!" yelled the man with the Cabriolet, laughing at their shared plight. He finished sealing up his ragtop and approached.

Mars nodded to the man, then turned her attention to her car, stretching her arm into the sunroof reaching for the lock. She was inches away but still couldn't reach, so she slid off the car and began tearing the seam of the garbage bag. When she looked up, the man was next to her, oblivious to the downpour.

"Locked out?" he yelled over the noise of the rain.

"You got it," she answered.

"Let me help you with that!"

Mars held the plastic bag over her head. The stranger reached in through the sunroof, but he also was unable to reach the door.

"It's just a little too far," said Mars.

"Wait a minute. Let me try something else," he said.

Mars stood back and watched. The stranger went to the front of the car, climbed directly up the hood, and straddled the windshield. From the top of the car, he reached in through the sunroof. She watched through the window—his arm stretched and just barely reached the door lock. *Click.* He'd done it.

Mars laughed with delight and then opened the door, climbed over the seat, and got the keys. She started the engine and closed the sunroof. Then she killed the motor and climbed out.

"Thank you!" she shouted over the rain. "Come on in!"

The man followed her into the bakery. She closed the back door. They were both drenched.

"That storm sure snuck up on us. Brrrr." Mars shivered and stomped her feet to warm herself up.

"Surprised the heck out of me!" the man said with a smile in his eyes. He had a direct, friendly manner. Something about the man made Mars feel comfortable and relaxed.

"Thanks for saving me from my own foolishness," she said.

"Don't mention it. Good thing we didn't discover it an hour from now!" The stranger extended his hand. "Alan DeVries."

"Alan, I'm Mars Chittenden." She shook his hand. He grasped her palm lightly and moved it up and down only once, looking into her eyes. She was used to rural men's rougher handshakes. The stranger seemed cultured to her, perhaps wealthy. There was a gentle quality about him. Although he had been driving in the cold, his hand felt warm.

Mars was drenched. Her wavy red hair stuck to her head making her look like a wet rat; her once-nice silk blouse, now soaked, clung to her torso; and her stocking feet were covered with mud. Before the rain she'd tied her hair in a knot with two bright green chopsticks as decoration. She tugged the sticks out and flung her hair back out of her eyes.

Mars walked behind the counter, her favorite spot.

"Cup of herbal tea?" she asked. "I'm going to have one."

"No, thanks."

"Can I give you some muffins? Or how about some delicious cupcakes? Just baked them." Mars had always felt that no favor should ever go unreturned. It was bad business and bad Karma to let someone do something for you without reciprocating.

"No, thanks."

She shook out her hair and caught a glimpse of her reflection in the glass case. Her blouse was soaked to transparency and clung to her skin. All that protected her from nakedness was a lacy wisp of a brassiere. She swallowed. Butterflies. She turned to the stranger. He was looking back at her. He had seen it all. Drops of rain on her eyelashes blurred her vision.

"I'll be right back," she said. Mars darted into the tiny bathroom cum broom closet at the back of the shop. She closed the door, took off her blouse and wrung it out in the sink. She picked up a dish towel and dried out her hair, then rolled the blouse up in the towel. She removed her bra and shook it out, spraying droplets on the mirror. Mars heard the back door open and close. *Is that guy robbing me?* she thought.

Covering herself with the balled-up blouse, she leaned her head out the bathroom door. Hanging on the bakery pan rack was a red University of Massachusetts sweatshirt.

"I figured you'd be cold, and I have all these dry clothes out in the car, so . . ." came the man's voice from the front of the room.

"Thanks!"

Mars grabbed the sweatshirt, then went back into the bathroom to finish drying off. The sweatshirt was warm and cozy—just what the doctor ordered. *Some robber.* She combed out her hair, humming to herself.

When she emerged, dryer and warmer, a father and two kids were walking out the door of the shop. DeVries was behind the counter.

"I didn't know how to do your register, but I helped those folks. Your sign says eighty cents a muffin, and they wanted a dozen, so here's the $9.60." DeVries moved from behind the counter to the customer area.

"They're only $4.99 a dozen!" Mars said, laughing.

"Well, don't tell them. They thought it was a good deal."

"I can't thank you enough! Don't you want some muffins? Fresh bread?"

The man who called himself DeVries smiled and shook his head. "No, thank you. Actually, I was going to try and scare up some dinner. Can you make a recommendation? I wasn't planning to stop here in . . . what town is this?" he asked, laughing.

"Welcome to Endocino," said Mars, shivering. She poured some hot water into a biodegradable paper cup and dropped in a caffeine-free fruit and almond tea bag.

"Is there a place in town that has good soup? That'd hit the spot in this weather," asked DeVries.

Mars bit her lip. "There's only one restaurant and one coffee shop open during the off-season, and both are closed Monday nights. But maybe you'd like to . . ."

He cut her off before she could offer dinner.

"What's the closest open restaurant?"

"That'd probably be the truck stop in Bonita, about fifteen miles down PCH. But why don't you come . . ."

DeVries interrupted. "PCH?"

Mars laughed. "Pacific Coast Highway, that main road at the edge of town."

"How do I get there?"

Mars was about to make a pitch for DeVries to join her for dinner when the oriental bells on the door jingled. Roslyn Tabor, Mars's best friend, pranced in, still in her blue-and-white waitress uniform. Seeing that Mars had a customer, she stood at the door and waved with the tips of her fingers. Mars waved back, then turned her attention to DeVries. Roslyn put down her umbrella and undid her rain bonnet.

"Where was I?"

"The restaurant."

With her friend in the shop, the intimacy seemed gone, and Mars lost her nerve. She got a pencil and paper and drew a map. "Take PCH down to where it goes into the next town. There's not much between here and there, so you can't miss the huge truck stop. I don't think it has a name—just a big sign that says 'Eat.'" She turned to Roslyn. "What's the name of that place?"

Roslyn stepped forward. "You mean that den of horrors in Bonita? The place where they use motor oil to cook the potatoes? That place is far too miserable to have a name." Her voice turned dramatic. "The Restaurant That Dare Not Speak Its Name."

DeVries laughed.

"She's sending you to be poisoned? What'd you do to her?"

Mars scowled. "It's not that bad."

"When was the last time you ate there? Have you *ever* eaten there?" Roslyn demanded, a teasing challenge.

The man held up his hand. "That's okay. I can drive on past there. I'm not *starving,* just thinking about dinner."

Roslyn looked him over. "Why don't you eat with us? We're having . . ." She turned to Mars. "What're we having?"

Mars glared back at Roslyn. "A little chicken."

Roslyn grinned. "Roslyn Tabor."

"Alan DeVries."

"New in town?" she asked.

"Just passing through, probably."

Roslyn should have known better, thought Mars. Roslyn had been invited to dinner that night, and in fact she ate at Mars's home more often than not. Mars had wanted to invite the man. Now Roslyn had stolen her thunder.

DeVries saw the look in Mars's eyes.

"You're very kind, but I can't impose on you."

Roslyn protested. "Nah, there's really nothing decent for forty or fifty miles. In this weather, that could take till midnight."

"That would be kind," said DeVries, adding, "are you sure it's okay?"

Mars was silent.

Roslyn grinned sheepishly. "Sure it's okay. We'd love to have you."

Mars gave in. "Let me just close up, and then we'll go. I

still have to balance the register and mop up this mud. I'll do the dough machine in the morning."

"Let me do the floor," offered DeVries, heading toward the mop.

"No, no, I'll do it," said Mars, but before she could stop DeVries he had already gotten behind the counter and picked up the mop. Mars had a superstition about accepting favors, particularly from strangers. She felt that it put the recipient at a disadvantage. She pressed a few keys on the electronic register, which printed out the day's total. By the time she had folded and filed the paper tape, counted the drawer, and locked the cash into a little safe, DeVries had finished mopping the floor. Roslyn sat on one of the four chairs in the customer's area of the shop and freshened her makeup.

"I still have to pick up Farrell. Why don't you ride with me, Roslyn, and, Alan, you follow."

"I don't want to impose . . ." said DeVries.

"Don't worry about it. We'll enjoy having you," said Mars.

Roslyn looked up from applying liquid eyeliner. "Yeah, it'll be fun."

As soon as Mars and Roslyn were in the car where DeVries couldn't hear them, Mars turned angrily to Roslyn. "Who asked you to invite that guy to my house?"

"What's the big deal?" asked Roslyn.

"If I had wanted to invite him, I would have," Mars said.

"The guy is good-looking, the right age, probably single, probably well-off, and you were going to send him to the truck stop, Mars. Maybe you'll thank me later," said Roslyn.

"You're going to be matchmaker for me. Oh, thank you for finding me a man, Madame Roslyn," said Mars, with singsong irony.

"I did it for myself—I hear you bitch 'there's no interesting mehhhhn in Endocino,' six nights a week. So when one comes to town, let's at least get a good gander so we don't forget what a single man looks like."

"Why are you so worried about *my* love life? What's going on with yours?"

"I'm still seeing Chad. You know that," Roslyn said.

"How long's it been?"

"He's supposed to be coming pretty soon."

"That'll be nice."

Mars decided not to press the point that Chad was an incredibly lousy boyfriend and hadn't been to town in three and a half months. It would have been cruel. Chad owned a semi and ran lumber from northern California down to the mills south of Endocino. Roslyn had been seeing him once or twice a month for about a year for a couple days of beer and soulless sex. He always told Roslyn that in a few years he would retire and settle down with her. He hadn't been through town for three months, the longest he'd stayed away at a stretch. Mars figured he wouldn't come back. They rode to her son's school in silence.

Farrell was waiting outside his school holding a brightly colored skateboard and jumped into the car. Mars waved back to the Cabriolet following.

"Who's that guy?" Farrell didn't waste much time before becoming sullen.

"He's someone who helped me fix my car. He's coming over for dinner."

"Does he have to?"

"Yes, he does. If I wanted to get your approval, I would have asked." Farrell was getting to *that* age, and Mars was in no mood to be second-guessed by a teenager.

She turned off the main highway and drove up a narrow dirt road that led to her home. The Cabriolet kept up with her the whole way. Mars pulled into the gravel driveway of her home, and Farrell jumped out into the rain and opened the garage. Mars pulled in. DeVries parked behind her in the driveway.

Mars's home was a U-shaped ranch house with a detached "granny shack" that sat in the back. There were only five houses on the quarter mile of dirt road: hers, Roslyn's, a retired military man who was perpetually in the hospital, and two summer homes for tourists.

DeVries followed them in through the garage. Mars looked at her home with new eyes. A man in the house, a real, eligible, *potent* man, made everything look different.

The Indian flower painting she had impulsively purchased only a week before looked dopey to her now.

"Here, leave your shoes, I'll go get you some slippers." She disappeared into the back of the house and returned with a pair of man's slippers she'd had for years.

"Thanks. They fit perfectly."

Roslyn pulled a large green bottle of wine out of the refrigerator and got three glasses off the counter.

"Thanks again for having me over for dinner," said DeVries.

"Don't thank me. Thank Roslyn—she's cooking," said Mars with a mischievous grin.

Roslyn set the wine bottle down. "What am I making?" she asked.

"You'll just have to surprise us," said Mars. "I'd love a glass of white wine while you're up, Roz. I bet Alan would too."

DeVries and Mars walked out to the family room area adjacent to the kitchen.

"Sit down, relax," said Mars. She did a quick pickup job, grabbing the shoes, catalogues, and the half-completed sweater that she'd been crocheting in front of the television.

She went back into the kitchen and threw them into a big box in a closet.

"What in the world do you mean, me cook?" asked Roslyn.

"You can cook. You invited him," Mars said with a smile.

"What is there to eat? All that I saw in the freezer is three chickens. Is there anything easier out in the garage?" asked Roslyn.

"Nope. The big freezer broke. You're on your own."

"Okay. You win. I'll cook. But you have to eat it."

Roslyn started rummaging around in the closet. She found a passable-looking package of spaghetti and started pulling out other things. Mars picked up the wine bottle and went into the family room.

"Sorry about all the commotion, Alan. That's just life in the small city."

"That's okay. I was just thinking about how perfect your life seems. You've done what so many people I meet just talk about—you run your own business, live in a beautiful part of the country . . . you really have the world by the tail."

Mars blushed. She rarely met men who weren't intimidated by her independence, much less admired it. "Well, it's not always rosy. It's a lot of hard work," said Mars.

"Yes, but you seem willing to do what's necessary. I really admire that in a person."

"What do you do, Alan?"

Roslyn, who had been eavesdropping while preparing food in the kitchen, stepped closer to the family room to hear the reply. DeVries didn't see her—the couch he sat on had its back to her.

"Well, you could ask, 'What *did* I do?' " said DeVries.

Mars tried to politely listen, while Roslyn made a thumbs-down gesture and frowned at her, unseen by DeVries. Mars tried to avoid Roslyn's eye but could see her mouthing the word "unemployed."

"Until three months ago, I was working for a large brokerage firm in New York. I was with them almost eleven years."

"And then . . . ?" Mars asked.

"I was in charge of five really important clients. I was making more than a hundred thou a year before bonuses."

Roslyn raised her eyebrows and made a big thumbs-up sign. Mars tried to ignore her.

"But I realized that all my creative energy was going toward selling Miracle Shavers to people who didn't want them. The money was what they call 'golden handcuffs.' One day, I ran into an old friend who had taken a low-key, low-paying government job. But he had a life."

"What?"

"He had a wife, two kids, time to himself. No matter how much money you have, everyone has the same amount of time. And I lacked any real life outside of work. I thought: What if I just walked away? So I did. I cashed in my stock, sold my condo, and headed West. It's what I always wanted to do anyway. So I'm just puttering around right now, loving it."

"So that's it? You're just driving around the country?"

"I plan to stop wandering; I'm just trying to find the right place. When I was a kid, my family took a vacation in northern California. It was the best two weeks of my life. I thought I'd give it another look," said DeVries. He drank the last out of his glass of wine.

Roslyn made two emphatic thumbs-up, then went back to the kitchen and threw some spaghetti into the boiling water.

Dinner was soon ready, spaghetti and canned tomatoes. For all her time slinging hash, Roslyn still hadn't figured out the first thing about cooking. DeVries seemed to enjoy the food a great deal, though.

About halfway through the meal, Roslyn brought up the constant rains that were plaguing Endocino, and Mars's son, Farrell, silent till then, spoke up. "I heard the Manley bridge went out. Won't have it fixed till the weekend."

The Manley bridge connected Endocino with all parts south. There were alternate routes, but they meant going north then turning back south on another freeway. You could get to San Francisco in two hours using the bridge or in six if it was out.

"Where'd you hear that?" asked Mars.

"On Rock-99. They have traffic reports and that was the big news."

"Wow." Mars looked worried.

"The rains have slowed down a little. Don't you think we should check the Ridenours' house? They asked us to look after it while they were gone, and I know they were worried that it might rain," asked Roslyn.

"What?"

Roslyn stared at Mars with a slight smirk of significance.

"Oh! The *Ridenours'* house. Yeah, okay." Mars nodded.

"We'll be right back. You can read or watch TV or whatever you want to do," Mars said to DeVries.

"Would you mind if I took a shower?" he asked.

Mars thought it was Karma that she'd cleaned up the bathroom the previous weekend.

"Sure, go ahead. Let me get you some clean towels."

She led DeVries down the hall to the bathroom.

"Thanks."

DeVries ducked out to his car and came back in with a slick leather suitcase, then headed for the bathroom. The two women put on raincoats and went outside. As soon as they left, DeVries joined Farrell in the kitchen.

"Well, Farrell, how long do you think it'll take them to check the neighbor's house?" asked DeVries, rubbing his hands together.

"Maybe ten minutes. They're really going to smoke a joint, but Mom doesn't want me to think she uses drugs, so they say they're going to check on the neighbors. I've seen them," said Farrell, hoping to win the man's trust.

DeVries ignored the confidence. "Ten minutes, eh? In ten minutes, I bet you and I can clean the kitchen up."

"Do we have to?"

"I wash, you dry."

"Okay."

The boy wanted to get to know DeVries, and he was interested enough even to wash dishes.

Mars and Roslyn trudged around in the rain, sharing a big umbrella. They'd already pulled the wooden pipe out from its hiding place under the water meter.

"What are you going to do with him?" asked Roslyn, taking her third puff on the little pipe.

"I don't know. I just don't have room in my life for a man right now."

"Are you stubborn or stupid? When the gods send you a gift like this, and you turn him away, they don't send you any more."

Mars finished off the load. The wine, the pot, the rain, and the weirdness of the day combined to make her feel exceptionally light-headed. She laughed.

"You think I should ask him to stay the night?"

"If you don't, I'll have you committed."

"I hate you when you're right. What about Farrell?"

"He can come over and watch videos at my house."

"It's a school night."

"Rules are meant to be broken, right?"

"Thanks, Roslyn."

They both laughed. The rain picked up, and they went back to the house.

All the dishes were dried and put away. The table was cleared. And the garage door was open. Mars leaned in.

"Hello?"

"We just about have the freezer fixed. The compressor

motor was clogged with grease and wouldn't move. I took it out and cleaned it up. We ought to be on line in just a few minutes."

Farrell and DeVries were putting the final bolt on the garage freezer. Farrell handed the older man tools, entranced at his ability.

"Thank you, thank you." Mars's mouth dropped open.

Roslyn grabbed Mars by the shoulder and dragged her back into the kitchen out of earshot.

"Anything it takes to keep him here is worth it," whispered Roslyn emphatically.

After a dessert of stale cookies and instant coffee, Roslyn invented an errand and suggested that Farrell come with her. Farrell liked to go to Roslyn's house, because she let him watch whatever he wanted on cable TV and even drink the occasional beer.

"Can I stay over at Roslyn's tonight?"

Once in a blue moon, children ask the right question. Mars wondered if he'd been coached by Roslyn.

"Is your homework done?"

"I don't have any tonight."

"Sure. Roslyn, don't let him stay up too late."

"Never in a million years!" Roslyn and Farrell both laughed.

"I'm going to take that shower now," said DeVries. He disappeared into the back hall. Farrell filled a knapsack with comic books and headed out the door.

"You can start the car, but don't drive, okay?"

"Sure!" he said, heading out the door.

"Let me know what happens," said Roslyn, giving Mars a quick good-bye kiss on the cheek.

"Probably nothing, okay?"

"Let me know." Roslyn backed out the door, winking at Mars.

Mars listened outside the bathroom door till she heard flowing water, then ran into her bedroom. She frantically changed the sheets on the bed, then looked in her closet. The only thing that was sexy without being obviously seductive was a flowing, flowered dress she'd gotten from Roslyn. She closed the bedroom door and stripped off the sweatshirt DeVries had loaned her. She held it up to her face. It smelled like a man. She felt warm, like she was standing by one of her ovens. *What if nothing happens?* she thought. *Forget it. No one can say you didn't try.* She sprayed some Temptation on the nape of her neck and crossed her fingers, slipping on the dress.

When she entered the family room, DeVries was reading *Mother Jones,* perched on the chair as if ready to spring up. He had changed into khaki slacks and a brilliantly colored sweater. A fire was just starting to crackle in the fireplace.

"Sorry to leave you out here," she said. "That was a fast shower."

"I wondered where you all went."

"Would you like a glass of wine? All we have left is red wine."

"Well, if I have to be driving in this rain, I probably shouldn't . . ."

"Do you have to be someplace tomorrow?"

"No, not really."

"The Manley bridge is out, so you really can't get anywhere tonight. You could stay on my couch if you wanted." She tried not to sound too hopeful.

"If it's not imposing on you . . ."

"Not at all." His gaze met hers; his eyes were deep and hypnotic. She held the look until she felt self-conscious, then turned away, blushing.

"I'd love a glass of wine, Mars."

She fumbled with the corkscrew. Mars felt like she was on a first date. She saw DeVries standing by the record player.

"Can I put on a record?"

"Sure, whatever you want."

She guzzled a glass unobserved, then poured two more.

The opening bars of "Whiter Shade of Pale" by Procol Harem were playing as she entered the room.

"I'd forgotten I had that record! That's one of my favorite songs," Mars said, handing DeVries a glass of wine.

"It's my favorite, too," he said, sipping the wine.

"Do you dance?" he asked.

Mars laughed. "Well, I used to."

They danced slow and barefoot in her living room, without speaking. He led, steering her around the small floor. Mars hadn't pressed against a man for so long she hoped she didn't do anything wrong.

When the song ended, she still held him.

"Can we dance some more?"

"I'd love it."

They slow danced through two albums and one of her party tapes, hardly speaking. After the Moody Blues' "Nights in White Satin" faded away, she took his hand and silently led him around the room, switching out lights. They kissed in the firelight.

Mars made love that night for the first time in several years. Afterward, DeVries didn't fall asleep right away like so many men do. He held her close.

"It feels too right," he said.

"It's kind of scary," said Mars.

"I feel alive for the first time in many years," he said.

"If you want, I hate even to ask . . . so many men are scared by this question, but if you want to stay, you can. If you don't want to, I'll understand."

"You mean tonight?"

"I mean a little while. Just . . . stay. If you want to."

Her heart pounded. There was a long pause.

"I'd love to."

Mars had many strange dreams that night. So much had happened so fast.

7

Web was late. The day was overcast, and he'd slept through the alarm. The digital clock read 8:41, and his office hours were supposed to begin at 9:00. He threw on a shirt and some trousers and dashed downstairs dragging a cordless shaver across his face. The cereal bowl on the table meant Joyce had gotten up and made it to school okay. Mud paced back and forth, nervous, edgy, his toenails clicking against the hard kitchen floor. Web poured some Purina into the dog's bowl, then he jammed a couple slices of bread into the toaster and stuck a cup of day-old coffee into the microwave for himself.

He dialed the receptionist at his building. No answer; the student temp didn't start work till 9:00 A.M. *Who comes in early?* He examined a list of numbers scrawled on a pad next to the phone and dialed one.

"Wallenberg."

"Matt, this is Web. Can you put a note on my door? I'll be a little late for my office hours this morning."

"Sure, no problem. What's up?"

"Just overslept."

"You expecting anyone?"

"Yeah, there's a student who wants to get into one of the graduate courses. Renny McDonald, I hear he's a really sharp kid. He'll probably be late anyway. If you see him . . ."

"Gotcha covered Web. You going to the lunch with the Russian mathematicians?"

"Jesus! I forgot all about them. Dobrokiev has written me a bunch of letters. I've got to be there."

"See you when I see you."

"Unless I see you first."

"Bye."

Another day totally shot, thought Web. McDonald, then the Russians (who would want a long lunch with lots of drinking), and by that time it'd be three or four o'clock. He selected a blue sport jacket, stuffed a tie into his briefcase, and set the house alarm. Walking out the door, pushing a whole piece of unbuttered toast in his mouth, the headline of the *Chronicle* on the mat caught his eye: "Girl Doesn't Return from Grandma's House."

Standing in the open door, Web picked up the paper. The subheader read: "Is there a big bad wolf?"

A 19-year-old Vallejo woman, Annabell Norris, disappeared during a two-mile walk through suburban streets and has not been seen for four days. The recovery of a pair of underwear believed to belong to Norris, as well as her purse with nothing missing, has led Vallejo police to suspect foul play. Fear has gripped this normally tranquil community.

On Sunday Norris visited her grandmother, Sandra Bligh Warner, as she has done every week for the past year. When Norris failed to report to work for the second day at the building supply warehouse where she works as a bookkeeper, a supervisor called the woman's apartment. A roommate said she believed Norris was still with the grandmother.

Mrs. Bligh Warner doesn't believe Norris simply ran away. "She didn't seem depressed or sad," said the woman. "In fact, Annabell was excited about a promotion at her job and was preparing for exams at Solano Community College . . ."

The article continued on an inside page, but Web was transfixed by the photo. The girl was pretty, with large blue eyes, and her prom photo showed long, dark hair. Web's concentration was abruptly interrupted by the shrill electronic whine of his house alarm. He dashed inside to the closet and entered a four-digit code into a keypad, but the noise didn't stop. Mud whined and tried to escape the painful piercing sound by placing his paws on his ears.

Web picked up the phone and dialed the alarm company.

"Security Corps. May I have your code?"

"Two-three-nine-oh."

"I need the false alarm password, please, not your entry code."

"Just a minute."

Web rifled through a kitchen drawer. He couldn't remember what word he and Joyce had agreed upon. He finally found the contract he'd signed when the system was installed. Joyce had picked the password, which was written on the bottom of the sheet.

"Hubba Hubba," Web yelled over the shrill oscillating whine.

"Would you please repeat that, sir?"

Without inflection, Web repeated the words: "Hubba hubba."

The operator paused, and Web heard keys clicking on a computer. "Mr. Sloane? Thank you."

The alarm went off.

"We have already notified police," said the operator. "Because you didn't call inside of two minutes, there may be a fifty-dollar false alarm penalty, unless you are there when police arrive."

"Okay."

"Thank you for choosing Security Corps."

Web wrote "Hubba Hubba" next to the number of the alarm company. Fifty bucks a pop was expensive, and the alarm system was only a week old. He decided to wait a few minutes till the police arrived.

Mud trotted over to Web's side.

"Hell of a bad start for only just getting up, huh, boy?" he asked the dog, patting him on the head.

Mud adjusted his head until Web's hand hit the magic spot.

Mud followed Web to his office and sat outside the door. Web took the newspaper into his study, then turned to the continuation of the article. The girl was the proverbial "good egg," studying to get her CPA. Not a wild partier. Didn't have a boyfriend. Web clipped the article out of the paper and tacked it to the only open space on his two bulletin boards. In just a month since meeting Maria de

Rivera, he had accumulated quite a collection of what seemed to him suspicious occurrences.

Norris was the third girl missing in a month, but the papers hadn't made any connections. The other two stories had been buried on back pages, possibly because Kuwait and Iraq had dominated the news so long. He checked his moon-phase watch. 9:22. He'd give the police another ten minutes, then just eat the fifty-buck charge; he couldn't show up much later than 10 A.M. and expect to accomplish anything.

Web considered the articles pinned to his bulletin boards. What impact might they have on Joyce if she wandered into the study? It wouldn't be good. He pulled down the papers one by one, placing them into a manila folder.

> "Nursing Student Runaway"
> "Student Still Missing"
> "Tico Officials Make No Progress"
> "Teenager Gone: Bicycle Recovered"
> "Day Hiker Doesn't Return"
> "Search for Day Hiker Continues"
> "Woman Missing in Forest Not Found"
> "Weather Halts Forest Service Search"

Examining the articles, Web noticed a striking similarity among the photos of the three girls. Although from different towns and different backgrounds, they could have been sisters. *They could be Joyce's sisters.* Web put the three newspaper photos in the top of the file.

When he finished, the police still hadn't arrived, so Web scrawled a note, reset the house alarm, and drove to his office at Berkeley. Mud watched through the front window as his master left.

A tall scarecrow-thin kid with long blond hair was sitting outside Web's office, marking up an article with a highlighter pen and tapping the keys on a laptop computer. When he saw Web he stood up.

"Hey, are you Sloane?"

"You're Renny McDonald?"

"Yeah."

"C'mon in."

Web flipped on the lights and sat down. The student dumped a backpack, several loose books, and the computer on the ground and slouched into the chair opposite Web's desk.

"You know, we usually don't let undergrads into The Ethics of Information."

"Well the deans said I hadda try to get in."

"Which deans?"

"Well, the discipline guy, Dean Couger. I got into some trouble. I, uh, like hacked the university network, and they said I hadda either take your class or maybe face suspension."

"You're *that* McDonald?" Web felt the blood rise in his face.

"Yeah, I guess so."

Over the summer someone had taken over the eleven campus mainframe computers from a payphone, locked out more than a hundred users, and somehow tied the machines together. All just to make computer-generated psychedelic pictures. It had been in the student paper for a week until they caught the guy. This guy.

"You can't just walk right in to this course because a dean told you to. It's a demanding class."

"Well, I read your books."

"Which ones?" Web wanted to call the kid's bluff. His textbooks were not light reading.

"You know, the four published ones, and I also found your dissertation stashed in an on-line database. They were pretty cool."

"When did you do this?" Web squinted his eyes. McDonald was making an outrageous claim.

"Uh, last weekend."

"Mm-hmm. Last weekend. Did you understand what you read?"

"Yeah, I think I got it." The kid bit his lower lip and scowled. "Well, no, not exactly. I kinda got hung up on a couple concepts."

"Well, did you understand anything?"

"I got the gist but got way confused mainly 'cause you

start out in the first two books with a probabilistic kinda structure for queries into large or infinite data sets, then in the third one, what's it called?"

"Meaning from Chaos." Web listened intently, ready to call the boy's bluff.

"Yeah, in that one you get real structured, with these bitchin' multiple-criteria data queries and command sets, almost like a neural network, and then in the last book you like do this back flip to stab and grab again with no allowance for structured query at all, like you gave up on neural nets? That kinda blew my mind. And I think there's a typo, one of the information probability formulas is upside down. I freaked at first, thinking, whoa, this is over my head, but figured out it must be, like, the typesetters or something, right?"

The kid held out a page halfway through Web's fourth book. A formula was highlighted, and numbers were scribbled all over the page in a juvenile scrawl. Web's eyes grew large as he stared at the boy. He took the book from McDonald and spent the next half hour discussing his ideas with the kid. The formula hadn't been a typo, but an error that Web himself, the peer review board, and three years of grad students had missed. Renny McDonald, who looked like a rock and roller and talked like he had grown up in a mall, had plowed through fourteen years of research in a weekend and nailed the mistake on a quick reading.

At 11 A.M. Renny looked at his watch and stood up.

"Sorry, but I gotta go to band practice."

"It's been nice meeting you, Renny." Web had heard of computer prodigies like this but never before met one in the flesh.

"Do you think it would be okay if I, like, took your course, you know, even though I'm like an undergrad?"

"I think we could make room."

"Really? Thanks, man. If I got kicked outta school my old man would have a cow."

"Thanks for stopping by."

Web watched the student disappear into the hall, then closed his office door and sat down. His in box was full of university paperwork; he moved the whole tray to the floor.

Then Web pulled out the manila folder from his briefcase and reread the articles, searching for any nuance that might allay his suspicions. He cleared off his desk and arranged the articles in a new order. All the photos were placed at the top of his desk. Below that he laid out the stories, organized by victim. He was about halfway through covering the desk when there was a knock at the door.

"It's open."

Wallenberg, a muscular middle-aged man with a tanned bald spot, walked in.

"Web, we have to go."

"Oh, the Russians!"

"Yeah. It's in five minutes. Let's jog."

"Let's walk and be late."

"Wimp," said Wally, challenging.

"Wimp? Okay, let's not jog. Let's run, full out," said Web.

"Okay. I'll walk."

Wallenberg perused the articles on the desk while Web was pulling on his sport coat but did not comment. Web was embarrassed by his friend's silent, judgmental gaze and covered his desk with a newspaper. On the walk to lunch with Wally, Web forced the conversation to neutral topics— small talk and dirty limericks. He was relieved that the mess on his desk did not come up.

Web got back to his office at four o'clock. It was all he could do to get away from the Russian mathematicians, who kept toasting him and repeating how much they loved him. The Russians were an emotional bunch for math heads. Web's work had been very well received in the USSR, and this was the first group of Russian scientists to meet him in person. But he was bored by them; due to the lag in translation, they were still reading papers five and ten years old.

The articles on his desk quickly drew Web's attention; they held a powerful sway over him. Though a little tipsy, Web knew he had to do something soon or throw them away. *"Knowledge must lead to action."* Web's own words. He dug through his files till he found a letter from an old friend. An office phone number was printed on the stationery. Web lifted the phone and dialed.

"FBI, Special Agent Reynolds's office."

A woman's voice. Web was surprised. "Does Jack have a secretary now?" he asked.

The secretary ignored him. "How may I help you?"

"May I speak to Jack Reynolds, please?"

"Who is calling?"

"Web Sloane."

"One moment, I'll connect you."

There was a long lull; intermittent beeps reminded him that the call was being recorded.

"Reynolds."

"Jack, this is Web Sloane."

"Web! How the hell are you? I thought you were living in Seattle."

"I moved down here about six months ago. I remembered you'd been transferred here."

"So, do you want to get together for a beer?"

"That'd be nice, but I wanted to talk a little business first."

"Can you tell me on the phone?"

Web hesitated, remembering that the call was being recorded. "I'd rather meet you in person."

"How 'bout tomorrow afternoon? There's a very dull meeting I'd love to skip."

"Sure."

"I'll meet you in the lobby."

Web arranged and rearranged the photos on his desk, drawing lines between the faces. He wanted to be fully prepared the next day so he could convince Reynolds of what he believed.

8

"*Hey guys, tonight on Dial-a-Date we promise to finally have the ideal woman: a blind, deaf nymphomaniac millionaire who owns a liquor store.*"

Mars laughed at the stupid jokes that the morning disk jockey cracked on the classic rock radio station, even though they were sexist and she'd heard them a million times before. She was a little tense that morning, worried about Alan. The month since he moved in had been truly magical. Her sense of humor had come back to her. Just having such a warm, helpful *man* around had made her feel constantly giddy, like a teenager with a big crush: a one-month high that she hoped to ride forever.

She was tense because of the previous night. Alan hadn't been quite able to perform in bed. *Perform*. Mars hated the Dr. Ruth sterility of the term. They'd enjoyed a very nice evening just watching TV and smoking a joint. When they retired, Alan appeared to respond to her advances, then suddenly became nervous. When she realized what was occurring, Mars tried to console him by telling him how wonderful he was and that the sex was just icing on the cake. Alan clammed up, angrily staying on his side of the bed all night. She felt a little sorry for him.

She didn't sleep well and went into the bakery early to make something special. Next to her on the car seat were some fresh croissants, still warm from her oven. Mars wanted to bring home a peace offering. She really didn't care about his occasional impotence—this was only the second time it had happened. From what the radio therapists said, it was no big deal. The croissants were meant to be a gentle way to show that there were no hard feelings on her part. *God, I'd hate to lose him.* If he liked the breakfast in bed, maybe they'd crack a bottle of champagne, make mimosas, and just stay in bed all day. The bakery can remain closed once in a while for the sake of love.

There was a note from Farrell on the refrigerator. Roslyn had picked him up and was going to feed him breakfast at the diner before taking him to school. On tiptoe, Mars crept back toward her bedroom. In the hall she kicked off her shoes and fluffed up her hair. She wanted to climb right into bed with Alan. Slowly she opened the bedroom door. The bed was empty. *Oh my god.* He was never up before eight. She looked around. The big basket where Alan kept his dirty clothes was empty—all thirty pairs of socks, all the shirts and slacks, gone. None of his things were around. Mars sat on the bed. Nothing that good could ever last, she thought.

The front door slammed. Footsteps came closer down the hall. Mars wiped her eyes. The bedroom door opened.

"Alan! God, I was worried about you!"

"I just threw in a load of laundry. No big deal."

Alan was wearing shorts and a sweatshirt. He placed a box of detergent on the dresser.

"Come on over here, you big lug, you." Mars did her best Mae West imitation for his benefit, placing her hands on her hips and hiking the hem of her skirt up around her waist.

"Mars, I really can't, I have a lot of things to do today." He bounced from foot to foot, standing his ground.

"Well then, soldier, I'll just have to come get you, won't I?" Her Mae West was colored with a tinge of desperation as she walked toward him, swinging her hips. She put her arms around him and nibbled his ear. Alan kept his arms stiff by his side and backed up till he was pinned in the corner, before lashing out.

"No, NO! I have a busy day."

She quickly dropped her grip. There was a brutish quality about his anger. She'd never seen him like this. Mars backed up across the room.

"Okay, I'm sorry. At least have a croissant. I just got them from the bakery."

"Toss one."

She grabbed one of her carefully made pastries from the bag and tossed it to him, underhand.

"Thanks. Looks good."

Alan quickly scurried out of the room. Mars collapsed onto the bed with a sigh. *He's getting bored with me. I can tell. I'm not good enough, I'm not good enough.* She heard the slam of a car door, the engine starting up, Alan's tires grating across the gravel. Mars laid on the bed for a long time, replaying in her mind what she might have done wrong in their month together. *Was he gone for good?*

Usually Mars could lose herself in work, but today everything seemed to be going in slow motion. Nothing came out right, and even her favorite customers just came and went in a blur.

At 3:15 the phone rang while she was totaling an order of cupcakes for several girls who'd just gotten out of school.

"Mrs. Chittenden? This is Dr. Svoboda, the guidance counselor at your son's school."

"Yes? Is something wrong?"

"Can you talk, Mrs. Chittenden?"

"Just a moment."

Mars put her hand over the phone and addressed the group of teens. "Those are free today! But only if you eat them outside."

"Thanks, Mars!" the older one said and the girls left, giggling at their unexpected windfall. Mars followed them out and locked the door.

"Dr. Svoboda?"

"Yes, I just wanted to tell you that one of our teachers noticed a lot of activity around your son's locker today . . ."

"And?"

"Well, he had quite a few of these adult magazines."

"What?"

"Pornography. And he was charging a quarter for other kids to have a look. We took the magazines away, and he's not really in trouble just yet, but you might want to have a talk with him."

"Pornography? You mean, like *Playboy* or something?"

"No, it's a bit harsher. A *lot* harsher. I can hardly look at some of this stuff actually. Your boy may have some very serious problems. He's made quite a bit of trouble here."

Mars felt her blood pressure rocket up. "Farrell is not a

troublemaker. I don't know what he's done, but you must be exaggerating."

"Well, I've known him for three years, and he seems to be a good kid. But sometimes the ones who seem best turn out to be the worst."

"Dr. Svoboda, you are talking about my son. I don't like the tone of your voice."

Svoboda sighed; parents never believed him. "This could just be a phase, so I'm not going to do anything but warn him." He sighed. "This time."

"Okay. I'll be right over. Thanks, Dr. Svoboda, for letting me know."

"We try to help."

Mars locked the register, turned off the lights and ovens, and put up her Back in One Hour—Thanks for Waiting! sign. All the o's in the hand-drawn sign were happy faces. But Mars was scowling. She sped across town to the school. *The nerve of that man.* His words kept echoing through her mind: "Sometimes the ones who seem the best turn out the worst." *What a jerk.*

Svoboda was filling out grading forms when Mars stormed through the door.

"Mrs. Chittenden? Would you like a seat?"

"It's *Ms.* I think I'll stand."

"I can see you are upset and you should be. Farrell could turn out to be quite a problem if this continues." He wore a bureaucratic smile.

"I don't know you, but Farrell is not a troublemaker. This is the first time he's had trouble of any kind, and I think you should get off your high horse about it."

He opened a file. "Well, according to my records, in the third grade he got in some fights. It says here, 'Must constantly observe on playground.'"

"Third grade?" Mars's mind reeled. *"Third grade?* You're talking about something that happened seven years ago. He got in a fight when he was a tiny kid, and you keep a record of it now?"

Svoboda didn't modulate his tone. He was used to dealing with angry parents. "We just try to keep a record of repeated behavior . . ."

"May I see your file?" She grabbed the folder off his desk.

"I'd like to keep this and this and this." Mars pulled out the records of elementary school, the yellow form indicating Farrell had once gotten in a fight.

"Those are school records, Ms. Chittenden."

"Not any more. Please give me the magazines."

Svoboda didn't dare refuse. He handed over two large envelopes.

"Those pictures are quite harsh. I hope at least you'll have a talk with your son." Svoboda added hopefully.

"I think I will. And I think I'll talk to my friend on the school board about you keeping personal files on children that rival the KGB's. Goodbye, Dr. Svoboda."

Mars walked out, racing between the lockers to daylight. She remembered the claustrophobic feeling of being in high school all too well.

In the parking lot, she stared at the envelopes with fear for a long moment before opening one up.

Quite harsh.

Dr. Svoboda had been right. Each magazine she pulled out had a garish fluorescent-colored title page. *Three Men and a Babe. Little Oral Annie. James Bondage and the 007 Girls.* Inside the cheaply printed pages were brightly lit photos of explicit sex acts peppered with advertisements for 976 numbers and prostitution services. Mars felt the blood drain from her face as she looked at them. Huge close-ups of genitalia, sometimes belonging to several men and one woman, were in every magazine.

Although the captions were about sex, the images were primarily ugly portrayals of the sexual humiliation of women. When she opened the second envelope she let out a desperate "Oh, my God." The magazines were European, and every picture portrayed young girls being tied up with tape, rope, or wire, older men performing unspeakable acts upon them. Bad European teeth grinning beneath black leather hoods. One, *Blood Sisters,* had two naked girls, no older than fifteen, being whipped with straps and barbed wire. On each page, the whipping got crueler. The wounds didn't look like stage makeup.

Mars's hands shook. She got out of her car and threw both of the envelopes and Farrell's records into the school dumpster. Worried that someone would find them, she reopened the dumpster and buried the envelopes as deep in the trash as she could. Mars got in her car and sped home.

Farrell was already there; his knapsack was in the middle of the kitchen table. She marched down the hall. His bedroom door, covered with stickers and a big Bart Simpson Hey, Man—No Adults Allowed sign, was closed. She knocked. No answer.

"Farrell, it's Mom."

"I'm taking a nap," came the reply.

"Please open the door. I want to talk to you."

She heard footsteps, the *click* of the lock being undone. The door opened slowly. Farrell looked pitiful; he had been crying, and his eyes were still bloodshot.

"C'mon out, angel, I just want to talk to you."

He followed her to the kitchen and sat at the table. She sat across from him, and Farrell grabbed his backpack and held it in front of himself, as if for protection.

"I talked to Dr. Svoboda at school."

"Yeah, I know."

"I saw the magazines he took from you."

Farrell slumped on the knapsack. "You did?"

She nodded. Farrell was ashamed.

"Was that all of them?" she asked.

"It's all I have now."

"Were there more?"

"I had another bag here, but I burned them when I got home in the charcoal grill."

She didn't know where to begin. Mars knew she should tell him why they were bad; she should punish him; but a question was burning in her mind that she had to know the answer to first.

"Where did you get them? From another kid?"

"I don't wanna tell," Farrell said, tears welling up in his eyes.

"Look, if you're worried about getting one of your friends in trouble, don't. You'll probably be doing him a favor if his parents talk to him."

"I didn't get 'em from another kid."

"Where? Where did you get these?" Mars nervously twirled a strand of her long red hair in her hand.

"Do I have to tell?"

"Yes."

"I know I'm not supposed to go into his room, but I did."

"Whose room?"

"Alan's." Farrell pointed out the window to the garage that Alan had converted to his personal workroom.

Mars was caught completely off guard. First, the previous night's *performance* problem, now dirty pictures. She stared out the window at his garage as if in shock.

"What is it, Mom?" Farrell sensed something big was wrong.

"Did you really get them from his room?"

"Yeah. I'm sorry. I shouldn't a' been in there."

She wanted to know more.

"How many did he have?"

"I dunno, I was just fooling around and saw them and so I took 'em."

"He doesn't know you have them?"

"I don't know. They were under the bed."

Mars had heard enough; she was angry and bewildered.

"Go to your room."

"What?"

"I said, go to your room. Stay in there till dinner."

"Okay, okay, I'm going."

Farrell disappeared down the hall, glad to be off the hook temporarily. Mars forgot all about her talk about sex and women and being respectful. She poured a glass of Gallo red and picked up the phone.

"Roslyn?"

"Hey, Marsy, where are you? I was supposed to pick up the bakery stuff and it said you were closed."

"Can you take a break if I come in?"

"We're just about to start dinner rush."

"Please?"

"Rupert will kill me."

"It's important." Mars distractedly chewed on a fingernail.

"Rupert will live. Bring our bread, and I'll just leave the suckers to starve."

"Thanks."

"Bye."

Mars slugged down the wine and hit the road.

The diner was packed. Mars set the box of bread and baked goods down at the counter and caught Roslyn's eye.

"Just a minute, honey."

Roslyn clutched her stomach and waited till Rupert, the balding expatriate Englishman who owned the diner, saw her.

"Rupe, doll, c'mere."

"Yes, what is it, Roslyn?"

"I have to take a break."

"We're full and have a line! Bloody hell, I only have two other waitresses for all the tables."

"C'mon, Jan can cover the counter for a little."

"No! What is it?"

Roslyn leaned in and spoke in a stage whisper.

"You know . . . female trouble." She patted her gut and grimaced.

Rupert blushed. "Oh, sure. Fine, fine. Take your break. Do you need me to boil some water or something?"

"No, that's okay. Thanks."

Roslyn turned around and winked at Mars. She wasn't exactly lying when she said female trouble. She knew Rupert would rather do cartwheels on the counter in his underwear than discuss menstrual cramps, real or imagined. The befuddled Englishman was so predictable. *Boil some water?*

Roslyn listened to Mars's story intently, sipping a diet Coke as the two women sat in the car.

"So what're you telling me for?" asked Roslyn.

"What should I do?"

"I'll tell you—exactly nothing."

"But last night and then this morning and now these dirty magazines . . ."

Roslyn put her hand on her friend's shoulder.

"Did those magazines look new?"

"No."

"Alan was traveling for weeks, maybe months. He probably got horny on the road."

"But they're so obscene!" said Mars.

"Think of it as a good thing. Most men, out on the road, they'd just screw anything that moved. But I bet he kept to himself, you know, no road bimbos, just looking at them pictures and jerkin' himself off," said Roslyn.

"That's good?"

"Sure! That means he doesn't have a girl in every port, like some traveling men I know. He probably bought them before he even met you." Roslyn sounded sure of herself.

"But they're not erotic, they're just disgusting. And Farrell found them." Mars was still upset.

"Okay, Mars, maybe you do have to tell him to keep them away from Farrell. But it doesn't mean he's a raging pervert or something. A guy goes into a strange town, goes to a liquor store or whatever, and just buys what's ever there. It doesn't mean a thing."

"I don't know, Roslyn."

"Look. Didn't he fix your fridge? Paint the house? And let me tell you, you've been a lot happier since he's been around, at least from what I can see. Why do something that could send him packing?"

"You're right. I guess I love him."

"Sure you love him, Mars," said Roslyn. "So don't read too much into it. He's a good guy."

The two sat in silence.

"Was one of 'em really called *Three Men and a Babe?*"

"Yeah."

The two friends laughed hard.

"I guess it is funny," Mars said.

"Sure it is. Don't take it so hard."

Mars gave Roslyn a big hug. "Thanks for keeping my head on straight. You always seem to know the right thing to do."

"Yeah, except in my own life."

"Oh, Roslyn."

They hugged again, then Roslyn got out of the car and returned to the hellish dinner shift.

When 7:30 P.M. arrived and Alan hadn't returned home, Mars went ahead and ate dinner with Farrell. She had her little talk with him over chicken and dumplings, and he seemed to understand what she said about girls and love and sex.

"Do I have to get in trouble?" he asked warily when she was done talking.

"I just want you to write an apology to the principal. Put in there some of the stuff we've talked about."

"Do I have to?"

"Yes. I want to read it before you give it to him, though."

"Okay, Mom."

Mars was dozing in front of the TV watching Arsenio Hall when Alan came home.

"Hi, Mars." Alan set down a brand-new briefcase and pulled a beer out of the fridge. Then he sat in the overstuffed chair next to the couch.

"Hi, Alan. You're out late."

"Hey, what the hell. I got a new job today!"

She could see that he was drunk. "What?"

"I got a new job. I'm going to be working part-time."

"Where'll you be working?"

"You won't like this." Alan sucked on the Bud Dry.

"Where?" Mars fidgeted on the couch.

"At the Vine County sheriff's office."

"The cops?" asked Mars, unbelieving.

"He's cool, he's really cool. We went out for some beers after he hired me," said Alan.

"So what're you gonna be, a narc?" Mars sat upright.

"Nah, nothing like that. He just had two girls quit on him, and he doesn't know how to run the computers. I'll be just doing some computer work, which I love anyway. I learned all about computers in the—at my last job."

"Are you sure it's cool?"

"Yes, I'm sure. He was quite generous, too. Make my own schedule, as long as it comes to twenty hours a week. Pays $15.50 an hour plus benefits."

"How come they went for that?"

"He's just stuck in the cold. No one has any idea how to run the thing, and I met him last week in the line at the carryout. So I'll have total autonomy."

Mars sat upright on the couch and pushed her dress over her bare legs.

"I thought you didn't need to work. You know, all that money from the stockbroker company."

"I don't really need the money. But it sounds interesting to me. My uncle was a cop."

"I didn't know that," said Mars.

"I start in a week and a half."

Mars didn't want to confront him about his job on top of everything else. "I guess congratulations are in order," she said glumly.

"Damn straight." Alan finished the beer and immediately fetched another from the refrigerator.

"Alan . . ."

"What's up?"

"We have to talk about something."

"Yeah?" Alan leaned forward on his chair.

"Farrell got into your room, you know, the garage. I told him he shouldn't go in there, but . . ."

"What did he do in there?" He cut her off. There was panic in Alan's voice. He slammed his beer down and pushed the large chair back.

"Nothing. He just found some dirty magazines and took them to school . . ."

Alan's face went blank for a moment. Mars thought she saw a look of concern on his face, but it could have just as easily been the wheels of thought spinning in motion.

"Ah, those magazines, ah. Those magazines, they, one time, when I was driving, ah, I gave a ride to a hitcher, you know, hitchhiker, who seemed like a nice enough guy. And he left them in the car. I opened up a couple of them and they were disgusting."

"I know!"

"I'm sorry Farrell found them. I always meant to throw them away but just forgot completely about them."

"I'm sorry, too. I told him not to go back there, but boys will be boys."

"It won't happen again, Mars," he said solemnly.

"Thanks. I was a little worried."

Mars got off the couch and slid onto Alan's lap.

"I love you, Alan."

"I love you too, Mars."

"C'mon, let's go to bed."

"Let's do."

That night, Alan fell asleep almost immediately; he didn't even get the opportunity to experience a *performance* problem. Mars stared at his face for a long time before drifting off herself.

When Farrell got off the bus the next afternoon, he saw Alan sitting on a folding chair in the middle of the gravel driveway, his arms crossed on his chest.

"Hi, Alan." Farrell made a quick, jerky wave and made a beeline for the house door.

"Not so fast. I just want to talk to you for a minute." Alan tried to sound friendly.

"Um, I'm supposed to go over to Danny's and stuff." Farrell moved slowly toward the door.

"It'll just take a minute. C'mere." DeVries made a broad beckoning gesture.

Farrell cautiously approached Alan and stopped a few feet away, gripping his backpack in front of his chest with both hands.

"What?" Farrell bounced from foot to foot.

"I just want to talk to you about going into my room. That's all." Alan spoke in patient, measured phrases.

"Hey, I'm sorry, okay?"

"You know why it's wrong to get into other people's things?"

"I already got in trouble at school from the principal and the guidance counselor and also in trouble with Mom. I don't hafta hear it from you, too." Farrell's eyes grew large.

"Farrell, you got *me* in hot water too. Don't ever go in my room. Understood?" Alan's temper was rising.

"It's partly your fault, man. You shouldn't have that stuff in the first place."

"It's my room and I don't want you going in there."

"That used to be my workroom and now I can't even go in. They said whoever's stuff that is is some kind of pervert, and I don't think you should even live back there."

Farrell turned toward the door. Alan leaped up and grabbed his shoulder.

"Read my lips. That's my room now. And if you ever go in there again, you'll regret it. You'll find out what 'sorry' is."

"Leggo my shoulder." Farrell wriggled in the man's grip.

"Say 'I won't ever go in there again.'"

"Shut up, you pervert!" yelled Farrell.

"Say it." Alan's fingers dug into Farrell's flesh. "Say 'I won't ever go in there again.'"

Now real fear was rising in Farrell; he tried seriously to break away, but Alan's iron grip seemed to sap his strength.

"I'll never go in there again!" Farrell bleated.

Alan dug his fingers in deeper. "If I ever catch you again, I'm going to take your precious skateboard and saw it right in half."

Farrell turned pale at this new threat. "You wouldn't!"

"Just try me."

DeVries loosened his hold. Farrell broke away and ran into the house, slamming the door behind him.

9

The FBI office in San Francisco was a tall stone government building in the midst of downtown, with no sign, just the street number. Web walked in through revolving glass doors and crossed the lobby to a large counter where two men in suits sat. Two visible video cameras were pointed at him; he suspected there were more hidden surveillance devices elsewhere.

"I'm Web Sloane. Jack Reynolds is expecting me."

"I'll page *Special Agent Reynolds.* Please take a seat."

Web sat in a government-issue padded chair. Moments later, an elevator door opened. A handsome black man, a little younger than Web, wearing a neatly tailored navy blue suit stepped out.

"Web Sloane—"

"Jack, you're looking great!"

They shook hands. Reynolds handed him a badge. Web's name was already typed onto it. Web put on the badge. Reynolds opened the elevator with a card key and Web followed.

"You have a secretary now, nice suits, and you're in San Francisco—not bad for a kid from Seattle, Jack," said Web.

Reynolds smiled broadly. "I've done all right. The company has been pretty good to me, I guess. So how's your wife . . ."

Web flinched at the mention of Alice. Reynolds instantly realized his faux pas. "I'm sorry. I mean your daughter?"

Jack Reynolds had been one of the primary FBI investigators on the Bundy case and was the lone voice at the FBI recommending adoption of Web's computer database, SKID. In the late seventies the two men had seen each other almost daily, until Reynolds was transferred to San Francisco.

"Joyce is doing fine. She finishes high school this year."

"Great, great. College?"

"Ah, well, we're working on that." Web grimaced.

"None of my business."

After passing through two additional card-key doors and past a secretary, they arrived in Reynolds' office on the top floor. It had a spectacular view of downtown San Francisco.

Reynolds sat at his desk, idly bending paper clips.

"What's up, Web?"

"There's some funny stuff going on up in a little town called Tico, and I wanted to see what you knew about it."

"Tico, Tico, what county is that?"

"Vine County. Your bailiwick."

"Only my bailiwick till they open a new district office next year. Go on."

Web told him of the two bodies found, the missing girl, and the strange stories he'd collected from the newspapers. Laid out end to end it sounded pretty convincing to Web. But Reynolds didn't budge.

"So, what do you think the FBI should be doing?"

"I wonder if you could look over the shoulder at the Vine County sheriff and see if he's missing anything. Or maybe take up the case." Web leaned forward, hopeful.

"Can't do it," Reynolds stated firmly.

Web leaned forward, irritated. He hadn't expected to be turned down so quickly. "Why not? I mean, what if the sheriff's not doing his job . . ."

"Web, that attitude's out-of-date. The FBI can't second-guess every Podunk sheriff in the country. Law enforcement is built around trust between agencies. We give support to local lawmen and give 'em full use of company services when they ask us to, but unless it's a federal crime, we can't barge in and take over. That kind of thing is obnoxious, presumptuous, and ended with J. Edgar Hoover. We're a lot better off for it."

"I have some doubts about this Block character. Have you ever met him?"

"Block? The sheriff? Sure I met him. In '82 his brother was busted for growing pot and transporting interstate. That was my case."

"So what happened?"

"The brother's in jail. But as far as we could tell, Block wasn't involved at all. I interrogated him at length and talked to neighbors and co-workers. He cooperated as fully as anyone could in a case involving a brother."

"Is he a good cop?"

"Sheriff's an elected post. Block's popular with the locals. And from what I see, he seems like a pretty good cop." Reynolds looked down while speaking, twisting a paper clip so hard it broke.

"Off the record, what do you think?" Web knew there was something Reynolds wasn't saying.

Reynolds stood and closed the door, then moved next to Web and spoke in a hushed voice.

"Off the record? Block's a redneck bigot and a drunkard. He throws these big barbecues to raise campaign funds and is tight with all the growers who use illegal immigrants on their vineyards. A little too tight, for my taste. But I don't think he's incompetent, nor do I think he breaks the law. He probably does a better job than most, 'cause he knows practically everyone in his county by name."

Web pushed his argument harder. "Don't you think it's bigger than just Vine County? What about the missing girls? Do you think we have another serial killer? That's what I really want to find out."

Reynolds stood, shook off his jacket, and stared out the window as he spoke. "Web, you're a damn good professor. But you can't start reading a few newspaper articles and decide there's a serial killer running amok. What you're doing is what happens to our first- and second-year agents. They dig a little and start seeing connections everywhere. But when you've been at it awhile, you realize that mostly it's just isolated incidents and the connections are coincidence."

Web clenched his fists. "You saying it's in my head?" he spat out challengingly.

Reynolds didn't answer directly. He turned to Web and leaned forward. He wanted to speak as plainly as possible. "You suffered some terrible losses from a killer. So you read the paper, and articles about missing girls leap out at you. If you'd been robbed, maybe you'd notice burglary stories. I'm just saying that we have a lot more information than you do, and we move in at the first credible, unimpeachable sign of anything that looks like a pattern and falls into our jurisdiction. We can't have our men chasing ghosts."

"So you can't get the FBI involved." Web scowled and closed his manila folder.

"Web, I can do practically anything. But I won't waste resources and time just because you're a nice guy." Reynolds sat back at his desk.

"Do you think you could grant me access to FBI files on the cases? Nothing top secret, just give me a look at what you get over the transom."

"I'd like to, Web, as a friend, but there's confidentiality, and frankly, I think we have the best people in the world analyzing things anyway. You have better things to do."

"You're just going to ignore it, Jack?"

"That's not what I said. But you can't go seeing psychokillers under every rock, Web. I think you're just putting two and two together and getting five."

Web stood up, insulted. He felt a throbbing in his forehead; a migraine was coming on. "I'm acting crazy?"

"C'mon. Of course not. You're just concerned. I'm concerned, too. But there are already mechanisms set up to deal with each of your questions."

"Will you at least keep an eye on Block?"

"Watch this."

Reynolds picked up the phone and dialed.

"Dorinda? There were two murders in Vine County, unidentified bodies. I think we sent Toriyama from forensics up there a while back. It's being handled by their sheriff. Tomorrow morning, put everything we have on my desk . . . okay. Thanks, Dorinda."

Reynolds put down the phone. "It's great having people working under you. She'll have to stay late digging that stuff out. I'll take a look tomorrow. But I'll bet you dollars to donuts it's not a federal case."

"Thanks, Jack." Web was mollified a little.

"Still want to go for that beer?"

"I'd like to, but not tonight. I have a long drive."

"Okay. Don't be a stranger. I've got to walk you out."

Web drove straight home rather than going back to the office. It was nearly six o'clock; the throbbing had grown to a constant pain from his neck to his forehead. About a mile from home he pulled into Safeway to pick up that night's dinner. A beat-up old red Peugeot parked next to him. When he climbed out of his car, he heard an unctuous voice speaking the Queen's English with a hint of an Indian accent.

"Good afternoon, Web! Funny chance occurrence, this!"

He looked over to the car: It contained Ramiah Bose. Web hadn't seen him in class since Joyce's big night out when she wrecked her car and spent the night at his house.

Web forced a smile. "Ramiah—hi. Nice to see you." It wasn't.

Bose wore jeans and a tweed jacket and looked at the world through John Lennon-style granny glasses. He lit a clove cigarette and walked around his car.

"I'm sorry I missed the last two lectures. I had some guests from Oxford visiting." Bose couldn't resist a chance to mention Oxford, where he had earned a degree before coming to Berkeley's Statistics Lab.

"Well, we missed you, too," Web said, hoping his voice lacked any trace of irony.

"Say, I was going to the Old Vic tonight to catch a Fassbinder film. Perhaps you and Joyce would like to join me."

"I'm really busy, Ramiah."

"Perhaps just Joyce?"

The thought of his daughter dating a man in his thirties caused a wave of fury to grip Web. He had an urge to punch him but held it in check. He stepped closer to the student and spoke softly, with a hint of threat in his voice.

"Ramiah, you're a good student. But I don't want you going out with Joyce. She's seventeen years old, and you're . . ."

"I'm thirty-one this year. But I'm not "dating" Joyce. We've just gone out for coffee and talk a few times."

This was news to Web. He thought the ill-fated party was the only time she'd seen him.

"Listen: Joyce is in her senior year of high school. She should be seeing kids her own age. You can miss my lectures as often as you want, and I can't do a thing about it, but Joyce is my daughter and I don't want you seeing her. *Capisce?"*

"Web, she'll soon be eighteen and permitted to do anything she wants. I don't think you can treat her like she's a little girl."

The words landed on Web's ears like fingernails on chalk. *Nobody* told Web how to raise his daughter. "I can make your life very difficult, Bose," said Web.

"Is that a threat?"

"That's a promise."

Web was shaken. He got back into his car.

"Aren't you going to do your shopping?" Bose asked as Web rolled up his window.

"I think we'll eat out tonight."

Web gunned his engine and drove out of the parking lot. Bose finished his clove cigarette and swore at the professor once he was out of earshot. Then he headed for a pay phone.

When Web entered his house, carrying a bag of fast-food chicken, Joyce hung up the phone and scowled at him.

"Hi, Joyce! I got Pollo Loco."

Joyce stood silent, steaming.

"Okay, what is it?" Web put down the yellow bag and folded his arms.

"Dad, you can't tell me what to do."

"I just got home! I haven't told you anything."

"I'm talking about Ramiah." She moved so that the kitchen counter was between them.

"It's about time you talked about Ramiah."

"He told me what you said."

"Already?"

"Yes. You can't tell me who to see and who not to see."

"Joyce, I'm talking about your best interest. Ramiah is more than thirty years old."

"What you did—it's so embarrassing!" Joyce's voice raised an octave. She was furious.

"Why didn't you tell me you were going out with him?"

"I didn't 'go out' with him. We just went to a couple concerts."

Web massaged his temples as the level of deception was made clear. "A couple concerts? Ramiah said it was a few coffee shops. How much are you telling me?" It sounded to Web as if both Ramiah and Joyce were practicing some serious spin control.

"It's none of your business."

"How long have you been seeing him?"

"I'm not *seeing* him. We're just friends."

"Well I don't want you becoming friends."

"Dad, why not? He's the only intelligent guy in this whole town."

"Joyce, I want you to tell me straight who you're going out with and when."

"Get serious!"

"Then you're grounded. For the next week, you can just enjoy the company of your dear old father."

"Dad! I have tickets to a concert!"

"You have to try to sell them."

"I'm almost eighteen."

"But you still live here. Understood?"

"No." She opened, then immediately slammed shut a cupboard door. Inside, something made of glass shattered.

"You want to be grounded for two weeks?"

"You're so unfair." Joyce ran out of the kitchen and stomped up the stairs to her room.

Web sat in the kitchen, alone, waiting for Joyce to return. When it appeared that she wouldn't, he opened the chicken and nibbled at a few pieces. Food didn't ever taste good alone, especially after a fight. Mud lay outside the kitchen, quietly watching. Web pulled off a few scraps of chicken for the dog. When he leaned down to set them on the floor, the pain in his head burst like an overfilled water balloon. Mud nervously took the scraps and ran back to hide behind the couch.

Web hated being tough but feared the consequences if he weren't. What bothered him most was that Joyce had been seeing Bose and hadn't told him about it. Web thought Bose was a bad influence on Joyce: a glittery layer of pretentious education concealing a core of sleaziness. Fascinating to a young, naive girl, but ultimately bad for her. And Web would do whatever it took to keep Joyce from seeing him.

The next morning Web was awakened by the phone.

"Hello?"

"This is Jack."

"What time is it?"

"It's about 7:30. I just finished reviewing the Block file. And for kicks, and because you're a friend, I checked out two of the missing girls."

"And . . ."

"Block's doing a by-the-book job at least, if not better. And the other two are garden-variety missing persons."

"So you don't intend to put an agent on it." Web gripped the phone so hard his fingernails turned white.

"I think it would be a foolish use of company resources. The local yokels are doing perfectly well without us."

"Did you look at the photos?"

"I have them here. All three girls are lookers, but so what?"

"They all look alike."

Reynolds let out a long, exasperated whistle.

"Web, I could find you forty-five runaways who look almost the same and do it before my coffee break. Young girls look like young girls. There's no way we can become involved. Leave the law enforcement to professionals, and I promise I won't try to teach college. But this is America. You can do whatever you want, Web."

"Great. That'll do a lot of good."

"I gave it my best, Web. There's not a lot I can do. Hey, let's still get together for a beer."

Web didn't even hear the words. "Sure. Bye."

He slammed the phone receiver down.

Am I crazy? Do I see bears and serpents in the sky where an intelligent person just sees random points of light?

The thought was disturbing, but his instincts were more powerful. He wouldn't give up.

10

The essential American soul is hard, isolate, stoic and a killer.

D. H. LAWRENCE

The shrill whine of metal on metal awakened Mars with a start. She was surprised by the sound; the noise of the modern world rarely penetrated her cul-de-sac. She peered through the curtains into the backyard. Alan's Cabriolet sat in front of his workroom, the garage. The shriek stopped, and Alan leaned out of the backseat of the convertible. Mars threw on her robe and went outside to see what he was doing.

"Good morning, Alan—I missed you in bed this morning." She tried to sound as cheery as possible. No need to even hint at *the performance problem.*

"'Morning. Had some stuff to do." He rummaged through his toolbox and pulled out a screwdriver bit.

"What are you doing out here, anyway?" she asked.

"Taking out the passenger seat. You know, so I can fit more cargo into the car." He snapped a bit into the drill.

"It's such a nice car!" she said, caressing the fender.

"Well, I'm more into practicality than aesthetics, anyway. I can always put the seat back in if I don't like it." He pulled on safety goggles and leaned under the passenger seat. There was a loud metallic screech followed by the clink of a bolt flying out.

"Damn! Where'd that bolt go?" he asked, groping in the gravel.

Mars knelt beside him. The bolt was in plain view, right next to the tire. She saw that Alan's eyes were bloodshot and unfocused.

"Here you go." She placed the bolt into his toolbox. Her pot pipe was in there, as well as her metal box of marijuana. *He's been getting high already this morning,* she thought. The box was nearly empty. Three days earlier Mars had put in a full ounce of pot—a three-month supply for her because she only got high once or twice a week.

"Alan, I really don't want you smoking pot in front of Farrell."

He gave her a cold stare, holding the drill in his hand like a gun.

"I don't even think he saw me."

She stood up.

"I know it sounds hypocritical, but Farrell's only fifteen and I don't want to set a bad example."

Alan grinned and gave the drill a quick burst. *Wheeirrr.* "It's not as if he doesn't know about you and Roslyn firing up a toke every once in a while. Hiding it just teaches him to be hypocritical."

"He's my son, and I don't want you doing that in front of him. Understood?" She folded her arms on her chest defiantly.

Alan repeated her wishes in monotone. "I promise to be good and only get high in secret and never show Farrell"— he turned his head toward the house—"what we really do."

Farrell stood just outside the door, dressed for school. He'd heard every word.

Mars shouted to her son. "Farrell, don't you have to catch your bus?"

"I'm going, I'm going, Mom."

"I'll pick you up at four. Better run!"

Farrell trotted sullenly around the house, disappearing toward the road where his bus would pick him up. Alan ducked under the seat and started the noisy drill again. Mars unplugged the power cord; the drill wound down and stopped.

"Hey! What's the idea?" Alan emerged from under the seat and sat on the edge of the car, reaching for the cord. Mars dropped it on the ground.

"You seem pretty unhappy the last couple days. What's wrong?" she asked.

"What's wrong? You're asking *me* what's wrong?" His tone was low, challenging.

"Yeah." Mars was worried. The safety goggles stretched Alan's eyes into giant orbs, making him appear alien. Dust and grease were smeared on his arms, hands, and shirt.

"I'll tell you what's wrong. You've totally changed. When I first came here, it was 'oh, Alan, you can stay and do whatever you want.' Now, you're giving me a hard time about everything."

"What did I give you a hard time about?"

"Just now, 'don't smoke pot in front of the boy.' And if I stay out a little bit, maybe grab a beer, it's 'where have you been?' "

"When I ask where you've been, it's just curiosity— maybe it means I care. I'm not being nosy, Alan."

"Well it sounds nosy to me."

"I'm sorry."

"And another thing. I don't need you grimacing every time I mention my job."

"I was just surprised. God, you just don't seem the type for police work."

"Well, I am." He dropped the drill into the toolbox.

"You don't have to be so mean."

"I just don't want it to be like my life was before. I came out here to have a little freedom to move around, a little space. I don't need to be told what I can do and what I can't. I'm an adult. I can make my own choices."

He peeled off the goggles and dropped them in the back seat. They left deep red impressions around his eyes.

Mars became aware of another side of the man that hadn't emerged before: nasty and self-centered. She thought it must be true what she'd heard about New York stockbrokers. They'd sell their own mother to make a deal. Before, she couldn't believe that's what he had done, but now she could see it. Alan had that "I'll do anything to win" look. He even looked a little bit like Michael Milken.

"Whatever you want, Alan." She angrily trudged into the house to cool down.

As she searched for a dress, Mars saw a sampler that Roslyn had given her years earlier. It said, "If you love someone, set them free. If they don't return, it was never meant to be." It was corny, but reassuring. Roslyn had originally given her the sampler during her breakup with Farrell's father. Mars kept it partly because Roslyn had made it by hand and partly because she believed its message. She dried her eyes and returned to the backyard. Alan had the car seat on the ground.

"I'm sorry we've been fighting so much."

"I'm sorry, too. I think we've been together too much too soon." Alan was guardedly cheerful.

"What do you mean?"

"You know, just cabin fever. I was thinking maybe I should get away for a couple days. I have some business to deal with in Oregon, and this would be a good time to take care of it. Now, before I start this job."

Mars thought it over. She hadn't expected him to say this. *Was he going to abandon ship? Leave her alone?* But she had to let him.

"Okay, if you have to. But I'll miss you, Alan."

"Don't try to pressure me to stay."

She had hoped he might say "I'll miss you, too."

"I'm not pressuring you Alan. Do whatever you want. It's fine by me."

"I just want you to understand that."

The chill in his voice scared her. Mars felt a burning in her eyes. Tears were forming.

"You'll come back, won't you?"

He leaned close to her, then whispered in her ear.

"Of course I'll come back. You won't meet a handsome millionaire while I'm away?"

"No, no." She giggled through her tears. They embraced. She didn't mind that he was getting grease and dirt on her clean dress.

"Wanna come down to the shop for some breakfast? I have some great French bread today."

"Nah, I should get going."

"You mean today? When you said you wanted to take some time away, I didn't think you meant right now!"

"I think it's best. I start at the sheriff's next week."

"I hate good-byes, Alan. When will you be back?" Mars bit her lip.

"Couple days. Maybe three. But soon. Don't worry."

"Okay."

She plodded out to her car as if going to her own funeral.

Then she drove away without looking back. She had a terrible feeling he was gone for good.

Alan smiled and waved, standing with his arm in the air like a scarecrow, as Mars drove down the road. As soon as she disappeared around the bend, he felt buoyant, free, as if a weight had been lifted from his shoulders. Alan hadn't planned to leave so soon. He had planned to think out a careful justification for his trip, but one had been dropped in his lap. He could do anything he wanted.

He went into the house and turned on the stereo. It was set to Farrell's trendy teenage rock station, but he quickly tuned in a classic rock station. *"That's* music," he said aloud, as Led Zeppelin blasted out of the stereo.

Alan grabbed a beer and drank it in the shower. He downed another while he dressed. Singing to every song, he grabbed a grocery bag and filled it with supplies for his trip. From the broom closet, he pilfered a bottle of Gallo; then, he saw behind it a long-forgotten bottle of Popoff vodka nearly full.

"Need that, too."

He rummaged around in a kitchen drawer, pulling out a roll of duct tape and a length of copper wire. DeVries peeled off a piece of tape and tested it for stickiness on his arm. It stuck well and pulled up a thick clump of hair when he peeled it off.

"Ouch!" He smiled.

Examining his bag, he thought for a moment, then returned to Mars's room and took several wire hangers from her closet. Going outside, he threw his bag into the trunk of the Cabriolet, next to the crowbar and his suit bag. One thing was missing. *TV Guide.* He ran back into the house and grabbed a copy, then checked to see that everything was in place. Then he left a note on the table:

> *Bye, Mars. I've gone north to Oregon just to take care of some business. Don't you worry, I'll return to this special home of yours. Give my regards to Farrell.*
>
> > *Love,*
> > *Alan*

He crossed out "yours" and wrote in over it "ours." "That should keep her happy," he said aloud.

It felt good to be on the road again. Pacific Coast Highway was the ultimate drive, and it was a clear, beautiful day. He tooted as he drove by the bakery.

About seventy miles north of Endocino, he entered a small town. Tall Pine had been a booming lumber town in the twenties, but the capriciousness of railroad routes cut the city off, and the lumber mills moved on. Only a few small shops, a diner, and a gas station remained.

Alan liked the town. He looked at his watch. It was 12:30. He wanted to make a number of stops and leave before 2:00. First he went into the general store, which offered an eclectic mix of hardware, groceries, movies on video for rental. In the back was a little lunch deli counter. On the door was a sign: VISA/MasterCard accepted.

Alan had recently received a Visa card that he ordered from an advertisement inside a matchbook. "You CANNOT be turned down!" promised the ad. It *was* a Visa; but he deposited five hundred forty dollars to get a card with a five-hundred-dollar limit. A rip-off, he knew, but it would give him two things: legitimacy and a paper trail.

He filled up a hand basket with Spam, tuna, some shavers and shaving cream, and supplies for his car: a beverage holder, antifreeze, and two quarts of oil. Alan sat behind the lunch counter.

"Hello?"

An elderly woman got up from the cash register and walked to the deli counter with the aid of a cane.

"May I help you?"

"Hi! I was just going to get these groceries, but then I saw your wonderfully laid out deli."

"What'll you have?"

"What do you recommend?"

She laughed. "We don't often get folks asking for recommendations. Personally, I like the smoked turkey and tomato."

"You look like you know your sandwiches. I'd love a large one of those."

She went about making the sandwich, slicing off thick chunks of meat from a large turkey breast.

"Are you from the East Coast? I thought I heard something in your voice . . ." Alan asked her, pumping up the boyish charm.

"Came out from Massachusetts eleven years ago," she said, spreading mayonnaise on a slice of white bread.

Alan winked at her. "Where? Let me guess. Martha's Vineyard."

"Close. Nantucket. That obvious?"

"I love the accent. I grew up in Missouri, but my family spent many summers on Cape Cod." He extended his hand. "Alan DeVries."

"I got your turkey all over my hands so I won't shake. Phyllis Donnely."

While he ate, they talked at length about Martha's Vineyard, Nantucket, and Massachusetts. DeVries was especially careful to listen more than talk; he knew almost nothing about the area. But Phyllis seemed genuinely pleased to run into someone who would listen so patiently to tales of her childhood on the Cape.

When he finished the sandwich, he licked his lips.

"That was one heck of a turkey and tomato. You know how to make a good sub, Phyllis."

"Well, I try."

"I have to be hitting the road now."

He pulled out his wallet.

"Visa okay?"

"Sure."

He walked over to the register as Phyllis hobbled behind him.

"Could I ask you a big favor?"

"Just metcha, Alan. How big?"

"Well, I'm on a company expense account, but the business trip doesn't officially start till tomorrow. I was wondering if you could put tomorrow's date on the slip. That would let me get reimbursed without the usual hassle."

"Who you working for?"

"Big oil company. They have me doing a survey of roads up here."

"Screw the oil companies, I say. Sure, how 'bout day after tomorrow?"

"That'd be even more helpful."

He examined the slip and added a two-dollar tip. Phyllis took it back.

"Well, thank you very much, sir. I hardly ever get tips in here. It's been a pleasure."

"A pleasure, Phyllis. Hope to see you again."

"Bye."

Alan spent another hour in the town, buying gasoline at the Sun Oil Company, and some shirts, suntan lotion, and several pairs of socks at a tourist shop. He persuaded both proprietors to let him postdate his credit card. Then, he got back in the gray convertible and headed south, passing through Endocino again, going in the opposite direction. He got on the 101, drove straight through San Francisco, and headed for Monterey.

Alan pulled into the ritzy seaside town of Monterey as the sun was going down. He drove around the main part of town, past people coming out of diners and going into movies. The town was closing up. He looked at his watch. *Prime time.* Twenty to eight. In a half hour, families all over the nation would be settling down, turning their attention away from their yards and streets, and staring at "Cosby," "The Simpsons," and "Cheers." *"What I do differently, what he did wrong, is to be thoroughly prepared. He didn't know that the most important tool to a professional voyeur is a thorough knowledge of the television schedule,"* he thought.

With the top down, he had an unobstructed view. The sky was growing darker; people hadn't yet closed their shades. He went out of the main part of town and drove inland, looking for a suburb. Any suburb. He selected the neighborhood with care. Too poor, and the houses are close together and people drink out on their porches: a problem for his work. Too rich, and the owners would be cautious and more likely to have dinner guests going in and out. He went by the elementary school and found a street he liked. Middle class. Medium-size homes. *He would have picked these houses, but he would have messed it up.*

Via Paseo was nearly perfect. The street gently curved, making it hard to see a suspicious vehicle. He parked in front of a darkened house. Alan got out and pulled a leather bag from the trunk. Besides the things he'd pilfered from

Mars, it contained binoculars and a pipe wrench. He pulled out a gray overcoat. Pinned to the breast was a badge that read "Sunnyvale Gas and Electric." Too bad he was a hundred miles from Sunnyvale; hopefully no one would get an opportunity to read the tag anyway. He pulled headphones of a Sony Watchman over one ear. The most popular television shows in the country were just starting, debilitating the entire nation for an hour. He knew he could move about undetected during the programs; he would just have to stay low during commercial breaks when folks got up to get Coke and popcorn.

DeVries walked straight through to the long stretch of uninterrupted backyards, his secret freeway. There weren't many fences; people trusted one another. America's Funniest Hour was just beginning. He made no attempt to conceal his movements as he trampled through grass, gardens, patches of ivy, and patios. During the programs, there was no need. He peered in windows at family after family glued to the set. A mom and two kids. A yuppie couple. An old man and his lap dog. He came upon a large yellow house with a glass patio door. From his vantage point behind the rusting swing set, he could see a group of girls. He lifted the binoculars. Four teenage girls. A slumber party. His heart skipped a beat. *Bill Cosby was having an argument with his wife about his daughter's dress.* The girls were playfully fighting, whacking one another with pillows. Three were wearing pajamas; one had on a sheer nightgown. A door adjacent to the TV room opened. *Damn. Here comes Dad and Big Brother with pizza. I'm not going to get caught the way he did.* He lowered the binoculars.

And now a word from our sponsors. People would be milling around. He sat on the ground next to a sandbox and waited. Honda. AT&T. *We'll be right back*—he stood up—*after these important messages.* Prudential Insurance. He leaned against the swing set again. Dad walked over to the window but didn't look out. A dog barked. He looked ahead—two houses ahead of him, a yellow labrador strained at a chain, barking at him. Move forward and risk the dog? Or go back? *And now we return to our program.* Move ahead. No one would pay attention to a dog with so many good shows on.

Four houses down he saw a redwood fence. *Keeps the neighbors from seeing in.* He tried the gate. It was unlatched. He tuned the Watchman; no commercials. Cosby was doing a monologue; Bart Simpson was playing a supposedly obscene rock song. Inside the fence he could see straight into a den. All the other lights in the house were out. Inside was a young woman, nursing a beer, watching television. He tuned his receiver until the sound he heard matched up with what he saw. It was a miniseries with Richard Chamberlain. The girl wore a pair of panties and a tank top. He waited till a commercial break to find out if she was alone. She moved into the kitchen and pulled something out of the fridge. She was a looker: long hair in a pony tail. A voluptuous figure; her breasts jostled under the thin tank top, arousing him. No shoes. No one else there. He grew short of breath. Pay dirt.

Quickly he moved around to the front of the house. He had twenty-five minutes left in prime time before people stretched and let their dogs out. He dumped the Watchman and binoculars into his bag. Then he rang the bell.

There was no answer. He rang it again. The door opened a little ways; a chain held it partially closed. The miniseries girl peered out.

"Hello?"

"Hi. I'm from the gas company. There's a leak in the neighborhood and we're trying to trace the source." He stood straight and spoke in a deeper voice than was natural.

"I don't have gas. My stove and hot water are both electric."

I. She said "I." She lives alone. He hardly heard her sentence.

"Sorry about the problem. We just need to look at your stove and furnace." He smiled.

"I just said I'm all electric." She gripped the door.

"The big gas pipe goes all through the houses."

"The what? You mean the main?"

He grimaced. "Yes. The gas main goes under all the houses. I just need to do some tests with some scientific apparatus. It'll just take a moment. If I don't, there is a risk of explosion."

She closed the door. He heard the chain come off, then the door reopened. She was less beautiful close up; she had a scar over her left eye. Nevertheless, he was breathing hard. No going back.

"Could I see some I.D.?"

He pushed the door open. She stood in his way.

"Could I see some identification, please?"

He had planned for this.

"Sure, hold this bag for a moment."

He handed her his bag. It was heavy, and she held it with both hands. From his vest he pulled out a stun gun. It was off. He flipped the switch. It took a moment to charge. She saw it.

"What are you doing?" She backed up, still holding the heavy bag.

"Stand still." He thrust the stun gun at her neck. He missed. She dropped the bag and moved backward.

"Go away! Go away! Go . . ."

He moved in quickly. *ZAP*. The stun gun touched the bare skin on her leg. She dropped unconscious to the floor. *He didn't have the advantages of technology. Love these little toys.* Quickly, he closed the door. He removed the package tape from the bag, pulled her wrists together behind her back and put several layers around them, then through her wrists, securing her arms. He methodically taped her feet together. He dragged her into the living room and dropped her on the floor. Then he grabbed a blanket and threw it over her.

Moving back to the foyer, he hoisted his bag and went out the front door, making sure to leave it unlocked. He put on the Watchman and strolled back to his car, then drove to the front of the house.

Bart Simpson was talking about freedom of speech. He tuned the dial. *Bill Cosby had admitted that the dress wasn't so extravagant.* Prime time was almost over. He would have to move fast. He opened the trunk. Casually, he sauntered up the path and admitted himself. He could hear sobbing and Richard Chamberlain.

The girl had awakened. She had rolled across the floor and crawled toward the front door. Her eye caught his.

"Who are you? What are you doing? Don't rob me. I hardly have anything."

"I'm not going to rob you."

He had other plans.

She screamed. He taped her mouth shut and changed the channel. *Homer Simpson was singing with his son's rock band.* He still had a couple minutes. Alan pulled out the stun gun, and when it had charged gave the crying girl a jolt. Then he turned off the television, rolled her into the blanket, and lifted the mass. His back hurt. He stumbled out to the car and threw her in the trunk. As closing credits rolled on America's Funniest Hour, he grabbed her purse so friends would think she had taken a trip, closed the door to the house, got back in the car and disappeared into the night, whistling the theme from "The Cosby Show."

Thursday nights were always slow at the Monterey Big Screen Sports Lounge, but during the tourist off-season, the cavernous beer-soaked room looked equally ridiculous and lonely. Louise Jenkins cursed her friend who had talked her into switching from the Elbow Room: "Sports, think of it, Louise—lots of young, single men—and big spenders, too! I heard one waitress got a five-hundred-dollar tip when a customer won a bet on an A's game!" In her three months at the Big Screen, Louise had succeeded only in meeting the drunken frat boys who stiffed her and depressing widowers drowning their sorrows in Lite beer and ESPN.

The slim, brown-haired waitress didn't even look up from the register when the stranger approached. "I'm closing, mister, I can't help you. Try over there—" she pointed to the other bar.

"I don't necessarily want a drink. I just wanted to talk to you." The stranger's voice was mellifluous and intoxicating. Louise dumped an uncounted stack of dollars into the drawer and looked up. "Hello . . ." Her face flushed. The handsome stranger had an immediate and profound effect on her.

"How about one on the house though?" Louise's own voice sounded ridiculous to her. She hoped she didn't scare him off. Louise turned her back on the man and took a deep breath. *When your ship finally comes in, just make sure you're not at the airport,* she thought.

"Johnny Walker?" he asked.

"Sure." She poured from the expensive Black Label bottle.

"Thanks. You look like the person to recommend some offbeat distractions for an out-of-towner," he said, catching her gaze.

Louise couldn't place his accent: Canada? New York? Australia? Wherever he hailed from, the man appeared to be educated and good-looking. *And he drinks Johnny Walker,* she thought. Louise liked that he said "offbeat." She thought she knew every obscure night spot in Monterey and wanted to tell the stranger everything at once. "You mean like music clubs? I know a really cool after-hours blues bar and a great down-and-dirty rock and roll band who plays tonight."

"Great minds think alike. That sounds perfect. How would I find this place?" He stared deep into her eyes.

"Okay, okay. This is really weird, but I'd like to cut out and go see Angelz Fury—they're the band. It's almost dead in here. I'm going to go lie to my boss so I can leave right now. If he asks, you're my cousin, and our grandmother's ill. Okay? And oh, my name is Louise."

"Hi, Louise. I'm your cousin Alan."

"Nice to meet you, Cousin Alan." They shared a laugh and a long handshake.

Louise ran back into the walk-in fridge, where Cleveland James, her boss, was doing inventory. "Cleve, my cousin just walked in. I haven't seen him in eight months, and he says his mother, my aunt, is feeling poorly . . ."

Cleveland cut her off. "Look, Louise, you don't have to make up any funny stories to tell Cleveland. If you want to go, just go. I'll close out your register."

She laughed and gave him a quick kiss on the cheek. "Thanks, Cleve."

Louise's boss followed her out of the walk-in to get a look at this "cousin." From across the room he looked about like any customer, except maybe better dressed. He watched as Louise put on her jacket, then as she followed the man out of the front door.

Cleveland James never saw Louise again. A month later he mailed her final paycheck, but it was never cashed. Waitresses were flaky that way. Cleveland figured she'd just taken a better job or maybe run off with that guy. It had been the slow season anyway.

The air was chilly from the cool ocean mist that had blown in. The yellow light from the high parking lot lamps dripped down in long cones disappearing near the ground. Alan and Louise walked across the parking lot to her car. She was delighted to meet a cute guy on such a lousy night.

"So, Alan, what brings you to Monterey?"

"Ah, just business. I work for a venture capital firm that hopes to take over a chain of furniture stores out here . . . it's pretty boring. Do you really want to hear?"

"It sounds pretty interesting to me. You get to travel a lot?"

"More than I'd like. It's not that much fun. Let's get going."

"Sure. You want me to drive?"

"No, what if I drive, you navigate." He pulled his keys out of his pocket.

"Here's my car. I don't mind driving," she said, tapping the hood of her AMC Gremlin.

"I'd rather drive. I don't like leaving my car behind."

"Okay. I want to get something. Why don't you go get your car and meet me here?"

"I'll wait."

"I have to change . . . I hate this stupid waitress uniform," she said.

"That's okay, I'll wait."

"All right. Just turn around."

He stepped a couple feet away and turned toward the main building. Louise got into her car and climbed into the back seat. She opened a bright pink gym bag and pulled out a pair of jeans. In the cluttered automobile she had little room to wriggle out of the skirt. When she got it off, she peeked up through the back window to see if Alan was still there.

Louise saw that he stood like a sentry, staring straight into the car. A stern scowl had replaced his warm demeanor. He clenched his hands and he bounced nervously from foot to foot. She rolled down the window and leaned her head out.

"Hey, Alan, I told you not to look!" She laughed.

His scowl disappeared, and he transformed into the friendly man she had met.

"Sorry, I forgot. I thought I heard someone over there."

"It's okay. Probably nothing you haven't seen anyway—polka dot underwear. I'm almost through."

She pulled on her jeans and put on some cowboy boots, then checked her makeup in the rearview mirror. *Not bad.* Louise picked up her purse and got out.

"Let's go, dude!" she giggled as she walked over to where he stood.

"Yeah, let's go," he replied, distracted. She followed him to his car. The convertible top was down.

"Nice convertible. What happened to the seat?"

"Oh, I took it out. You'll have to sit in back."

"We could still take my car."

"No, that's okay."

As she got in the car, she saw that a woman's purse was on the floor in the back.

"Hey, Alan, what's this?" She held it up.

"I found that on the beach today. I keep meaning to turn it in."

She leaned forward to get out of the car.

"You're married, aren't you. I knew it. I knew something had to be wrong."

"I'm not married at all. Look at the I.D.—she has a different name and everything."

Louise opened the purse. The California driver's license showed a blond girl in her twenties named Sophia Baker. "Okay, what's your last name then?"

"DeVries. I have no idea whose purse that is."

He leaned over the seat and winked. "Let's go, okay?"

"Okay."

Louise inspected the purse as they drove out. The strap was broken, and there was something wet on one side. As they went under a light, she saw that it was red.

Nail polish. Exactly the kind of bimbo who would lose her purse would spill nail polish all over it, she thought.

He drove out of the parking lot onto the side road leading into the country. He gunned the engine on the unlit road.

"Alan!"

"What? I can't hear you. Top's down."

"You took the wrong road! You should have gotten on the other one. *WRONG ROAD!*"

"What?"

"I said you're on the wrong road!"

"Oh. Wrong road."

He pulled over next to a large field and killed the engine, then turned off the lights.

"It's hard to hear you with the top down. Could you help me put it up?"

"Sure. I'm pretty cold anyway."

She climbed out of the passenger side as he went to the back of the car and opened the trunk.

"We ought to get going. The club closes at two."

"Oh, yeah, two o'clock, huh." He pulled something out of the trunk.

"I need this to close the top," he said. She couldn't see what he held.

"Okay. Grab that handle with both hands. That one, there." He stood behind her as she reached for the small red handle. She heard the whistle of something moving quickly through the air and felt a surge of pain in her shoulder and neck. Then she fell to the ground.

"What are you . . ."

Before she could complete her question, he grabbed her hair and slapped a wide piece of packaging tape over her mouth. She realized blood was coming from behind her ear. He expertly taped her wrists together. She saw the lights from a vehicle approaching them. Louise pulled herself up and moved toward the road.

"Don't run."

The truck honked its horn but kept moving.

Louise felt another sharp blow to her shoulder and fell to the ground. Half-conscious, she watched Alan tape her feet together. Then she was dragged back to the car and thrown into the empty space where the passenger seat should have been. He closed the top and started the car. He tuned in the classic rock station and started singing to a song. It was a long drive, and Louise floated in and out of consciousness as her head bounced against the floorboard. During the moments she was awake, she prayed.

* * *

She woke up to hear the car rattling along on a gravel road. It was a steep incline and her hands and feet had both fallen asleep. The car slowed to a crawl, then stopped. Cold air blew in as the man opened his door, then pulled back the top. He opened her door and lifted her out. She tried struggling, but her limbs were useless and her head throbbed from the bump. Louise saw a summer cabin with a light on. The man dropped her on the ground. The cold gravel scraped the skin on her arm.

When he came back out of the car he held a scarf. She tried screaming but could make no sound. He tied the scarf around her eyes and carried her up some steps, then laid her down on a soft surface—a camp cabin bed? She felt a handcuff clamp her wrist to the metal frame. Louise cried.

For a long time there was no sound. Louise stopped crying and listened hard. She wriggled on the bed, trying to break free. But there was no way to move, what with the tape and the handcuffs. Rubbing her head on the plastic mattress, she moved the tightly knotted scarf down so one eye could see out. It was a two-room cabin; she could see into another room, but it was dark.

The man walked back in, carrying a beer. He had changed into blue jeans and a T-shirt. He walked past her like so much furniture and flipped on a light in the next room.

Oh my god.

Her view was obscured by the door, but she could see a woman's arms and long, blond hair. The hands were tied around a radiator. The man went back outside, leaving the door to the next room open.

From the room she heard the crescendo of a long anguished cry. The words were muffled. *She must be gagged,* thought Louise. The tormented cry grew louder, sounding like the roar from an injured animal. Even though obscured, Louise thought she heard the woman trying to form words: *"Help me! Oh, mother! Help me!"* No one responded to her pleas.

The moaning stopped. Louise tried not to look into the room but could not avert her eyes. The half-seen captive began to struggle with her bonds. The woman's upper arms were fastened securely with packing tape on one side of a radiator; her wrists tied with rope on the other. The net effect was as if the captive were embracing the radiator, held by bonds on either side. Louise stared at the woman as she contorted and smashed her forearms into the radiator, then screamed horribly. *The radiator must be on,* thought Louise. But the tape was giving way.

Repeatedly the woman pulled her arms back, then shoved them into the hot radiator, using it as a wedge to break the grip of the tape. Each time her arms touched the hot metal, she screamed louder, eventually breaking into short sobbing cries that never ceased. But she was succeeding; Louise could see the tape giving way, bit by bit. *Come on, just a little more, just a little more.* Louise silently cheered on the woman.

The last bit of tape broke. Louise could see blood and welts on the captive's arm. *Yes! Yes. Almost free. Almost free!* Louise thought. The sobbing became a whimper. Only the rope held her now. Louise saw the woman stretch her arms into an inhuman position; pressing them against the boiling steel. She raised her arms up, a little higher, a little higher . . . then yelled, a desperate, hopeless shriek. She could not reach over the radiator. The screaming continued nonstop as the woman writhed on the floor.

The man stormed back in, carrying another beer. He glanced at Louise; she lay very still. He went into the other room, yelling at the top of his lungs.

"Shut the fuck up! What the fuck are you doing!"

Louise saw him kick the woman, then slam the door. The woman's cries sounded frenzied. Time seemed to slow down to a crawl. The animalistic screeching sounded as if it would go on forever.

When she thought it could not get worse, the cries became words. He must have taken the gag off.

"Don't do that please don't do that. No. No. NOOOO!" She heard a loud thump. The words metamorphosed to gurgles, as if obscured by water.

The door opened and the man went back outside. He didn't look her way. She glimpsed into the other room; the woman was alive. She saw the arms twitching on the radiator. Something shiny covered the floor. Something red. *The gurgling wasn't caused by water. It was blood.* A door closed. The man came back into the cabin. He held a large pipe wrench. He went into the room. The door closed. Louise heard a dull pounding noise, once, twice, three times. The screaming became louder than ever before. Louise knew the screams could be heard for a mile away; *if anyone is out there.* Then she heard a clang as something hit the radiator. The screaming stopped. Louise could hear only the crickets in the night, and the wind rustling through the trees.

Louise cried. The man opened the door a crack and stepped into the room. He calmly sat and sipped his beer; unaware that she could see him. Specks of blood covered his shirt. Suddenly he turned toward Louise and said, "Make yourself comfortable. It's going to be a little while."

Louise knew what would happen. She stared at the ceiling. She thought about her best friend. Her mother and father. She wondered what her little niece, who was just learning to talk, was saying now.

Louise had envisioned her death many times before. Sometimes she thought it might come in a fiery car crash, quick and painless. In dreams she would fall off a cliff into a deep, black ocean. Once when she was in love she had talked with her boyfriend about living to a ripe old age; when their bodies deteriorated, they would eat a wonderful meal capped off by poisonous mushrooms, dying in each other's arms. But in all the times Louise thought about dying, she had never thought it would be like this.

The next day Mars Chittenden came home to find Alan in the driveway, vacuuming out his car. He was full of vitality and energy as he almost danced around the Cabriolet, whistling to himself. She felt a surge of gratitude that he had returned.

"Alan! How was your trip?" she yelled, running out of her car to greet him.

"It was just lovely, just wonderful. I got myself a computer, and . . . it's all so boring. I'm just glad to see you again."

He threw his arms around Mars and gave her a big, enthusiastic kiss. She felt a wind of good feeling blowing in, warming everything.

"Oh, Alan, I'm so glad you're back. I missed you so much."

"It was only two days, but Mars, let me tell you: I missed you, too."

That was what she wanted to hear. He seemed renewed by his days away. Her sampler was right: You've got to set free the one you love. Gone was the cold, distant Alan she'd seen before the trip. He'd returned as the man she loved.

"C'mon in. You can finish that later."

The vacuum and car sat in the driveway all night. Mars sent Farrell over to stay at Roslyn's house. They ate pizza and drank the mimosas she'd planned to make the week before. Then, they made love twice—once in the living room and once in the bedroom. She was so glad he was back.

11

The recent rains had washed the smog out of the air. In the newly transparent atmosphere, the bright sun created hard-edged shadows, making the world look polished and clean. The Sloanes' backyard had an innocent, unreal allure, like the childhood memory of a school playground. The dirt in Web's garden plots glistened with moisture. No flowers had emerged, yet the gardens were well tended and full of the promise of life. His hopes for them to succeed went beyond the desire for decoration; to him, the garden's eventual success would indicate that his new life in Berkeley would also flourish.

Web and Joyce took turns whacking tennis balls across the backyard, bouncing them into the fence for the amusement of their hyperactive pet. Mud lived up to his name, digging through their damp gardens to fetch the spit-soaked ball, then depositing it at their feet like priceless booty. Web teased him, hiding the ball behind his back. Mud misunderstood and knocked Web to the muddy ground in an irrepressible canine hug.

Joyce howled with laughter.

"My dear," she drawled in a lispy French accent, "you look divine in earth tones. That's what they're wearing in Paris this season, you know."

Ever the opportunist, Mud took that moment to shake himself off, soaking Web from head to toe in dirty water.

Joyce helped her father off the ground.

"I think he likes you, Dad," she said, eyeing the dog with a mischievous grin.

Web laughed. The dog served as an intermediary between Web and Joyce, helping them get around barriers that had grown between them. Web saw the side of Joyce that was full of vitality and love, a side that was often kept hidden from view.

Web picked up the ball and threw it across the lawn at Joyce, who dodged Mud's diving leaps then threw the ball back to her father. Web chased after the dog, wrestling him to the ground in an explosion of wet earth. The game degenerated into a euphoric free-for-all, father and daughter throwing mud at each other as Mud danced enthusiastically between them.

Their game was interrupted by a familiar female voice with a Spanish accent. "Hello, Web."

Maria de Rivera walked into the backyard. She had on a brilliant red sundress that heightened her color. The breeze swept her raven hair to one side exposing her long neck and elegant shoulders.

She had appeared so suddenly and seemed so out of place, there was an otherworldly quality about her. Web froze in his tracks; he couldn't help staring at her as she approached.

Joyce discerned something unfamiliar and unsettling in her father's eyes, a look that she had seen only on the faces of boys her age. She turned to see what had caught his attention. Maria waved to her.

Suddenly, Mud dropped his ball and made a beeline to greet this new playmate. Web leaped after the dog, falling to the ground but retaining a firm grip on the beast's collar.

"No, Mud. *No!*" he yelled.

Web dragged the dancing dog to a chain at the back of the yard and fastened him securely. He received an unwanted shower when Mud shook himself dry, then Web sheepishly crossed the yard to Maria.

"I'm kind of a mess," he said, blood rushing to the back of his neck.

"No need to apologize. I was not supposed to be here for another hour, but my first appointment was canceled. I watched you for a long time. That dog is a *diablo,* but such a lover."

He turned to his daughter. "Joyce, this is Mrs. de Rivera. I think you two have only met on the phone."

"Yes, *Maria* and I spoke the other day," said Joyce.

"Would you like to come in and have a soda while I shower?" asked Web.

"I can come back later . . ." Maria offered.

"Nonsense. Come on in and Joyce will keep you company for a few minutes."

Ordinarily, Joyce would have objected to her father volunteering her time, but she was suddenly quite curious about this woman. What did Maria have that caused her father to act so . . . so weird?

Web slogged up the stairs. Joyce and Maria sat at the kitchen table.

"Would you like some coffee, Maria?" Joyce stood up and started to pour some water into the Mr. Coffee machine.

"Thank you, but you do not need to make coffee. Whatever you were going to drink is fine," replied Maria.

"That's what I always drink," she said emphatically. Joyce filled the machine carefully—she had made coffee only a few times before. She tried a conversational gambit. "Have you heard of Jack Kerouac? The famous poet? He only drank coffee, you know."

"But he died of alcoholism, not coffee, I've heard." Maria winked conspiratorially.

"In the early days, he drank only coffee." Joyce flipped the switch on the pot. "Well, that's what I read."

While the beverage brewed, Joyce sat across from Maria, arms folded, "girl talk" fashion.

"So what brings you to our lovely abode, Maria?" she asked.

"I am just following some leads that may help find my daughter. The usual," said Maria.

"Your daughter's missing?" Joyce leaned forward, her interest suddenly piqued. Daddy-O hadn't mentioned *that.*

"Your father did not tell you?"

"Oh, right, yeah, he said something about it. I forgot—what happened to her?"

"She went for a bicycle ride one night and did not come home." Maria related the tale very plainly; she'd told the story a hundred times before.

"Oh, I'm sorry." Joyce tried to sound more concerned than curious. "You know, my older sister was . . ."

"Yes, I know. That's why I contacted your father. *Mi madre* . . . my mother once said, if you have an illness, do not go to the doctor; first, go to someone who had the same illness."

"That's pretty wise. Coffee's ready," said Joyce, setting two steaming mugs down on the table.

"I also forgot—what exactly is my father doing for you?" asked Joyce.

"I am surprised he did not tell you. He has dedicated much of his time helping me organize the search for my daughter Tanya."

You're such a jerk, Daddy-O. You could have at least told me, Joyce thought. "He ought to be real good at that. All he's done for the past ten years is leave me to look for Vicki," Joyce said, unable to disguise the bitterness in her voice.

Maria looked at her quietly for a moment, then said, "Of course he did. If you were missing, he would look for you, too."

"That's exactly what he always says," said Joyce.

"He did? When?" asked Maria.

"About a million times. When I was a little girl, after my mother died, he always was someplace far away—Utah, Colorado, anywhere but home. He never took me. I was practically raised by baby-sitters. If I complained, he always said he was looking for Vicki and he would do the same for me," Joyce said.

"It must have been hard on you," replied Maria.

"I didn't even know how unusual it was. After my sister was missing five years, we had her funeral. I was about ten, and Dad said it was time to put it behind us. I didn't even cry because I was glad it was over."

"And was it?" said Maria.

"No, he never stopped looking; but after her funeral, he just stopped telling me about it. I guess I'm not really that surprised he didn't tell me about you. The truth is, I don't even care any more. It's what I grew up on," Joyce replied, staring into her coffee.

"I am sorry if it seems I am taking him away from you, Joyce. Your father has been a great help to me. No one took me seriously—the police, the FBI, the missing person bureaus all brushed me aside—but your father listened. My daughter Tanya is just about your age," said Maria.

Joyce didn't flinch. "You don't have to apologize. I'm seventeen now. He's going to do whatever he wants and I can't stop him. I just wish he'd told me."

Maria was trying to think of an answer when Web trotted down the stairs, his hair slicked back like a big-band crooner.

"Maria has been telling me all about the help you've given her," Joyce said, watching to see how her father would react.

Web looked sternly at his daughter. He felt slightly guilty; he had breached a promise of sorts with Joyce.

"Well, let's not start a fan club just yet. We have a lot to do this afternoon," Web said, sitting down, a little edgy.

"We do? What are we doing?" Joyce asked, putting down her cup.

"It won't interest you, Joyce," said Web. "Maria and I are just going to go into San Francisco and ask some questions." He bit his lip.

"I'd love to come! I haven't been into town for weeks," said Joyce, pressing the issue in a way she knew would upset her father.

"She should come with us. I would enjoy her company." Maria said.

Web saw he was outflanked. "Okay, but we're not going shopping in Chinatown like we usually do."

"That's all right. I just want to help any way I can," Joyce said.

"Well, better grab a sweater. It's going to be chilly," Web replied.

Joyce stood up, worried. An afternoon with her father and Maria initially had been enticing, but trepidation gripped her. Having won the invitation, she suddenly didn't want to go at all. It might be *just a little too weird.*

"You know what?" she began, slapping her forehead in a cartoonish gesture. "I almost forgot that Margaux and I are supposed to go to the movies this afternoon. Gosh, Dad. I'm so sorry, but I guess I can't go with you after all," Joyce said, her eyes darting from Maria to Web.

She turned to Maria.

"It's been a pleasure meeting you, *Maria.*"

"Nice meeting you, too." Joyce shook Maria's hand, then darted upstairs.

From the privacy of her bedroom window, Joyce watched Web open the passenger door of his car for Maria. *Daddy-O never opens doors for people,* she thought. She didn't know what to make of this woman with a missing daughter.

From the outside, Hardware Hypermarket looked like any of the large gray warehouses in San Francisco's industrial district. Web drove past three times before noticing the sign in the parking lot: "Hardware Hypermarket—Insanely Great Technology at Insanely Low Prices." He pulled into a space near the back of the crowded parking lot and stopped the car.

Web and Maria were there because fourteen hundred dollars had been charged to Maria's credit card at the store three weeks earlier. Maria had discovered the charges the previous Thursday when reviewing her monthly statement. Soon after her daughter disappeared, Maria had canceled the two charge cards that carried Tanya's name but had forgotten about the duplicate MasterCard on her account that Tanya also carried.

Maria called Sheriff Block immediately. He relayed the report to the San Francisco police, who sent two officers to investigate. SFPD had only learned that a man had used the card. They didn't have much information beyond that. Maria wanted to visit the store in person and see if the police overlooked anything. If she could find the man who used the charge card, she might be closer to finding Tanya.

Maria and Web walked toward the store. Even the parking lot was a hubbub of activity. Two disheveled men in their twenties examined some equipment in a car trunk, negotiating loudly. As Web and Maria entered, a father and son walked out, excitedly unwrapping a computer game.

The whole facility seemed more like an enormous grocery market than an electronics store. Web and Maria went straight to one of the eleven registers, where an agitated college-aged checker was flashing a light pen across dozens of parts as a balding customer pulled them out of his cart.

"Pardon me," Web was unable to catch the boy's attention. As the checker kept ringing up items, Web stepped in and placed his hand on a box of disks that the checker held.

"Excuse me. We have an appointment with the manager."

"Yeah, right. Just a minute."

Without looking up, he continued ringing up the merchandise. After a series of high-pitched beeps, the machine made a deep buzz. The checker lifted a phone.

"Price check, station eleven." His eyes turned upward, away from Web and Maria.

"We want to see the manager," repeated Web.

"Hey, just a minute. I'm right in the middle of something," said the checker, avoiding direct eye contact.

Maria grabbed the boy's arm. "This is an important matter involving the police." He turned to face her and she stared him down.

"Don't have a tizzy. He's right in back. Furthest door, can't miss it."

Web and Maria walked through the turnstile into the cavernous store. The checker muttered *"assholes"* loud enough that they could hear him.

The aisles were piled high with cartons of every brand of computer, monitor, and electronic doodad still on forklift palettes. A few aisles were blocked off, turning the store into a labyrinth of hacker toys.

Web said to Maria, "You could get lost in here," then thought: *the perfect place to make a large purchase without being remembered.*

They found a door covered with stickers from electronics manufacturers and science fiction movies. In the middle of the stickers was a sign that simply said "The Big Cheese." Web knocked impatiently.

A lanky thirty-ish man in jeans and a "Grateful Dead" T-shirt opened the door.

He simply said, "Yeah?" Nothing about him seemed managerial.

Maria stepped forward, extending her hand. "I am Maria de Rivera."

The manager slouched against the wall. "I'm Ed. Look, I'm really busy today. We have Beginner's Night on Monday and that might be the best thing for you . . ."

"We have an appointment," Web said tersely, "and we're not customers."

The manager folded his arms in front of his chest. "Look, I'm real sorry. Maybe you made an appointment with Roland, but he called in sick and I have a lot to do." Ed's small frame half-disappeared behind the door frame.

"I don't know if Roland told you, but this is police business," said Web.

"Oh. Oh." Ed closed his eyes and leaned his head back. He appeared to be hung over. "And you two are police, right?" He started to close the door. Web blocked it with his weight.

"You charged more than a thousand dollars on this woman's card. Illegally. We only want to find out how that happened," Web said through the opening.

"You have to take that up with senior management. I'm only the weekend guy," droned the manager.

"We are not going to make another trip," said Maria. "Unless it's with the police naming you as an accomplice." The tone of her voice let him know she was serious.

Web pressed the door open, and they entered the tiny office. There was only one chair besides the manager's and it was piled high with computer print outs. "Look, sorry about my office, but . . ."

"There is no need to apologize." Maria tried to take the edge off the situation. "I only wish to speak with the clerk who sold the computer. I want to ask him about the person who used my credit card."

"I don't know if I can do that," said the manager.

"You can introduce us now," said Web, "or wait till the police come. And they will come."

The manager cracked his knuckles. "Right, of course. Do you know who that was? Like I said, the regular manager isn't here." Ed slouched into his chair.

Maria looked in her daybook. "His name is Jamie Walker."

"Jamie, yeah, Jamie. Hold on." Ed picked up the phone and pushed a button. "Jamie, to the manager's office." His voice reverberated through the store. Ed nodded slowly, closed his eyes, and rolled his head back. "He'll be right here. Want a vitamin?"

"No. Thank you." Maria answered.

Ed opened a jar of large vitamin tablets and swallowed one without the benefit of water. Maria and Web exchanged glances.

The door opened, and a heavyset kid, no older than twenty, leaned in.

"You called me?"

His weight and blotchy skin gave the impression that he'd subsisted on nothing but Doritos and Dr. Pepper for most of his life.

The manager stood up.

"Jamie, this is, uh . . ." He couldn't remember the names of the people he'd just met.

"I am Maria, and this is Web."

Jamie entered the room and closed the door, eyeing the two with suspicion. The little office was crowded and stuffy.

"So ask away. Whatever he can tell you." Ed leaned back in his chair and started to put his feet on the desk, out of habit, but stopped short of doing so and instead wriggled uncomfortably in his chair.

"Jamie, my credit card was used to purchase some equipment," Maria said gently, trying to put Jamie at ease. "I would like to know everything you remember about the customer."

"God, it was like three weeks ago. I already told the police anyway the other day," he mumbled.

She smiled at him. "Yes, they told us how much help you were—said it was rare that a man had such a keen memory. Isn't that what they said, Web?" Web nodded.

Jamie spoke hesitantly, like someone who eschews human contact for the comfort of a computer screen. "Okay. You know we get a lot of guys in here, but this one seemed . . . kind of like a novice. Uh, so I answered some of his questions. He bought a whole computer, you know, the works—CPU, modem, monitor, and a bunch of beginner books."

"Such a memory!" Maria pumped up the charm. "What else? Anything about the man who bought it?"

Jamie nervously chewed on his lip. "Well, except for his questions, he looked a lot like our regulars. Jeans, T-shirt or maybe a flannel shirt. I think he was kind of heavy, or . . ."

"Or what?" Web had the scent; there was a detail the boy half-remembered.

"Well, I noticed at one point that he had on two pairs of jeans. We get some weird guys in here, but it was real hot that day. Maybe he forgot he got dressed—got dressed again. I thought it was funny." Jamie laughed without opening his mouth, producing a snort.

Maria flashed her white teeth and laughed throatily, as if to say she appreciated the dry wit.

"That is kind of funny, Jamie." Maria wanted him to loosen up. "Do you think perhaps he was purposely hiding his appearance?"

"Well, you know, now that you point it out he coulda been doing that. Yeah. I guess so."

"Do you remember anything else?"

"Not that much really. We were really busy that day." Jamie gnawed on his pinkie, then pulled it out of his mouth and wiped it on his jeans.

Web saw that they weren't getting much more useful information from the clerk. "We'd like to see the order form and whatever he signed."

Ed, the manager, spun his chair around. "Actually, we do everything electronically. We run the mag strip on the card and the machine does everything else. There's no real signature to give you . . ."

"You're kidding." Web had never heard of this.

"Nope. The owner thinks everything should be connected with everything else, the paperless office thing."

"Can we at least get the serial numbers of the equipment he purchased? There has to be some sort of record," asked Web, exasperated.

"Sure. I'll print it all out for you." Ed started punching away at keys on his terminal.

"Can I go?" Jamie seemed uncomfortable.

"Could I have your home phone number in case I think of another question?" asked Maria.

"Sure, okay."

Jamie scribbled his phone number on a torn strip of paper and gave it to her, then nervously left without saying good-bye. Ed pulled a copy of the receipt out of the laser printer on his desk and handed it to Web.

"Is there anyone else who may have seen this man?" Web asked.

"Not that I can think of. We gave the police the grand tour yesterday and Jamie was the only one who remembered much." Web examined the receipt. In bold letters at the bottom it was marked "Will Call/Warehouse."

"What's this?" Web pointed to the marking.

"Well, big orders have to be picked up at the warehouse," replied Ed.

"Did *this* customer have to go there?" asked Web, aggravated at the omission.

"Yeah, I guess so." Ed crossed his legs uncomfortably.

"Did you tell the police about it?"

"I dunno. I wasn't here Friday. That woulda' been Roland who talked to them." Web thought the manager was hiding something.

"Where is this warehouse?"

"It's about six blocks away. The facility here isn't big enough to handle all the product at this location, so we use a warehouse annex," said the manager, slipping into corporate-speak.

"How could we get there?" Web demanded.

"There's nothing for you there. I don't think anyone working there would know much at all." Ed chewed on a pen until the top cracked loudly in his mouth, then sheepishly tossed it into the trash can.

"How do the customers get there?" Web asked angrily.

"What's the big deal? We give them a little map. They pick up their purchase."

"Give me one of those maps, please."

The manager still hesitated.

Web stood up to his full height. "Now," he said.

"Okay, okay. Here it is." He pulled from his drawer a preprinted map with a dashed line indicating the route to the warehouse about a mile away. Coupons for future sales were printed on the reverse. It looked like plenty of customers were sent to the warehouse—but not the police.

Maria and Web compared notes as they drove to the warehouse.

"Pretty strange, this warehouse," said Web.

"Yes. I find it odd that the manager I spoke to yesterday called in sick," said Maria.

"Something's not quite right."

They drove across two sets of railroad tracks and pulled around to the back of an old red brick building. Several men bustled around, unloading a delivery truck. Web and Maria went to a door marked "Will Call." Maria rang the bell and the door opened with a loud buzzing sound. They entered. A pale balding man wearing a blue jumpsuit sat behind a counter.

"You here to pick up something?" he asked.

"No, we just want to ask a few questions," Web said, approaching the counter.

"You a cop?"

"No, I'm not. My name's Web Sloane. This is Maria de Rivera."

"What's the deal?" He was visibly annoyed.

"My credit card was used by a man to purchase some computer equipment without my knowledge. He picked it up here. I was wondering if you could help us identify him." She handed him the form that the manager had printed for them.

"This was picked up three weeks ago. The loader was . . ." The man tapped some numbers into a computer. "It was loaded by Jesus Alvarez. He's, ah, not even here anymore." The man threw up his arms.

"Were the police here yesterday?" Alarms went off in Web's mind: He detected a lie by omission.

"Nope. Should they have been?"

"They sure should have. You just give things to whoever drives up?"

"Nah. They have to have one of these forms here," replied the clerk defensively.

"Thanks for your time," Web said, rapidly steering Maria out of the building. He knew what the omission was.

"Why did you leave so soon?" Maria asked, puzzled at Web's quick exit. "There might have been something we could have learned . . ."

"He was worried about the INS. They didn't bring the police because they use illegal immigrants." He headed toward the loading dock.

"Imigra. How can you tell?" asked Maria.

"A hunch is all. Let's ask some questions without that manager following us around," said Web.

The loading dock workers drank coffee and ate doughnuts standing around a catering truck. Web approached a muscular man who wore a red flannel shirt and jeans.

"I'm looking for Jesus Alvarez. Is he here today?"

The man swallowed a bite of doughnut. "I don't know no Jesus Alvarez." He turned away.

Maria put her hand on the man's shoulder and spoke to him in Spanish, using friendly, measured tones. Web picked up a little of the small talk. The man was Salvadoran. Maria commented on the great seafood she had once had when visiting El Salvador. The man was pleased and bragged a bit about his homeland. Then Maria got more serious, obviously changing the subject. The man shrugged his shoulders and replied but spoke so fast Web could not understand.

Then, to Web's surprise, Maria lost her temper. She let loose a long harangue in Spanish, shaking her finger at the man.

He threw up his arms. "Okay. Okay." He whistled, then yelled into the warehouse. "Jesus!"

Maria turned to Web. "You were right about illegals. I had to let him know we weren't *imigra,* but that if he did not cooperate, I would not hesitate to call them."

"What's he say?"

"The boy still works here," she replied. "The manager lied to us."

A kid no older than fourteen, wearing a seed company cap, jumped down from the loading dock and approached them. He looked very worried.

Maria greeted him and started asking questions in Spanish. The boy loosened up. Maria turned to Web.

"Can you buy him a candy bar and a Coke? It's to show we're not out to get him," Maria asked.

"Sure."

Web went to the roach-coach and bought the items. He stalled to give her some time alone with the boy. As he walked back, he saw Maria smile. He handed the boy the food.

"Web, get a pen. I want you to write some things down."

Maria translated from the boy's Spanish as Web took notes.

"He drove a gray car. A convertible," she said.

The boy saw Web taking notes and suddenly spoke in thickly accented English mixed with Spanish phrases.

"Yes, it was a bad-ass *chingadera* car too. *Es un BMW.*"

Web understood BMW and repeated it. "A gray BMW?"

"Sí. Fue un, it was a, you know, no top?" The boy waved his hand in the air.

"Convertible?" Web asked.

"Sí, sí." He continued to speak in Spanish, and Maria translated the highlights.

"He is not certain it was a BMW, but it definitely was a convertible. . . ." Maria listened to the boy, and translated, "He remembers the man because he was very picky about his car . . . he did not want a scratch on it."

Web wrote it down, then asked Maria.

"Why does he remember this man?"

She asked the boy, then translated the answer.

"It was unusual for him to be so fussy . . . because the car seemed kind of beat up. It had the front seat missing. Then he tipped him twenty bucks . . . two days pay."

Web's pencil slipped and he stabbed himself in the hand. He suddenly felt dizzy and stared at the boy as if seeing a ghost.

A missing car seat might be innocuous enough in a beat up old car. But not in a new BMW. The kind of person who drove a BMW didn't let it stay in disrepair.

"Ask him if he's *absolutely sure* about the seat," Web asked.

Maria put forth the question. The boy answered in English.

"Yes sir. No seat. The car was . . . no top and no seat." He lapsed back into Spanish. Maria asked him some more questions.

The answer unnerved Web; he didn't hear what was said next. *Theodore Bundy had driven a car with one seat missing. The place where the seat went was where he put girls' bodies. That way they couldn't be seen by passing cars.* Another Bundy coincidence. *Or was it by design?*

It wasn't until they were driving home that he was overcome with a sense of dread. *If there were a copycat murderer, and he had studied Bundy in detail, he may have taken the seat out of his car to be more like his twisted idol. Copycats were like that. And that would mean that Maria's daughter might have been one of his victims.*

Maria snapped him out of his reverie.

"Web, the light is green."

"Oh, yeah." He stepped on the accelerator, pushing the car to fifty miles an hour on the city street.

A primal rage surged through Web's consciousness. The hunter within him was awakening from its dark slumber, unleashing the volatile elements of his mind that were called upon only in times of crisis. The dangerous and consuming mental reserve allowed him to make connections unseen to the ordinary mind; it was the kind of superhuman force that allows a mother to lift an auto to free her trapped child. Left unchecked, though, it could destroy him.

He sensed the presence in the world of a fierce adversary who covered his tracks almost completely, yet left teasing hints that might be detected only by an initiate: by someone who had suffered firsthand the limits of human perversity and terror. Someone like Web Sloane.

Maria stared at him, frightened by the faraway gaze in his eyes.

Later, in Web's kitchen, Maria hung up the phone with a deep sigh of gloom.

"The San Francisco police took the information and thanked me. There's not even a specific detective assigned to it—the dispatcher just added our notes to their file."

Web stood up from the kitchen table. "No one even assigned to it?"

"They are treating it as a mere credit card fraud report.

Nothing about Tanya at all." She kept her hand on the phone, as if touching it would somehow relieve her despair.

"Let's call Block," Web said, rubbing his hands together. *"He's* working on a missing person, not credit card fraud. I'll call him.

"That would be kind. I am sure he is tired of hearing from me."

Web dialed and was quickly connected to Sheriff Block.

"Working Saturdays still, Sheriff?" Web asked.

"Who's this?" came the gruff reply.

"Web Sloane. I met you a month ago."

"Ah, yeah, right. The professor," chuckled Block with glee.

Web was surprised and pleased that Block remembered him.

"So, Professor, did you catch my man yet?" Block inquired, a bit of challenge in his voice.

"No, but we got a good lead. You remember the credit cards?"

"SFPD already filled me in. Beat you to the punch," Block said, "and you thought I was sleeping on the job."

"We found out something more."

"How 'bout dropping the other shoe, Prof?" asked the sheriff.

Block hung on every word while Web related the details surrounding their discovery of the illegal immigrants working at the loading dock and, more importantly, the gray convertible, probably a BMW.

"Hot diggity, Professor! You did dig something up. Give me your number and I'll call you back. I want to run this description by DMV to see if anything fishy comes up."

After hanging up, Web turned to Maria.

"The sheriff's hooked and says he'll call us back this afternoon."

Maria lit up. "I do not like that man, but he is said to be hardworking."

"That's more important than table manners from my experience," said Web.

Maria laid her head on the table. Web sat across from her.

"Maria, it'll be a little while before he gets back to us. If you'd like to take a nap, we have an extra room. I could keep it quiet around here for a little while."

"That is very kind, but I think I should be getting home soon. It's almost five o'clock and I have a long drive."

Web sensed the exhaustion and confusion that Maria was experiencing. There was no one she could lean on.

"Maria, why don't you take a nap, and we'll go to dinner tonight. Give yourself a little time off. If you like, you can stay in the guest room and drive home tomorrow," Web suggested.

"No, I would be imposing on you," Maria replied.

"It would really be my pleasure. You're not imposing one bit," said Web.

"There are so many things to do . . ."

"Give yourself a break. A night off can do wonders once in a while."

She smiled. "You sound like you speak from experience. I accept. Thank you. Now, where can I take that nap?"

While Maria was resting in the upstairs guest room, Block called back.

"What did you find out?" demanded Web.

"Bad news and some not so bad news, Professor. I got through to the right bureaucrat down at DMV, and there's, uh, 22,541 convertible BMW's in California."

"That many. Jesus. We're looking for a needle in a haystack."

"Yeah, but here's the not-so-bad news. Only 3,601 are listed as gray. That don't mean our computer shopper didn't paint his gray down at Earl Scheib."

"What do you do now?" Web wanted to hear something reassuring he could tell to Maria.

"DMV's sending me all the lists. All the BMW convertibles. And all the gray ones. If something is hot or if the registration has expired, or even if they have too many parking tickets, it will be flagged. Just one more arrow in my quiver," he said.

"Good enough. I'll tell Maria later." Web hung up.

Web read the paper while he waited for Maria to wake up. What had once been a relaxing Saturday ritual was now an anxious ordeal, as he combed the front pages, City Section, and local roundup for signs of new disappearances. Today he was fortunate—nothing more than the typical robberies, gang shootings, Middle East wars, and political scandals.

Maria wandered downstairs. She had taken the combs from her hair, and it fell softly around her face, giving her a relaxed, vulnerable appearance.

"What did you find out?" she asked Web.

"Block is getting every registration card for convertible BMWs in the state."

"How many are there?"

"A lot." He didn't want to give her the number; it was too depressing. "But only a fraction are listed as convertibles."

"That is something. What do we do next?"

Web stood up, lifted by a sudden inspiration.

"Maria, did you cancel that credit card?"

"No, not yet. I probably should." She looked at Web with anticipation.

"Don't cancel it. I have a friend at MasterCard in St. Louis who can put a tracer on it. If someone uses it again, he'll call us within one day, maybe sooner, before the police are notified. It might cost you money if it's used, but it could help find Tanya."

"Good idea. Did you tell the sheriff about all the stolen goods?"

"I figured SFPD would have."

"They may have, but I would not count on them. I'll call them back." She dialed the sheriff's direct number.

"Vine County Police."

"May I speak to Sheriff Block? It is Maria de Rivera."

"He's not in at the moment, Ms. de Rivera. May I take a message?" The man on the phone spoke solemnly, a disinterested bureaucrat.

"I just wanted to give him the serial numbers of some equipment that was bought with my credit card."

"I can forward that information if you like," said the voice on the other end of the line.

Maria read him the serial numbers from the Hardware Hypermarket invoice, thanked the man, and hung up.

"I just like to tell them everything as soon as I know.

Ninety percent may be worthless, but you never know which ten percent will be useful," she said to Web.

"Right. Good thinking," said Web.

Alan DeVries hung up the phone. He tapped a pen on the desk, thinking.

Late in the day on Saturday was Alan's favorite time to work; usually, no one else was at the Vine County sheriff station besides the dispatcher, who sat in another room. He could accomplish everything he needed to do without interference.

He carefully transposed the numbers and descriptions given by Maria as he entered them into the computer. At a glance, the alterations would be imperceptible without a direct comparison to the original documents. They could be mistaken for simple typographical errors, but the invisible alterations would keep the computer from matching the goods purchased with a stolen credit card to the computer he had at home.

12

Web took Maria and Joyce to dinner at Lucky Golden, his favorite Korean restaurant. The restaurant was decorated in dark wood, with massive tropical fish tanks in each of the six dining rooms. It was quite a lively production: Raw, marinated beef was brought to their table, where they cooked it themselves on a gas grill at the table's center. Maria felt thoroughly relaxed for the first time in recent memory.

The manager, a handsome Korean man wearing a tuxedo, came to their table when they were partway through the meal.

"How is everybody? Do you like it?" he asked.

"It is absolutely perfect. I have not had so much fun in a

long time," Maria said, addressing the waiter, but really speaking to Web.

"Another drink, anyone?"

Web took the lead.

"Sure, I'd like another glass of red wine," said Web.

"I would too," said Maria.

The manager turned to Joyce. She looked at her father and Maria, then said in a matter-of-fact manner to the waiter, "I'd also like a glass." The waiter nodded. As he left, Web turned to Joyce and spoke in a soft voice.

"I don't think that's a good idea. You're underage."

"Just one drink with dinner won't kill me." She smiled pleasantly.

Maria spoke up. "In some countries, children drink wine at half her age—this is a special occasion."

Web allowed himself to be persuaded. He wanted Joyce and Maria to be friends. In fact, he desired it more urgently than he cared to admit.

After dinner, the conversation turned to careers. Maria explained her job in real estate sales.

"My husband, I mean my ex-husband, was a builder, so sales was a natural occupation for me. It turned out I had a knack for matching up a family with the right home. I have done quite well in good times and bad. Home prices have almost quadrupled since we moved up there."

Joyce leaned forward. "Don't you feel tremendously guilty? I mean with all the homeless people around nowadays, how can you sell a house for millions of dollars? Shouldn't that be spent on shelters for fifty families?"

"Joyce . . ." Web tried to stop her. He envisioned the evening degenerating into an embarrassing fight.

"No, it's okay," said Maria, drawing on her complement of diplomatic skills. "I think you have a legitimate question. Selling expensive homes provides jobs for people in construction, in building repair. If forty men work several months on a house, I think each of them is kept out of poverty, too."

Joyce was feeling uppity. "Yes, but aren't those workers exploited by the ruling class? Why shouldn't they live in the homes they build?"

"Honestly, at the rates they are paid, I do not think it is exploitation." Maria folded her napkin.

"I've read some books that say one of these days the laborers are just going to rise up and smash the bourgeois ruling class that's holding them down. I just wondered what you thought of that." Joyce delighted in being bad; she looked over the green tea ice cream with a glint in her eye.

"To tell you the truth, I do not believe that will happen. I have read Karl Marx, too, and like many others I believe his ideas are a hundred years out of date."

"But what about all the poor people in America . . ."

"Joyce, that's enough." Web angrily cut her off, then summoned the waiter.

"Our check, please." He turned to Maria, embarrassed.

"She doesn't really mean what she's saying," Web said to Maria, growing flustered.

"Of course she means it," said Maria, taking sides with Joyce. "She's not a child." She turned to the girl. "Are you interested in helping the homeless? Perhaps you might work in the shelters or participate in fund-raisers."

Joyce was caught off-guard. "I guess I really haven't done that much," she said. "It's like that song where they say 'Everybody's talking about the weather, but nobody ever does anything about it . . .'"

Maria laughed. "There is plenty you can do. I bet with your initiative and intelligence, you could make a real difference."

As the two women discussed ways Joyce could become involved with the homeless cause, Web marveled at how Maria had defused a potentially ugly argument with Joyce. It made him aware of his own shortcomings, of what he thought was a critical gap in his parenting abilities: He didn't know how to fight with his daughter. Maria had a unique ability, simple yet ineffable, something Web would always lack. It was to him the essence of feminine mystique.

That night, Web and Maria stayed up late, chatting on the foldout sofa bed in the guest room where Maria was to stay. Joyce had mercifully opted to stay downstairs and watch "Saturday Night Live."

"Joyce just loves to find new ways to run me through the wringer," said Web.

"Don't take offense, but I think you keep Joyce at a distance."

Web spoke quietly, reflecting. "You mean I'm too strict, don't you."

"No, not exactly." Maria put her hand on Web's arm and took another approach. "Where is her mother? Are you divorced?"

Web exhaled deeply. He hadn't told her about Alice. The subject touched something deep in him; he didn't confide the tale to many people.

"When our older daughter, Vicki, was missing, we spent day and night searching for her. After several months, Alice, my wife, became very distraught and collapsed of exhaustion." Web stared at the wall, thinking about his long-dead wife.

"Yes? And then what happened?"

"Alice checked into a hospital near our home. She had good doctors, psychiatrists, the best of care. But nothing could bring her out of the depression. She was a broken woman." He spoke in a near whisper. "After two weeks at the hospital, she took an overdose of sedatives. Officially, it was an accident." Web stared off into space.

"Web?"

"I'm all right."

He paused a moment to gather his composure. "I've always held Ted Bundy responsible for her death. Before Vicki disappeared, Alice was cheerful, determined, a strong woman. She had given up a career teaching college to raise our girls, and they were her whole life. There were so many things she took care of, so many little things she did . . ." Web realized he was rattling on and took a breath. "Sorry. I'm boring you with this, Maria."

"No, you're not. I want to hear." She held his wrist.

"One of the most important people in the world to her, our daughter Vicki, disappeared without a trace. I know I can never be what she was, but I try to be as good a father as I can with Joyce. It's just not the same."

"The same as what?" asked Maria.

"I'm not supportive emotionally. I realize it, and yet I can do nothing about it. When she's crying or angry, when she needs me the most, I can't do anything. I just freeze up and wait until she's back to normal." Web wiped his forehead, then continued.

"Joyce is totally different from her sister. It might be the times, or because her mother isn't here, but she's constantly testing me, always trying to be difficult."

Maria leaned away and looked at Web. "You cannot compare her to her sister. Joyce is her own girl. Of course she tests you. She is a teenager. My daughter, Tanya, is like that too. She will do something bad just to see how I react."

Web listened intently. Hearing Maria's troubles, with her own daughter gone, made him suddenly have a greater appreciation for Joyce.

"What kind of things did Tanya do?" he asked.

Maria froze. The impact of what Web said took a moment to hit him. He said *"did."* As if Tanya were dead. The question hung in the air like a dirty joke.

"Hope is all I have." Maria pleaded with Web.

"Maria, I'm sorry." He looked away.

She took a deep breath. "No! It's not possible. I will *not* believe it."

She stood and threw back her head in an imperial gesture. *"Your* daughter died and *your* life came apart, but that is not my life. I will not believe she is dead; you cannot drag me into your pit of despair!"

Then without knowing his intention, Web grabbed her—his hands clasped her hard by the shoulders. He shook her once so hard her head snapped back sharply. She tried to pull away.

Then with sudden realization, he stopped himself. Their eyes locked.

It was the anger, the deep tidal rage, he had felt the day they had shown him the videotape of Bundy's confession. Web had never expected to experience that again. He thought it was gone with Bundy himself, but it had only lain waiting, dulled and slumberous, beyond his awareness.

Now Maria's stinging words had brought it roaring back to life. And God knew what he had nearly done to her because of it.

In sudden realization, he pulled her body against his. He

felt her own frustration, palpable as blows, as profound sobs racked her body. He held her tight against him, conscious of her heartbeat and the strange electricity of another's body against his own, her breath against his ear. He murmured over and over, "I'm sorry. I'm so sorry."

Slowly, her tears subsided. They sank onto the sofa bed. Soon she lay gently on his shoulder. Softly he put his hand on her head, running his fingers through her hair, soothing her. Her sobs metamorphosed into the languid rhythms of sleep, and he laid her limp body down on the bed. She was asleep, exhausted.

He considered getting up but thought it might disturb her rest. He knew it was the warmth of her body that was irresistible to him. A need that had been suppressed for years was at last met; like a man who tastes his first water after days in the desert, he had forgotten what it was like to share a bed. He thought, *I'll just stay until she's really asleep and then leave her. Just a little longer . . .*

Web was soon asleep by her side.

At 6 A.M. a flood of sunlight in the guest room awakened Web. Maria's warm body was draped over him, and she slept very soundly. He gently escaped from her grasp and slipped downstairs to his office. He didn't want her to think he had taken advantage of her.

He dialed a St. Louis phone number.

"MasterCard Information Services Department. Newman speaking."

"I'd like two double-cheese, double-anchovy pizzas. And a quart of Coke." Web waited for a reply, smiling.

"What? Who is this?" The connection was noisy with static.

"Hey, you deliver, right? I said two double-cheese, double-anchovy pizzas." Web spoke in a nasal voice this time, imitating a teenager.

The man on the other end of the phone grew impatient. "This is MasterCard ISD. I think you have the wrong number."

"I just want a goddam pizza, goddamit!" Web laughed.

"Sloane? You asshole. Where the hell are you?"

Web spoke in his normal voice. "Nailed me, Will. But I still want those pizzas."

The two had shared an office at the University of Washington when Web was a junior professor and Will was his head teaching assistant. During the two years as officemates, they had received hundreds of pizza orders from students who dialed a number incorrectly listed in the student phone book. The pizza gag had lived for twenty years, and each year at Christmas Web and Newman sent one another chef's hats, pizza boxes, and every other kind of pizza paraphernalia imaginable.

"I dialed your home number. What's it do, ring through to work?"

"Yeah, the guru never sleeps." Newman sounded tired.

"I thought you'd given up working on weekends."

"Only during emergencies, which only happen on weekends, four times a month." Will sighed. "So where the hell are you, Sloane? I called you about a month ago, and your number was disconnected."

"Berkeley. I moved last summer. I thought we sent you a change of address and a funny letter."

"Right, right. Now that you mention it you did. It's probably buried on my desk at home. So, let me guess. You want to get me out of here and give me a killer cushy job as a professor, fly me to California, and double my pay."

"I wish I could, but I'm looking for a favor, Will."

"Big surprise. Let me check your favor account . . . it seems you're overdrawn. But we'll make an exception for you I guess." Newman thought "favor account" was the funniest joke in the world.

"You're still king of the system, right?" Web asked.

"I designed it. I can do anything."

"I want you to track a card for me. Put a tag on it in case anyone uses it."

"What's the deal?"

"The daughter of a friend of mine has been missing for several months. A couple weeks ago, someone used her card for the first time. We think if we can find whoever is using the card, we can find her daughter."

"Hmmm." Newman hesitated. "Gimme the number."

Web read him Maria's credit card account number. Newman tapped a few keys.

"Maria de Rivera . . ." Web could hear the clicking of computer keys again. "San Francisco Police Department just reported that it was stolen. We're supposed to pull the account."

"I know what you're supposed to do, Old Man." Web used Newman's college nickname. "But she's a lot more interested in finding her daughter than worrying about charges on her card. I just want you to reinstate the card, tag it, and call me whenever someone uses it."

"This on the level, Spider?" Two could play the nickname game.

"Absolutely. It would mean a lot to me."

"Let me tell you what I'm not allowed to do," said Newman.

"You're not going to help?" Web was frustrated at his friend's refusal to cooperate.

"Just shut up for a minute. There's a little matter of federal law we can't break. So, I'm *not* going to reactivate the card. Then, I'm *not* going to put a trace on it that will ring into the goddam pager they make me wear. Additionally, I *won't* see that you get called within a few minutes of the card being used. And if you want me to, I *won't* raise the limit on the card."

"Credit limit raise seems like a good idea."

"Web, you're about the only asshole in the world who I do these things for. Except of course I won't do any of them, right?"

"Well, I'm not going to send you a bottle of good California wine for your troubles." Web knew Will loved a good wine.

"How about not sending some Beaujolais nouveau? I hear that's the new trend for you wimpy Californians."

"That's what I won't do then, Will. Thanks for your trouble."

"I didn't do a thing."

When Web left his office, Maria was walking down the stairs. She had brushed her hair and put on makeup and looked well rested, refreshed, ready to face the world. Web wondered whether to mention that they had slept together.

"Good morning, Web," she said tenderly.

"Good morning, Maria. Want some breakfast?" He had a strong urge to kiss her.

"I would love nothing more than to have breakfast with you. But I must get back home." She sat on the steps.

"You sure? I could put on some coffee." Web liked having a woman in the house.

Mud trotted out from the kitchen and approached Maria. He rubbed against her legs, and she leaned down and scratched his ears. Mud turned on his side, blocking her path. Web smiled.

"He just wants you to rub his stomach. He loves that."

She scratched the dog's stomach. Mud closed his eyes and held out his nose in a position of perfect tranquility.

"He's so sweet," said Maria. "But I really must leave."

"Let me walk you out, then."

They walked in silence to her car, which was parked on the street. Mud followed, a few feet behind. A shiny covering of dew made her car glisten.

"I called my friend at MasterCard. He'll tell us if anyone uses your card again. Probably within minutes."

"The police said I had to cancel . . ."

"We kind of went around the police. I think it's more important to find Tanya than to follow some rules." Web leaned against the car. Maria stood right in front of him.

"Web, thank you so much for everything. I really enjoyed myself. You were right—a night off can do wonders."

"Maria, believe me, the pleasure is all mine. You're welcome any time you wish to come."

He gave her a hug good-bye, then walked around to the driver's side of the car. She opened the door but didn't climb in. The golden morning sun made her face glow.

They hugged again. This time it was more than a simple good-bye hug. Maria whispered into his ear.

"Thank you, Web. I didn't mind . . . it was very nice when you . . ." She didn't want to say it.

"Yes," he said, gathering her hair in one hand.

He held her tight for a long moment, inhaling the warmth of her body. Then suddenly she was in her car, closing the door.

"Good-bye," she said.

Maria drove down the suburban street. Mud chased behind the car through two front yards, then froze and wistfully watched her disappear, holding one paw tenuously in the air. Web walked slowly back to his house. It was such a bad idea to get involved with this woman. He asked himself if two people who met under such tragic circumstances could become close, or if they would simply be haunted together.

13

In the back room of the Vine County sheriff station, Alan DeVries read the hastily scrawled instructions left by the last operator of the computer database and typed in codes that he hoped would connect him with the FBI.

```
VINE.02198> telnet FBI.SKID /08113
Dialing . . .
CONNECT.
----------------------------------------

          Federal Bureau of Investigation
      SKID Serial Killer Identification DataBase
                    File 08113
**All Record Update/Changes Routed to Vine 02198**
----------------------------------------


AUTH CODE: Baby Blue
WELCOME VINE COUNTY #02198
USER LEVEL: TOP PRIORITY
```

The password Block had given him hadn't been changed. Alan now had full authority to view and change files. He wanted to find out how much was known and what connections had been made, if any. DeVries knew Block would soon be coming in, and he was supposed to be entering stolen car reports, not fooling around with SKID. He tapped furiously into the terminal.

FBI.SKID> SYNOP/08113/SCREEN

Within seconds, a thorough overview of everything known by all law enforcement departments about his case scrawled across the screen. He was ecstatic; in the wrong hands, this system intended to aid the police could be the greatest criminal tool in the world. He scanned the reports, trying to memorize as much of their content as possible. To print them out now would be far too risky.

```
JURISDICTION: Vine County Sheriff Station 02198
    RELATED REPORT SUMMARY/See individual files for
further information.
    03/17/90: 10-187 HOMICIDE. VICTIM: Jane Doe
90-4.
VICTIM: Jane Doe 90-5; SUSPECT: None. CHARGES
FILED: None. SUSPECT DESCRIPTION: None.
    04/19/90:   10-207   POSSIBLE   KIDNAPPING/
MISSING PERSON (See Vine 08116). VICTIM: Tanya de
Rivera (minor); SUSPECT: None. CHARGES FILED: None.
SUSPECT DESCRIPTION: None.
    3/14/91: 10-33 CREDIT CARD FRAUD (SFPD B-1109
Jurisdiction - transferred to VINE 02198). VICTIM: Maria
de Rivera, Tanya De Rivera (minor) (See 4/19/90). SUS-
PECT: None; Charges Filed: None; SUSPECT DESCRIP-
TION: Male Caucasian, 20-40, Possible Dark Hair,
Possible Glasses, Medium Build, Height Unknown,
Weight Unknown. Seen driving gray convertible BMW,
passenger seat removed. FRAUDULENTLY OBTAINED
PROPERTY: Computer, Additional Electronic Gear—
Maker & Serial Numbers: . . .
```

Alan DeVries studied the computer screen intently. *I'm in the driver's seat here,* he thought. In two weeks at Vine County sheriff station, he'd accomplished several objectives. First, complete jurisdiction had been given to Vine County for all cases related to the two Jane Does as well as the Tanya de Rivera missing person case. That meant that no law enforcement authority anywhere in the country could change or update records without Vine County's approval.

Without my *approval,* thought Alan, laughing at the exquisite irony. No one else at the station knew how to use the computer. The other departments had been happy to hand off the case; it was considered a bureaucratic hassle. In addition, he'd garbled enough numbers to make tracing the computer equipment impossible. And he knew exactly how far ahead of the authorities he was. The hundreds of pages of records synopsized in front of him contained his favorite words over and over again: *No suspect.*

Alan was debating removal of the line about the missing car seat when he heard a door slam behind him. He turned around. It was Block. With a deft touch of the fingers, Alan tried to make the reports disappear off the screen. An error message came onto the screen and the computer issued a shrill beep. The records were still visible; a flashing warning asked for an authorization code. Block walked up right behind him.

"I hate that goddam machine, Alan." Block watched as Alan frantically typed in various codes in an attempt to make the incriminating screen before him disappear.

"Yeah. It's really, uh, poorly designed," Alan replied, worried.

Without looking at Block he tried two other code combinations. Nothing could stop the alarm. Finally, he switched off the monitor. He turned around. Block was chuckling.

"Don't take it too personal, Alan. You're not the first person to get zillions of beeps outa' that peckerwood contraption. In fact, you probably have figured the friggin' thing out better than anyone before you. Don't let it tweak you." Block punched him on the shoulder.

Off the hook, for the moment, Alan thought.

"Okay. I'll get it." He smiled sheepishly at Block.

"Scooch over, I'll share my ignorance with you. I know how to stop the beeping, anyway." Block reached for the switch on the monitor. Alan grabbed his hand.

"No, that's okay. I learn the system better if I make my

own mistakes." He tried to look like a serious problem solver.

"Here, I'll just show ya' . . ." Block had his hand on the switch.

"No, no. If I can learn this system the hard way, you'll never have to touch it again. If you tell me, I'll always run to you with questions. I'll figure it out."

"That's damned dedicated of you. How you doing entering the month's reports?"

"Ah, a little behind. But I don't mind staying tonight till they're all in." Alan looked at the stack of papers. He hadn't accomplished a bit of legitimate work. All he had done was study his own file in SKID.

"Whatever it takes. If you really set it up so I don't ever have to touch this high-tech abortion, you got yourself job security till you croak." Block laughed.

"What?" Alan was shaken.

"If you master it, there's no chance of ever being fired. In fact, we'd probably just handcuff you to the damned machine so you can't even quit." Block guffawed.

Alan didn't catch Block's joke, set off by the reference to handcuffs.

"I'm trying as hard as I can. I'll get it," he said, unnerved.

"Sure you will. You're doing fine, Alan. Don't take it so hard. Things have been going a lot better since you got here."

"Thanks. In no time we'll be computing like NASA."

Block slapped him on the back and left.

As soon as Block was gone, Alan turned the monitor on again and stayed there till he'd figured out every possible security code. The month's backlog of stolen car reports languished on the desk. He hoped no one would discover them.

On his way home from the sheriff's station, Alan stopped by the Mars Bakery to take care of some business. He had timed his visit carefully; Mars usually made deliveries around three o'clock.

"Hi, Alan! What a surprise! How's it going at the sheriff's?" Mars stopped kneading dough on the counter and wiped off her hands. There were no customers.

"Terrific. He said I was the only one who could work the computer," Alan said, trying to sound enthusiastic.

"Great!"

"Actually he told me"—Alan did his best imitation of Block's down-home style—"ain't another soul can figure out that peckerwood contraption, boy!"

Mars laughed. "I was just going over to the coffee shop and the grocery to deliver some pastries. Wanna come with me?" she asked, taking off her bright red apron.

"I have to drive out to pick up some gear tonight and was hoping just to grab a cup of joe before leaving."

"Ah. What're you getting?"

"Some VW stuff. There's a dealer in Greenfield." He fidgeted. He needed some time alone in the bakery.

"You can drink your coffee in the car and come with me . . ."

"I'd rather just hang out here, if that's okay." He sat down at the small table.

"Sure. No problem. Could you watch for customers? I'll only be gone about forty-five minutes and I'd rather not close." She put several boxes of bread on the counter, ready to carry out to the car.

"Okay—but I'll probably be gone before you get back."

Alan walked her out to the car. As soon as she was gone, he went back into the bakery to finish his business.

First, he quickly wolfed down three pastries, washing them down with a cup of coffee. Then, he rang up a bogus customer on the machine. He entered $179.00. Then he entered $1.79. Alan walked over to the door to see if anyone was approaching. They weren't. Quickly, he pulled nine twenty-dollar bills from the register and stuffed them in his pocket. Then he corrected his mistake: voiding $179.00 twice should make everything come out within a few pennies of the correct figure, and leave him one hundred eighty bucks richer. He left Mars a note, jumped in his car, and headed for Greenfield, seventy-three miles away.

The grease-smeared kid in the service bay of the Volkswagen dealer looked the car over woefully. He hated to see a thing of beauty so defaced.

"Someone did a pretty darn savage job ripping this seat

out. I reckon I'll hafta weld it back in—bolt's sheared right through. Can have it for you tomorrow afternoon," said the kid.

"Can you do it tonight?" Alan pleaded, hopefully.

"No way, mister. We close in another half hour, and I got to finish out that Vanagon over there."

"I'll kick in thirty in cash for you personally, besides the regular cost of the job."

The mechanic sighed and leaned on the car. He pulled off his baseball cap and out fell long, dark hair. Alan eyed him carefully.

"Well, that's against the darn rules, and I could get in a lot of trouble taking thirty bucks. A hotel would cost you about fifty if you stayed overnight, and then you'd have to buy breakfast and dinner, too." The mechanic rolled his fingers in his hands, looking slyly at his fingernails.

Alan liked the way the mechanic did business.

"Well, I'd like to save that breakfast money."

"I reckon I could stay late and have you out of here tonight."

Alan reached for his wallet. The mechanic stopped him and pointed over to the manager, who could see them plainly.

"Maybe I could find a fifty accidently left in the glove compartment."

"No problem."

Alan put some bills in the glove compartment, then gave the keys to the kid.

"I want it to look new. Like the seat was never out."

"I'll take care of it." The mechanic smiled.

Alan read *Field and Stream* for the next couple hours, thinking about how careful he'd been. *"Ted Bundy never would have been this smart. But Alan DeVries knows better."*

14

In his office at the university, Web anxiously scanned the *San Francisco Chronicle*, snapping the pages as he pored through their contents. He contemplated the man who had used Maria's credit card. If he was the one involved in Tanya's disappearance, while he was in town he might have taken the opportunity to indulge his horrific passion. Web hoped he was wrong but feared he would find a story about a missing person or a murdered girl in the papers within a week. When he discovered no such story, Web felt relieved but strangely disappointed.

With Tanya still on his mind, Web laid out the photos that held such a fascination for him. He was as familiar with the pictures of young girls as a kid is with his baseball cards; their edges were tattered from use, and with a glance at each face he could rattle off any number of depressing statistics— date missing, circumstances of disappearance, what each girl's future might have held if she hadn't vanished into thin air.

There was a quick tap on the door, then Wallenberg barged in.

"How's it going, Web?" His bearded colleague saw the photos but said nothing.

"Decent, I guess." He didn't look up.

Wally pushed the photos aside and dumped a canvas bag onto Web's desk, which landed with the loud clink of metal.

"There's your 'biners, and I also threw in some 'biner brakes and a couple chocks." He opened the bag and dumped out several aluminum rings and other assorted rock-climbing gear.

"Oh, jeez, that's tomorrow?" asked Web.

He had forgotten his promise to go climbing with

Wallenberg. Once, Web had gone climbing at least every month but hadn't gone on an outing since leaving Washington State.

"Pick you up at 6 A.M.?" asked Wally, chipper.

"I don't know, I had planned on working in the garden this weekend." His flower gardens were sorely lacking for care and attention; Web had been looking forward to pulling weeds and erecting a new fence to keep squirrels away from his bulbs.

"You can't back out this weekend. Goldsmith sandbagged me, 'cause of that damned astronomy TV show he's working on, so if you don't come, I'm stuck. C'mon, yesterday you said you'd go."

"There's just too damn much to do. I don't want to spoil your trip, but . . ."

Web tried to shift the photos on his desk around so they wouldn't be so prominent. Wallenberg leaned against the wall and scowled.

"Web, I'm kind of worried about you."

"What do you mean? I've got two great classes. I'm doing some vital work."

Wallenberg grimaced, then waved his hand over the desk. "Don't humor *me,* Web. You're not doing a bit of academic work. What's all this business with the newspaper articles, the girls, all that bullshit?" The way Wally phrased his question made Web feel sordid, perverse.

"Just something I'm doing to help a friend. None of your business."

"It looks to me like you're refighting the last war. I'm no psychologist, but if it's what it looks like, you're replaying what happened with Vicki, only with this other woman's daughter."

Web leaned forward, defensively.

"That's not it at all. I just have some rather specialized knowledge, and I'm using it to help one mother."

"I never see you doing anything else, Web." Web didn't answer. Wally continued to preach at him.

"There's a lot you've been neglecting. Next week is your Chancellor's Request lecture. Do you know what that means?"

"I have a good idea of what I'm going to say."

"That's not good enough. Chancellor's Request is the ticket to the big time. The guys who do well get a department chair or their own department. The guys who screw up or recycle some freshman talk fade away. Remember Jerry Walker, the econ professor?"

Web nodded.

"Well, he totally washed out at his CR lecture. He was hung over and just blithered in that British accent."

"But he's tenured!" said Web.

"You're new to Berkeley. Let me tell you something: There's tenure, and then there's clout. Walker's tenured all right, but they imported a guy from Harvard to head his department. Walker should have had that job."

Wallenberg leaned on the desk, examining a photo. "I want to see you do well. Spend some time on your presentation. Spend some time with your daughter, for Christ's sake. Don't fritter your time reliving the search for Vicki. She's gone. Get on with your life."

Web was angry. "Wally, that's enough. I don't need you telling me what to do."

"Okay, fine. Make your own decisions. You won't hear another word out of me. But I couldn't watch you spinning into the void without saying something."

Web stood up. He wanted Wally out, and he wanted him out now. He picked up the climbing gear from his desk.

"Here's your equipment. Sorry I can't go."

Wallenberg took the gear from Web and left without saying good-bye. Web closed the door and immediately began studying the photos again, searching for some clue, some overlooked detail, that might lead him to the murderer. In spite of his friend's advice, he didn't touch the Chancellor's Request notes until the day before he was to present it.

The following Thursday Web sat in his office sweating out ideas for the important lecture. He had selected a title: "Intuitive Thinking to Draw Order from Chaos." Web knew he could glean material from two papers he wrote on related subjects, and he'd done enough additional research to push onto new ground. What he had decided during the sleepless night before was to pack his presentation with visual aids—slides, charts, pictures. He had one day to prepare them, which was only possible if he worked from morning till night and took advantage of the university's computer graphics department.

While he sketched out the first chart, the phone rang. He debated whether to answer it, then decided he had to in case it was something relating to the lecture.

"Sloane."

"This is the University Message Center. You've got several calls that haven't been returned." It was the cheery voice of the career operator at the Berkeley switchboard.

Web nervously chewed on a piece of paper. "Let's hear them."

"Will Newman from MasterCard, actually, three times today. Said, "the card's been used." Also, Wallenberg and four calls from Eubank at Personnel."

"Thanks."

Web didn't even write the messages down; *screw Personnel, screw Wally.* His hypothetical person had reared his head again and used Maria's credit card. He dialed Maria's number.

"Maria, this is Web. I just got a call from MasterCard."

"Dios mio, Web. It's good to hear your voice. The Sacramento police just called me." There was an uneasy hesitation in her voice. "They've got my card in their possession."

Web's heart raced. "Do they have a suspect?" he asked.

"No, just the card." Maria sighed. "They want me to . . . try to identify a body." She sighed.

"Jesus. I'm sorry, Maria."

For a moment, Web considered the sorry state of his visuals for the next day's lecture. *The Chancellor's Request makes or breaks you,* according to Wally. He briefly imagined the smell of Maria's perfume. He wanted to see her; he couldn't let her do this alone. *Lecture be damned,* he thought.

"I'll meet you there."

"Web, you do not have to do that. I will be okay."

"I have to."

There was a long pause.

"Thank you, Web. It would mean a lot to me."

Nothing was as stressful as the macabre call to a morgue. Three times in his search for Vicki, Web had answered such a request; each occasioned conflicting emotions that shook him to the bottom of his soul. On the one hand, he would wish that it weren't his daughter, that there was still a glimmer of hope to find her. But there also was a selfish desire that became harder to suppress: that they *did* have her body, that the search was over, that he *knew*. There was no reconciling the two conflicting impulses. He assumed Maria was going through the same catalogue of fears and hopes and he wanted to comfort her.

It was about eighty-five miles to Sacramento. Web left immediately, hoping to beat the rush-hour traffic.

Web waited in the large front lobby of the decaying North Sacramento police station. He was surrounded by upset citizens reporting stolen cars, reclaiming delinquent children, and bailing out loved ones. After reading every pamphlet in the room, from "What to Do after a Car Accident" to "AIDS Prevention Tips for New Prisoners," the man at the desk finally called his name. He was ushered to a small room with two couches, coffee, and donuts. The door closed behind him with an uncomfortable click. He noticed a large mirror on one wall; someone was probably keeping an eye on him. All he had to read were the same damned pamphlets. After an interminable wait, the door finally opened. It was a Detective Tsumuru and Maria. The trails of tears lay upon her face like old scars. Tsumuru, a trim Japanese-American man in his forties with clear eyes, stood his distance and watched.

Maria hugged Web. "Thanks for coming, Web."

Tsumuru smiled at them.

"I'm sorry I had to stow you back here, Mr. Sloane. I needed to give her an opportunity to say she really had asked you to come. I didn't know if you were an angry ex-husband or maybe even the press."

"No problem." The cold reception didn't surprise Web; he considered it a sign of a cautious, thoughtful detective, unlike some he'd seen who would spill everything to the first person who asked.

Tsumuru led them in silence out of the building and

across a parking lot. A gust of wind blew dirt across the asphalt like black snow from purgatory, whirling into the air then disappearing. Maria abruptly stopped; Web took her hand and she was able to continue. She squeezed his hand as they entered a white, signless door.

The acrid odor of formaldehyde greeted the grim procession of three as they moved down a tiled corridor. Muzak emanating from an unseen source gave the surroundings an air of unreality; a short circuit somewhere made it start and stop at random. Tsumuru halted before a frosted glass door labeled Viewing Room. He pressed a button, then the door buzzed open. He turned to Web and Maria.

"I just want to ensure that everything's in order before you come in."

Web caught a glimpse of the eerie white room and felt a draft of cold air as Tsumuru disappeared inside. Maria's nails dug into the flesh on his hand.

"It'll be over in a minute," said Web, rubbing her forearm. Maria stood silent, her face drawn tight, frozen like a figure in a wax museum. Web tried to catch her eye, then looked away when he saw her odd stare. She looked at the wall, but her eyes were focused as if watching something miles away.

The door buzzed again and Tsumuru admitted them. A curtain was drawn across half the room. He spoke in a whisper as if afraid to disturb the dead.

"I'm only going to show you the face. There's been a train wreck, and . . ."

Maria cut him off.

"Let me see, please." She pulled away from Web and stood next to the curtain. Her hands tightened into fists, and she stood tense, as if expecting to be hit.

Tsumuru pulled back the curtain dividing the room. A young female medical technician stood by a gurney on which rested a body covered by a sheet. Tsumuru nodded at the technician. She peeled the shroud just enough to reveal a face.

Maria gasped.

It was the body of a man. He had matted graying hair that looked as if it were glued to his head. Crude stitches scarred the side of his face from the neck to the left ear. He was so pale as to appear green under the flickering fluorescent lamps. Web looked away from the body and toward Maria.

She breathed in deeply, then exhaled hard. Her face reddened.

Tsumuru turned to her. "Well?"

Maria said nothing but closed her eyes and flung her head back.

"Are you all right, Ms. de Rivera?" Tsumuru asked, taking a step toward her.

Without warning she slapped her open palm across the detective's face, then punched him in the chest. He recoiled and backed across the room.

The tension that had built up inside Maria for half a day suddenly erupted to the surface. "You son of a bitch! Why are you showing me this man? All this time I thought I was coming to look at the body of my daughter! Why? Why did you not tell me?"

With a gesture from Tsumuru, the medical technician quickly covered the body and drew back the curtain.

Maria ran out of the room. Web followed her into the hall, Tsumuru a couple paces behind.

"Maria?" said Web, hoping to console her.

"Go away! I want to be alone for a few moments. Just go away!" Tears streamed down Maria's cheeks, and she ran out the door of the building into the parking lot.

Tsumuru and Web stood in the hall and watched the door snuff out the bright sunlight streaming in. The detective spoke first.

"I'm sorry. I thought she was informed . . . I'm terribly sorry."

Web stared at the detective as if he were from another planet.

"How could you let her . . . didn't you know she's been looking for a daughter? What did you think?"

"I thought *someone* had told her. When we spoke on the phone, it seemed as if she knew. But it's my fault. I should have made sure. I . . ."

"Who the hell was that?" demanded Web.

"That was the man who had her credit card. A transient. He was killed in a train wreck, and we thought she might recognize him."

"Jesus Christ. She doesn't care about the damned credit card. She's looking for her daughter."

"I know that. I talked to Vine County. That's why we asked her to come."

"I'll talk to her. We'll find you inside," said Web, as the two walked out the door.

"Okay."

Maria sat in her car, eyes closed, head back. Web stood a distance away and watched her for a long time. When she finally looked out at him, she had regained her composure. Web quietly explained the situation, and they went inside to meet Tsumuru at his desk.

Tsumuru began by apologizing for his failure to inform Maria about the body. She accepted his apology tersely.

The detective doodled on a pad of paper as he spoke.

"Wilson Forest was the man who had your card, the man we looked at. He lived in a hobo camp out in East Yolo, near some railway tracks. My suspicion is that he just found the card and possibly used it, but when I heard there was a missing person I thought you should have a look at him. These drifters come from all over—riding the rails from town to town whenever there's trouble."

"Do you think he abducted Tanya?" asked Web.

"Absolutely not. He was in our jail two months before she disappeared and was only released a couple of weeks ago. That's not to say he didn't know the kidnapper . . . if she was kidnapped. He might have known Maria or her daughter somehow. It's hard to say."

"How did he get my credit card?" she asked.

"That's what we'd like to know."

He handed Maria a black-and-white picture from a photo booth that showed four poses of two men. The faded photo strip was taped together from several fragments; brown smears of dried blood obscured the image. The shredded picture was macabre testament to the violence of the train accident.

"Wilson's the one on the left. Maybe you know the other guy?" Tsumuru bit his lip and watched her face for a reaction.

"I do not recognize him either." She handed the photo back.

"Can I take a look?" asked Web.

"Sure."

Web studied the picture. The two men were clearly hard-luck cases, but they were mugging broadly for the camera. The trip to the photo booth was probably a bright moment in their otherwise dreary lives.

"Who's the other guy?"

"It's another sad sack. His name was Chad Mertz."

"Why's this photo say 'Al & Me' if his name was Chad?" Web asked, reading some scrawled handwriting on the back of the photo strip.

"Just some hobo gibberish. I thought it said 'All of Me.' Could have been a nickname, who knows?" said Tsumuru.

"What do you know about Mertz?"

"A couple of years ago, Mertz was found dead in an abandoned warehouse that had burned down," replied Tsumuru.

Maria watched Web. She could see the wheels in motion in his mind as he questioned Tsumuru.

"Did you know much about him?" Web asked, staring at the images before him.

Tsumuru retrieved the photo. "Forest just had the usual transient's rap sheet—drunk and disorderlies as long as my arm, couple of fights, petty theft. He would get arrested, dry out doing a thirty-to-ninety, and be okay for a couple months. I think he liked jail—a lot of these guys do. He was probably just hopping a train to go to warmer climes and slipped."

"What about Mertz?" asked Web. "Is he a suspect?"

"For one, Mertz died before your daughter disappeared. Sacramento police never had any business with him, but he'd been in recurring trouble in Florida, mainly a lot of bad checks. He skipped from a prison for the criminally insane in Florida and high-tailed it out here. Just to die in a fire."

Web and Maria stared dumbly at the detective.

"I won't take a lot more of your time. I just want to show you his effects. If he had your credit card, maybe he had something else, maybe something that belongs to your daughter."

From beside his desk Tsumuru produced a large cardboard carton laden with police identification stickers and numbers, then drew off the lid.

"I thought there was a tiny chance some of these things might have belonged to you or your daughter."

One by one, the detective pulled out shreds of blood-stained clothing encased in large Ziploc bags. A pants leg with one tattered edge. The remainder of the pair of pants. Three fragments of a shirt with grease and brown smears along the torn edges. Maria turned away, but Web stepped forward, fascinated.

"Any paperwork?" asked Web.

"Just a wallet. He had his parole card, a California I.D., Maria's credit card, and those photos."

At the bottom of the box was a pair of shoes, each in its own Ziploc bag. One was crushed and stained with blood; the other looked practically new.

"New shoes?" asked Web.

"Probably stolen. You never know." Tsumuru handed the shoe to Web, who examined it. The heel was almost new, and the shoe leather was still shiny. Web turned the shoe over in his hands.

"Johnson Supply Company," Web said, reading from the price sticker.

"Yeah, I saw that. It's a place out in East Yolo. I'm sending a guy out there tomorrow to talk to the owner," said Tsumuru, taking back the shoe.

Maria and Web watched in silence as the detective put the scraps of clothing back into the box. He walked them out to the front lobby.

"Ms. de Rivera, I'm going to keep the credit card as evidence. I recommend you cancel it. We've already notified the company."

"That's okay." she said.

"Thanks for your time. I don't think anything else will come up. If no one identifies him in ninety days, we bury him and close the case."

"Thanks for all your help, Mr. Tsumuru. Could we get a Xerox of that photo?" asked Web.

"Sure." Tsumuru walked inside and a moment later came out with a clean photocopy of the blood-covered photo strip, then handed them each a card emblazoned with a tiny detective's shield. They walked out to the parking lot. The cold, dusty wind blew harder than before.

"Now what do we do? I feel like we accomplished nothing at all," said Maria.

"Do you have to be back home for anything?"

"I was going to spend the night here. What do you have in mind?"

"I'm going out to the Johnson Supply Company. See what there is to see."

"The police are going tomorrow," she said.

"Yes, but I might see something that they wouldn't know to look for." In general, Web trusted the police; but the hunter within him would not be satisfied with second-hand reports. Something compelled him to see for himself.

"Then I will go with you," she said.

Maria and Web drove out to the shabby suburb of East Yolo in separate cars. The road marked a journey into economic despair through a mixture of agriculture and housing developments hidden behind graffiti-covered walls. The town had a desolate quality; although many homes were new, the developments were isolated from each other by fields of strawberries, soy beans, and lettuce. No children played in yards. It looked like a brand-new ghost town.

Johnson's General Store was a holdover from the days when the area had been completely rural. The building was a converted train station. The train had long since ceased coming to East Yolo, and grass had grown over the tracks. They pulled into the angular parking spaces in front of the store. Theirs were the only cars. Neon signs for Miller Beer and Budweiser glowed next to a large poster promising Seed and Feed. Trash and beer bottles littered the front of the store.

Web got out of his car and walked over to Maria's. She rolled down her window.

"This is the place. Looks closed."

"What should we do?"

"I don't know. I can't come back out here tomorrow. I'd really like to talk with the owner, if possible," said Web.

Maria got out of her car.

"Not much of a place, is it?" she asked.

"Depends on whether you're a yuppie or a transient. It's probably one-stop shopping for drifters," said Web.

They got out and walked up the steps to peer into the windows. No one was in there, but the store was obviously still in business.

"What do you think we should do?" asked Maria.

"Let's start calling Johnsons. Chances are we can find him."

Side by side at the dual pay phones in front of the building, Web and Maria dialed families named Johnson. There were two columns of Johnsons; Maria began with A. Johnson, and Web started at the end of the list with William W. Johnson.

The seventeenth name that Maria dialed, Francis X. Johnson, was a direct hit. She tugged on Web's sleeve. He finished his call and listened.

"Yes, it was my credit card. I think it may have been used in your store." She listened, then continued. "No, no, you are not in trouble. We just want to talk to you."

Maria scratched out a note on a page torn from the phone book and handed it to Web. It said, "He is drunk."

Maria persuaded the man to let them talk to him in person, then wrote down directions to his home. They drove together in Web's car through blighted streets into the older part of town. Johnson's once-white clapboard house hadn't been painted in decades. The lawn was a jungle of weeds, in the center of which rested a decrepit pickup truck eaten through with rust holes, looking like a faithful animal waiting to die.

Web and Maria tried the doorbell. Nothing happened. Web rapped on the door with his fist. A man's voice yelled something unintelligible. Web knocked louder.

"Go 'round. It's broke," said the voice.

A moment later a gaunt old man with an unkempt head of long gray hair, wearing overalls but no shirt, appeared from around the side of the house. His face was a blaze of red, like a baby left in the sun. He yelled over to them.

"I said, come on 'round. Front door's busted."

They followed the man around the side of the house, navigating the weeds and a mine field of dog excrement. He led them through a sliding-screen door into a sort of rec room, which had a couch, a La-Z-Boy chair, a fridge, and a wet bar. A large beagle sat under the wet bar furiously chewing its hairless stomach; the strong odor in the room suggested that it wasn't very well housebroken.

"Francis X. Johnson." The man extended his hand.

Web and Maria introduced themselves.

"Have a seat. Sorry the store's closed—I'm a little under the weather. Have a drink?"

"No, thanks, we have to drive," said Web.

Web and Maria sat on the couch. There was a damp spot under Web, and he slid down to a dryer cushion.

"Mr. Johnson, do you accept credit cards at your store?" Web asked.

"Yeah, I pretty much have to, and it's a goddam hassle. You people aren't from one of the banks . . ."

"No, I am looking for my daughter. I think a credit card I gave her may have been used in your store," said Maria.

"You sure you're not one of those agencies? 'Cause if you are, I don't know nothing."

"We're not. Here's my card." Web pulled out a business card that gave his Berkeley office address. Maria handed him a realtor card. He looked them over carefully, stretching his arm as far as it would go, then put on a pair of reading glasses. Satisfied, he lowered himself into the La-Z-Boy.

"So, what do you think? She ran away or something?" Johnson's words were slurred, and he punctuated his speech with flicks of his hand.

"I do not know," said Maria. "But it is possible that either she or someone else used my credit card at your store. It might help me find her."

Maria handed a photo of Tanya to Johnson, who pursed his lips and stared at it a long time.

"Can't say I've seen her. Pretty girl, I'd remember."

"What about this man?" Web swapped the photo of Tanya for the Xerox of the photo strip showing Forest and Mertz, the dead drifters. Johnson examined it closely. A momentary flash of recognition crossed his face. He looked away from Web and Maria.

"Nope. Nope. Not me. I never saw either man." Johnson

tried to light an unfiltered cigarette; he couldn't get his lighter to start and fumbled through his pockets for matches. Finally he got it lit, then handed the photo back to Web.

"That's it? That's all?" Johnson asked, puffing wildly.

Fury was growing within Web; the man was lying. "Mr. Johnson, if you did recognize one of the men and lie about it, you could be implicated in a murder and a kidnapping. We don't give a damn about the charge card." Web spoke slowly, deliberately, through gritted teeth. He wanted to make sure Johnson understood the threat.

"Let me be sure. Let's have another look."

Johnson looked at the photo again, this time through his glasses. He made a big show of closely reexamining the photo, squinting, running his finger down the sheet of paper.

"I wasn't *lying* before, but now that you mention it, I think this fella on the left came in last week. Bought some stuff on a credit card." Ash fell from his cigarette to the floor.

He had identified Forest, the man hit by a train.

"Do you know what he bought?" asked Web.

"I don't."

"Would you have a receipt?" asked Maria.

"That'd be in the store. I could show you tomorrow."

"This is urgent. We would like to look at it now," said Web, a tinge of warning still in his voice.

"I can't really drive, you know, at night," said Johnson. The truth was that he was too drunk.

"We'll drive you. It shouldn't take too long." Web was very firm.

"I gotta put on a shirt. I'll meet you out front."

"We'll wait here." Web knew that if they went outside, the man might just refuse to come out. Johnson disappeared into another room, then came back out with a shirt on. The group of three drove back to the general store.

During the drive, Johnson wouldn't stop talking. He was disturbed at being caught in a lie and prattled on endlessly about the difficulties of running his store until Web finally asked him to please shut up.

It was growing dark when they got into the store. Johnson opened the metal gates in front of the door a crack, and they slipped in. He switched on a single bulb rather than the main store lights. They worked their way back through rows of canned food and batteries to the long counter behind which the liquor resided. Johnson pulled out a metal box and set it on the counter.

"The charge slips are all in here." He dumped out several dozen yellow and white slips of paper.

"I'm supposed to call these in every day but you know I get real busy in here. So I have a girl who does 'em once a month or so," babbled Johnson. He pulled out slip after slip, examining them in the dim light at arm's length.

Maria called out. "That's it." She recognized the imprint of her credit card. Maria found it odd to see something familiar in these dark, alien surroundings. The total was three-hundred fifty-six dollars and change. A badly scrawled signature that read "Mary Rivers" was on the receipt.

Johnson put on his glasses and held the slip up to the light. "Yeah, that'd be the one."

Web suspected something fishy. "Why did you let a man charge on a card that had a woman's name?"

"That guy said his aunt had come to town and told him to get whatever he wanted. Times is hard. I can't really turn down a big sale like that. Look, I'm real sorry about your card." Johnson scowled defensively.

"Do you have a record of what he bought?" asked Web.

"Yeah, I sure do." Johnson pulled out a metal receipt machine, the type that makes a carbon copy and is advanced with a pencil. He opened the box, and rolled out several feet of receipts.

"That was last week. How much was it?" asked Johnson, nervously.

"Three hundred fifty-six dollars," replied Maria.

He unreeled the paper across the dusty floor.

"Here it is."

Web read the receipt.

8 pair socks	$24.00
1.5 liter Jack Daniels	$18.99
Hack saw	$17.99
Blades	$11.54
Axe	$12.99

Two pair handcuffs	$36.88
55-lb. sack lime	$14.45
Shoes	$220.00
Camper map	$2.50

Web stared at the paper, trying to determine the intent behind the purchases. A buzzing in his mind told him something wasn't right. First, a 55-pound bag of lime required a car. Something a transient didn't have.

"How'd he carry the lime?"

"Just lifted it. I don't know."

"Did he have a car?"

"I figure he must have."

"What kind of shoes cost two hundred twenty dollars?" Web had found the question to make Johnson break.

"Ah, jeez, I'm real sorry. I shoulda known better." Johnson was quite upset.

"Come on. What is it?" Web pointed accusingly at the mysterious figure on the charge slip.

"I told you business is real hard. The shoes are only fifty bucks, but the guy wanted to get some cash. I'm really not supposed to do that, so I told him he could have one-fifty and I'd keep twenty for myself. I thought he was for real, I really did." Johnson burned his lip on his cigarette.

Maria cut him off. "No, no. We do not care about the money. Can you remember anything else at all?"

"Not really. You're not going to turn me in?"

"It is my credit card. I will not press charges, but the police will be here tomorrow. All I ask is that you cooperate with them fully." said Maria.

"Yeah, no problem. I'll tell them everything they want to know."

Web read the sinister list. Lime—used for disposing of bodies. Handcuffs—the intent was obvious. A hack saw *and* an axe. No homeless man would have this shopping list.

"These handcuffs—why do you carry them?" asked Web.

"I don't know. I sell a few pair every now and then. I have all kind of stuff—hunting knives, jackknives, you name it. My knife distributor just brings 'em in and it sells." Johnson sat on a stool behind the counter.

"Can we get a pair of the handcuffs?" asked Web.

"They're $18.44," said Johnson.

"The way I see it, you owe Ms. de Rivera better than three hundred dollars."

"Okay, okay." He opened up the jackknife showcase and pulled out a pair of handcuffs.

"What about this 'camper map'?" asked Web.

"I got a whole rack of maps. I don't remember which one it was." Johnson pointed to a magazine–book stand filled with maps.

"I want to get three complete sets."

"Ah, jeez, I'm trying to run a business."

"Thank you for your cooperation," said Maria, as Web began pulling three of each map off the rack. There were ten different maps: a total of thirty.

"That it? That all you're going to take?"

"The way I figure it, you're getting off easy," said Web.

"Easy's a relative term. You got to take me home, now."

"Let's go."

After dropping a very upset Francis X. Johnson off at his home, Maria and Web discussed what they had found while they drove back to Maria's car.

"Do you think he knew something he did not tell us?" asked Maria.

"He was just a drunk. He doesn't call in his charge cards, he doesn't open the store when he feels like staying home and drinking. He probably told us everything he could remember," said Web.

"It was quite an odd shopping list," she said.

"A bum doesn't need most of the stuff on that list. Plus, this Forest character was in jail when your credit card was used to buy computer equipment. I think he was buying for someone else."

"Who did he buy for?"

"My guess is the same guy who bought the computer equipment told Forest he could have a bottle of liquor if he'd buy him some stuff. That way, if there were trouble on the card, only the hobo would be implicated. Forest probably picked up the one-fifty just because he could get away with it."

They pulled into the dark gravel parking lot of the general store once again.

"I'm going to stay overnight in Sacramento. I want to talk to the police tomorrow," said Maria.

"I'd like to stay, too, but I have a big lecture to give tomorrow."

"Thanks for coming." She got out of the car. Web got out to say his good-bye standing up.

"Here, give these maps to the police. They probably mean nothing, but you never know."

"I want to be with them when they question Johnson tomorrow," she said, accepting the maps.

"Good idea. Tell them everything we found out tonight. Tsumuru seemed like a good guy; he might figure out something new."

They hugged good-bye for a long time. Neither one wanted to stop, but both knew they had to. Web stood outside his car till Maria had pulled out, then sped out of town in hopes of getting home in time to put a little work into his presentation. In spite of his best intentions, he fell asleep in his office at home, staring at his presentation, fifteen minutes after returning.

15

Web awoke before dawn, mouth aching from a night of anxiously grinding his jaws together. He brushed his teeth, grabbed a frozen bagel, and headed for the campus. Speeding down the East Shore Freeway, Web felt giddy and wide awake even with just two hours of sleep. A construction crew blocked the campus entrance near his office, so he parked on the opposite side of the campus and walked. The fog formed an opaque dome with him at its center, and as he briskly traversed the dewy paths of the deserted campus, fragments of buildings appeared and disappeared in the mist like half-forgotten ideas.

The click of his heels reverberated down the hallway as

Web entered his office. He looked at his sketches for his presentation; in one second he decided that the lecture would be a piece of cake. He knew the material better than anyone in the world, so well it bored him. The greenish fluorescent light of his office and the damp heat from the ancient radiator conspired to rob Web of his heightened mental state. He turned out the overhead light and opened the window, pacing back and forth across the dark office to prepare for the Chancellor's Request lecture. The Board of Regents, the heads of every department, and the dean of the university would be there, in addition to the chancellor. And Web had only a few words scratched onto a piece of paper as a guide. It would be just three hours till he spoke. Focusing his mind, Web tried to recreate the clarity of thought he had experienced the night before. The title of the lecture was "Extracting Meaning from Chaos." There were no visual aids. He would be on his own. He scratched out a rough outline, hoping it would fill the bill.

He put on the suit he kept in the office for occasions like this and examined his reflection in the glass of the window. *This is your chance.* Little wonder that surveys show the number one phobia to be fear of public speaking.

He plodded down to the lecture hall as if going to his own funeral. On the way he passed a student recreation room; a TV blasted away with no viewers. Web pulled the TV off the table and took it with him. On the short walk to the hall he passed the physics buildings. He set the TV down outside, ran in to a freshman laboratory, and swiped a large electro-magnet. Now he was prepared.

Seated at the table in the front of the hall, he watched the room fill up. There were some people he knew, like Wallenberg and the professionals from his department, but for the most part he saw strangers. They chatted among themselves, laughing, trading papers. *The toughest audience in the world, sharpening their knives.* The lights dimmed. The chancellor introduced Web. There was polite applause. Web stood up.

He said nothing at first. Web just pushed the television set to the center of the room, flipped it on, turned to a station filled with static, then pumped the volume all the way up, filling the room with white noise. Web shouted so he could be heard over the television.

"My lecture is titled 'Extracting Meaning from Chaos.' A TV set, not tuned to any channel, spews out random information. Half the pixels black, half the pixels white, in an ever-changing pattern. The perfect picture of chaos." He let the noise blare out for an uncomfortably long time.

"Is it possible to learn anything from such a random display?"

Then he picked up the electromagnet. Swinging it in front of the set, the black and white specks of the picture swayed and distorted into weird patterns, following the magnetic field. The sound oscillated from a shrill whine to a low purring sound. The overeducated crowd in the hall sat silent, wondering if the speaker had lost his mind.

"The government spent 24 billion dollars on a supposedly invisible bomber, the Stealth. They designed this plane so that the world's most sensitive radar cannot detect it. To someone looking where he's supposed to look, it creates no discernible trail." Web swung the magnet in front of the set again, making a psychedelic distortion pattern.

"But residents of the desert where the tests are performed complain that when the Stealth bomber flies over, the picture on their televisions becomes distorted for fifteen or twenty seconds." He shouted over the static coming from the set. "They can then go outside and have a look at this secret airplane as it flies overhead."

Web turned off the set and lowered his voice to a stage whisper.

"That static is not random noise; it contains valuable information. With two TV's, it is possible to triangulate the bombers' speed and direction. With no military clearance, anyone could buy machinery to detect the one-billion-dollar invisible airplane. You can get a Stealth detector at Sears & Roebuck for about three hundred bucks."

The professors laughed nervously; it caught Web off-guard. He looked out at the audience. *Got 'em in the palm of my hand,* he thought. He scratched some equations onto the board.

"How did this major flaw escape the designers of the

airplane? Because they depended on conventional wisdom. Because they used standard computer models."

Web paused for dramatic effect. There was a nervous ruffling of papers coming from the back of the room. "Because they went by the rules. Information is all around us. It is utterly meaningless unless analyzed in an original fashion with intelligence and creativity."

Web had reached Lecturer's High. He dove into the highly technical part of his talk and started speaking about intelligent pattern detection, drawing examples from cryptography and astronomy. He decried "number crunchers," the grinds who use standard algorithms and methods for analysis. He showed in several ways that it was easier to fool an educated person, who knew the "rules," than it was to fool a novice.

Web furiously covered the chalkboard, drawing out one case study of a code-breaking team. The code had stymied high-level cryptographers for three months, because they depended too heavily on supercomputers and an army of mathematicians. Eventually it was broken, but by the one woman in the group with a background in literature rather than mathematics: their typist.

While he spoke of mathematics and codes, Web was thinking to himself about crime detection. Many of the phrases he used about cryptography were perfectly applicable to the disappearance of Maria's daughter and the bodies found near Tico.

The conventional wisdom is the easiest to fool.

In detecting patterns, creativity should always take precedence over the "harder" mathematical analysis.

When a searcher looks only for what he found before, he will never find anything new.

As he built his presentation to a crescendo, Web's eye caught the clock. He had gone a half hour over, speaking without notes for a full ninety minutes.

"That is as concise as I can be with the new material I have. I'm sorry I ran over, ladies and gentlemen. Thank you for your patience."

Web sat at the table and slugged down a glass of water. There was a painful, embarrassing silence in the auditorium. Murmuring among themselves, his audience simply picked up their belongings and filed out. There was no applause, no indication of their reaction to his material.

Only Wallenberg approached the stage.

"Wally, thanks for coming," said Web, wiping sweat from his brow.

"Real interesting, Web. Gutsy . . . interesting." Wallenberg didn't make eye contact. "Drop by sometime."

Wally shook Web's hand. Formally. The way a stranger might, not a friend of fifteen years. "Good luck, Web." Then he left.

Web glumly sat, holding his head in his hands. He strained to pick up the television set.

A door opened behind the podium.

"Dude, want some help?"

Web turned around. It was Renny McDonald, the hacker forced to take Web's class. He wore torn jeans and a Bride of Reanimator T-shirt.

"Renny! What on earth are you doing here?"

"You won't get me in trouble, will you?"

"Trouble?"

"Well, these deals are supposed to be for the chancellor and professors. But I wanted to hear what you said so I hid up in the projection booth." He pointed up to a glass-paneled room above the chalkboard.

Web laughed. "What did you think?"

McDonald lifted his hand, removed an imaginary hat, and bowed to Web. "Maestro! Wizard! Fearless leader! I thought the sixties spirit of protest was dead. But dude, you really put it to them hard! Buh–rah–voe!"

Web stared at the boy as if he spoke a foreign language. "I was talking about pattern detection. What do you mean, 'spirit of the sixties'?"

"Heck, it's been in the student papers for weeks. You don't have to act like you don't know."

Web grew pale. "What?"

"Didn't you see all those protestors in front of Berkeley-Livermore last week? Berkeley's bidding on a multibillion-dollar Strategic Defense Initiative contract from the DOD. Those guys in the back two rows—all of 'em were Defense

Department spooks. When you slagged on Stealth, I could see their faces—they totally freaked! No offense, but I didn't think you had the nerve."

Web felt dizzy. His mind reeled. "Oh, Jesus! Oh, shit!" He sat down. Web saw his career flashing before his eyes. *That* was the reason for the cold reception.

"Prof?" Renny asked.

"Goddam, goddam, *goddam!*" Web kicked a chair across the floor.

"You didn't know?"

"No one told me the Star Wars guys would come to my lecture."

"Well, dude, you stuck to your principles and did the right thing. That's what's important, right?" asked Renny.

"Yeah. Right. And I'll probably be out of a job in a week."

"Look, I'll help you move the TV if you want."

"Sure. Thanks, Renny."

In silence the man and the boy lifted the television and returned it to its rightful owner. Three professors who had attended Web's lecture stood in the hall, chatting. When they saw him approach, they ducked into a classroom and shut the door.

Web sped home angrily. His lecture had been letter-perfect in content, a political fiasco: the perfect metaphor for his whole teaching career. He had wondered how the bureaucrats would stick it to him, but no longer had to worry since he'd served them his own head on a plate. Later, sitting in his office at home, he smiled. Now that he had all but committed career suicide, he could dedicate himself to what he did best without worrying about university social climbing. There was a certain freedom in being an outcast: You can say "screw the rules" and follow your instincts.

Web had been on a roll for two days. According to his intimate knowledge of his mental cycles, he knew these flashes of insight wouldn't last much longer. In his office at home, he thumbed through the ten maps that he'd obtained from Johnson, the drunken store owner. The hobo had purchased one map. If his hunch were correct, the bum acted as an agent for the same man who purchased computer equipment with Maria's credit card. The same man kidnapped Maria's daughter, Tanya. And left the bodies of two young girls in the woods. It was a tenuous thread, a leap of faith, to link the two events. However, he held something that could confirm his hypothesis.

What he had to find out was: *Which of the ten maps?*

Three maps were for recreational vehicle owners: typically purchased by geriatrics looking for a hookup where they can park a mobile home. He set them aside. If one man were responsible for the crimes, as Web thought, that man, that *hypothetical person*, probably would not buy an RV map.

There were seven left. Four were road maps: *Western States and Provinces, Northern California, California,* and a map of the whole country labeled *U.S.A. by Car.* Would his killer, his kidnapper, need so general a map? No. They were for tourists from out of state or someone just embarking on a trip. The hypothetical person already knew his way around fairly well. Web set those aside, leaving three maps.

Web unfolded *Winston's Guide to Hot Spring Recreation.* It was a crudely drawn map, with sketches of natural hot springs accompanied by commentary from the author. Would his killer want this map? Web had been to several places that were mentioned. Obscure hot springs were often populated sparsely, sometimes only a couple people at a time. He pictured in his mind the scenario in which the hobo had purchased the goods. Without accompanying the homeless man, how would this *hypothetical person* request such a map? If the killer had gone in the store himself, it would be a candidate, but Web still ruled out *Winston's Guide.* It was too specific, too strange.

He spread out the two remaining maps on the floor and tacked *Northern California* on the wall. Both were USGS topographic maps, giving detailed pictures of areas in two different northern California state parks.

Which map?

Annadell State Park or Mount Diablo State Park?

Web closed his eyes. He knew why this hypothetical person bought the maps. It was not to forage for victims; it was to dispose of bodies. He remembered what Theodore Bundy had once said: *If there's no body, there's no uproar. If you leave nothing behind, no one even thinks to look. The discovery of a body mobilizes police and puts pressure on to find a suspect at all costs.* This killer might have learned the same lesson.

He looked at the maps again. Annadell was heavily traveled; lots of camping hookups, lots of day-hikers. Mount Diablo was more isolated, although still accessible by a main road. There weren't many tourist attractions, thus, there weren't many people.

If Web wanted a map to show him where to dispose of bodies, he would pick Mount Diablo. Simply by process of elimination.

He got out a Magic Marker and the map of California. He put an X where Tanya had disappeared. He put another X where the hobo was killed, then put marks where the two bodies were discovered and O marks for every unexplained disappearance that seemed to Web something more sinister than a runaway.

Then he outlined Diablo State Park on the map. All of his marks fell outside the square. If his intuition panned out, he had a Stealth killer on his hands. The police looked for someone who habitually visited the same places repeatedly. And ninety-nine times out of a hundred, the police were right.

But that one-in-a-hundred killer more than made up for it in unchecked destructive force. Some could evade discovery by moving constantly, second-guessing the law. Men like Bundy and John Wayne Gacy knew police procedure and successfully evaded standard searches for years. Men like John Lee Lucas, propelled by inner demons, moved erratically from state to state with no discernible pattern. A man who didn't want to leave tracks would buy a map of an unfamiliar park just to find a new dumping ground. Web assumed that his hypothetical killer was such a person.

There was a knock at the door.

"Daddy-O, I didn't even know you were home. How'd the big lecture go?" said Joyce.

"Really swell. By speaking my mind, I alienated every high-powered connection I could ever hope to make."

"You did?"

"Unfortunately, yes. But I spoke honestly."

Joyce's eyes lit up. "I'm so proud of you!" She ran in and kissed him on the forehead.

He chuckled. "Joyce, you sure know how to say the right thing. But moral victories don't pay the rent."

He quickly folded up the maps and chucked them under his chair.

Web's daughter looked so healthy, so robust, she seemed to glow. Joyce wore black from head to toe, but everything about her was vibrant and alive. Full of energy, curious, naive; she stood at the doorway where the magic of childhood intersects with the beauty and strength of adulthood. In short, she was becoming a woman.

"What'll we have to celebrate?" she asked. "All I saw in the cupboard were three cans of Ken-L-Ration. How 'bout dog food with its own juicy gravy?"

Web laughed. She could always make him laugh.

"All beef and no by-products!" she said, reading from the can.

"Tasty!" he said. "But I bet you have a second choice in mind."

"Well, I was just looking at the take-out menu from a new Szechuan place that could possibly persuade me not to steal Mud's dinner." She loved Szechuan but knew her father usually claimed it upset his stomach.

"Well, hmmm, it's that or dog food?"

"Szechuan it is then. I'll order." She won. She always won, but tonight Web didn't care. Joyce trotted out of his office.

"Um, Joyce, ask them . . ."

She finished the sentence for him. "If they have anything that's not so hot."

"Yeah. Right."

They ate in the living room, watching "Suspect at Large," the police show. The show claimed to have uncovered new evidence that Elvis was murdered, even providing a composite sketch of the murderer. Mud licked off the plates when they were through, then hopped up on the couch and fell asleep, violating months of training, as if he knew he could get away with it this one time. Web felt wistful, reflective. It would only be a few months before Joyce might be gone from their home for good, either to college or maybe just to her own place. He tried to get her into a game of Scrabble, but she had homework.

"Joyce, you know you only have a few more months in high school," he said as earnestly as possible, hoping to lead into something more serious.

"Oh, my God! Like, I forgot!" she said in her best Val-speak, bugging her eyes out.

"I was just thinking, we haven't been camping since moving to Berkeley. I wondered if you'd humor the old man for one more trip."

Joyce had once loved camping but felt she had outgrown it. Even so, maybe one last outing wouldn't be so bad, just for old time's sake.

"Um, well, okay, Daddy-O. When?"

"Next weekend?"

"Let me pencil you in." She pretended to put down a note in an invisible daybook. "Where are we going?"

"Somewhere new. It's called Diablo State Park."

"Sounds good to me! I'll probably have to buy some new boots and maybe some other new stuff next week. Is that okay?"

"How much?"

"I don't know, boots are expensive. Maybe two hundred?"

He handed her a credit card. "Is this what you were asking for?"

"As a matter of fact, yes. Thanks, Daddy-O. Oh, I also need a couple new skirts. Can I get them, too?"

He did a double take. Everything translated into an excuse to shop, and shopping always multiplied on itself; but now that Joyce would soon be leaving, he didn't mind.

"Sure. Just let me know what you buy."

"You'll see it. Thanks!"

She ran up the stairs. Web wondered about the wisdom of taking her to Diablo on his macabre search. In any case, it would be a good chance for a last father-daughter trip.

16

The weather had been picturesque when Joyce and Web left Berkeley in the predawn hours, but now, at Diablo State Park, tempestuous storm clouds began to form. Bolts of lightning struck in the distance, followed by low rumbling of distant thunder echoing through the mountains.

"Dad, do you think it's really a good idea to camp in this weather?" asked Joyce as her father systematically drove stakes around their large nylon tent. Web squinted at the black sky in the distance. A cool breeze started to blow, making the tent flap like a loose sail. Mud circled the camp, nose in the air, engrossed by the smorgasbord of new and exotic odors in the woods.

"It could blow over real soon. Let's give it a little time and see what it does." He pulled the tent taught and began unrolling the waterproof tarp that went on top.

"Grab an end. We might just need this." Web kept an empty grin on his face like a statue of Fred MacMurray.

"The radio says the storms might get worse tonight," said Joyce, taking an end of the tarp. They set it loosely over the top of the tent, and Web attached a rope to one corner, preparing to pull it taught when a sudden gust yanked the tarp out of his hands and blew it across into a tree. A bolt of lightning struck close enough that the thunder followed immediately afterward.

"Daddy-O . . ." pleaded Joyce.

"If it gets much worse, we'll go. It'll be okay."

Web grabbed the fluttering tarp and with Joyce's help fit it back over the tent. A few drops of rain hit the ground, then rapidly multiplied, as if someone had turned on a faucet.

The two threw their backpacks and provisions into the tent as another bolt of lightning struck nearby. "Get in the tent! I'll finish putting the tarp on!" Web yelled over the beating rain. Mud frantically ran in circles, catching the rain on his tongue.

Joyce reluctantly crawled into the dim tent that smelled like an old pair of socks and wrapped herself in a blanket. She knew her father could ignore all common sense once he made up his mind to do something. He probably would stay in the tent during a force-ten gale. Joyce reflected in frustration that he'd string her along, promising to leave if it got bad, but that he really intended to stay the whole weekend.

"I can't believe I missed the Faith No More concert for this," she sulked, as the rain and wind whipped the little tent around. After much pounding and pulling, Web eventually came in, rubbing his hands together. He looked like he'd just climbed out of a swimming pool. Mud shook himself off in the vestibule.

"We're anchored solid as a rock. I used ten-inch stakes for the guy wires, so it's secure," Web said cheerily. He plopped down on a foam cushion, dripping water all over the floor of the tent.

Grabbing a towel from the backpack, he mopped himself and the floor dry, then spread out a map.

"There are two good places we could go for a hike . . ." he said, running his finger across the topographic map. He hadn't told Joyce where the map came from or what he was looking for.

"We're not going to do much hiking if it keeps raining like this, Daddy-O," said Joyce, fiddling with a Walkman.

"Remember when we were at Mount Hood and got in that blizzard? I said it would blow over and it did," Web reassured her.

"We almost died of frostbite that weekend," Joyce replied as she put on her Walkman and drowned out her father with the bleak strains of Morrissey.

Web ran his finger along the ridges on the map. *There were two spots good for getting rid of unwanted baggage,* he thought. One, Deadman's Swamp, was just west of the main entrance to the park, through the most heavily traveled tourist section. Where all the day-hikers would go. Even if his *hypothetical person* had a weird sense of humor and enjoyed the dark joke implicit in the name, logistically, it would be a bad choice. If the *hypothetical killer* were truly careful, he would realize that any *cargo* deposited in Deadman's Swamp might be found quickly.

Muir Point seemed the most sensible spot. Web had pitched the tent less than a mile from its steep cliffs. As he examined the map, everything else around him faded from consciousness, including the rain, the tent, and Joyce sulking under her headset. All he could see was the map.

He might enter here, off a back road. He might drive all the way to the footpath that leads to Muir Point. Then it's a scant fifty yards to the scenic view point marked on the map. Good place to get rid of cargo.

Web didn't notice that Joyce had removed her headset and watched him intently. Mud howled at the noise.

"Dad . . . Daddy-O!"

"Hmm. Yes?" He looked up.

"That thunder sounded awfully close!"

"It'll blow over." He hadn't heard the noise.

"You sound like a broken record! 'It'll blow over, it'll blow over.' It's getting worse, not better."

"Let's just give it another hour. I was hoping to at least get in a little hiking today. If it's still pouring at dark, we'll strike the tent and go home."

"Oh, right. I think it's a total waste of a good Saturday, sitting in a smelly tent." Joyce angrily replaced her headphones.

After a few minutes, the storm relented. Web poked his head out of the tent and looked at the bruise-colored sky.

"Hey! It's not raining any more," he yelled with glee.

Joyce opened the back vent of the tent and peered out of the screen.

"Swell! It looks like Mud City USA to me."

The dog sat upright at the mention of his name.

"Don't be such a downer. Let's just take a little hike. We can bring our ponchos and get back here fast if it picks up again."

"No, thanks. Pneumonia isn't my kind of disease," Joyce replied.

Web crawled back into the tent.

"Well, I'll go by myself then. I'm going to go down the fire road about a half-mile to a scenic view point. Maybe get a good view of the storm, maybe go down a path. I should be back in an hour or so."

"Whatever." Joyce pulled out a copy of *Spin* and put her headphones back on, chewing on a Snickers bar.

Wearing a poncho, plastic pants, waterproof boots, and gators, Web trudged out into the forest. The whole earth smelled good; he loved the air just after a thunderstorm. Mud excitedly leaped up in the air, running behind, beside, and ahead of Web in an erratic path like a beetle on a string.

A few steps away from the tent, Web had second thoughts. *If the man who bought the maps and used Maria's credit card came here once . . . ,* he thought, *. . . Joyce shouldn't be alone in a tent.*

Web leaned in the tent, startling his daughter.

"Joyce, I'd really prefer if you came with me."

"Get serious," she said.

"I want to climb down a cliff face about a mile from here. Maybe if you waited in the car at the top."

Joyce rolled her eyes.

"You can drive," he said.

That was the bait. She put on a poncho and grabbed some reading material to take with her.

The fire road was all mud; Joyce had a hard time navigating it. Twice the car got stuck.

"Is this really such a good idea?" she asked.

"It's good practice to drive in bad conditions," he said, thinking, *If my car with Joyce at the wheel can make it through here, then a convertible BMW could, too.*

They stopped at a shelter: a park bench, map, trash can, and two outhouses underneath a wooden roof.

"I'll be back in about an hour," he said, taking the map. Joyce watched him walk toward the cliff, then returned to a big article in *Spin* about the untimely demise of a Grateful Dead keyboard player.

Scenic View signs directed Web to the top of the cliff. A deserted Park Service shelter offered men's and women's latrines and several picnic tables. Web walked to a section of fence overlooking a vast chasm. The view was spectacular; the low ceiling of black clouds spread out over the rock formations and tree-covered mountains in the distance, coloring everything a brilliant lavender. Then he looked straight down.

Topographic maps don't lie. A steep drop of at least two hundred feet opened up directly below the fence. Park service signs warned Stay on Marked Paths Only. Web paced in front of the fence. Mud stayed by his side, nose to the ground, trying to follow a scent.

If I wanted to get rid of something heavy . . .

He picked up a trash can and carried it along the edge. Mud tilted his head, puzzled. There were spots where the fence was too high to lift something large without slipping, but Web soon found a spot where the rock jutted in. Standing there, trash can in hand, Web wondered if someone else had thrown heavy objects over this cliff.

Web put down the trash can and picked up three large tree branches, then carved his initials, WS, into each using a pocket knife. He moved to the incline and heaved one stick off the edge of the cliff. Mud began to run after it but stopped at the cliff's edge. It tumbled end over end down the incline, hit a large rock, and then swerved off into a knot of trees. He threw the other two sticks from slightly different locations. Each followed approximately the same path down.

Web pulled out the map and ran his finger along the squiggly topographic lines. He could reach the point where the sticks had landed; the path would be circuitous but reasonably safe except for one sharp drop. Web climbed over the fence, ignoring the sign about staying on marked paths. Mud anxiously paced back and forth at the top of the cliff, sniffing the air for danger as his master descended.

The gullies were muddy, but Web traversed them easily. When he got to the steepest part of the walk, just a hundred feet or so away from where the sticks had landed, he mistakenly grabbed a thin birch tree for support. It pulled out of the wet dirt, and Web flew down the slick, muddy incline.

"Goddam!" he yelled. His voice echoed off distant hills. A sharp prickly bush abruptly halted his journey.

A sharp pain shot through his right wrist. He held the hand in front of him and stretched it out. He could move it forward but suffered extreme pain when he tried to pull the hand back up. *Just a bruise,* he told himself, suspecting it was probably something more. He was too near his destination, and too curious about what he might find, to give up now. The hunter within egged him on, oblivious of the pain, focused solely on the question of whether there were bodies at the bottom of the cliff.

It should be just about a hundred yards over there, he thought, looking off toward a depressed area of earth. Walking along a narrow strip of level land, he found his way through the tangled shrubs. Entering a tight knot of trees, he spotted a familiar stick. WS. His initials. This was the spot. He quickly found the other two sticks.

A gust of cold air howled through the trees. Web nervously glanced around. This was a sort of collection point for everything that fell down the hill. There were hundreds of beer cans, soda bottles, and a broken cooler, all of which had apparently been thrown off the cliff. But no bodies. No clothing. Nothing except trash left by campers.

Back in the car, Joyce became bored reading about REM and Morrissey. She foraged around in the backseat of the car looking for something else to read. A folder fell to the floor, and photos and maps spilled out of it: Web's secret collection.

Joyce flipped through the photos, then through some writing of her father's. A spiral notebook was filled with her father's neat block letters.

Supposition: A highly organized serial killer may be at work.

Supposition: The maps purchased at Johnson's General Store used to decide where to dispose of bodies.

Conclusion: More research is necessary. Explore Diablo State Park, esp. cliff at north end.

She threw it into the backseat.

All this bullshit about a father-daughter camping trip and he just wanted to look for bodies! she thought. She was tempted to pick up and leave right then.

* * *

In the canyon, Web leaned against a rock with his right hand and groaned. His wrist was swelling like a water balloon, and the drizzle began to change to rain. He realized he had to make it to the top as quickly as possible without full use of one of his hands. It was a slow struggle upward.

Just as he neared the top, the rain picked up to a torrent. He slipped again, landing on the injured hand. Pain shot through his arm.

Choosing an alternate route, Web struggled up to level ground. He ran down the muddy fire road, back toward Joyce. Mud found him and ran alongside, worried, whining. As Web saw the car, he began shivering violently, realizing that he was quite cold.

Joyce was listening to the radio when Web rapped on the window. She looked up at him and unlocked the door. He entered and dripped all over the car seats. Mud leaped into the backseat and hunkered down, gnawing a burr embedded in his leg.

"Are we having fun yet?" Joyce asked, challenging.

"It wasn't so bad," said Web. He couldn't tell her what he had been looking for. He collapsed onto the passenger seat of the car.

"What happened to your wrist?" cried Joyce, startled at her father's hand, which looked like an overripe eggplant.

"I guess I bruised it," said Web, slightly dazed.

"That's more than a bruise. Let's get you to a doctor."

Web stared at his wrist. Joyce realized he must be in a slight state of shock. Fortunately, she had learned first aid just about every year since she'd been ten, thanks to her panicky dad. She kicked into action.

"Put this over your shoulders," she said, draping a jacket from the backseat over her father. Then she pulled up his sleeve to get a good look at his wrist. It was the color of blueberries and twice its normal size.

"We have to get you out of here right now, Dad."

"What about the tent?" Web asked, slightly dazed.

"We'll come back. We're going to a doctor." Joyce figured they would just let the tent rot, but she knew enough not to upset him by spelling it out.

* * *

The emergency room personnel in Walnut Creek praised Joyce for her levelheadedness when they discovered Web's wrist was broken in two places. They released him after two hours, his wrist in a cast, a bandage on his arm, but in general, fine. He didn't even take the pain killers they had given him.

Joyce drove in silence from the emergency room toward their home, speeding down the freeway.

"You might want to watch that speed, Joyce. The road is pretty slick," Web suggested.

"I'm driving. I'll get us home however I want," she said, then turned on the radio.

"Sorry about the camping trip ending so soon," he offered.

"Oh, bullshit, Dad. You just told me it was a father-daughter trip so you could get me to come. So I wouldn't get in trouble."

Web turned down the radio.

"That's not it at all, Joyce. I really wanted to . . ."

"Dad, I found your folder with the pictures of dead girls in it. And I found your map. You were looking for bodies up there. After all this time, after all the speeches about how you were going to put Vicki behind us, you wanted to look for bodies. And that's the deal with Maria, too."

"She's in a tight spot. She needs someone to sympathize with her," he said.

"Yeah, right, Dad. So you find the only woman in five hundred miles with a missing daughter. But we're still putting Vicki behind us. Sure. I'm not stupid."

"Look, that wasn't the only reason we went to the park. I did think it would be good to spend some time together."

"So you left me in the car alone in a place where you think a psycho is running around loose. That's what I call quality time."

Joyce pushed the car beyond seventy miles per hour. Web didn't say anything more about her driving, and they rode in silence for the next hour. When they got home, Joyce sped up the driveway, put up the garage door, and ran out of the car and into the house.

Web yelled after her.

"Joyce? Joyce!"

She was gone, locked away in her room, out of reach. Mud, tail between his legs, shot away from Web and hid behind the couch.

On the following Friday, while waiting in a doctor's office for a checkup on his wrist, Web stared at the television news playing silently in the waiting room. A reporter stood in a forest somewhere; shaky handheld footage showed body bags being carried into an ambulance.

Web leaped out of his chair and turned up the volume, startling an old lady with a walker who was enjoying a two-month-old *Reader's Digest*. The On-the-Spot Reporter was in midsentence.

"The unidentified women's bodies, ironically, were found in a spot called Deadman's Swamp. We talked briefly with Park Ranger André Thiodolou at the scene."

The view shifted to a ranger. "There are no suspects at this point in time. I'm afraid that's about all I can report, except that the main entrance to the park will be closed for the next twenty-four to forty-eight hours as we dredge the rest of the swamp."

"Reporting at Diablo State Park, I'm Terri Knots, Newswatch 16."

Web frantically flipped channels, trying to find another news report. Nothing was on except soap operas and game shows.

Web walked to the nurse's station.

"About how long do you think Dr. Crite will be?"

"Probably another forty-five minutes, at least," she said, glancing into an appointment book.

"I'll have to come back in tomorrow. I think my wrist is going to be okay, anyway."

Web ran out the door. The woman in the walker muttered under her breath to the nurse, "That rude, rude man."

Driving toward home at high speed, Web listened to more details on the AM news radio. One of the two bodies had been positively identified as Annabell Norris, from Vallejo. Web mulled over in his mind where he had heard the name before; it was definitely familiar. In a traffic jam, he reached into the backseat and pulled out his briefcase, flipping through his notes while driving. When he read the name, he almost crashed into the van in front of him and slammed on the brakes, sending papers flying through the car.

Annabell Norris was the girl who worked in a building supply warehouse in Vallejo who'd disappeared during a short walk several weeks earlier. He had two newspaper articles about her and a photo.

From the first moment Web read the newspaper article, he had suspected that Norris had been abducted. And, he had correctly guessed which park the unknown abductor used as a dumping ground. The news story was just one more piece in the puzzle. Someone out there was responsible for the abductions and deaths of several young girls, possibly including Tanya de Rivera. The volatile, unstable, but extremely sensitive part of Web's mind was coming into its own. He was beginning to understand how this "someone" thought.

17

Mars Chittenden felt sorry for herself as she fretted around her bakery. It was her thirty-ninth birthday, and none of her friends had planned anything special. That morning, neither Farrell nor Alan had even mentioned the occasion in spite of the multiple hints she had dropped in the weeks preceding. She had at least hoped for Farrell's usual badly made birthday pancakes, but that morning he had merely run out to catch his bus, late as usual. He added insult to injury by telling her that he would be staying after school to skateboard with his buddies. Alan left shortly thereafter, earlier than usual, without the slightest hint that he remembered or cared what day it was; he even said that he was going to down some beers with his boss that night and not to expect him for dinner. And Roslyn was out of town, visiting her parents.

Mars's self-pity turned quickly to anger and she could hardly concentrate on the croissants she was supposed to be making. *Haven't I made Roslyn a big, fancy dinner on* her *birthday the last ten years in a row? Didn't I take Farrell to a Giants' game and a waterslide on* his *birthday?*

"Some people are users, and others just get used," she said aloud. She smelled something burning. Thirty bucks worth of croissants went up in smoke.

The hell with it, she thought, yanking the tray out of the oven, dumping the smoldering food straight into the trash bin. She turned off the oven, flipped out the lights, and closed up an hour early. The week before, Mars had read a book about self-nurturing. Its message was that a woman has to take care of herself, and by God that's what she intended to do.

She cranked the volume on a Windham Hill tape in her car stereo as she drove to the grocery. She wanted to get the makings for her favorite meal of halibut tacos, smoked oysters, and mashed potatoes, and she intended to purchase exactly one serving. Alan and Farrell could forage for themselves.

As she entered the Endocino Ralph's, Mars spotted a familiar gray convertible in the parking lot. Alan's car. *What the hell is he doing here? He told me he was working.*

As Mars approached the store, she saw Alan walking out the door on the opposite side. He was dressed up—the new shirt she'd gotten him and a bolo tie. Their eyes met for a moment—she saw the flash of recognition in his face. But then he turned his head and pretended not to see her. He waited by the door for a moment, then was joined by a woman. Even from a distance she could see the woman was younger than herself. And dressed to kill. She saw Alan grab the woman by the wrist and drag her around to the far side of the building. Into an alley. *He's hiding.* The way he held her as they ran was far too intimate. She was no mere acquaintance. *He's having an affair with her,* she thought.

Tears quickly came to her eyes. *That son of a bitch. That goddam prick. Of all the nerve, out with a bimbo on my birthday, and he tells me he's drinking with his boss.* She chose not to run after him. That wasn't her style. Instead, she would throw all his junk out onto the lawn when she got home. Piece by piece.

But only after she ate her lonely birthday meal.

Mars had to set down her grocery bags to open the front door. Besides her favorite food, she'd bought a six-pack of Anchor Steam and a bottle of the most expensive champagne the store had to offer. *Nurture, schmurture,* Mars thought. She was going to take the bull by the horns, get good and drunk, and chuck that asshole Alan out.

She kicked the door open, dropped both grocery bags on the table, then headed directly for the cupboard. She reached for a glass.

Something was wrong.

Most of the glasses were missing from the cupboard.

Had she been robbed?

She heard some noise coming from the family room. Mars spun around. No one was there.

"Hello?" she said tentatively. She grabbed a large knife from a wall rack and walked down the two steps into the family room, tiptoeing toward the noise.

The room lights suddenly came on and the door from the garage flew open.

"Surprise!"

Alan, Farrell, Roslyn, and her British boss Rupert leapt out from the garage door wearing party hats and blowing on noisemakers.

Mars felt simultaneously ridiculous and furious. The knife looked absurd in her hand.

"You guys! I nearly had a heart attack," she said, collapsing into the couch.

Roslyn laughed. "Yeah, you should have! You nearly ruined your own party. When on earth have you ever closed the shop early? You almost spotted me and Alan carrying your cake out of the grocery store."

"Oh, Jesus, I'm such a dunce!" she said, blushing.

Alan gave her a big hug and kiss.

"Happy birthday, Mars!" He slipped something around her neck.

"What is it?" she asked.

She looked down. It was the Zuni turquoise necklace that

she had wanted for months. She couldn't believe it. Alan understood her hints and gotten exactly the right necklace. No "nearly right" gift. This was the piece of jewelry she had lusted after.

"Oh Alan!" She gave him a big kiss, then slumped back into her seat.

"You guys have no idea what was going through my head. I thought you had completely forgotten!"

"Well, maybe we didn't! Happy birthday, Mars," said Alan.

Mars loved her party; they made her fish tacos, just as she had hoped, and a carrot cake. They drank lots of wine. After Rupert left and Farrell went to bed, Mars, Roslyn, and Alan shared a joint.

"Just the usual suspects left," joked Alan.

"Let's turn on the tube," suggested Mars.

"TV? It's your birthday," said Roslyn.

"So I can do anything I want. And right now I want to see what's on."

Wielding the remote, Mars rapid-fired through the channels, calling out what was available.

"News, news, 'Masterpiece Theatre,' or 'Suspect at Large.' I vote 'Suspect at Large.'"

"Is that the best there is?" asked Roslyn. "I have a videotape in my car."

"Nah. I think Clinton Bernard is kind of cute. Let's take a look."

"Do we have to?" asked Alan.

"It's my birthday."

"You're right. 'Suspect at Large' it is," he said.

Half-stoned, they watched the first part of the show, about a transvestite bank robber. Alan cuddled up to Mars, stroking her hair; it was a special treat for her, since he was often standoffish when other guests were in the house. At the commercial break Alan got up. He was in the kitchen warming up a frozen pizza when the second story came on. He stood at the edge of the kitchen and stared at the television, transfixed by the story.

"Just three days ago, the skeletal remains of two young women were found in prophetically named Deadman's Swamp, here in Mount Diablo State Park," announced the

lifelike voice of Clinton Bernard in an archly melodramatic tone. *Police have promoted the notion that the unfortunate women were victims of a camping accident, but in a 'Suspect at Large' exclusive, reporter Marge Godfried reports new evidence that the campers were victims of a violent criminal.*

The story cut to a reporter at the park standing in front of ambulances as covered body bags were loaded. Continuing, the reporter detailed all the sensational elements of the story that the news media had been able to pry out of police and park rangers, embellishing it with wild speculation by the so-called reporter: *Is a satanic cult operating in this picturesque state park? Or a deranged killer, moving freely about, someone who could even be your next-door neighbor?*

Smoke poured out of the oven. Alan didn't move an inch from his vantage point in the kitchen.

"Alan, something's burning!" yelled Mars.

"I'm watching," he said, never removing his eyes from the set.

"Alan, you've got to take those things out!"

"Just a minute. It's almost over," he said.

Mars began to rise from the couch.

"I'll get them. Sit down, it's your birthday," said Roslyn, walking into the kitchen. Alan blocked her.

"I said I'd get them. It's no problem," Alan said.

"They're burning, Alan. They won't wait for a commercial break."

"I'll get them!"

He ran to the oven and jerkily yanked the pizza out, slamming it on the table.

"Okay then." Roslyn returned to the family room, eyeing Alan warily.

"Cool your jets, Alan," yelled Mars into the kitchen.

He stomped down into the family room and turned off the television set.

"Hey, turn it on," said Mars. "It's not over!"

"I hate watching this kind of crap, and it just makes me very upset," said Alan.

"It seemed like you were interested enough a minute ago," said Roslyn.

"Well, I wasn't. It's like stopping at a car accident. They shouldn't show it at all. It should be banned."

"It's not that bad, Alan. Let's just watch the end of the show," pleaded Mars, flipping on the television with the remote controller.

"No! I'm not going to watch that kind of stuff."

Alan grabbed the control from her hand and turned off the set.

The women exchanged knowing glances.

"Okay. I guess we won't watch that one," said Roslyn. "Look, I have a tape in my car that I was supposed to return. Wanna watch that?"

"What is it?" asked Mars.

"A comedy. *Spring Ski Break.* I didn't have time to watch it. As long as I'm paying four days' rental, we may as well watch that," she said.

"Okay. Let's watch that then," said Alan.

Roslyn picked up her keys and went out the back door.

"What's the matter, Alan?" asked Mars, worried.

"It's the TV show. That's all," he said, folding his arms.

"You could have said something earlier. Just chill out a little. It's my birthday. Don't ruin it."

She put her hand on his shoulder. Alan leapt away, as if she had touched him with a hot poker. She wondered what set him off. The day had been an emotional roller coaster: first, she thought that her friends had forgotten her birthday, then that Alan was having an affair. The party had cheered her up somewhat, but now Alan was being a jerk. She felt exhausted.

Roslyn bounded back into the room holding a videotape. She looked at the depressing tableaux of Mars and Alan both staring off into the distance.

"Hey guys, what is this? A funeral? C'mon, I got a tape," said Roslyn in an attempt to recapture the party spirit.

She inserted the videotape into the player. Mars sat up straight; Alan continued slumping into the opposite corner of the couch.

"It's one of those shows for teenagers that's so stupid it's funny," said Roslyn, trying to cheer them up.

They watched *Spring Ski Break,* a sequel to a sequel filled with slapstick comedy about teenagers drinking and trying to get laid. There was a recurring gag about twin girls, one promiscuous and the other a prude, and repeated wacky ski wipeouts with girls and boys finding themselves in apparently compromising positions.

The movie took Mars's mind off of Alan's nasty mood swing. She and Roslyn sat on the couch laughing. Alan sat on the floor near the television with his back to them.

During a ridiculous scene where dozens of girls and boys wound up in the same hot tub, Mars saw Alan wringing his hands. He was making a guttural grunting noise.

"Alan, what is it?" asked Mars.

"It's this movie. I think it's even worse than that television show. Sex. It's all sex. How can those girls run around in their underwear at that ski resort? It's totally repulsive."

Roslyn laughed. "Yeah, I bet it really bugs you."

He exploded with rage, yelling over the rock music in the movie. "It is! What in the world are they thinking? How can young girls do that? It is incredibly dangerous. Why? Why do they let it happen?"

"It's only a movie, Alan. Get serious," said Mars, disturbed at his outburst.

"But it's based on reality, isn't it? They let girls nowadays do that, don't they? Unsupervised, promiscuous, running freely," he said, almost yelling.

"It's just actresses, Alan. Keep saying to yourself, 'It's only a movie, it's only a movie,'" said Roslyn.

"I know it's a movie, but I think this sort of shit really happens. Their parents don't even care. Who lets it happen? Why aren't those girls scared?" he ranted.

"What's to be scared of, Alan? Teenage boys?" said Mars.

"You just don't understand, do you? You don't even care about what happens to them."

"Alan, nothing's going to happen. It's not like they just invented spring break or anything. It's been going on as long as there were kids with hormones. Roslyn and I used to go to Tahoe every year in high school and it was ten times worse than this movie," said Mars.

"Why did you do it?"

"Because it was fun?" suggested Roslyn.

"I'm surprised nothing happened," said Alan.

"Yeah, we wish something had happened. That's why we went!" said Roslyn, laughing.

"You went where? Tahoe?" Alan asked.

"Tahoe. You know, ten kids to a car, fifteen to a hotel room. Just to blow off steam."

"I think it's disgusting," he said, turning off the television. Roslyn saw that the night was not going to get better.

"I think I'm going to go," she said, rising from the couch.

Mars walked her to the door. The two women spoke in hushed voices.

"Think he's okay?" asked Roslyn.

"Yeah. It's just a mood swing, or maybe he drank too much. I'm sorry this had to happen," said Mars.

"Don't apologize. It's your birthday. I almost had a lovely time," said Roslyn.

"Thanks for everything, Roslyn."

"Take care, love." She kissed her friend on the cheek.

Dreading every step, Mars returned to the family room where Alan had not moved an inch.

"Alan, you don't have to be such a jerk when company's here," she said.

"I didn't get that movie. It was Roslyn's fault," he said.

"No, it wasn't. There was nothing wrong with the movie. You just had a fit over nothing."

He sat immobile on the floor.

"I'm going to bed," she said after an interminable silence.

"Happy birthday then," spat Alan. "I'm going to sit out here a while longer."

"You do whatever you want, Alan."

Mars ran down the hall to her room and locked the door behind her. She caught a glimpse of the lovely necklace he had given her. *How could a guy sweet enough to get me this nice necklace turn into such a jerk?* She flopped down on the bed. *Every rose has its thorns,* she thought. Then she cried herself to sleep. It had been an especially trying birthday.

Alan DeVries tiptoed down the hall and looked through the keyhole into Mars's bedroom. The lights were out and he was sure she was asleep. Then he returned to the family room and turned on the television with the sound down low.

Roslyn had left the *Spring Ski Break* tape behind. He fast-forwarded the movie to the hot tub scene and watched it eleven times in a row. *All those young girls frolicking at a ski area.*

Mars had said they went to Tahoe in her youth. He pulled

down a map of northern California. Tahoe was less than a four-hour drive. He checked the freeways and plotted out a course.

Then he fast-forwarded through the movie, stopping at a scene where a girl skies down the steepest hill in the nude, on a dare. He froze a frame where she was going over a ski jump while dozens of men looked on. Breathing heavily, Alan unfastened his trousers, staring at the fuzzy freeze-frame. It took only a minute to satisfy his powerful need.

He fastened his pants, then pulled the movie out of the tape deck. That which moments ago had been erotically thrilling now filled him with rage. He smashed the videotape under his foot, then unwound the reels of magnetic tape. He threw the shreds of plastic and tape into the kitchen trash can, then buried them under the ruined pizza.

Then he went back to the family room and looked at the map again. His finger kept coming back to Tahoe, as if drawn by a magnet. Simply thinking about a place where he could ski and meet young, drunken, beautiful horny coeds again aroused him sexually. He rubbed the bulge in his pants and thought about how he could arrange a trip. *Tahoe.* The name on the map alone was enough to carry him through to ecstasy a second time. He wiped himself off and slept on the couch, dreaming of snowy mountain slopes.

18

Web was not surprised to find himself back in a classroom at the University of Washington, although it had been over a year since his resignation. He was teaching an introductory course in Boolean logic, the method of analysis mathematicians use to eliminate or include elements in a group, using the terms *either, or,* and *and.* He had been invited to speak as a guest; the students were beginners.

"You could have a set that includes all men who are bald," he explained to the class, *"or* who are named Herbert. It would be much larger than the set including all men who are bald *and* named Herbert, because the former set would include all men with hair who are named Herbert. Are you following me?"

The students didn't understand and stared at him as if he were speaking Latin. And they kept referring to the principles he discussed as *Bundian* logic.

"Tell us about *Bundy-an* logic," a student said. As he scanned the befuddled faces in the room, Web could not identify who had asked the question.

"No, no, it's called *Boolean* logic. *Boolean!*" Web yelled, frustrated at the misunderstanding of a simple term, so fundamental to his point.

"Tell us about all men named Bundy who kill young girls! Who is included in that set?" someone in the front row asked.

He looked at the student. It was a young girl. Why did she look so familiar? It was Maria's daughter, Tanya. *Why is Tanya here in Washington? Has she been here all along? Why didn't she call home?* he thought.

Closely examining the faces in the class, he realized that all the students were girls. He did not know why, but he recognized every one. *Old students? Friends of Joyce? No. These are the girls whose photos are in my file!* he thought. It was so simple. Those girls weren't missing. They were right here in his class on Boolean logic.

"We have to know about *Bundian* logic," another girl said. "We don't care about anything else."

"Won't you listen? That's not what we're studying," he yelled. But they stared at him blankly, as if they knew themselves to be right. He wondered, *What class is this? Have I forgotten even the simplest concepts? Why do I feel so stupid?* He waved his hands in the air, flabbergasted.

Web woke up from the nightmare when his hand smashed into his bedside lamp.

The sheets were kicked to the floor. His back was soaking with sweat.

What did it mean?

Web knew dreams could provide insight unavailable to the waking mind or reveal ideas that were too terrifying to be considered consciously.

Rutherford arrived at his basic conception for the atom in a dream, Web thought. *Dreams can be of value to the waking mind.*

But what is Bundian *logic?*

He closed his eyes.

In Boolean geometry, one might draw a circle representing all numbers divisible by three. Then, another circle representing all numbers divisible by six. The areas where the circles overlap would be connected by and: *the numbers divisible by three* and *two.*

The application of a rule to a set of facts or objects. Some will be included, others excluded.

Maybe that's what Bundian logic is.

Web could postulate a hypothetical killer but lacked a model to predict his behavior. Is it someone who kidnaps girls in a rage brought on by some external circumstance? The phase of the moon? The football team that won that weekend? Fights with his mother?

Or was it someone who was simply insane, who acted without knowing why himself?

There were too many false correlations that could be drawn. But he had dreamed about "Bundian" logic. There had to be a reason. What if he was looking at a Bundy copycat? There was the car with the seat taken out: *just like Theodore.* The mysterious purchaser of maps had also bought eight pairs of socks—*Bundy had a sock fetish, always buying or stealing several pairs at a time.* There was the appearance and age of the victims—all young girls, all with long dark hair. And now there were bodies, dumped in remote locations. Was it someone who had studied Bundy? Or a maniac driven by similar forces? The voice in the back of Web's mind rapidly fired questions, as if from a Gatling gun.

He threw on a pair of pants and went downstairs to his office, intrigued by the dream. He would assume "his" killer operated like Theodore Bundy once had. He might be wrong but wanted to follow the argument to its logical conclusion.

Killing at random, but choosing the same type of victim time and time again. Always in full control of his faculties. Never leaving a messy crime scene, just a vacuum where his victims had disappeared, seemingly into thin air.

One other element of the modus operandi represented a leap of faith. Bundy had usually covered his tracks by arriving safely at home the same day as a killing, creating an alibi. If this new killer operated similarly, then no murder site, no dumping ground, nowhere he had visited would be further than a six-hour drive from his home. Sure, it was possible that this new entity might move around, change residences. Web wasn't ready to consider that possibility. The assumption Web was going to make was that this person had stayed in one place. A locale no more than a six-hour drive from anywhere his handiwork had been found.

Web spread out a map on the floor of his office. He had already drawn "X" marks on the areas where several girls had disappeared. Now he added new X's at Mount Diablo State Park, near the store in East Yolo, and at Hardware Hypermarket in San Francisco.

Examining the roads from each of dozens of points, he drew rough ovals out to approximately a six-hour drive in every direction. The circle from Mount Diablo State Park was much smaller than most, because the twisted back-woods roads prevented one from driving very fast; six hours of driving would equal 150 miles. The circle from East Yolo was larger than average, because a good interstate freeway went nearby—in six hours, someone could drive 350 miles. He drew similar circles around every X on his map.

When he finished, Web saw a graphic picture of where his Bundian logic might take him. Where did all the circles overlap? There was only one area partially inside all of the circles. It was near the center of some six-hour circles and at the extreme edge of others: Vine County was less than a six-hour drive from every X on the map, clearly delineated by Web's mental exercise.

He knew the area well. Tico, where Maria lived, fell inside every circle, as did Endocino, where the county sheriff had his headquarters. About a dozen other unincorporated towns fell inside his circles, too.

Web dressed, hurriedly ate a predawn breakfast of toast and coffee, and drove toward Tico. There was very little traffic on the roads.

At 7:30 he pulled into an Independent USA gas station and called Maria. Her phone machine answered, and he left a message.

"Maria, this is Web. I . . ."

She picked up the phone. "Web?" The screech of electronic feedback came from the answering machine as she turned it off.

"Where are you?" she asked.

"I'm going to be in Tico in about an hour. I just wanted to talk to the sheriff and perhaps that guy on your task force . . ."

"Peter Rowan. I'd like to meet you, Web, but I am preparing to leave for New York."

Web felt a surge of disappointment. He had hoped to see Maria during his visit.

"What's there?"

"Covenant House. Tanya was always fascinated with New York, so I want to at least talk to them."

Web recognized the name of the organization run by the Catholic church to shelter and assist runaway children; he had talked with them on dozens of occasions during his search for Vicki.

"When do you leave? Could I meet you for breakfast?"

"My girlfriend will be here in a few minutes to drive me to the airport."

"Oh," he said. She sensed his disappointment.

"But that doesn't mean that I would not have loved to."

After hanging up, Web felt slightly foolish. He had driven to Vine County because of his discovery; but now he realized that his real goal had been to see Maria. Now that she was not going to be home, he felt slightly out of place. He dialed another number.

"American Hotel. Peter Rowan speaking."

"Peter, this is Web Sloane. I'm in town."

"How are you, Web?"

"Pretty good. You still working on finding out who left two bodies outside Tico?"

"Besides running a hotel, a restaurant, and a volunteer fire department, I've spent every waking moment on it."

"Then I have some maps you'll want to see."

"Can you meet me for breakfast at the hotel?"

When Web got to the hotel room command center, Rowan had laid out an enticing selection of croissants and fruit. He looked like he hadn't slept in weeks.

Web spread out his maps and explained the thinking behind his overlapping circles. Rowan squinted his eyes and ran his finger over the map.

"Why wouldn't the circles come together anyway? I mean, if your information all comes from up here, then the leads we find would be centered around here," said Rowan.

"Except for the information I found on my own or with Maria, I've gotten most of the stories from San Francisco newspapers and *USA Today*. If the source of the news were an issue, the epicenter should be San Francisco, not a hundred miles north."

Rowan stared at the map as if it were a used car he was considering purchasing, running his finger across every "X" mark and examining Web's circles.

"What does this mean, then?" asked Rowan, lighting a long brown imported cigarette.

"Let's interpret the circles conservatively. Maybe only a half, or a third, of these disappearances and murders are connected."

"That's fair," said Rowan.

"But no matter which ones you eliminate, you still have a rash of atypical disappearances and the four girls' bodies left in the woods."

"Four?"

"Your two, plus the ones found in Mount Diablo State Park."

"And . . ."

"And it seems to me that our prime candidate lives somewhere in the Vine County area."

Rowan was unimpressed. "That narrows it down to only a quarter million people."

"No. It cuts it down much further than that."

"How so?"

"You can eliminate half the population right off the top—serial murderers are almost invariably male."

"Okay. A hundred thousand."

"You can scratch out anyone older than about fifty or younger than sixteen. That puts it down maybe to fifty thousand. The man who used Maria's credit card in San Francisco was white. We're down to maybe thirty-five thousand."

"So you want to talk to every white male between the ages of fifteen and fifty that lives in Vine County?"

"You've forgotten something that will get us down to maybe ten guys out of those thirty-five thousand, Peter."

"Yeah?"

"He drives a gray convertible BMW. I'd like you to come with me to tell Sheriff Block."

Rowan suddenly stood up, waving his cigarette.

"I don't know if that's such a good idea."

"Why?"

"Block has some sort of beef with me."

"So what? He's still a public official. He still has to listen to you."

"Why don't you go by yourself?" said Rowan.

"I'm not a citizen of the county, and besides, you should be in constant touch with him."

"Why don't you go with Maria?"

"She's out of town."

Rowan stubbed out his cigarette and exhaled an eerie blue cloud of smoke.

"I'll go with you. But it won't do any good."

In the lobby of the house that served as sheriff headquarters, Web asked to see Block. On Rowan's advice he didn't mention his companion.

A buzzing sound admitted the two men into the sheriff's office. Block was on the phone and motioned for Web to sit down. He looked at Peter Rowan as if he were about to kill the man. Block's appearance had radically changed since Web had last seen him—the long hair and beard were closely trimmed, and he wore a neatly pressed suit. Web figured out why—a reelection poster graced the wall behind him. Block hung up the phone.

"Hi, professor. You didn't tell me you were bringing a little friend," he said, addressing Web but ignoring Rowan as if the man were invisible.

"I've been working on this as hard as any citizen, Sheriff Block," said Rowan, taking offense.

The sheriff nodded. "Yeah, yeah, tell me about it. What do you have?"

Web spread out the map of northern California and explained the story to the sheriff, going through the argument that led him to believe that one of the few white men in Vine County who drove a BMW convertible should be a good suspect.

Block grinned broadly.

"I like the way you always come in here telling me how you solved the case. Just give me the name . . ."

Rowan cut him off. "This represents some serious research! How long would it take to ask questions of a few people in the county? It's worth a try, don't you think?"

"Rowan, as long as I'm still sheriff, I'll do things my way. I've already run checks on every BMW convertible in the state! I think it's a goose chase but occasionally you catch a goose so I'm going for it."

Web seethed with indignation. He bit his lip to prevent himself from screaming at the man *you stupid son of a bitch!*

Rowan spoke. "It's a waste of time looking at the whole state. Why not start here? There's good evidence that a suspect might be found here in Vine County!"

"I'm not ignoring Vine County, Rowan. But unless you and your bunch of swell fellas down in Tico unseat me in November, I'm in charge here."

"What the hell?" asked Web.

Rowan jumped back into the fray. "You calling me names? What do you mean by swell fellas?"

"Well, Petey baby, I didn't mean anything worse than the little cartoon of me you guys faxed around that says 'Redneck Justice.' Now if you're done, I've got work to do," said Block.

Web stood up. "What about the maps? You're not even considering . . ."

"I'm considering everything, professor. I'm just considering some things a little more than others. The door out is behind you. Watch that it don't hit you in the ass."

In the parking lot of the sheriff station Web confronted Rowan. "What is going on between you and Block?"

Rowan sighed. "I'm backing another candidate for sheriff in November. Block knows it and he's sore as hell. He's run unopposed the last two elections. I didn't fax that cartoon around, either, but he still blames me for it."

"What cartoon?"

Rowan sighed. "The absurdities of small-town politics. It seems so stupid to explain it to an outsider. Just a picture of him with the words 'Redneck Justice.' It's just all bullshit, I don't even know who started it. But you see why I'm not going to support him for reelection."

"I don't give a good goddam about any election. He's sheriff now, and if you want any progress, you have to work with the man."

"I try to, but he hates my guts."

"You shouldn't antagonize him."

Rowan made an audible groan and got into the car. They rode back to Tico together without speaking, listening to Rowan's opera tape.

Rowan and Web parted at the old-fashioned hotel. Web started to drive back toward San Francisco, then decided to make a slight detour. A man in nearby Green Grove owed Web a favor, and he intended to collect.

The two bodies in the woods had been left more or less in the Spring of 1989. Perhaps Web's *hypothetical person* had to fill up his tank that night. Web pulled into O'Brien's 25-Hour Gas Station.

O'Brien was working beneath a pickup truck when Web walked into the service bay. In the adjacent waiting room a pregnant woman sat knitting, watching "Donahue."

"Mr. O'Brien?" Web asked.

"Just a minute. Hold on."

O'Brien slid out from beneath the vehicle on an oversized skateboard.

"I'm Web Sloane. I don't know if you remember me or not . . ."

"Can't say that I do," said O'Brien.

"One night about six months ago I drove your daughter and her boyfriend here . . ."

O'Brien cracked half a smile. "Oh yeah. It's no longer 'boyfriend.' He's her fiancé now." He yelled into the other room. "Jeannie!"

The pregnant woman was the same girl he had stumbled over at the murder site, and she looked about six months' pregnant. The leather and lace was gone, replaced by a baggy lime-green dress. She peeked into the service bay.

"Hi?" she said, not immediately recognizing Web.

Web waved, then spoke quietly to Mr. O'Brien.

"I don't really need to talk to her. I wanted to ask you something."

"It's okay, Jeannie," O'Brien said. The girl returned to her knitting. "What do you need?"

"I'd like to look at your gas slips from last March and April," Web said.

"That's kind of confidential information, Mr. Sloane. You with police or something?"

"No. I'm conducting an independent investigation."

"Let me call the sheriff's office. If they say it's okay, then fine."

"I'd rather you didn't talk to him."

"You a private investigator or something?"

"No. But I think someone who bought gas here could have been the same one who left the bodies on the hill."

"I don't know. I mean, you just walk in here and start asking to look at my records. I can't allow that."

Web bit his lip. His eye caught the girl in the waiting room.

"Your daughter could have been in a lot worse trouble if I hadn't brought her home that night."

"What are you suggesting, Mr. Sloane?"

"We brought her here instead of to the police or something."

"You making a threat against Jeannie?"

Web gritted his teeth, flustered. "No, not at all. I'm just saying you owe me one. Man to man."

O'Brien didn't reply but instead just washed his hands in the service bay sink.

"Mr. O'Brien?" Web asked.

The mechanic dried off his hands. "Okay. You can look at them. Favor's a favor."

O'Brien let Web sit at his desk and piled dozens of shoe boxes in front of him.

"These are the receipts. I don't know what you'll do with them."

"Could I photocopy them?"

"I'd rather you looked at them here."

Web began with a box labeled "Mar. 1990/Wk. 1." Handful by handful, he pulled out the charge slips and carefully copied down license numbers. An hour later he had filled four pages with license numbers and had only gotten halfway through the first box. His hand ached from the transcribing. Web went outside to relax and stretch his hand.

Two cars were filling up with gas: a station wagon and a Mazda Miata. The cashier collected payment from the station wagon, then gave the driver a token. Web watched as the car pulled around to the side of the station, inserted the token into a coin changer, and drove through the car wash.

Then Web saw the Miata driver paying. The driver smiled and chatted with the station employee a moment, then the attendant handed him a coupon. The driver walked over to his car, put the convertible top down, and drove away.

Web approached the cashier, a young man with long blond hair.

"What pump?" asked the kid.

"None, actually. What was that coupon you gave to the guy in the Miata?"

"Dollar off. See the sign?"

He pointed to a faded sign: Free Car Wash with Fill-Up. Handwritten below that was: Convirtables Get $ Dollar $ Off on Next Fill-Up.

O'Brien spotted Web talking to the attendant and ran over to him.

"Mr. Sloane, you can't leave my records spread out all over."

"Sorry. I was just relaxing my eyes. How's that work?" asked Web, pointing to the sign.

"Get a token, go through the wash," said O'Brien.

"No, the dollar off," asked Web.

"It's just good business. If I can't give 'em the wash, at least give 'em something. Repeat customers are my life blood."

"What if a worker just starts giving out the dollar off to his friends?"

"Thought of that, too. See here?"

O'Brien pointed to a receipt. There were two boxes printed on it.

"Car wash gets the left box checked. Dollar off gets the right box checked and they have to initial it. That way I know who is giving out coupons. You gotta watch every dollar in this business."

"That's great. Thanks. One more question. Are there any other 24-hour stations around here?"

"Not for about sixty miles on this road. Those late hours are hard, but it keeps me in the black. I call it '25' hours 'cause it feels longer than a day."

Web laughed and returned to the office.

He had a new key to the receipts. Only fifty-two receipts in March and April were convertibles. He copied the license numbers down, thanked O'Brien, and drove back home.

First, he faxed the numbers to Block with an explanatory note saying he should cross-check the numbers with the plates he got from the Department of Motor Vehicles. Then Web called the DMV himself. After an extended hold period, filled with recorded messages about road closures and traffic safety, he finally got an operator.

"Vehicle ownership is a public record," she explained. "We will identify vehicles by license number for a $2.50 service charge. Each request must be mailed separately and accompanied by a money order. It usually takes about thirty to sixty days for each request to be processed."

It took the rest of the afternoon to purchase the money orders, print the request letters, and mail them, but Web felt that he might be on to something important. The list of names he would get from the DMV might contain the name and address of a killer.

19

Joyce climbed the stairs of the North Berkeley Graduate Student Apartments, soaking up all the fascinating sensations the old residence had to offer. The building itself represented something mature and alluring to her; the people who lived here, she imagined, were impassioned thinkers, libertarian and nonjudgmental, pursuing intellectual dragons behind these plain apartment doors. She felt a kindred spirit with these graduate students, more than with kids her age who were entering college as freshmen; she believed the bohemian spirit was very alive within these walls.

As she worked her way to the fifth floor, Joyce tried to notice the details that a poet might see: graffiti reading "To think is to live," written on a fire door; the smell of incense leaking from one apartment, steak cooking from another; a broken light fixture, filled with dead bugs. The ascent to Ramiah Bose's apartment was like a trip into a deeper part of herself, and she felt more thoughtful, more sensitive, more alive, *more in touch with the universe itself.* By the time she knocked on Bose's door, Joyce tingled with fervor for all things strange and dangerous.

Bose answered the door wearing blue jeans and a smoking jacket. He kissed her on the cheek to greet her. When her grandmother did that, she thought it corny, but when Bose did, it seemed exotic, refined.

"Don't just stand there, my dear, come in," he said.

"Thanks, Ramiah." She put her books down on his coffee table, then sat on a cushion on the floor. Bose owned hardly any furniture; just the cushions, the big coffee table, and a futon rolled up in the corner. She liked the elegant simplicity, and the art on the walls, mostly posters from art exhibitions, seemed chosen by a master hand.

"Glass of wine?" Bose asked.

Joyce hesitated. "I thought we were going to work on the SAT stuff," she said. "I don't think we ought to be getting drunk."

Bose laughed. "That's something you haven't yet discovered in life—that one can have a glass of wine without planning to get drunk."

Joyce smiled. *Ramiah's so cool.* "I guess if you put it that way . . ."

He poured two glasses of chianti, setting one down in front of her. "There. It won't kill you, nor will you turn into a pumpkin."

"Thanks, Ramiah." She sipped the wine. It made her feel like she was glowing, warm.

"So. I wanted you to help me with the mathematics part tonight. I got a little hung up on some of the geometry . . ."

Bose laughed. "You're in such a hurry! Get right down to work, no time for small talk?"

"Oh, right. I'm sorry," she said, grinning sheepishly.

"So how have you been, Joyce, dear?" Bose said in his best Oxford accent, lighting a clove cigarette.

Joyce didn't know what to say. She didn't like to talk about the little things from her *regular* life when she visited Bose; telling stories about school plays or life at home took away from the exotic feeling inside her.

"I don't know. Just these SAT's and stuff, I guess," Joyce said, finishing the glass of wine. Bose filled it right back up.

"Which university? If you're taking these achievement tests, you must have chosen a college."

She shrugged her shoulders. "That's just it. I don't even *want* to go to college right away. I just want to live a little first, you know, see some of the world or something."

"Then why are you knocking yourself out?" he asked with a flourish of the cigarette.

"It's my dad, I guess. He says I have to go to college, and . . . I don't know. It's just what you're supposed to do."

Bose grinned and whispered to her.

"You'll soon be eighteen, darling. You can do *anything you want.* If you do what your father tells you to at this age, in a few years you'll be doing what someone else tells you to do, and then one day you'll find you lived your *whole life* fulfilling the wishes of others."

Joyce grimaced. Bose's picture of the world sounded oppressive. As the effects of the wine kicked in, she began to feel more comfortable talking about herself.

"Bosey, I wish it were that easy. But you know my dad, and everything—I pretty much have to go to college next year."

Bose held her hand. It was very strange; he had hardly ever touched her before. But she didn't mind, really.

"It's very easy. Just say 'I don't want to go.' That's it. Then do what you want to do."

"If only he was as understanding as you are. I mean, he hardly knows me! I feel you really know me, the *real* me, Bosey. He's always trying to make me like my *perfect* sister, the one who died."

The words came tumbling out of Joyce, aided by the wine. "He always liked her more. My dad never was satisfied with anything *I* did. He always searched for Vicki and made sacrifices for her and talked about her . . . but he didn't even come to my school play. I just want him to know I'm not a dummy, I'm better than she was. I *have* to go to college. It's what he expects."

Bose looked her straight in the eye. "If you don't want to go, let's not waste time preparing you for something you have no desire to do."

She hesitated. "But what could I say?"

"Say, 'I don't want to go to college.' That's it. The simplest, most elegant words in the world. That's what being an adult really is. Sticking up for yourself."

A tear came to her eye, which she tried to wipe away. "Oh, Bosey, you have such a way of seeing through these difficult things. You think so clearly. That's what I should do, isn't it?"

He took her other hand.

"Of course it is."

Joyce felt a mixture of fear and anticipation, like the first time she rode on an airplane. There was a threshold she had crossed somewhere; she didn't feel like a kid any more. A new identity was asserting itself. She associated the feeling partially with Bose, but more with the way he made her feel.

Like a real adult. She stared dumbly at him, not knowing what to do.

Then he kissed her. He knew what the feeling was, even before she did.

They held the kiss a long time, not saying anything. When Bose got up to dim the lights, she was going to say something to protest, like she had done with other boys. Joyce had always thought she'd save herself until a special moment. And this time, with this man, seemed like just that moment.

Several hours later, Bose invited her to spend the night, but Joyce knew she couldn't do that. Bose drove her home in his beat-up Peugeot, and she would forever associate its smell of burning oil with her first night of lovemaking. They had a long good-night kiss in front of the house; Bose didn't stop the engine. Joyce peered out the car window at her house and saw that her father's light was on. It seemed a hundred miles away.

"Bosey, I have to tell my father that I'm not going to college. Would you come in while I do?"

His eyes momentarily darted back and forth; the shadow of a scowl crossed his mouth. "I would hate to ruin such a special evening on something so drab, Joyce."

"Please?" she asked, kissing him quickly. "I really need you to help me face him . . ."

"Dearest, you have to stand up for yourself. That's what being an adult is. I could come with you—but it's much more important for you to brave it on your own." He grinned slyly and gripped the steering wheel, as if anxious to leave.

"I . . . I guess you're right." She opened the door. "Thank you for . . . a lovely evening."

"Thank *you*. I had a jolly wonderful time."

The way he said *wonderful* was odd, as if they'd just played a round of golf instead of the *ultimate,* but Joyce didn't think of that till much later.

"Bye, Bosey."

"Good-bye."

As soon as she stepped on the curb, he gunned the engine and sped away.

Joyce walked slowly to the door of her house, notebooks

pressed against her breasts. She didn't want to lose the magic she felt; she wanted to think about life and *everything* that night. She stood in the cold air, gathering her courage, looking at the flower gardens. When a neighbor's car pulled into an adjacent driveway she suddenly felt foolish and went inside. Web was waiting up on the couch.

"How'd it go? You studied pretty late." He seemed like an alien life form, sounding so cheery.

"Um, Dad," she began.

"Yes? Trouble with the math?"

"No, that's not it at all. I just wanted to say—"

"Don't worry about the tests too much. You'll do fine— they look at the whole person, not just the scores."

"That's not it," she said, teetering between bravery and buckling under.

"What? What do you mean?"

Joyce hesitated a long time, her fingernails digging into the vinyl notebook cover, then spat it out. "I don't want to go to college."

She couldn't believe she had said it. In her own house. To her own father. Joyce heard the words as if another girl had said them to someone else's father.

"What? That's ridiculous. I thought you were studying . . ."

"I was. But I stopped. I changed my mind. I don't want to go to college and never did and you can't make me." Joyce started to lose her nerve. It wasn't as easy to say as she had imagined when Bose was coaching her.

"Joyce, what happened? We've talked about this a lot of times and you always said . . ."

"You always *wanted me* to say. But I don't want to go. And I don't want to talk about it and that's final!"

"We will talk about it and it's not final. What happened to . . ."

Feeling cut off and disoriented, like she'd jumped out of a window but not yet hit the ground, Joyce ran to her room and locked the door.

Ramiah Bose didn't call the next day. Or the next. Or the next. Joyce felt her world coming apart at the seams, but she didn't want to call *him*. He had to call *her:* didn't it mean anything at all to him? She successfully avoided her father through a variety of ruses for four days: play practice at school, locking herself in her room, spending time with her girlfriends. But when a week passed and Bosey hadn't called or written or stopped by or *anything,* she hit rock bottom.

She was staring blankly at an English text lying open on the table, rereading for the third time a passage from Chaucer without understanding it, when her father came into the room.

He sat down across from her. She thought she knew why. "Joyce, what happened?"

"I don't know, Dad. I just don't know."

"The other night, when you got back from Margaux's . . ."

She didn't want to correct him and say where she'd really been was Bose's apartment.

"That night, you said you didn't want to go to college. And since then it's as if you've been hiding."

"I'm sorry, Daddy-O," she said softly. She didn't know what to say, she was so mixed up.

"Is it true? About college? Is there something else you'd really rather do . . ."

"That's just it. I don't have the faintest idea what I want to do. It's like everyone expects that you graduate from high school and instantly know what you want to do for the rest of your life. I'm not like that." She felt a drop of moisture in her eyes. It was very hard being honest with her father but strangely satisfying, like a swim in a cold river.

Web exhaled deeply. Her answer wasn't what he had hoped to hear, but it wasn't the Hari Krishnas, either. He had considered the situation thoughtfully since her announcement and come to a difficult realization.

"You don't have to go," he said.

"I don't?"

"No."

"But what should I do?"

Web laughed, but it was a laugh that brought them together, not one of ridicule. "I thought you had some big secret plan. Like joining the circus, maybe."

Joyce laughed with him, then sniffed. "No, it's not that. I just don't know at all. You always said I had to go, but I didn't ever decide for *myself.*"

"What about a compromise?" he suggested, playing with the lid on the sugar bowl.

"Like . . . ?" Joyce smiled. Her father seemed really to listen to her.

"What about this. Take the SATs, but don't kill yourself over it. Try college for a year. I'll pay. After a year, if you like it, continue. But if there's something else you'd rather do I'll back you all the way."

Joyce was overwhelmed. "Anything?"

"Well, maybe not the foreign legion, but who knows? You might see a lot of things at college that you never expected would interest you."

She sniffled and laughed. Just by discussing the subject, it was as if a cloud had cleared away. When it wasn't being force-fed, college suddenly seemed like someplace interesting, someplace fun. If she was just *trying it out,* it wasn't as intimidating as if she had to go and get perfect grades and be the perfect daughter and turn into a lawyer or doctor or something.

"Well, it sounds better than the circus, Daddy-O."

"Shall we shake on it then? Or would you rather go out for milk shakes?" he asked.

Joyce smiled. "Both?"

They shook hands, a broad imitation of executives closing an important business deal. Then they went to Bob's Big Boy and enjoyed two chocolate-malted milk shakes. And talked, not about college or life plans or what Joyce was supposed to do, but about stupid little things like the upside-down name pin on the waitress. Joyce felt like an adult.

20

Mars Chittenden smelled the clean sheets as she lovingly pulled them off the clothesline: She called it her solar clothes dryer. Saturday laundry provided some of her favorite sensations: the feel of soft, freshly laundered cloth in her fingers, the ineffable scent of the fresh air married into the sheets, and the dance of the linen in the breeze.

Alan had taken Farrell to some kind of skateboarding convention, and she had the house to herself the rest of the day. The dishes were done, she was almost finished with the laundry and had planned a barbecue for later in the evening. A perfect early-spring day.

Inside the house, her old, scratched-up record of Gregorian chants resonated through every room. Part of the reason she liked the old album so much was that no one else could stand listening to it. It was a rare treat to pump up the eerie voices to full volume.

She pulled the old Batman sheets off Farrell's bed and threw them on the floor. She noticed the mattress sagging in the middle. It had not been flipped over in six months, so she dragged it off onto the ground. Out fell a half-dozen glossy magazines. She leaned the mattress against the wall and picked up one of the magazines. It was called *Lesbo Dildo Lust* and was illustrated with an appropriately graphic color photo. Her pulse raced. The magazine was shiny and new. Mars knew all she wanted to know. Farrell hadn't gotten these from a friend at school. And now she knew Alan's lame tale about a hitchhiker leaving dirty pictures in his car was a lie.

"Goddamit, GOD DAMN IT!" she yelled although no one was there to hear. Mars grabbed the magazines and ran into the kitchen, where she dumped them in the trash can. She immediately pulled them out, went outside and threw them into the barbecue she had set up, doused them liberally with Wizard lighter fluid, and dropped in a match. For a few moments, the flames curling into the air held her transfixed. When the magazines were burning sufficiently, she walked over to the converted garage, Alan's room.

Though Alan had changed the locks, Mars knew where he hid his spare key, having seen him use it dozens of times. She looked down the road. *Should I go into his room?* Briefly, she considered how it might violate his privacy, but her hesitation dissolved into fury as she thought about his lies about the hitchhiker and how he had supplied her son with ugly smut, not once but twice. Mars lifted the potted geranium next to the door and pulled out the key. She let herself into Alan's room.

The room smelled of mold and soured towels. Mars had been in the room before, but not in several months. She flipped on the light, a bare ceiling bulb, and looked around, not knowing what to expect. Alan's bed, which he used only on the rare nights he didn't sleep with Mars, was neatly made. Her old workbench had been converted to a computer table. He had repainted the old dresser they had purchased at a garage sale. But she saw nothing unusual or out of place. No dirty books.

Mars stepped outside to see if someone was coming. No one was there. Bits of burned paper floated through the air from her grill, toward the remaining laundry. She looked at the clothes—mostly Alan's. *Fuck 'em.* Mars went back into Alan's room. She opened a drawer in the dresser. Suddenly she felt uncomfortable, like a burglar breaking into a stranger's home. There was nothing in the drawer but several dozen pairs of new black socks, still in their wrappers. She slammed it shut and looked in the other drawers. Clothes, paperback novels, change, and receipts, but nothing unusual. A creepy feeling came over her. *It was too normal, too boring.*

She glanced around the room. Protruding from under the single bed was the corner of a footlocker. She was immediately curious about its contents; what was in there? Mars felt her stomach churn with guilt. *I shouldn't,* she thought. She looked in the last drawer. More socks. And a footlocker key.

THE STRANGER RETURNS

I guess I was meant to open it if Karma gave me the key just when I was thinking about it.

The metal corner screeched on the cement floor, leaving a chalky white streak as she dragged the footlocker out. As in a dream, the key fit perfectly. She opened the latches on either side of the foot locker and lifted the lid.

Inside, porn magazines filled the box up to the very brim: *there must be hundreds of them.* Titles that made *Lesbo Dildo Lust* seem tame by comparison. She shifted the magazines, trying not to disturb them so much that her intrusion would be detected. *Why does my Alan look at these?* she wondered, as she stared dumbfounded at the pictures.

His lies were even worse. *Should I confront him?* Then she realized that the entire footlocker was not full of magazines; they were simply resting in the top drawer, a shallow tray that rested in the box, where a GI might put his watch and wallet. Cautiously, she tilted up the tray.

The glint of metal caught her eye. Lifting the tray a little more, a hack saw was visible, and . . . *is that a pair of handcuffs?* The unmistakable sound of a car coming up the gravel driveway broke her concentration. Panicked, she dropped the tray back into the footlocker, slammed shut the lid, and kicked the box back under the bed.

She looked out the door, afraid of what she might see. A tourist in a Mercedes-Benz was turning around in her drive. The car pulled out and zoomed away, belching diesel particles.

After the car disappeared, she ran back into the room. *That could have been Alan! What would he do if he caught me in here?* she thought. She then restored the footlocker key to its drawer and tried to put everything back into place. She straightened out the footlocker, left the room, and hid the key back under the geranium.

The idyllic Saturday had been completely destroyed. The adrenaline still pumped through her veins. Now, her clean laundry was peppered with specks of burned paper, she had discovered her boyfriend in a lie, and to top it off her Gregorian chant album had a new scratch and repeated over and over *"Miserere Requiem."*

Glumly, Mars returned to Farrell's room and finished changing the sheets. The fun was gone; it was now drudgery. *Screw the barbecue,* she thought. *They can eat leftovers.* She made her bed, then laid down and watched the end of a show about dolphins on PBS. She fell asleep during a rerun of "Fantasy Island."

When she awoke to the sound of running water, it was dark, except for a light coming from the hall. She groggily climbed out of bed and left her room. Alan was obviously back, judging from the shoes dumped in the hall.

"Hello?" she yelled in the direction of the shower.

"It's just me," came Alan's voice. "Farrell's staying over at Pete's."

She chose not to reply. The anger she felt before the nap reasserted itself like a migraine headache that won't go away. Farrell's friend Pete, in her opinion, was a budding redneck and his parents were practically John Birchers. *She* would not have allowed her son to stay at their house. *Who the hell does Alan think he is, giving Farrell that kind of permission?*

She walked to the kitchen and stared at the mess Alan had left; he had made himself a hamburger and left bread, cheese, greasy pans, and plates scattered over all three counters. *The hell if I'm going to clean it up,* she thought. Mars was hungry and pulled out a canteloupe, some carrots, and several cucumbers. She was angrily slicing the cucumbers, the knife making a *whack, whack* sound against the cutting board, when Alan walked in, a towel wrapped around his waist.

"Hi, doll," he said, leaning over to kiss the back of her neck.

She jumped away, as if he were a snake, and continued slicing without turning to greet him.

"Someone has a bug up her ass," he grumbled, then pulled down a bottle of rum and poured himself a long shot.

Mars turned around, still holding the long knife in her fist.

"Alan, we have to talk about Farrell."

"What's to talk about? He's over at Pete's. I told you that."

"He shouldn't be at Pete's. You can't just pretend to be his father and give him permission to do this, do that, whatever mood hits you."

"What's the big deal? It's Saturday. He's sleeping over there."

"He's my son. This is my house." She stabbed the knife into the cutting board. "And I make the rules."

"Excuse me. I guess I misunderstood. Any other *rules* I should know about?"

"Don't be an asshole, Alan. Yes, there are. I found more of that bondage crap in his bed."

"Snooping around?"

"I wasn't snooping around. I was changing the sheets, if it's any of your business at all."

He leaned against the counter and took a long sip of rum. "Are you saying I gave him smut? That proves he probably got it from a friend, because I threw out all that stuff from the hitchhiker . . ."

"Bullshit, Alan. Don't lie. I'm already mad enough without you lying. You know he got it from your room, so don't make up any more stories."

"What? Do you have any proof?" he said, eyes wide in mock indignity.

"Proof? What is this, the Supreme Court?" she said, offended at his childish pretense.

"Yes, proof. What did you do, snoop around my room, too? I thought we had an agreement . . ."

"If you have to know . . ." She hesitated, vacillating between confessing her break-in and swallowing his bullshit. It was an easy choice. "Yes, I did. I went into your goddam room. You walk all over *my* room and *my* house, so don't act so hurt."

"I thought privacy was an important thing to you," he said, like some lawyer.

"Alan, you lied. About the magazines, about the hitchhiker, and just now you lied again," she said.

"So what if I have some dirty magazines. So I tried to keep them out of your sight. What's the big problem? It's perfectly *natural*. It's perfectly *normal* for men to get turned on by stuff like that," he said, finishing the rum.

"Alan, I don't give a damn what you look at or when. But

when you lie to me about it, and when you won't even . . ." she didn't know whether to bring up sex.

"Won't what?" he asked, challenging her.

"Won't even touch me in bed anymore, that's what. I have needs too, and I can't get off looking at dirty pictures. You've turned into a lousy lay, Alan. I don't know why, but . . ."

"Fuck you," he said, pouring another drink. "You don't even consider the pressure *I'm* under. You don't even think *why* I have to have those magazines. You just think *me, me, me and Farrell,*" he said, pouting as if he had suffered some great indignity. "So don't give me a hard time about it."

Mars looked at him as if he were an alien imposter. This was not the man who moved in with her months earlier. The more he talked, the more upset she became.

"Stop it! Stop talking. I don't want to hear another word." She turned away from him, facing the window over her sink.

"Maybe I'm tired of hearing you, too. Maybe I'll just take a little break. I have some business in Oregon that I have to wrap up, so you can just count on seeing me later."

Mars heard the door slam and watched out the back window as Alan threw clothes from his garage room into his Cabriolet, then lugged the footlocker and put it into the backseat. He sped out, throwing up rocks from the driveway.

The house was silent. Mars turned off all the lights and lay down on the couch, crying herself silently to sleep.

21

Eleven miles from home, he pulled the Cabriolet to the side of the road and extracted a tattered map from the glove compartment. Placing it under the dashboard light, he quivered with anticipation as his finger traced the route he intended to take. Reno, Nevada, was only six hours away. There, he could rent a room and sleep all day. Lots of gamblers did just that, and in Reno, no one would blink an eye if he paid cash and registered under an assumed name. But Reno was just going to be a rest stop. After a good long nap and a big breakfast, he intended to head for his final destination: Lake Tahoe. Where college kids would be vacationing on their spring break. *Smug, snotty brats who think they're too good for me.*

He opened the convertible top and drove back onto the road, then pulled a joint from his breast pocket and lit it. The cold night air blowing against his face at sixty miles an hour contrasted with the hot smoke he sucked into his lungs. The night was full of possibilities, and he felt young and free. After taking the last hit from the joint, he flicked it onto the road and watched it explode into sparks. One thing was missing, he thought—*music.* He flipped on the radio. The first chords of "Born to Be Wild" blasted out, like an electric confirmation that the night was his. He pounded his fist on the dashboard and swerved the car in time to the music.

They are so stupid . . . they caught HIM because he was sloppy that's the only reason . . . but they haven't even seen me. How can they let it happen again? It's because they're so gullible and foolish they think that because they make the rules no one will break them . . .

He laughed aloud and choked on the wind rushing into his dry throat. He gagged and spat out of the car onto the rushing pavement. Then he lit a Marlboro.

Why do these GIRLS go to Tahoe or Fort Lauderdale or any of those places don't they know that it's dangerous but of course they don't take it seriously because they think everything is theirs and no one will challenge them. These are the people who put alarms on their cars and burglar bars on their houses and lock their money away in banks and tear up the carbons to their credit card receipts but they are so STUPID the GIRLS go off to a ski resort where they drink and sit in hot tubs totally unclothed and say to the boys "you can have me but YOU cannot." But they are WRONG.

I will have them and I will move around undetected because no one is looking. Anybody could do it but most are so stupid but I'm the one that will have them and pick and choose the ones I want and no one will stop me. What will they say THEN? It's all their FAULT because they are so

STUPID they let it happen and they will be sorry and I will win by breaking their rules I will have them they will be mine and it is their fault.

He arrived in Reno at 4:00 A.M. and registered at the Sands Hotel & Casino under the name of Tom Kingsley. *A brilliant fuckin' name,* he thought. *Who the hell could remember a name like that? Lord knows I'm sick of being Alan DeVries anyway.* The desk clerk didn't even ask for identification. Hundreds of other people would check into the enormous casino hotel that night, and his would be just another bleary-eyed face mixed in with the mob.

Before going to his room, "Tom Kingsley" *I've got to remember that's my name that's the name I'll use* walked through the casino, where late-night gamblers were stationed randomly about at slot machines, like night-shift workers on a noisy factory floor. He positioned himself at the bar, slightly elevated above the pits, sipping a beer, scanning the crowd. He stared hard at a woman in a tight gold lamé gown. *I could have you in a minute but I won't. The cocktail waitresses scurried about in little short skirts, but they didn't interest him. You would give yourself to me if I asked and who cares about a slut waitress at a casino anyway? I wouldn't even take them. I've got bigger plans. The waitress is Little League. I want to win the Super Bowl.*

He finished one beer and got another, staring at gambler after gambler frantically stuffing quarters into machines and yanking on levers. He grinned slyly. They were like the mice from one of his college psychology experiments, trying to find the lever that gives out cheese and receiving instead only electric shocks. *You are all safe—why should I take a beat-up Chevy today when I can steal a Porsche tomorrow?* "Tom Kingsley" returned to his room and slept soundly till 3:00 in the afternoon, the sunlight blocked out by heavy velvet curtains.

He got the $2.99 prime rib special for his late breakfast and hit the road to Tahoe. He was full and happy and had a strong sense of his mission.

The terrain on either side of the road quickly changed from the dry, flat high desert plains of Reno to the tree-covered mountains leading to Tahoe. When he hit the snow line, he pulled over to fasten chains on the tires. The cold air carried the scent of pine trees. *Nothing like mountain air,* he thought. *Like Christmas year-round . . . so brisk, so wonderful. What a day for . . .* He didn't complete his thought; he knew what he had to do. *What a day!*

The winding road led him to Heavenly Valley ski resort. *I haven't hit the slopes for a long time . . .* He parked in the crowded gravel lot and sauntered into the smoky lodge bar. After guzzling two Irish coffees in quick succession, he kicked off his shoes, then scanned the people sitting in the lodge. Tired skiers getting loaded after a day on the slopes packed the room to overflowing. No one paid much attention to him. He walked over to the entrance in his socks. *Lots of them walk around in their socks.* Near the door were several dozen skiers' boots, and he casually picked a pair that were about his size. He didn't look around or act suspicious; *if someone asks, I'll just say I thought these looked like mine.* Without missing a beat, he stole the most expensive looking jacket from the rack, ski pass still attached. Outside, he had to try on four pair of skis until he found a set that would fit his stolen boots. In the commotion at the bottom of the hill, with people busy getting their skis on and off, no one gave him a second look.

Riding up the chair lift, he found a pair of goggles and a fuzzy ski cap that pulled down into a ski mask in the pocket of the jacket. *Perfect.* Using a ruse to indulge his passion for skiing was like double ecstasy; he got to pull one over on the gullible leisure class and enjoy the exhilaration of speeding downhill in the snow, a sensation denied him for many years.

After two runs, it was nearly dark. Every joint in his body was sore from the three wipeouts he had suffered as well as being somewhat out of shape. *Just one more run.* There was a long line to the chair lift. He skied along the line, holding up his hand.

"Single? Single?" he yelled, looking for someone close to the front of the line who would share the ride up the chair lift.

"I'm riding alone!" yelled a girl wearing a brand-new two-tone yellow and black ski jumpsuit. Betsy Foote's mother had always taught courtesy; it would turn out to be a lethal lesson.

He moved up next to her in line. "Thanks. I don't think I would have gotten in another run before dark if I were further back in line," he said.

"No problem," said Betsy, looking him over. He was an older guy—thirty-five or forty—but still kind of cute. What would the sorority sisters say if she was dating a distinguished older man? She smiled.

They stood in silence for the last moments before getting on the chair lift. As they ascended side by side, he introduced himself.

"Jim Kingsley," he said, extending his mitten. *Damn, it's Tom, not Jim. What the hell.*

"Betsy Foote," she said.

"Skiing by yourself?" he asked.

"Well, I came up here with two girlfriends from college, but they wimped out about an hour ago."

"What college?"

"USC."

Fucking University of Spoiled Children.

"They waiting in the lodge?" he asked.

"No, I'm just going to take the shuttle bus back."

"Don't bother with that. I'll ski down with you and then give you a ride."

She smiled nervously. "I don't know, I'll just take the shuttle."

He tried another tack.

"I know we just met and everything, but I hate to see a fellow Trojan wait in line for a smelly old bus."

It worked. *Reel her in.*

"You went to SC?" she asked excitedly. "When?"

"Class of '81," he said. *Hope that's plausible.*

"Really? My brother was class of '82! Didja know Don Foote?"

He thought quickly. "Tall, kind of quiet at first, but a real cool guy once you got to know him?" he asked.

"Yes! That's him!"

Every college-age guy in the world is kind of quiet at first but a real cool guy once you get to know him.

"He was in a couple classes of mine," he said.

"Wow! Small world! He was a Deke. You a Deke, too? Oops, here we are!"

Before he had to answer a *goddam fraternity question,* the lift dumped them out at the top of the run. He was sure he had her hooked.

"Well, nice talking to you, Betsy," he said, loitering at the top of the hill, trying to look sweet.

"Nice talking to you . . . uh,"

"Tom." *Or Jim? Who gives a damn she didn't even remember.*

She screwed up her face into a smile. "Y'know, can I still catch that ride from ya'?"

"For a Trojan? No problem. See ya' at the bottom." He waved his hand, trying to form the Trojan "fight-on" sign, but messed it up and instead gave the Texas "hook-em-horns" symbol with his index and pinkie finger.

Betsy stared dumbly. "You mean this?" she asked, waving her index and second finger limply.

He laughed nervously. "I just wanted to see if you were really from USC." Then he waved the fight-on sign, correctly this time. Betsy laughed and skied away.

He watched her go down the hill a little before launching himself. She was a very showy skier, zigzagging back and forth in a dazzling display of prowess. *Probably has the money to ski fifty times a year,* he thought. His sore muscles hampered his skiing, so he went down in a clunky, oafish-looking snow-plow style, swerving from side to side of the hill, faster skiers constantly passing him. *Go ahead pass me hotshots. I'm into a much more dangerous sport than skiing that none of you would dare to play.* As it grew dark, he was one with his thoughts, sliding through the snow toward the inevitable. The time had come to act. When he got to the bottom of the hill, his mind was so focused it was like skiing a foot above the ground.

Betsy grinned widely and waved the USC fight-on sign to him as he came down the last hundred feet. He stared at her and tried to look slick as he approached but succeeded only in falling flat on his ass. *Damn.*

She skied over, giggling, and offered a hand up.

"There you go." She helped him up.

"You gotta get some better wax or something," she said.

"Sure," he said, distracted. "Let's get going."

"Wanna get a hot chocolate first, Tom?" she asked.

"No, I have to be on my way," he said without looking at her.

"Okay," she replied, wondering why he had gotten all uptight.

They kicked off their skis at the edge of the parking lot and walked across the gravel to his car, parked in a dark corner of the lot, close to the road. He opened the trunk.

"Let's put your skis in here." He placed her skis in the trunk, through the hole in the backseat of the Cabriolet built specially for that purpose, then put in the skis he had stolen.

He opened the passenger door for her, and she sat down in the car. After hearing the door slam, he scanned the parking lot for activity. Half-dollar-size snowflakes were falling. They were virtually isolated even though hundreds of skiers were barely fifty yards away. *Let's do it,* he thought, walking around to his door. *Now is the time to get going.*

He got into the driver's seat and turned on the engine.

"Gotta let it warm up."

"Yeah, of course. You gonna wear your goggles all day?" she asked, giggling.

Will she see me? Who cares. He took off the goggles.

"Let me get my driving glasses," he said, then leaned over her and reached into the glove compartment. He pulled out the stun gun.

"What's that?" she asked, backing up.

He didn't answer but jabbed the two prongs into her neck, the only exposed skin on her body. She momentarily yelped then slumped over in her seat. *Advantage—me!* he thought. *It's so much easier than I thought it would be. Damn, I'm good.*

He set the stun gun down between the two seats and put the car into gear.

The speedometer pegged up to thirty-five miles per hour and created a high-pitched whine as the tires spun against the slick ground.

Shit.

He looked at the girl again; she was waking up. He shocked her twice more with the stun gun, then reached around to the backseat and opened his footlocker. Removing the top tray, he pulled out the handcuffs. He couldn't manipulate the key so he took off his mittens. The steel froze to his finger, tearing off a bit of skin. *Damn.* He threw the handcuffs down, pulled out the pipe wrench, and swiveled around to the front seat.

She's wriggling around. Fucking stun gun doesn't work too well in the cold.

He swung the cold iron down on her wool cap. It made a crack that reminded him of a ballplayer hitting a home run. He watched impassively as she jerked violently in an epileptic fit induced by the blow. The convulsions stopped as suddenly as they had begun. Quickly, he fastened the handcuffs around her wrists.

Bitch is gonna bleed on my car, he thought, as a dark spot grew larger on her cap. He pulled out an old Indian blanket from the trunk and wrapped it around her head, then covered her body with it.

He turned his attention back to the car. Alternately jamming the transmission into forward then reverse, he succeeded only in digging himself deeper into the hole. He got out and reconnoitered. The car sat several inches deep in ice-covered gravel; nothing would move it.

Standing behind the bumper, he pushed hard but only succeeded in straining his back. He paced, trying to think of a way out, when a big red four-wheel-drive pickup truck happened by.

What if he sees my cargo.

But . . . what if I'm stuck here when the parking lot is empty?

He smiled widely and waved at the truck, which pulled over behind him.

"D'you think you could give me a push?"

A big blond man with sunburnt skin and a broad mustache leaned out of the truck.

"Sure, no problem."

The truck positioned itself behind his car.

He got behind the wheel of the Cabriolet, leaned out, and made a circle with his left index finger and thumb, indicating for the driver of the truck to begin pushing.

He felt the car jerk forward and threw it into gear. The wheels spun momentarily, then found their traction.

He gunned the car and turned in a wide circle, till he was facing the truck. He saw the driver exit the truck and approach his car.

Should I open the window or should I get out?

He opened the window. The blond man stood next to him.

"You okay then?" he asked.

"Sure. Thanks for the push."

The pickup driver pointed to the *cargo*. "She sure is a solid sleeper."

"Yeah, long day on the slopes."

A long trail of dark red liquid leaked out from beneath the Indian blanket. *Should I say something or should I deal with that man . . .*

When he looked up, the driver of the truck was gone.

Close fuckin' call. He rolled up the window and switched on the heat. Then he wiped up the blood from the blanket using Betsy Foote's scarf.

Let's get on with it.

He looked at his map of Tahoe, trying to pick a suitable place. Six miles away from the ski resort was a boat launch. *Who the hell would be at a boat launch in the winter? It's great to be brilliant.*

He parked the Cabriolet at the top of the long steep driveway leading to the boat launch. The virgin snow confirmed that no one else had been to this place, at least since the last snowfall. He left the *cargo* in the car and walked down the drive to confirm he was alone. Leeward Wind Boat School consisted of two corrugated steel shacks, padlocked and boarded up for the winter. No one anywhere near.

He felt invigorated, alive; the large, delicious snowflakes in the blue winter dusk were eerie and beautiful. Across the frozen lake the lights of the casinos flickered temptingly. He stared off at the distant neon like Gatsby watching Daisy's docklight, comprehending that he could never be one of the beautiful people, that *they* would never accept him. Unlike Gatsby, he wasn't content to wait: *You can gamble all day, but a real man takes what he wants. A man like me can get away with it.*

He worked his way up the slippery driveway to his car. The passenger door was open. *She* wasn't in the car; *the cargo has been misrouted.* He grabbed his pipe wrench from the back seat and locked the car, then saw how easy it would be to find her: A path of crushed snow dotted with blood led to the road. He walked quietly, like a ghost. He was right behind her before she noticed.

When she saw him, she emitted a shriek that echoed against the mountains. He grabbed her from behind in a headlock and stuffed part of the Indian blanket into her mouth.

"C'mon, we have to go," he said, grabbing the handcuffs. She resisted, kicking and screaming, but he just yanked on the handcuffs and dragged her down the driveway like a disobedient horse. Several times during the climb down she fell to her knees. When that happened, he simply jerked on the handcuffs and she slid on the snow, the cold steel biting into her wrists. If he had looked at her face, he would have seen tears and terror. But he didn't look. It would have been too horrible. He might have made some sort of connection.

When Betsy realized the futility of struggling, he was able to force her to walk faster. He led her several hundred yards out to the middle of the frozen lake. *Ah, what a beautiful, beautiful night,* he thought. It wasn't hard to undress the girl except for her thermal undershirt, which caught on the handcuffs, *brand-new probably cost a hundred bucks.* He had to rip the shirt in two.

Naked, facedown on the ice, she shook with cold as much as fear when he violated her. It took longer than usual to satisfy his desires, and she kicked and flailed, so he knotted the scarf around her neck, drawing her head up like a dog wearing a choke collar. He pulled tighter and tighter on the scarf, and her chokes and sobs grew softer and shorter as her air was cut off. It seemed to him that she stopped struggling at the same time his need was relieved; *it's sort of like coming together,* he thought, then the notion was obliterated by a rush of ecstasy. He dropped her body onto the ice and zipped his pants. He walked around her lifeless body, still in the dreamy orgasmic grip, feeling satisfied as if he'd just eaten a big, juicy steak. She was beautiful. And he had had her in every sense.

The whine of a truck changing gears echoed across the lake. He looked around. The truck lights flickered across the white snow; it was at least a mile away. The eighteen-wheeler drove off and the noise faded away. *Sound travels out here,* he thought. Suddenly all he could hear was his own heavy breathing, and he was consumed with fear for his safety.

Jesus Christ you are as stupid as ever—people probably heard that from miles around. Hide it and get the fuck out of here. Got to get rid of this thing.

That *thing* would have celebrated her twentieth birthday if she had lived another six days.

Using the wrench, he bashed a hole in the thick ice several feet from her body. Freezing water splashed on his face as he frantically smashed the opening till it was about two feet around. He dragged her body over to the opening, and laid her next to the hole. He leaned in, putting his ear next to her mouth. *Is that her breath? Or just the wind? I think she's still alive. I didn't kill her. Good. She's still alive,* he convinced himself. He lifted her stiff body and lowered it into the icy water. She sank down partway into the water, then stopped. The arms wouldn't fit through the hole, so he unlocked the handcuffs and threw them aside. Then he pushed *it* through the ice and *it* sank down, the long hair bobbing for a moment before disappearing into the black, chilled water. *Gone forever.* He threw in her shoes, and clothes, but kept her parka. It was a nice one. *I could probably get twenty bucks for this.* He stuffed the handcuffs in his back pocket. *I might want to use these again.*

He inspected the ice around him. Nothing left. Then he looked at the casinos and grinned; *gamble away as if nothing happened motherfuckers.* He pulled a Marlboro out of his pocket, lit it, and began the walk back to shore. The snow had already covered the tracks they had made while walking out. No doubt the ice would freeze over again that night, eliminating all traces of his activity till the spring thaw.

The Cabriolet started right up. *I love Volkswagens!* he thought.

Once on the road, what was left of his fear was quickly replaced by elation, as he realized no one had any idea what he had just accomplished. *Put one over on them! Game, set, and match!* He flipped on an oldies station. A Beatles tune from *Sergeant Pepper* was playing. As the music rose, he could feel the synapses in his brain firing faster and faster. Everything was right. The sentiment in the song backed by the ever-rising orchestral crescendo coincided with the feeling of power surging through him. *I'd love to turn you on* . . .

He drove into town and marveled at the beauty of the neon lights reflected against the snow. *This is my night!* He drove along until he came to a hotel casino at the edge of the woods. He felt lucky. In his wallet he counted three hundred forty-one dollars. *I can turn one hundred into a thousand, it's one of those nights.*

He brushed his hair, threw the stolen parka into the backseat, and put on a blazer. Once in the crowded casino, he strutted up to a hundred-dollar-limit poker game and took a seat. The other players, a retired Jewish couple dressed as if for an opera and two Big-Man-on-Campus-type college boys, hardly acknowledged his presence.

"Mind if I sit in?"

The dealer, a forty-ish woman with skin like saddle leather, nodded curtly. He exchanged two hundred fifty dollars in cash for five fifty-dollar chips.

His first hand, a straight, lost him one hundred dollars to the BMOC's full house.

Goddam luck will have to come around next hand, he thought.

"Waitress?"

A beautiful young girl in a blue sequin vest ran right over to him. *This is the way to live.*

"Double Tanqueray and tonic."

"Straight or on the rocks?"

"Straight," he said, then added, "make it a triple, okay?"

"Sure."

He lost the next two hands quickly, reducing his pile of money to ninety dollars. He laughed nervously. The other players silently glanced at him.

"Just a bad run," he said.

On the next hand, he drew a full house on the first deal. *Knew my ship would come in tonight!*

He knew he could win. Quickly he bet all ninety dollars.

But then one of the other players raised the stake by fifty dollars.

"Hey, I thought it was a hundred-dollar limit," he said to the dealer.

"Hundred dollars per betting round. Three hundred per hand. Look at the sign."

There, printed right in front of his nose, were the rules.

"Okay. I need fifty dollars more worth of chips."

He reached into his wallet. He only had forty-one dollars left.

"Can I get credit for nine dollars?" he asked.

"Yeah, right." The dealer didn't even budge. No one got credit in a casino.

"What happens then?"

"You can't make the pot, you fold. That's the rules. That's been the rules for one hundred years."

"Jesus Christ!"

He slammed his cards down in the middle of the table, disturbing the pile of chips.

The BMOC glared at him. "Geez, it's only a game."

He squinted back at the rich kid.

The dealer raised a hand. A security guard walked over to the table.

"Problem?" asked the heavyset, mean-looking guard.

"Nah. Just an angry player," replied the dealer.

"You done playing?" asked the guard.

Those're your rules you should see my rules

"Yeah. I guess. No need to use force or anything," he said, shrugging away from the guard.

"Why don't I just walk you outside."

"I'm okay! I can walk by myself!" He glared at the guard.

"I'll just go with you, Mr. . . . ."

"You don't want to know my name." He climbed off the stool, headed across the casino and out the door. From the parking lot he looked back at the casino and saw that the guard was still watching him.

He had an urge to flip a bird at the man but restrained himself.

Shit. Goddam! Now he only had forty-one dollars left. He had been thoroughly humiliated at the card table. And he had no place to stay. He got into his car and stared out the window, contemplating how his fortune had changed in such a short time.

He looked up to see a gaggle of college-age boys and girls emerging from the opposite end of the casino, laughing and yelling. The light from a parking lot lamp struck one of the girls; she had long red-brown hair and shook it out before pulling on a ski cap. Her tight ski suit emphasized her slender figure. He caught a fragment of her conversation: She said, "I won a hundred fifty!" Listening to her brag was the BMOC who had taken his own money unfairly.

He smirked. He had a plan to get his money back. *And maybe a lot more than just my money. Poker is a gambler's game. I go for sure things, and the stakes are much higher. Maybe my luck will still come around.*

The students piled into a brand-new lime-green minivan. It started up and went out onto the main road that circled the lake.

He started the Cabriolet and followed at a distance, using only parking lights.

When the van turned onto a side road leading away from the lake, he turned off his lights completely and followed up the icy incline. A half-mile up the dark road the van stopped. He killed the engine on the Cabriolet, partially opened his window, and watched.

The procession of drunken students piled out of the van, and moved up a short walkway to a large ski cabin.

One one thousand two one thousand three one thousand, he counted to sixty slowly, then got out of the car. In his pocket was the stun gun. In his hand, a metal pipe.

Better go around the back. He pulled the stolen parka tightly around him. He didn't know what he was going to do. Maybe just get his money back. Maybe go inside, pretend he's a friend. *Let's just get a look.*

He took a few tentative steps toward the yard, groping in the night for handholds on the trees surrounding the cabin. He could barely see anything in front of him. Laughing voices startled him. He looked over toward the cabin; three boys walked directly toward him. He froze in his tracks.

The boys opened the back of the van and unloaded several

pairs of skis and boots. As they climbed the hill, one of them accidentally dropped two boots.

"Smooth move, queerball!" another boy shouted.

"Shut up. I'll get it in a minute," said the boy who had dropped the boots, hurt at the insult.

"I guess that's why we call you Princess Grace!"

All three boys went into the house, closing the door behind them.

Where the hell are they? He said he would be coming back out to get the boots but they are just sitting there.

A gust of wind cut through the ski mask, making his eyes water. His hands ached with cold. He realized that where he stood, out in the open, was the coldest place he could be. Nearer to the house, the wind wouldn't be so severe. But he would have to cross the open yard to get there.

In about fifteen seconds I could make it over there.

He ran for it. Halfway to the house, he tripped on a tree root submerged in the snow and crashed to the ground. The metal pipe flew out of his hand.

He couldn't see where it landed. *Couldn't have gone more than a few feet.* Laying on the ground he could hear his heavy breathing. The vapor from his breath formed ice crystals on the ski mask. He stood up and brushed some snow off his jacket, then crouched to the ground and felt in the snow for the pipe.

Has to be right here somewhere . . . He took off the mitten and felt through the cold powder on the ground. *Bingo!* he thought and picked up the pipe.

When he looked up, the clumsy kid was walking down the path toward where he had dropped the ski boots. He could see now that it was the same kid who had taken his money.

Princess Grace has returned . . . He hesitated. If Princess Grace looked over in his direction, he would be discovered. But if he moved, it might draw attention in his direction. *What to do.* He ran, ducking around the side of the cabin. He couldn't see to the front of the house and didn't dare look.

"Hey! Who is that?"

Footsteps crunched through the snow.

"Billy, if that's you I'm going to pound your face . . ."

The footsteps drew closer.

The steps slowed down. Princess Grace, BMOC, looked around the side of the house.

Seventeen pounds of cold lead crashed down on the boy's face, sending the cartilage in the bridge of his nose crashing into his brain and shattering the bone around his left eye socket. He fell immediately to the ground, pools of blood flowing out of the nasal cavity. A second blow shattered the right side of his cranium and partially severed his ear from his head. Four days later, a coroner would determine that the boy had most likely died instantly.

Holy shit. That was a stupid thing to do. Goddam. What the hell do I do with Princess Grace's body?

He stood in the silence of the snowy night. No one else was outside. Placing his ear against the window, he heard the murmur of normal conversation. No one knew what had happened just outside the wall of the cabin. He leaned the pipe against the wall of the cabin, then picked up the hands of the corpse.

Drag him into the woods. That'll keep him out of the way.

As he pulled the body away from the house, face down in the snow, he saw that he was leaving a two-foot-wide smear of blood in the snow.

Not a smart thing to do.

He pulled the body next to the cabin. Lighting a match, he saw that the back half of the cabin was elevated on stilts. He blew out the match, then tugged the boy back to the crawl space and dumped him there. He knelt next to the kid and pulled out his wallet. He extracted six one-hundred-dollar bills, leaving the small bills, travelers checks, and credit cards in place, then replaced the wallet in the boy's pocket. *It's just a game!* the boy had said to him earlier. *Well, I just won.*

He retraced his steps and brushed snow over the smears of blood, then returned to the crawl space and covered the body with a pile of snow and leaves.

The *thump, thump* of feet on the redwood over his head alarmed him. He sat perfectly still, crouched beside the dead Princess Grace.

Women's voices outside.

"Good night! Don't get too drunk, Randy!"

"G'night guys!"

Men's voices answering, inside.

"If you get too cold out there, Lisa, you can always crawl back in with me."

"In your dreams, Randy. Your *wet* dreams."

Laughter.

Do they hear me?

Footsteps going away.

They didn't hear me.

He scooted to the other end of the crawl space. There, down a fifty-foot path, he could see a second cabin. Three girls entered. He saw a light go on. The girls were stretching out blankets on cots. He saw them lift a sheet to cover the window facing the boys' cabin.

Wonder if you can see in the side.

He walked cautiously through the woods, around to the side of the tiny cabin.

They didn't even cover the side window they are so stupid. Guess that's why I'm a pro.

He stood by a tree and watched. It was a one-room cabin. One of the girls undressed. The other two were throwing wood on the fire.

Cute girl. Wouldn't sleep with "Randy" though. Saving herself? For me. He smiled at the thought.

She slipped out of her panties.

Holy shit.

She put on a flannel nightgown and climbed into a sleeping bag.

A second girl began undressing. Wearing only warm-up pants, she walked to the wall and turned off the overhead light. *Too much cellulite!* he thought. *Like her friend better.*

He crept up to the window. The girl wearing warm-up pants laid out her ski clothes on a chair and placed them next to the fire, then crawled into her sleeping bag.

His breath clouded the glass of the window. He could no longer see in.

I should leave someone is going to find that body I know it. But how often does opportunity present itself like this? Carpe diem. Seize the day. He smirked. *Seize . . . the night.*

He heard the door open. The third girl, no more than five feet away from him, walked to a woodpile outside the cabin.

Gotta move.

At the speed of thought he found himself on top of her, his hand across her mouth.

"Don't make a sound."

He didn't even realize that he was pulling off her ski pants, ripping off her jeans, anything. It was all kinetic motion, a frenzy of action. He gripped her mouth so tightly that blood flowed from the gash left by his fingernails. It took only a minute.

She was sobbing.

"Shut up! You're making too much noise!" he whispered into her ear. But she couldn't control it. He drew himself out of her warm flesh, never relinquishing his grip on her mouth. With his other hand, he drew her arm around behind her back.

"Put your head down. Right there!" he hissed into her ear, pushing her slowly down, his face next to hers.

She was confused and scared. He bit off her earlobe and forced her head onto the woodpile. Then he drew a log from the woodpile. He didn't look as he pounded it onto the back of her head.

In a second she was still. He rolled the body down onto the ground.

Can't cover this one up. Sloppy. I'm getting sloppy.

He pulled up his pants and walked back to the girls' cabin.

His heart was racing as he stood outside the cabin door. *They can hear me breathing. Too much danger. Too much risk.* He closed his eyes and counted backward from ten. A relaxing exercise he'd learned in prison. It worked. When he opened his eyes, he had regained his sense of purpose.

He pushed open the cabin door.

A girl's voice called out.

"June? Took you long enough."

He stepped in the direction of the voice.

"June?"

His eyes adjusted to the firelight. It was Miss Disgusting Cellulite. He felt the log in his hand and watched it come crashing down at the girl as if wielded by another's hand.

As he stepped toward the other girl, *the cute one,* he felt completely in control, as powerful as a boxer, as elegant as a dancer, as cunning as a spy. He had a gag on the cute girl in a split second.

Gonna take my time. Gonna seize the night. I'm in the driver's seat.

The next forty-five minutes were a primal experience. He simultaneously experienced the thrill of his horrible game and seemed to watch from the outside. While he was there, the time seemed to go by in an instant, like a fragment of a dream. It was like having his birthday and Christmas and the Fourth of July all at the same time.

The next thing he realized he was driving away from the cabins, speeding down the road around Lake Tahoe. *They'll never know what hit them only that a master, a true pro, was visited upon them.* He basked in imagined admiration, postulating that the people who discovered what he had left behind would attribute it to the work of a genius. *How could anyone but me accomplish so much, with four boys just a few feet away? In a crowded ski resort? It is a thing of beauty.*

He was wrong. No one who saw what he had done ever mentioned the word *genius.* His "thing of beauty" was never held up for critical admiration. Only the police report dared to describe what he had left behind.

. . . Karen Simmons, 19, and Lisa Packard, 18, both of Sunnyvale, California [Victim #3 & Victim #4], were pronounced D.O.A. at the scene inside cabin. Bodies discovered approx. 8:30 A.M. PST. Simmons found bent over at waist resting on bed; hands tied to feet with twine. Cause of death for Simmons determined to be massive brain damage caused by blow with log found at scene to sphenoid and upper cranium above right temple, multiple fractures, and hairline fracture in right orbit. Mandible separated from cranium; damage to left incisors. Sternum severed from ribs 4, 5 and 6; ribs 7 through 9 also broken, puncturing left lung causing internal hemorrhaging. Dental imprints ascribed to assailant discovered on both breasts; aureole severed on right breast, not found at scene. Two bite marks determined to be sustained while victim was alive; one presumed postmortem wound. Coital penetration both vaginally and anally; assailant achieved climax.

Body of Lisa Packard found prone, head placed facedown in cabin fireplace, left arm handcuffed to fireplace flue lever with Baker Model 109 police handcuffs; cause of death attributed to smoke inhalation and burns from fire. Eight point source burns (four sets of two pinpoints each), on neck, shoulder, stomach and face (see diagram) attributed to Meshan-Watkins Model 8040 9-Volt Stun Gun. Left foot crushed apparently with ski boot (see sketch). Traces of semen in vagina indicate positive penetration from same assailant; climax not achieved. Partial healing of burn marks and swelling around foot indicate that prolonged suffering occurred; victim was alive in fireplace for estimated forty-five to seventy minutes before death occurred.

22

As the murderer drove away from his crime, the distant sun rose over the hills outside Tahoe, filling his car with the eerie blue light of winter and melting the frost on the windows. Billboards of sequined women in headdresses promoting Reno hotels seemed oddly out of place at five in the morning. He pulled the Cabriolet to the side of the winding road to inspect it for any giveaways. Everything looked normal; there were no stains on the seats. Only the two pairs of skis in the backseat were suspicious. He got out of the car and slid the skis down the heavily wooded hill, watching them disappear into the dark pine forest, one by one. *I'll vacuum out the car when I get back,* he thought. Then he got back in the car and headed toward Reno, listening to the self-proclaimed Wackiest Morning DeeJay on an AM country station.

If I get gasoline and breakfast in Reno, it's totally believable that I was there all night. Who would know any different?

Pick up some keno stubs and chip receipts from the ashtrays and it'll look like I played all night.

After gathering several dozen gambling receipts, he ordered the Jackpot Breakfast at the Sands Casino Restaurant, slowly savoring the ham, bacon, eggs, pancakes, and hash browns, then drank several cups of coffee and flirted with the waitress. *She'll remember me. She'll say I was here.* He tried to stave off his exhaustion with the caffeine and Marlboros; the ashtray had a dozen butts in it when he finished. He left a big tip and said good-bye to the waitress by name. The room, which was nearly empty when he arrived, was now bustling with farmers attending an equipment show.

Driving west out of Reno toward home, he flipped through the radio dial, trying to see if any news stations had picked up on the previous night's activities. There was no mention; the top story was about a retired senator who had died. *I can be home before anybody finds out.*

He was delighted with himself. He had committed the perfect crime. There was nothing to suggest that he had been in Tahoe. No receipts. No one who saw him at a crime scene. *This is the way to go. Be smart. Be careful. Don't get caught.* No trouble at all. He had the perfect alibi in Reno and the paperwork to back it up.

As the sun climbed higher in the sky, he began to feel the warmth of the northern California sun. *Car's getting pretty damned hot.* He turned off the heater, but muggy air from the engine kept blowing over him. *Air-cooled car. This convertible is no VW bug and I bet the thing is malfunctioning, blowing engine exhaust all into the passenger compartment.* He made a mental note to have the car checked out on his return. He scanned the instrument panel to see if the car was overheating, but everything was in order. Still, the car felt hot.

He pulled off his jacket, then his sweater. Even putting on the vent didn't seem to help. *If I stop the engine, maybe it won't start again. I'll just keep driving and probably it'll be okay.*

The air felt unusually humid for winter, and the car was stuffy. He looked in the backseat to inspect for a water leak;

everything was dry. He unbuttoned the top button of his collar, but still felt warm.

Ate too damn much at that restaurant. That's gotta be it. He rolled down both windows and let icy winter air blast in his face. He lit a cigarette in an attempt to settle the queasy feeling coming over him. The smoke tasted weird, as if he'd never smoked before. It had a metallic taste, like he was chewing on aluminum foil.

It's gotta be the car. Exhaust is leaking into the passenger compartment. I'll just pull over and check it without stopping the engine. Gotta be something simple.

He swerved the car to the side of the road and leaned his head back on the headrest. *Just close my eyes for a second . . .* when he opened them, the cigarette had burned all the way to the filter, leaving two inches of ash precariously dangling. He dropped the butt out the window.

The nauseated feeling in his gut grew more severe, more pointed. *Indigestion? Did they give me some bad fucking bacon?* It was a struggle to draw each successive breath. *Poison gas. Has to be poison gas, a train derailed and now I'm choking to death.* He put his hand on his stomach and leaned forward on the wheel. The pain shot down his left arm, as if someone were drawing a cold knife against his skin. *Jesus Christ what the hell is happening.*

The pain expanded through his body like a flash fire. It came from everywhere and nowhere. He closed his eyes.

When he opened them again, he was in the emergency room of the Northern Plains Catholic Hospital. A nurse held his hand. He couldn't tell if he was lying down or standing up. From the bedsheets and pillow, he determined that he must be on a bed. *What is this how did I get here.* He flipped his head sharply to the side but was stopped abruptly by several tubes in his nose.

"You've suffered a minor heart attack, Mr. DeVries."

His eyes had trouble focusing. He was looking up at a young nurse who might have come straight out of central casting, right down to the little cap on her forehead. It seemed strangely funny to him.

"Whah?" he said, startled.

"You're in the hospital. Don't talk, Mr. DeVries."

"Caw me . . . Ted," he gurgled, feeling pain in his throat when he talked, unsure of where he was or how he got there.

"Just lay back and rest, Mr. DeVries. The doctor will be right with you."

Jumbled thoughts raced through his drugged consciousness. *I'm not Mr. DeVries . . . don't call me that . . . maybe Mr. DeVries had a heart attack and I'm really okay . . . got to stop them before they operate on the wrong guy.*

"Tad . . . name . . . is Ted . . ."

The nurse cut him off.

"It's too much effort for you to talk. Save your breath. Try to go back to sleep, Mr. DeVries."

He summoned all his strength. *They might operate and if they don't know who they're operating on, they might do something they shouldn't do.*

"Theo . . . doe . . . Wob-it . . ." he struggled to get the words out, past the tubes, through the phlegm. "Bun . . . nee." *They're going to cut me . . . got to stop them.* "Tad oh . . . Wob-it . . . Bun . . . nee."

"Don't talk, Mr. DeVries. Save your energy."

"Bun . . . ntee," he sputtered, then quit trying. It was no use. The drugs, the tubes, and his weakened condition conspired to keep the words from getting out. He stared at the flickering fluorescent lights, watching them go in and out of focus, then drifted back into unconsciousness.

Becky Jacobson, the nurse on duty, saw him relax into a deep slumber, then checked his vital signs. He would obviously live. Heart attack victims said the strangest things sometimes. Becky never gave them any credence. She chuckled to herself. A guy could be dying, and he says he wants a bunny rabbit?

23

An army of defiant weeds had taken Web's carefully planted gardens hostage. The tulip bulbs had been dug up by squirrels. Kneeling in the dirt by a Chrysler Imperial rose bush, Web tugged on a twig. It snapped like a toothpick. Dead. The sight gave him a sinking feeling in his stomach.

Pondering what to do next, he stared at the forelorn plot. In the fuss and fury of helping Maria, he had neglected his only personal project. He pulled one of his seven gardening books out of the shiny new wheelbarrow and flipped to the index. "Weeds, Pp. 43, 44, 51, 60, 80–85." He flipped to the first citation, but when he had only gotten halfway down the page, a disgusting sound stopped him.

Less than five feet away, Mud the dog was vomiting. The animal held his head sheepishly down, vomited again, then took a few steps away and laid on his side, panting.

"Mud, what is it, boy?"

The dog looked sadly up at his owner, his legs shaking.

Web ran into the house and flipped through the Yellow Pages till he found a twenty-four-hour veterinarian. He sped to the clinic with Mud, leaving his gardening tools and books in the yard.

Two hours and almost three hundred dollars later, Web learned that Mud had eaten a variety of bulbs in the garden, some of which were poisonous. "We just need to keep him overnight for observation," said the vet.

When Web arrived back home, heavy rain was soaking his new books and destroying the shiny finish on his gardening tools. Swearing, Web shoved the wheelbarrow into the garage and laid the books out side by side to dry. Angry, he stomped in the living room and plopped down on the couch, frustrated that his beloved gardens would have to wait another day. He flipped on the television.

A series of justifications ran through Web's mind as he flipped through the channels. *I'll just watch some tube and relax a bit.* He hardly ever watched commercial television. *"Jeopardy"* was on. *This is supposed to be mentally challenging. I'll just see if I can answer some of the questions.* But in the back of his mind, Web knew why he had the set on, even if he didn't want to admit it to himself. Driving home from work, he had heard television promotions for that night's "Suspect at Large" program. They promised to reveal new information about a crime that had gotten national prominence in the previous week. A crime that fit into a familiar pattern that no one else seemed to recognize. "Tune in tonight to see a police sketch of the Spring Break Murderer. Only on 'Suspect at Large,'" the deep-voiced announcer had said.

He reflected on how the cold-blooded media attached a catch phrase to a gruesome crime as if it were a new brand of toothpaste. "The Spring Break Murders." Like the "Central Park Jogger," the "McDonald's Massacre," or the "Hillside Strangler," it was a nickname that simultaneously glorified the criminal and distanced the public from the tragedy suffered by the victims.

Still he watched the commercials and waited for "Suspect at Large" to begin. The anchor, Clinton Bernard, was the same sleazebag who had confronted Joyce in his yard. Bernard appeared in front of a wall covered with FBI-style mug shots and police sketches, walking past the faces while intoning a prolonged, teasing introduction to his show like a perverse litany.

"All the criminals you see behind me have yet to be apprehended. Accused of the most heinous atrocities in human comprehension, these monsters still walk freely among us, their deeds unpunished. Look at these faces carefully. You may see them anywhere—at the grocery store or on a city street. In a crowd at a football game or next to you in a lonely elevator. For every one of them is a . . . suspect at large."

Web grimaced at the purple prose but attentively watched while Clinton Bernard, apparently half-man, half-marionette, shuffled papers during the ominous theme song.

"Last week, tragedy struck in Tahoe, disrupting the spring vacation of eight clean-cut honor students from UC Davis. By the end of one long, horrifying night, four of them would be dead—innocent lives snuffed out in their prime at the hands of a murderous cretin who still walks the streets of America, mingling with decent people as if he had done no wrong." Clinton Bernard stared into the camera, as if he personally suffered all the tragedy the world had to offer. Web hated the announcer.

"But perhaps this psycho's days of freedom are numbered. Investigative reporters for 'Suspect at Large' have unearthed a police composite sketch made by the Tahoe sheriff's department of a mysterious man seen playing poker with one of the victims earlier that grim evening. Before we go to our reporter on the scene of the Spring Break Murders, we have to ask every citizen of this good country to perform one duty in the name of justice for all. Memorize this face. Vindicate the innocent victims . . ."

They flashed a charcoal police composite sketch onto the screen. He did not hear what Clinton Bernard said next.

The police sketch was eerily familiar.

Web stared at the dark eyebrows.

The smug grin.

The slight wrinkles in the forehead.

The bushy dark hair.

The cold, emotionless eyes.

The air of confidence that came through, even in a drawing.

Jesus Christ, thought Web. *How can it be?*

Even considering the blurry details and the erasure marks of the police sketch, Web was shaken by the realization that the drawing could easily be that of Ted Bundy's twin. The hairline was a little higher, but other than that, the image was nearly identical to Bundy.

How is it possible?

They cut to a commercial of Bill Cosby pushing sugary pudding. Web fumbled around the videotape recorder and stuffed a tape into the machine. He couldn't remember how the damn thing worked. He pulled the manual out from under the tape machine and hurriedly read the directions.

Set the channel. Push record and play at the same time. He did what he was supposed to do and looked into the top of the machine. The tape was moving. The record light was on.

He watched the rest of the program, so transfixed by the show that when the phone rang, he let the answering machine pick it up. He hoped that they would replay the sketch so he could capture it on his videotape.

After fifteen minutes of repeating the details Web already knew from the newspapers, Clinton Bernard came back on the air and repeated his plea. They showed the drawing again, moving the camera across it in a cheesy video effect. When they pulled out to show the full face, Web just stared.

Bundy's twin?

He mentally tried out different theories, attempting to fit the facts to reality.

A copycat?

If someone who already had a screw loose realized that he looked a lot like Theodore Robert Bundy, then he may have decided to become the killer . . . or the other way around. The guy revered Theodore, followed his every move, and tried to make himself appear as similar as possible to his idol . . .

Or a relative. Like Gary and Thaddeus Lewdington, the Ohio brothers with a penchant for .22 caliber rifles . . . I never heard that Bundy had a full brother . . .

Or is it just me? Have I gone over the edge? he thought.

After the show ended, he went to a dusty bookshelf in the attic. In a black vinyl notebook, cracked with age, were yellowed clippings from newspapers and magazines ten years old that he had collected while searching for Vicki. He flipped to a picture of Ted Bundy, taken after his final capture. The mask of friendliness, the warm grin that covered up such a vicious heart, still infuriated him. Back in the living room, Web rewound the tape and played it again. He wasn't imagining this. Anyone would see the resemblance. *But how is it possible?*

Web picked up the phone and dialed a number. He felt like an imbecile calling Jack Reynolds at home after their last embarrassing encounter. He would pretend it was a social call.

"Jack, this is Web Sloane."

"I thought you probably hated my guts by now," laughed the FBI agent.

"Nah. I want to patch things up. Still up for grabbing a beer?"

Reynolds paused. "Tell you the truth, my wife's out of town. What're you doing tonight?"

"Nothing. Wanna meet at the Marriot?"

"Downtown?"

"Sure. I'm buying," said Web.

"No way. I'll pick up the tab," said Reynolds, laughing.

"I'll argue with you when I get there, but your money's no good tonight," said Web.

"We'll see. Catch you down there in, what, an hour?"

"Right."

When Web arrived at the half-empty hotel bar overlooking the city, Reynolds had already stationed himself at a corner table. The waitress refused Web's credit card, winking broadly at Reynolds. The two men swapped tales of daughters and baseball teams while drinking from one frosted pitcher of Heineken after another, carefully avoiding the subject both knew was taboo.

Finally, when he felt safely drunk, Web opened the Pandora's box.

"Did you happen to see 'Suspect at Large' tonight?"

Reynolds laughed. "I wondered if it was just coincidence that you called three minutes after it ended."

"Can you talk about it?"

"It's not in my jurisdiction, but it is a company case. We know he crossed a state line—California to Nevada. Can't talk about the case—especially to you. I can talk about the TV show, though."

"You told me to back off, to get back to teaching and all that," said Web hesitantly.

"I know what I said, but I came down here to meet you, didn't I? I'm not working now," said Reynolds, twisting a napkin in his hand.

"So what did you think of the show?" Web asked.

"Piece of doo-doo. Like all those shows. I hate them. But I watched anyway, just to see what they would show."

"You think the murders there are connected with . . ."

Reynolds cut him off.

"With your little notebook filled with pictures? Uh uh. No way."

"How come?"

"The girls up in Endocino were hit by what Quantico calls a 'Type 1 Methodical,' or 'Organized,' killer. A guy who plans things out and removes the evidence. Guys like John Wayne Gacy or Lucas are Methodical. These Type 1's usually kidnap the victim first, then hide evidence. Your textbook Type 1 is very careful. Very hard to catch."

He watched Web's face.

"Is this too much for you? I'm just explaining why we're sure it's different guys," asked Reynolds.

Web shook his head. "Not at all. I've read extensively about psych profiling. I don't see the relevance here, but I'm no expert."

"I'm no expert myself, but I did attend a three-week seminar in Quantico in 1980."

"What's the other type?" Web asked.

"I was going to get to that. The Tahoe victims were murdered by what we call a 'Type 2 Disorganized Asocial' killer—a guy who just gets all worked up and lets it all out in a rage. Richard Speck was a Type 2. Mr. Tahoe is a classic Disorganized Asocial. He was a slob—left a big mess, just seemed to be taking out his anger on the world. The guy in Vine County was a textbook Type 1. Different M.O. Different kind of suspect." Reynolds spoke as if addressing a novice FBI trainee.

Web took in the lesson but couldn't quite believe it.

"You can't just classify murderers into two groups like that and put up a wall between them. There *have* been killers who committed both kinds of murders. You know, a string of serial murders, then a crazed burst," said Web.

"From what I've seen and learned, they're strictly Type 1 Methodical or Type 2 Disorganized Asocial. Two completely different animals with different motives. We have separate methods for identifying and locating each kind," said Reynolds, the patient teacher pointing out the student's error. "I can't think of anyone who committed both types of murder."

"What about Bundy?" asked Web.

"What about him?" Reynolds asked, slightly startled.

"He killed in isolated incidents for years. What you call 'Organized' or 'Type 1.' But then, in Florida, he went four-plus bonkers and became what you call 'disorganized.' He's an example of a mix of both types, so it's not impossible."

"I guess he is the lone exception that proves the rule. Our profiling department has done case histories on four hundred fifty serial killers and found that the two types are fundamentally different. You just don't get crossover."

"But you do get crossover. At least, you have once. And you might be again right now in Vine County and Tahoe." Web said.

"Bundy was . . . an exception. I'll give you that much." Reynolds took a long slow sip of beer from his frosted glass. Then he leaned in close to Web, as if divulging the dirty secret of his profession. "I spent six years chasing him. He was technically a lust-driven serial killer in the broader sense of the classification. But he was unlike any of the others I've ever seen, and I've seen a lot. Theodore had a different axe to grind; he was an aberration among aberrations. He was smart as hell, knew a lot about police work, and had a degree in psychology."

Reynolds sighed. "My guess as to why he doesn't fit into the established pattern is that he *knew* about psychological profiling, *knew* we looked for two distinct types, and had the personal control to mix up his M.O. intentionally just to throw a wrench into the works. Your garden-variety serial killer doesn't have that kind of know-how or control. Every agent who had any contact with Bundy agrees that he transcended any attempts at classification. Something about him defied the ordinary rules, he was beyond studies of criminal behavior, beyond even the darkest reaches of abnormal psychology. Dozens of the best criminal shrinks *in the world* talked to him over the years and not one could get a reading." Reynolds looked down into his glass and spoke softly. "But we weren't trying to explain Theodore. We just wanted to stop the son of a bitch. And we did."

The FBI agent drummed his fingers on the table. "Just because one criminal in a million doesn't fit into the game plan is no reason to throw out the rulebook."

Web leaned in and spoke in the same conspiratorial tone. "I think our man is more like Bundy than you'd like to admit, and the murders *are* related. We've got some sort of copycat who studied Bundy's every move. Even tries to make himself look like Theodore."

Reynolds grinned. "Is this why you asked me out?"

"Yeah, I guess."

"Well, here I am. You got me. What do you want me to say? That for the second time in a hundred years we have a psychopath who has the intelligence and willpower to change his behavior?"

"Did you see the police sketch on 'Suspect at Large'?"

"Saw that sketch a week ago. The bureau is a little faster on the draw than network TV."

"Did you see any resemblance to Theodore?"

"Web, it was a police sketch. A drawing from memory. There are thousands of guys who look sort of like that."

Reynolds recaptured the chilly tone he had used earlier. "I don't want to talk business anymore. Bundy's been dead two years, but you're going to see him in every police sketch for the next fifty. Reacquaint yourself with reality. If you really can't sleep at nights, if this is driving you insane, get a shrink. Or go talk to someone who saw Bundy die. But don't start talking ghosts with me. I helped put him behind bars. I celebrated when the bastard fried."

Web cracked his knuckles. "I'm not talking about ghosts. It could be a copycat who idolized the guy. Bundy got hundreds of fan letters from people all over the country. He got marriage proposals, love letters. There could be one of them who wants to relive Bundy's life."

"Forget it. You're not going to draw me into this—this theory of yours."

"I know I told you this was a social visit. But the coincidences are overwhelming. I can't be the only one who sees the pattern."

"I'm not blind and I'm not stupid. I knew why you asked me out for a beer. I came because I wanted to talk to you before someone else arrests you for harassing the police. I've known you a long time, and I hate seeing a grown man run around like a nut. Next thing I know I'll see you downtown, passing out little typed tracts showing why the Pope is dealing drugs and that the Queen of England is a man," said Reynolds. "Don't make this another Anchorage."

Anchorage. Reynolds had to bring that up. Years earlier, during the search for Vicki, when Web was developing the first version of SKID, he drew from thin air a suspect that had relocated to Alaska. Web had gotten "hot" correlations on eight out of a possible nine characteristics. He persuaded the FBI and Washington State Police each to send task forces to Alaska, in dark, cold January no less. Six men plus Web spent nearly a month in Anchorage. They found a man and all but pronounced him guilty of the Washington murders.

Web asked, begged, to interrogate the suspect. Although it was against "official" rules, the FBI trusted Web and thought of him as one of their own. Five minutes alone with the suspect, and Web realized he wasn't guilty. Web loudly pronounced as much to everyone who would listen. The prosecutor was furious. Everything indicated the suspect, except Web Sloane's damned hunch.

After Web had satisfied himself that the Alaska man hadn't killed Vicki, he expected the various forces instantly to redirect their efforts to the original case. But inertia and the demands of bureaucracy kept them tied up in Anchorage. Web had many arguments with the FBI and the police.

Two months after his arrest, the suspect established an alibi: air tickets and hotel receipts showed definitively that he was not in Washington during the critical period. While he was later convicted of another murder, he wasn't the Seattle killer, just as Web had proclaimed. But by that time, Web had ruffled too many feathers, called too many influential people awful names.

The Seattle prosecutor and the bureau caught endless flack for the "irregular" escapade. Reynolds was relocated to San Francisco, although everyone knew he was blameless. Web had tracked down one murderer, but not the right one. His flare-up earned him the name at the FBI, behind his back, of "ninety percent Sloane." Ninety percent genius. Ten percent crazy. In secret, many law enforcement officials admired him, but his method was too chaotic for an organization of any size; working with him could put their careers in jeopardy.

A surge of anger tore through Web. He *wasn't* crazy. This *wasn't* another Anchorage.

"Go to hell, Jack."

"What'd you say?"

"I said go to hell. The pieces are there. You just can't put them together, because you expect everything to fit into a textbook pattern. Sometimes killers don't follow your rules."

Web jumped up, handed the waitress a twenty-dollar bill, and left the bar without saying good-bye.

Driving home, the phrase "reacquaint yourself with reality" sat heavily in Web's mind. He couldn't take Reynolds's insult lying down, that his interpretation of the murders was on par with the Pope selling drugs. Copycat? Brother? Fan? Look-alike?

Was it possible that Bundy had been innocent, and the real murderer remained at large, as Bundy had repeatedly insisted during his trials? Web knew about the notorious case of John Halliday and Timothy Evans. Halliday was responsible for a string of particularly loathsome sex murders in London between 1940 and 1950. Halliday murdered Evans's wife and fourteen-month-old daughter, then convinced Evans himself, a slightly retarded day-worker, to confess to the deed. Although innocent, Evans was tried, then hanged; Halliday continued his murderous rampage for several more years.

If another man had committed the crimes attributed to Bundy, then he would still be at large. It would make sense that he looked like Bundy; that would explain the eyewitnesses who picked him out of police lineups.

Bundy, innocent? Web's mind ground back to the videotape he had seen of the murderer's confession. *That one played saxophone.* It was a detail that no one except the man who killed Vicki could possibly know.

Web considered the chain of evidence. The man in the videotape had certainly killed Vicki. But the videotapes were made two weeks before the execution, by a minister, not by the prison officials or police working on the case. Web recognized the weak link: Was the man who confessed the same one who was executed? He had to know for certain.

One photo of the executed prisoner would be all Web required for proof. Then he would explore all the other explanations for the murders occurring in northern California.

He intended to eliminate theories one by one until what was left had to be the truth. He had to work by himself. Without the goddam FBI. Maybe he was crazy, but if he was to sleep at night, he had to know for certain that Bundy was dead.

That night Web called Delta Airlines. His schedule would allow him to spend four days in Florida. No one would miss him; UC Berkeley and Joyce's high school both had spring break the following week. Joyce was planning to spend it at her grandparents' house.

It took only three phone calls to set up a meeting with the prison doctor who had attended Bundy's execution. Web was friendly with the Florida State Police, because his daughter had been a Bundy victim and because he had helped them tap into the SKID crime-tracking system. Detective Reilly didn't even question why he wanted to meet the doctor—he trusted Web that much.

The drive to the Starke, Florida, prison brought up painful memories of his last trip there. Not much had changed; it seemed like the mammoth penitentiary had gotten a new coat of paint, but nothing could conceal the desolation of a building so filled with human misery.

He drove through two guard gates before leaving his car in a numbered stall by the outside wall. A guard escorted him through the front door; then he went through the metal detector three times. Eventually, they determined his Cross pen made the alarm sound. He left it in a plastic box with the entrance guard.

Dr. Wayne Kessler was squinting through half-glasses at a typed report as Web entered his office. The gray-haired doctor glanced up.

"Be with you in a moment, Mr. Sloane," he said officiously.

He dragged his finger down a page of the report, flipped to the final page, and signed it.

"Alex Kessler. Nice to meet you. Detective Reilly told me all about you."

"Web Sloane."

They shook hands, and Web sat in a chair across from the doctor. He tried to lean back, but it was nailed to the floor. They have to be mighty cautious in a high-security prison.

"Paperwork. It's all I do nowadays," said the doctor.

"I know what you mean."

Kessler shook some papers at Web. "Prisoner died of kidney failure. Eighty-eight years old. Decent old fella— he's been with us since 1955. Fought in World War I." The doctor grinned slightly. "Killed half a dozen people in a 1946 bank robbery."

"Strange business," said Web.

"Well, that's what you come to expect when you're a prison physician. What can I do for you, Mr. Sloane?"

"I was hoping to see Theodore Bundy's medical records. Especially the certificate of death. You were the examining doctor?"

"That I was. I remember Bundy well. I never knew what all the fuss was about; we had lots of worse criminals in here. Still do. But the media folks just loved him. What do you want with his records?"

"It's a long story, but . . . Bundy killed my daughter. I just wanted to . . ."

"You don't have to tell me more. It's a matter of public record. You didn't really have to come to me, but it would have taken a lot longer to go the Freedom of Information route."

The doctor pressed a button and spoke into an intercom. "Rick? Could I have the file on Theodore Robert Bundy? He's in the blue cabinet, you know, deceased."

A voice came back on the intercom. "Yessir, mein commandante. I vill haf the file for you in an instant."

He lifted his finger.

Kessler cracked one of his sly grins. "Rick's one of our inmates from the criminally insane ward. We try to put them to work where we can. He's not even German— actually a kid from Orlando. Don't let him scare you; the work is good for him."

"A rehabilitation program?"

"Well, sort of. We try to keep the mental patients doing productive work. It's a combination of rehabilitation plus the fact that our staff budgets keep getting cut. I can't afford as big a professional staff as I'd like, so I fill in with prisoners." The doctor smirked again.

A tall black man in prison blues marched into the room, handed a thick blue folder to Dr. Kessler, snapped a neat Nazi salute, then turned on his heels and left.

"These are just the medical records," said Kessler. "There's an entire filing cabinet elsewhere containing his legal records, psychiatric evaluation and testimony, and prison records. That's not my bailiwick. All I have are copies of the physical exams, the injuries, and the death certificate. I hope this is what you're looking for."

"This'll do fine, for a start," said Web.

The first page had the familiar admitting photo of Bundy, and the file was thick with records of various physical examinations administered during his decade on death row, as well as reports of all ailments. A bout with the flu took up three pages. A head injury, probably from a fight, took up ten. He flipped through several typewritten reports, straight to the back.

The last page was a death certificate, listing the cause of death simply as cardiac arrest. A photocopied sketch of a human body was marked with X's where the electrodes had touched his flesh and was signed by Kessler.

"Is this all? Shouldn't there be fingerprints or something?" asked Web.

"I examined him. I fill in the records and mark the time of death to demonstrate that the punishment is humane. His execution *was* humane, by the way. It took only one go-round, and I heard no heartbeat. I remember back a while ago when we had to jolt a poor man four times." The doctor winked nervously at Web; it was almost a tic.

"I was really hoping for a morgue photo—don't you do a photo?"

"Not in capital punishment cases. You know, the abolitionists see the burns on a body or how distorted the facial features get, and they'll have fits. I only did a quick-and-dirty autopsy, not the usual involved procedure. After all, there's no doubt about the prisoner's identity or the cause of death."

"You looked at him, didn't you?"

"Yes I did."

"And what did he look like?"

"His head was shaved, of course. One eye, the left I think, separated from the socket. See the crescent mark on the autopsy sketch?"

Web looked at the drawing and nodded.

"He bit off his lower lip and his tongue. And there were the usual third-degree burns from the electrodes, charred flesh on the head and leg. But don't share that with the anti-death-penalty nuts, okay?"

"You're *sure* you got a good look. It was Bundy, right?"

"Wasn't Mother Theresa. Is that all you wanted to know? That we executed Bundy? I would have told you that on the phone."

"What happened to the corpse?"

"It's right there on the form."

He looked at the Final Request for Condemned Prisoner paper. In Bundy's own handwriting, it said, "I prohibit any scientific examination of my body and declare that I wish my earthly remains to be cremated, the ashes to be entrusted to Reverend Jimmie Lee Gray of the Church of the Holy Saviour in Gainesville, Florida."

"Did you see him before the execution?" asked Web.

"A week before. He was in good health. Have to be, if we're going to execute 'em. One guy got a stay for three weeks so we could do an appendectomy. Was the scandal of the prison hospital. But Theodore was in good shape."

"I mean on *that day.* Did you see him on his last day?"

"Only after they strapped him in."

"Did you talk to him?"

"Not allowed unless the prisoner asks for it. Besides, by the time I get in there they have the leather mask covering his face. Privacy issues, you know. The ACLU liberals see to that."

"Who *did* see him that day?"

"His minister and the death room guards. Probably the warden."

"Could I talk to the warden?"

"Sure. Is that all you wanted?"

"Yes."

Web asked the same questions of Tom Barber, a wiry but handsome man of about fifty wearing an off-the-rack gray suit and black shoes. He had been stationed in his office the morning of the execution to deal with reporters and to wait for any last-minute stay that might have come from the governor or the Supreme Court. Of course, there had been no stay. But Barber hadn't seen Bundy die either.

"Who escorted him to the chair, then?" asked Web.

"The Capital Team," replied Barber.

"The what?"

"Specialists from Tallahassee. They take a three-week training course on how to prepare, what to do. A regular guard doesn't know how to handle the oddities of an execution."

"Why not?" asked Web.

"Prison guards make six dollars an hour. They think inmates will always behave like inmates. But a condemned man on his final walk might try anything. The Capital Team is drawn from the SWAT unit that guards the governor's mansion. They're real pros."

Barber tipped back his chair to close the door before continuing.

"We used to do all the preparation with our own guards. But in 1986, there was a kid who fought tooth and nail. Daniel Thomas Morris, his name was. Took seven of our guys fifteen minutes to strap him in, with thirty-eight witnesses watching the whole damn show."

Web stared at the warden in disbelief.

"So the guards escorting Bundy to the chair didn't know him?"

"Of course they knew of him, and the regular guards know Bundy. Capital Team is trained in the martial arts and in psychology, how to talk a guy into getting into the chair. Of course, Ted didn't give us no problems."

"Did the witnesses in the execution chamber see him strapped in?"

Barber lit a cigarette and stared Web down.

"No. Of course not. After we had that big fight with

Danny Morris, the anti-death-penalty folks picked up on it and had a field day. I can't blame anyone for struggling—hell, that's what I would do. So our Capital Team gets him in the chair, strapped in, mask on. Then they open the venetian blinds. The witnesses only see the execution. Saves everyone a lot of grief and lawsuits."

"So no one saw Bundy executed," said Web.

Barber leaned on his desk.

"That's not what I said. You sound like a broken record. Forty-two witnesses saw him die."

"*After* the mask was on."

"Yes, but they saw him executed. I don't know what your problem is."

"Do you think I could see the chamber?" Web asked.

"You're not going to write about it? I won't see a bunch of leaflets or something next week?"

"On my word."

The warden looked Web over cautiously.

"I suppose I could show you."

The warden escorted Web to the room where the grisly sentence was administered. The warden pointed out the various rooms and their functions. The chamber itself was not much bigger than a walk-in closet, with an old-fashioned wooden three-legged chair bolted to the floor. The executioner was stationed in another room behind the chair. The person who completed the lethal circuit had a special entrance and exit to preserve anonymity.

The spectator gallery faced the criminal. Witnesses had a separate entrance and sat in four rows of folding chairs behind the window. Double sets of venetian blinds blocked their view until the last possible moment. The warden's lecture was complete and well rehearsed. Plenty of people had toured the execution chamber previously, but none of them asked such an outrageous and obvious question: *How can you be sure you've killed the right man?*

An hour later, driving away from the prison, Web felt a sense of dread come over him. *No one who really knew Bundy saw him on his final day. Forty-two witnesses saw the execution of a man with a leather mask covering his face. There is no postmortem photograph. The doctor did not take fingerprints from the corpse. The men who escorted him to the death chamber were not personally familiar with the prisoner. And Bundy, according to his own wishes, was cremated within hours of the execution.*

Bundy had escaped from prison twice in his life. He never would have been caught again except for his own stupidity; he disappeared completely after the second escape, living in Florida under an assumed name, where he committed the most heinous crimes of his career.

Was there a *third* escape?

Web knew that he was the last person who could credibly put forth such an idea. Reynolds considered Web crazy for believing that a serial killer of any kind was at large. Any objective person would assert that a claim that Bundy might still be alive would fall into the same wacko-theory category as beliefs starring Elvis or John F. Kennedy, especially if the only proponent of such a theory was the father of one of Bundy's victims.

But as outrageous as the notion might be, *no one really saw Bundy die.*

If it were true, if Bundy somehow escaped, the refusal of sane persons to believe such a notion would work to his advantage. In this E-ticket scenario, the electric chair, believed to be the ultimate punishment, would have instead provided Theodore Robert Bundy with the perfect alibi. What law enforcement agency looks for a dead man?

24

The Reverend Jimmie Lee Gray agreed to meet Web later that afternoon at the minister's Gainesville home. Gray had spent the night before the execution praying with Bundy; possibly the last person truly familiar with the condemned killer to spend any length of time with him. Additionally, it was Gray who convinced Bundy at the eleventh hour to confess to the specifics of his crimes, and Gray was the person entrusted with his ashes.

Web was surprised to discover that the minister lived in a modest tract house in one of the suburbs surrounding Gainesville, a single-story stucco house with a small lawn, probably built in the fifties. A plump young girl in jeans and a pink blouse, wearing a cross around her neck, greeted him at the door and escorted him to the Reverend's study, a windowless room in the back that may have once been an extra bedroom.

"He'll be with you in a moment," the girl said, directing Web to a leather chair facing the desk, then shutting the door as she left.

Web noticed something unusual about the study as soon as he entered. Very few books were on the shelves—just some well-worn bibles and a dusty encyclopedia. Prominently featured around the study were photos of the minister with various celebrities: Anita Bryant, the governor of Florida, Rosalynn and Jimmy Carter, the Reverend Jesse Jackson. All the rest of the shelves were filled with audiotapes—*Books-on-Tape,* religious cassettes, *The Complete Spoken Word Audio Bible, King James Edition.*

The minister entered the study from an outside door and stared up at the ceiling a moment, as if in prayer. He wore overalls and his hands and knees were covered with earth. *Probably sixty or sixty-five,* Web thought. *Looks a little like Burl Ives. The perfect Southern gentleman.*

"Good afternoon, Mr. Sloane. Nice you could come." Gray's voice was as resonant as an organ in a country church and carried the warm accent of the Deep South.

"Nice to meet you."

The minister sat behind his desk.

"I'd shake your hand, but I've just been working in my garden. On a day like today, I just love to work the earth," he said, smiling.

"Yes—I love gardening too, though you'll see I can't really shake your hand," said Web, holding up his cast. The minister didn't react one way or the other.

"My assistant Sue Anne told me about your daughter . . . I'm so sorry. I prayed for you and her when I heard."

"Thank you." Web drew a deep breath. "I was hoping to ask you about Theodore Bundy. The final night of his life, in particular."

The minister stared at the corner behind Web's head, as if deep in thought. It didn't jibe with his direct one-on-one manner of speaking.

"Mr. Sloane, I know you blame Theodore for what happened to your family. It's perfectly understandable that you would. But God can forgive all men. I feel the boy is safe in His hands now. He was completely repentant in his last days."

Web grimaced. He didn't want a sermon.

"I was more interested in specific details. Were you the last person to see him?"

"Heavens, no. Guards led him away from the cell that terrible morning. And dozens of witnesses, you know . . ."

"But you were the last one who was personally familiar with Bundy to see him."

Gray leaned back in his chair. Still looking ahead, he reached into the top drawer of the desk and extracted a pipe and a pouch of cherry tobacco. He filled the pipe, tamped it down, and lit it before answering: the professorial stall.

"I had never thought of it that way before. He spoke to his mother on the phone, but I suppose the last friendly face he saw was mine. Why do you ask?"

Web didn't want to explain his entire chain of reasoning, so he chose to get the minister to talk in his own terms.

"Did he repent? I wanted to know what his *face* was like. Did he look different? Was he a changed man?" Web wondered if his gambit would work.

"He was a changed man. That I can tell you. But I can't describe to you what his face was like."

"What do you mean?"

"I've been blind for forty-one years."

Web blinked. He leaned forward, unable to respond. After a moment he sputtered out, "I'm sorry, I didn't know."

"No need to say 'sorry,' son, it's not your fault. I have long since come to accept it. It was how God directed me into the fold, I suppose. He works in mysterious ways. But," he chuckled, "I do get around pretty well. I knew one woman in my church for twelve years—even had her over for dinner a few times—before she knew. I can see a little—you know, shapes and movement. Between that and my assistants, I do all right."

Web's mind reeled. He made enough small talk before leaving so that he wouldn't seem rude, but he was obsessed with this new coincidence. *The last man to spend any time with Bundy was blind. And Bundy had specifically requested this minister over all others.*

As he stood up to leave, the minister got up with him.

"I have some tapes of my sermons you might find comforting, perhaps you would like to take a set with you."

"That would be very kind."

"You know, our church is a nonprofit institution, but I have to charge something for the tapes to those who can afford it. Do you think forty-five dollars for a set of nine tapes would be too much to ask?"

Web chuckled. "I'm not sure I have that much on me . . ."

"We take Visa and American Express."

"Sure. I'll take the tapes."

"It's been a pleasure, Mr. Sloane."

Sue Anne, the plump assistant, took his credit card and disappeared for a few moments. She returned, a frown on her face.

"Mr. Sloane, unfortunately we're out of the *Time of Need* tape set. Do you think you could pick another?"

"What others are there?"

"Come on down to the basement. I'll show you."

He followed her down the stairs to a storeroom piled high with boxed sets of tapes. He was going to pick one out at random when he noticed a display case on the opposite side of the basement. Prominently featured was a photo of Bundy holding a bible with his arm around Gray.

"Just pick anything for me," Web said, then walked toward the photo as if drawn to it. It was a miniature Theodore Bundy shrine—encased in a deep frame were several photos of the killer with the reverend. And an urn.

"What's in the urn?" Web asked.

"Those are the final remains of Mr. Bundy."

She called everyone "Mr." Just like *The New York Times.*

"Oh. Of course."

Web stared at the bizarre display of Bundy pretending to

be pious, not even noticing that the girl was right next to him.

"Mr. Sloane? Mr. Sloane, your tapes. I picked my favorite set, *Let God Purify Your Life.*"

"Thanks."

He took the tapes and quickly found his way outside.

Too distracted to drive, Web stopped at a coffee shop a mile from the reverend's home. An hour later he still stared at an uneaten pile of mashed potatoes, wondering if he was losing his mind. *Did Bundy die?* One side of him said "of course." But his irrational instinct began to see a more sombre picture, like a castle appearing through the fog. He had stumbled across a series of bizarre facts that could be construed as coincidences; but interpreted differently, they drew a far more ominous picture. He sipped at his iced tea.

Once, he'd attended a lecture by the Amazing Randi, the famous magician-turned-skeptic. Randi was a professional "debunker" who routinely offered one hundred thousand dollars to anyone who could demonstrate scientifically that ESP existed or that horoscopes were real or that UFOs had visited earth. The only proof he would accept was hard physical evidence. Randi had never paid out one cent. His motto was Extraordinary Claims Require Extraordinary Proof.

Web knew his theory sounded like something from a conspiracy buff. Any skeptic could drive holes through his suspicion that Bundy was still alive. He needed physical evidence to convince others, but more importantly, to convince himself.

What would qualify? What could convince a rational skeptic of even the possibility that the killer was alive?

Web was absentmindedly stirring his iced tea when he heard a cry. He looked up. A young Hispanic busboy, carrying too many things at once, dropped two full ashtrays on the ground, spilling them all over the floor next to Web's booth.

"I'm sorry, man, sorry." The boy was very worried about his stumble; he set down his tray of dishes and began sweeping up the ashes into a newspaper.

"That's okay."

Web snapped out of his absentminded reverie.

He knew what he must do. Only one problem: It was illegal.

Web's return flight didn't leave till late Sunday night. He spent the remainder of Saturday in the Gainesville library, reading old newspapers. He still wasn't sure he would have the nerve to go through with his plan, but staying in town left his options open.

Sunday morning he woke before dawn in the dingy Ramada room and ordered a continental breakfast and a Sunday paper from room service. Web felt tense and dry-throated as if he had a hangover, though he hadn't had anything to drink the night before.

What if I get arrested? he thought. Then he would look extremely foolish, and all his subterfuge about the trip being "scholarly research" would be exposed. He would have to tell his family and colleagues the true purpose of his trip to Florida.

When he opened the *TV Guide* he knew that he had gone beyond doubt. He would go through with the plan.

"Jimmie Lee Gray's Live Prayer-In" said the listing. The show went from 9:30 to 11:00 A.M. on a UHF channel. That meant that, considering travel time and makeup, Reverend Gray would be gone from his home at least from 9:00 A.M. to noon. A three-hour window of opportunity. But he had to know—would there be anyone else there?

He distractedly read other stories in the paper, killing time. At quarter of nine he picked up the room phone and dialed Gray's home phone. It rang thirty times. No one home.

Web dressed in blue jeans and a sweatshirt, the only casual clothes in his suitcase. He had to have some sort of physical evidence or admit that he was crazy. The risk of arrest was minor in comparison.

It was a twenty-minute drive to Reverend Gray's neighborhood. Web parked the rented Ford Escort on a street parallel with Gray's house and a block away. He sat in the car for a moment and surveyed the street. Some kids playing a block away. Not many cars. He looked at his watch. 10:08. He estimated that he had at least twelve minutes, even if someone called the police immediately. Longer than twelve, it was a gamble whether or not police had been summoned.

He walked up a driveway and through a backyard without looking side to side. As he entered the yard, Web slipped a gray gardening glove over his good hand, to prevent fingerprints. Everybody knows that's what criminals do.

Pretend like you have a purpose. Like you know where you're going. That will arouse less suspicion.

There were several small fruit trees in Gray's backyard. Web walked directly to the sliding-glass door and tried it. It was locked. He had a sinking feeling in his stomach.

He realized that he hadn't fully weighed the vagaries of breaking and entering. Web checked his watch. 10:08. Gray would be on television right now.

He walked along the back of the house and tried the kitchen window. It, too, was locked.

There were four additional windows to try, wells in the lower part of the split-level house, partially buried. One by one he tugged on each window. No luck.

10:14. I've been here six minutes. If a neighbor saw me he might be suspicious by now.

Try the front door? Too obvious. Right in view of everyone, too.

I've already come three thousand miles.

He went to the least conspicuous window, one in a well that was partially hidden by a large bush. Then he pounded the glass with his cast. His hand just bounced off. It wasn't as easy as it appeared on television to break a window. He turned his back to the wall and kicked the glass with the heel of his shoe, and the window gave way, shattering onto the basement floor.

Web looked around.

Did anyone hear?

He glanced at his watch. 10:16. *Four more minutes till I'm gambling.*

Web knelt, reached through the basement window, and unlatched it. He lowered himself into the basement. It took a minute for his eyes to adjust. The room was just as he had seen it the day before—bookcases filled with tapes and the photo of Bundy at one end.

He went to the display case. It opened easily. He lifted the urn out of the case and tried the lid. It wouldn't move. He set the lip of the urn lid on the edge of a table and pounded on the top with his gloved hand.

It must be welded on.

10:20. Gambling time.

He looked quickly around to see if there was something he could use to pry the lid off the urn. There was nothing but the religious tapes.

He set the urn down and went up the stairs. One by one he pulled open the kitchen drawers. Nothing strong enough to pry open the urn.

10:22. If someone saw him in the yard.

Gray is a gardener. There have to be tools in the garage.

He opened a door that he thought should go to the garage, but it was a closet. He tried another door—bingo.

A shrill *whoop, whoop* sound permeated the house.

They put an alarm on the garage door but not the basement window! Goddam!

10:23. He was already on borrowed time, but he'd never have another opportunity. Just better go through with it.

Scanning the garage, he grabbed a trowel. He ran back down to the basement.

Sitting on the stairs, gripping the urn between his shoes, he pounded on the edge of the trowel, trying to wedge it under the urn lid. The *whoop whoop* sound stopped and changed to a police sirenlike crescendo.

Web banged on the trowel and his hand slipped. The edge of the trowel smashed into his good wrist.

Should make a good bruise.

He turned the urn on its side and kicked the trowel.

The lid gave way.

He turned the urn upright and pulled off the top. Inside were gray ashes mixed with white flecks of bone.

Web pulled from his pocket a plastic bag he had taken from the hotel and tipped in some of the ashes. *How much do I need?* He dumped half the contents of the urn into the bag, twisted it shut, then stuffed it in his pocket.

He screwed the lid back on the urn and closed the display case.

10:27. He looked around. Ashes were spilled on the floor. Web ground them into the carpet with his foot. He ran up the stairs, quickly inspected the kitchen, then threw the trowel into the garage and slammed the garage door. He opened the sliding-glass door and went outside.

From the back porch he looked all around. Nobody was running to stop him. He closed the door and walked purposefully across the yard to his car, with one final glance at his watch. 10:28. The alarm had been going off just five minutes.

Calmly, he opened the Escort door.

A neighbor leaned out his door, but didn't seem to notice Web. He drove away, heart pounding furiously.

Web remained in a state of panic the rest of the day. When he checked out of the hotel, he expected to be arrested. When he returned the rental car, he thought he spotted a police cruiser and drove around the block twice before stopping. It wasn't till that night when he was safely on a plane bound for Berkeley that he realized he had gotten away with his little crime.

He ordered a Scotch and soda from the stewardess and remembered what he had learned from all his dealings with police departments: Nobody gives a damn about breaking and entering any more.

25

Web arrived home late Sunday night and was up early Monday morning to visit the university library. It was closed to students during spring break but open for staff and graduate students. He went straight to a collection of books on criminal forensics, buried in the basement of the stacks. The low ceilings and corridors of books made the area feel like a tomb.

What the hell can I prove with these ashes? Stealing them was impulsive. He didn't know exactly what he might find out, but he now held the only tangible evidence that Bundy was dead. Perhaps there was no serious reason to possess the contents of the urn; maybe it was just a perverse impulse to own the remains of his daughter's killer: a souvenir of death.

He had never visited the forensics section, which was for students in law enforcement and housed a grab bag of books on different specialties. Forensics was a weird mix of eclectic specialties like typewriter identification and blood typing. He pored through the books written by medical examiners but found nothing relevant. He then tried the section on evidence collection at crime scenes; again, he came up dry. Finally, he went to a graffiti-covered cubicle where a student, probably a Ph.D. candidate, was hidden behind dozens of thick books with titles like *Toward More Productive Arrests: Recent Supreme Court Rulings on Search and Seizure.*

"Could you help me a moment?" Web asked the thin, clean-cut student.

"Sure. What are you looking for?" The boy whispered, although no one else was in the room. It was, after all, the library, and a student in law enforcement followed rules even when they were irrelevant.

"I'm trying to figure out where I might look for information on identifying ashes."

"What kind of ashes?"

"Human remains." Web worried that his question would sound strange, but without missing a beat, the student replied, "I'd try arson. The back wall."

Of course. Arson.

Web found what he needed to know in an article reprinted from *Arson Investigator* magazine entitled "Achieving Positive I.D. in Total Burn Situations." It was originally written by Arson Detective, First Class William H. Hogan of the Chicago Fire Department in 1966 and updated several times since.

Although one hundred percent certainty in human incineration situations is never possible, techniques developed by the Chicago Fire Department can increase the likelihood of identification by process of elimination as elucidated below . . .

In technical language, the story detailed how the Chicago Fire Department had identified remains in two hotel fires that occurred in the early sixties. They relied on fiber identification and bone measurement for most of the successes, both of which were useless to Web, since he had neither fibers nor bones. But then an addendum to the pamphlet, added in 1981, explained techniques used in a refinery fire that had completely incinerated two workmen.

One of the bodies had been reduced to ashes. The investigator knew that he was one of two people: either the watchman's cousin or a second worker who was a prime suspect in setting the fire. The detectives had discovered that the ashes contained significant amounts of dental gold residue, which led them to believe that it had been the *suspect* who burned up, not the visiting cousin. Three months later, the cousin reappeared, having been in Haiti during the intervening time. Their ash identification had been correct.

This was something he could use.

He walked across the empty campus to his office and pulled out some old newspapers.

Dental evidence had figured prominently in one of Bundy's Florida murder trials. Dr. Ali Najeli, a dentist hired by the prosecution, compared a cast made of Bundy's mouth to bite marks left where the assailant had bitten off the nipples of a victim. Najeli had concluded that the bite pattern on the corpse's chest could be closely correlated to Bundy's orthidonture. It was a puzzle piece that helped convict Bundy of the murders in the Chi Omega sorority. From the testimony, it was obvious that Najeli knew every nook and cranny of the psychopath's mouth.

Two calls to long-distance information revealed that Najeli had relocated to Miami and had achieved some success, probably as a benefit of publicity from the trial: There were fourteen Najeli Smile Centers in the city. He called the Smile Center Main Office and in minutes was talking to the dentist.

"Yes, Mr. Sloane, I feel that I know the late Mr. Bundy's

mouth better than most. Why do you want to know?" The dentist had a hint of a Middle Eastern accent; Web thought perhaps he was Lebanese.

"Bundy confessed to killing my daughter. I am curious . . ." He thought better of explaining himself. "It would take too long to explain *why* I have to know. It's a strange question, but what kind of fillings did Bundy have?"

Najeli laughed. "Yours is not the strangest question I have heard. If you hold for a moment, I'll pull the records."

While on hold, Web was treated to recorded advertisements for the Smile Centers, backed by a sappy Muzak arrangement of "Smile." "No appointment necessary. Come into any of our fourteen convenient locations in Greater Miami and Dade County for every dental necessity. Local anesthesia or, for a small additional charge, enjoy Twilight Sleep as we make your teeth the best they can be. Smile centers also do cosmetic work . . ."

Najeli came back on the line.

"Mr. Sloane?"

"Yes?"

"He had partial crowns on 2 and 14, a porcelain cap on 6, and four amalgam fillings on 12, 16, . . ."

"I don't know all the technical dental talk. What I wanted to know was the *material* used in the fillings."

"Ordinary silver-mercury fillings. What we dentists call amalgam. The number 6 filling was a hack job, probably from the Utah or Colorado prisons."

"Silver-mercury. Dr. Najeli, were there any *gold* fillings? Any other materials used?"

"No sir. I am quite curious about why you want to know, but as a former public servant, I am quite happy to satisfy you. If you would like, I could send a copy of the impressions for an appropriate charge . . ." said Dr. Najeli.

"No, that's okay. You've answered my question. Thanks for your time."

It was almost three o'clock; Joyce was coming back from her grandparents' and would arrive at the airport within an hour. He would have to pursue the mystery of the ashes another day.

As he drove up to the US Air terminal, Joyce was waiting outside the luggage pickup, heavily laden with gifts from her grandparents. Web parked illegally in the red zone and quickly loaded up the car. As they sped away from the airport, an awkward silence hung in the air.

"So how were Nana and Grandpa?" he asked.

"They're fine," said Joyce.

"You got a tan, didn't you? Hot in Phoenix?"

"Yeah, I guess so."

"Were they mad I didn't come?" It had been a year and a half since he'd visited his in-laws.

Joyce didn't reply. Web looked over to see her staring glumly out the window.

"What's wrong, Joyce?"

"Nothing."

He racked his brain.

"Did I forget your birthday? I forgot your birthday, didn't I. I'm sorry."

"It's not till next week."

"Just testing." He tried another tack. "I'm so glad you're back. It's just so damn quiet with you gone."

"Yeah, I know." Her reply was aggressive, as if she wanted him to shut up. She turned on the radio, punched several stations apparently without finding anything to her liking, then switched the radio off.

Web was in the middle of the Golden Gate Bridge, fighting heavy traffic, when Joyce dropped the bombshell. Silent tears streaming down her face, she said, "I think I'm pregnant."

26

Nurse Becky Jacobson was on duty when the patient in room 127 gained consciousness for the second time. The doctors initially predicted he might not pull through, but Becky thought he was a fighter: She could tell who would make it and who would die. With staffing levels and funding dropping through the floor, the public hospital operated almost as triage. Becky spent fourteen dollars of her own money to purchase the stuffed rabbit that sat right in the patient's line of vision. That's what he wanted, after all.

She had orders to contact a woman named Mars Chittenden when he regained consciousness. Chittenden had been holed up in a local hotel for three days, ever since they found her name on a business card in the patient's wallet.

The patient opened his eyes briefly and glanced around the room.

"Where's my car?" he said.

"Your car is fine, Mr. DeVries. Everything is fine."

"I need to vacuum it out. There are things in there . . ." He tried to sit up.

"Save your energy, Mr. DeVries. Your car is fine."

"No! NO! It has to be . . ."

She pressed a red button on a panel next to the bed. Moments later, the resident on duty, Mylon Ellis, ran in the door.

"What is it?" he asked.

"The patient is panicking about his car. I don't know."

With the flip of a valve, he increased the level of sedation in the intravenous tap.

"I have to get out and clean . . ."

The patient relaxed and fell back into a deep slumber.

Nurse Jacobson noticed him twitching violently and turned to Ellis.

"Just dreaming. Pent-up dream deprivation. Sometimes trauma patients will REM for forty-five minutes or an hour once they get to the point where they can handle it. Call me if something else comes up."

The patient heard none of this.

He was four years old again.

Back in Pennsylvania.

Crying in the tiny room on the farm. He had just gotten a spanking and the poopy water bag from Mama. But it wasn't Mama. It was Grandma who did the punishment. They said he shouldn't call her Mama anymore. She was really Grandma. His older sister was going to take him away. But now he knew she was really his mother.

But it was still Grandma who made him bend over. She had caught him holding the cat's head in the watering trough, then pulling him out to watch him choke. He had been going on like that for a long time, pushing him under, then pulling him up at the last minute.

Grandma-who-used-to-be-mama watched him from the house.

She spanked him for hurting the cat.

But the enema was because he said Grandpa did it too. He had learned how to make the cat do water dances from Grandma's man, who used to be Papa but who he now had to call Grandpa. In his mind he would always confuse the name and call him Grandpapa.

"He does no such thing," she said, "and you'll go get me the bag in the bathroom for saying such horrible things about a fine man."

He cried the whole way he had to walk up the stairs to the bathroom and carry down the bad-smelling rubber. She gave it to him right in the barnyard, right outside where anyone could see.

And now he was crying alone in his room.

When the knock came.

It was Grandpapa. He closed the door and talked in hushed tones. He brought candy and a tiny glass of whiskey.

Grandpapa treated him right.

That day Grandpapa shared.

"She don't always know what she's doing. But it's not so bad to make the cats do the water dance or any of the other stuff either. Just don't let her know. Most folks can't understand. Tonight I'll show you how."

The whiskey tasted bad but he drank it because Grandpapa was confiding in him. Treating him like a real man.

That night Grandpapa showed him how to do it. They did two cats and a dog.

He felt bad for the cats, but Grandpapa said it was okay.

He could still smell the fresh-cut hay and the animal manure and the smell of trash burning out by the farmhouse.

But Grandpapa showed him how to hide his fun from the women.

"If you hide the damn dogs, then nothing happens. Don't mention it to the womenfolk. They never understand."

After Grandpapa showed him how to make a dog yelp in that funny way with alcohol and matches, they dragged the dog to the street and waited in the cold till an eighteen-wheeler truck ran him down. The trucker didn't even stop.

"See, boy?"

"Yes, Grandpapa?"

"Twas the trucker killed him. Twudden you or me."

When they had done making the cats do tricks, they put 'em both in a burlap bag and it was the cats' fault they didn't get out in the river.

Grandpapa showed him right. If a cat gets kilt on the road no one cares. So just put him up there while he's still breathing and your conscience can be clear. Don't tell any nansy-pansy women though. Just smile at the dinner table and talk about the weather and no one has to be the wiser. He was never caught again.

Mars Chittenden watched helplessly in the hospital room as Alan's head violently shook from side to side.

"He was awake a little while ago," said Nurse Jacobson. "He might wake up again."

"What's wrong with him?"

"It's just dreaming. It's a healthy thing, actually. Probably a good sign that there's no brain damage."

The patient heard none of this.

The appeals had run out.

He'd been on death row seemingly forever and there was no chance of parole and old sparky was waiting right down the hall.

It was time for the final psychiatric evaluation when a plan dropped into his lap.

In Florida you can't execute a crazy man.

Even though he never said he was crazy, they still had to make sure. The final battery of psych tests. To go in a record book somewhere.

He knew the psych tests. He used to give them when he was a psychology student in Washington.

So he could stall them. Give 'em a run for their money. Play crazy and they might take a week or two instead of one afternoon to certify him sane and ready for old sparky.

He was "under observation" in the pink-walled psych ward of the prison when he saw his opportunity to get out.

Two guards watched the main exit from the psych ward, twenty-five feet away from his cell. Each "client"-prisoner was in his own cell, and they could get toilet paper and matches from the trusty.

He got to know the trusty pretty well.

He was another prisoner, crazy as a lark but still in prison for passing bad checks. They let model prisoners be trusties, assistants to the screws. It was therapeutic.

Everyone called the trusty Khadaffi. The trusty called himself Khadaffi. But his real name was Chad Mertz.

Chad Mertz had made the stupid error of forging checks on a cocaine kingpin's account. It was his third arrest for forgery. But he believed he was the druglord. That's why he was in the psych ward.

Theodore Bundy recognized the mental condition the trusty suffered. Proximity replacement personality disorder. PRPD guys completely believed they were someone else. Some of them became Napoleon or Howard Hughes. They were technically called Aggrandizers. Others became Hitler or, like this patient, drug kingpins and Khadaffi. A deeply buried guilt complex made them believe they were villains. The worst villains in their consciousness.

He was nearly Ted's age.

For the two weeks Bundy was in the psych ward, Mertz

came to his cell at every free moment to hear stories about the exploits of the world's greatest serial killer.

Bundy didn't tell him his name. He didn't want him to know who he was. He just wanted to feed him information.

Ted told him details no one else knew.

Mertz always wanted to know more.

"What did he do then?" he would ask.

And Ted would tell him. Everything. All the details, the more horrible, the more perverse, the better. Even if he told, who would believe the story of a trusty who was likely to spend the rest of his life in institutions?

"Everybody hates him, don't they? He was very, very bad." Mertz would periodically say. But on the eighth day Mertz, without prompting, said, "Everybody hates me."

The groundwork being properly laid, carrying out the plan was the easiest part. Mertz had taken a bad fall one night. Bashed in his eyes and cut his ear. Bandages covered half his face.

The next morning Ted Bundy suffered a similar injury. At his own hand. Gave no explanation. The docs just attributed it to his trying to pretend to be crazy. Didn't even think that perhaps he had an ulterior motive.

Three days before his scheduled execution Bundy spent his last hours in the psych ward.

The timing had to be perfect.

If they could get the weed, the guards usually smoked a joint at around 3:30. Ted knew that. All the prisoners knew that. Boredom was the greatest job hazard for screws, and most of them fired up a doob when they could get away with it. At 3:30 the docs had their big meeting, and Mutt and Jeff, as the guys in the psych ward called the guards, usually disappeared for five or ten minutes and came back smelling of pot.

Ted gave them his best joint earlier that day. Said how much he liked them. They thought it was a gesture of respect from a dying man.

At 3:30 they split to the hall outside the room they were to guard.

Chad Mertz, as usual, was hanging on Ted's every word. Ted and Mertz had matching bandages.

Chad asked to be called Ted.

Ted obliged him.

Then Ted told him what a really evil, twisted, bad person would do in a mental ward.

And Mertz immediately followed his instructions, lighting a copy of USA Today *and holding it up to the smoke alarm. The alarm automatically opened the inside cell doors and closed down the room dividers with steel. That way the prisoners could get away from the source of the fire but still not escape. It would catch the guards by surprise and get them in trouble for smoking a joint. Better was the fact that it took a special key to open the dividers again and let them back in. Maybe four minutes till the supervisor ran down the corridor with the special key.*

After triggering the alarm Mertz hoped for praise from the man in the cell but instead got a kick to the head. Bundy pummelled the man till he was knocked unconscious.

It took forty-five seconds to strip out of his patient uniform, another fifty-one to strip Mertz, and less than a minute later Mertz was on Bundy's bunk, wearing Bundy's clothes. And Bundy, head still in bandages, just had to act crazy like Mertz for a couple hours.

He had escaped. But he was still in the prison.

They probably would discover Mertz was Mertz by day's end, during the routine attendance checks. But at the end of the day Bundy would be gone.

Escaping from the low-security psych ward, where the trusty/inmates were allowed to stay, was a piece of cake. The criminally insane trusties loaded the laundry trucks; the joke was that they were too crazy to try an escape. Bundy jumped out of the laundry truck into a swamp and was on a bus for Atlanta within twenty-four hours.

His training had apparently gone well. Mertz looked pretty much like Bundy, but not an exact match. The bruises and cuts helped cover that up. All the pieces were in place. With luck, the blind preacher would vainly attribute any change in "Ted's" behavior to a deathbed religious conversion.

But only in Bundy's wildest dreams did he think they would actually execute *Mertz. That was icing on the cake.*

When it happened, when he heard the news on television in

a hotel room in San Francisco, he felt no remorse for Mertz. He felt elation. Two thousand volts applied to the body of a poor nut arrested for passing bad checks freed him forever.

Ted Bundy is dead. Long live Ted Bundy.

27

As he approached the steps leading to his UC Berkeley office, Web saw a girl of about nineteen holding a two-year-old child. The baby shrieked loudly despite the girl's efforts to soothe him. The well-dressed college students entering the building unconsciously swerved around her as they happily bounded up the steps chatting with one another, avoiding the girl as if she were invisible. As he moved closer, Web briefly caught the girl's glance; she had dark circles under her eyes.

"Excuse me, sir, could you spare any change?" she asked, thrusting a dirty hand at him.

"Sure," he said, reaching into his billfold and producing a dollar bill. Web was shocked. She wasn't a student at all, as he had first thought, but probably was homeless. In his youth Web would have called her a *beggar*. He didn't usually give money to the homeless. *She's probably been here every day and I didn't even notice her.* Was this to be Joyce's fate? A pariah before her twenty-first birthday?

Joyce hadn't wanted to talk about her situation the night before, when they were driving home from the airport, or that morning, when she had raced off to school without saying good-bye. Now Web would have to force the issue. Everywhere he looked that day he noticed young pregnant girls and, worse, others who were tending babies.

Late in the afternoon Web called Joyce from his office.

"Joyce, there's a new restaurant that's getting rave reviews. I thought we could go there for your birthday."

"No can do. I'm going out with Margarita and the girls on my birthday, Daddy-O, but thanks for the offer."

"What about tonight?" he asked hopefully. He felt like a kid asking for a date.

"Sure, I guess. What's it called?"

"Caribbean Taste."

"Cool! See you later."

She hung up the phone abruptly. As worried as Web was, he was sure Joyce was even more distraught.

The loud Caribbean restaurant provided a colorful break from the typical night's activities. But during dinner, Joyce had avoided discussing anything except homework, her friends, and what was on television. Web had hoped she would bring up the subject but realized the ball was in his court.

They left the restaurant and were comfortably cruising on the interstate when Web decided to break the silence.

"We have to talk. I'm worried about you, Joyce," he said.

"Dad, what you mean is you're mad at me," she said. Then, deftly turning the tables on her father, she spat out, "I think we'd talk a lot more if you weren't gone all the time."

"What's that supposed to mean?"

"It's my senior year and you're always off on your little trips. It's as if you want to avoid me."

"It's a responsibility I have, Joyce."

"No, it's not. It's Maria." Joyce drew a deep breath. "You're always going to see her, trying to find *her* daughter. Well you've got a daughter, too." She pushed her body against the passenger window, as if trying to get as far as possible from her father.

"I have been away. I've been trying to keep it to a minimum. But I feel an obligation." Web looked away from the road to his daughter for a moment.

"Obligation? What did she ever do for you?"

"Joyce, it's not that kind of obligation, like a debt on a credit card. It's deeper than that. She needs help. Maria's going through something I would never wish on anyone. She has no one to sympathize with her and no one to turn to."

"What about me, Dad? Isn't it important to be at home, too?"

"It's the most important thing in the world, Joyce. You know that." He put his hand on hers.

"Well, I need you right now, too. I'm facing a lot of serious stuff now."

"I know. I want to talk to you about it."

"I thought you'd be angry or ground me or something," said Joyce.

"It's a little late for me to be angry. I just want to help you do what's right."

"Really?"

"Yes." Web slowed the car down. "When did you find out that you're pregnant?"

"I don't know. I guess last weekend. My period was late and everything."

"How late?" he asked.

"Like, up till now, over a week. I'm usually like clockwork." Joyce blushed. "Do we have to talk about this?"

"Yes we do. Are you sure? Have you gone to a doctor?"

"I called a clinic, but they won't even do a test until I'm six weeks past the last period. So I'm going in next week. But I'm absolutely positive. Remember Jennifer? She got pregnant last year and she told me all about it."

"It could just be nerves, you know. Sometimes girls are late," he said.

"I don't want you cross-examining me, too, Dad! It's true, I just know it."

Web bit his lip; she didn't need a lecture right now. But he had his doubts about her pregnancy. He knew from experience that one week late did not a pregnancy make. They pulled into their driveway, but neither got out of the car.

"Who is the father, then, Joyce? Does he want to help raise a child?" The words sounded very strange to Web even as he spoke them.

"He doesn't even know! I only told you and Jennifer. Um, the boy, um, I haven't talked to him for three weeks."

A vein in his temple throbbed. Joyce had been taken advantage of and Web wouldn't stop asking till he knew. "You better tell him. Who is it?"

She broke into sobs. Web gave her a handful of Kleenex. After blowing her nose, she sighed and said, "It's someone you know."

Her reluctance to answer was a red flag. "Did he force you to . . . ?" asked Web, already planning prosecution and violence against the unnamed boy if there was the slightest hint of rape.

"No! He didn't force anything. I was all mixed up. I was just visiting him like I always do and at one moment it just seemed . . . I don't know. We drank some wine . . . a lot of wine. I can't talk about it. It just happened. That's all there is to it. Can we talk about it more later?" Joyce blew her nose again.

"Who? Who was it?" Web gripped the steering wheel so hard his fingernails made an impression on the vinyl.

Joyce sighed and looked down at her feet. "Ramiah Bose."

Web had expected to hear the name of a goofy high school kid or some boy Joyce met at a party, but he was positively shocked that the snotty, thirty-something graduate student from his own class was *the one*. It made his blood boil.

"Bose? I thought I told you not to see him!"

"I know, Daddy-O, that's what makes it so much more terrible."

"You said you weren't dating him."

"We weren't exactly dating." It was hard for Joyce to draw breath. "We were just friends, but then one night I thought there was something more and . . . it just sort of happened." She looked off into the distance.

"And now he won't even return my phone calls. I left him dozens of messages, and it's like I don't even exist to him anymore. I think he hates me."

Joyce quickly got out of the car, like a cat that's been cooped up. She slipped into the house and ran to her room before Web could catch up with her. He ran up the steps; Mud, startled by the sudden intrusion, chased him up the steps, growling and nipping at his ankles.

Man and dog stood outside her locked bedroom door.

"Joyce, we haven't finished talking about this."

"I don't want to talk any more," she yelled.

"We've got to talk to Bose."

"I don't want to see him ever again!"

"Joyce, open the door."

"No! Leave me alone! I want to be alone for a while."

Web walked slowly down the hall, away from her door, his thoughts fixed on the graduate student who had used his daughter and then dumped her like yesterday's newspaper. Mud followed two steps behind, growling.

Web dialed Bose's number. He got an answering machine that played a clip of Jack Kerouac poetry followed by the machine's beep. Web opted not to leave a message.

Only a week earlier, Web had received the first installment of the student's dissertation, which sat unread in his briefcase. Now, he was suddenly interested in looking at the paper. Could he grade it fairly under the circumstances? He grabbed his briefcase and drove to Bose's apartment building to lay in wait for the man. His ire was raised; he wouldn't stop till he had satisfied the anger. Web's number one priority in life was the protection of Joyce. He had taught her self-defense; he kept a close watch on her grades, her friends, her activities, and her thoughts. Some would call it overzealous or even damaging, but after losing Vicki and his wife he couldn't help himself. He had to neutralize the newest threat: Bose.

The apartment building that to Joyce had seemed so exotic and intriguing struck Web as merely seamy. He walked up the four flights of stairs to Apartment 5B.

Web knocked on the door and got no answer; no sound came from inside. He sat on the floor outside the door and waited. He knew from experience that with a phone machine and diligence it was possible to avoid an encounter for weeks or even months. Web was in no state to wait. He wanted to settle his account right now.

To kill time, Web pulled out Bose's thesis, entitled "An Ethical Analysis of the IBM Antitrust Suits: The (Im)Morality of the Monopoly." Web glanced at the date on the thick paper. Bose would have been finishing it at almost precisely the same time he compromised Joyce. Web figured that he would have to give it to another professor for evaluation but still was curious to see what it contained. *Know your enemy.*

Eighteen pages into the paper, Web stopped reading. He flipped to the footnotes and bibliography, then went backward, glancing at a few pages at a time. He couldn't believe what he was reading. It was too good to be true. Web laughed aloud. He held in his hands Bose's Achilles' heel. It was the first time sloppy research had ever made Web smile.

Twenty-five minutes after sitting down, Web heard footsteps clunking up the wooden staircase. Two people. One of them with a loud, snotty accent that was British-by-way-of-India. His prey. He stood up.

A blond girl of about twenty-five in a tight leather skirt came up the stairs first, followed by Bose. Bose's wide smile melted when he saw Web.

"Professor Sloane. I didn't expect to see you here," he said.

"I know." Web stood in front of the door and stuffed Bose's dissertation into his briefcase.

"Mr. Sloane, this is my friend Lucinda." The heavily madeup young girl extended a hand laden with jewelry.

"Lucinda, you'd better go home. This is going to take some time," said Web, refusing to shake.

"No, no. Why don't we all come in," suggested Bose.

The stern look on Web's face alarmed the girl. "No, that's okay," she said, buttoning up her blouse. "I'll see you tomorrow, Ramiah,"

"You don't . . ."

"Bye." She stumbled down the stairs as fast as her high heels permitted.

"Fancy seeing you here, Sloane," said Bose, all semblance of friendliness gone. "Why don't you come in." The graduate student kept a close watch on the professor as he opened the door.

Web sneezed as the scent of cheap incense hit him in the face, then entered the cluttered studio apartment.

"I'd offer you a chair, but I don't have any," said Bose, apparently a little drunk.

Web blocked the door, his prey in his eyes. He didn't want Bose getting out.

"How long have you lived in the United States?" asked Web.

"Most recently, four and a half years, but I lived here for a couple years in the seventies. Why?"

"What do you know about statutory rape laws?"

Bose swallowed hard, then sat on the futon. "Oh, come now, what are you talking about?"

"You know perfectly well what I'm talking about."

"It is ridiculous to threaten me like that. If only you weren't so uptight, maybe——"

"You bet I'm uptight. You took advantage of the wrong man's daughter, Bose."

"Took advantage? Why, I did nothing wrong. Nobody was raped, Mr. Sloane. If you talked with your daughter you'd know that everything was mutual, and I'd say she enjoyed herself."

The words fell on Web's ears like jet fuel on an open flame. Web walked across the room and lifted the man up by his collar.

"Enjoyed herself? You disgust me. Statutory rape has nothing to do with consent. You seduced an underage girl by getting her drunk. Do you know what the penalties are, Bose? You could be convicted of a felony. That means jail in California." Web let go of Bose's collar.

Bose rubbed his neck. "Got her drunk? She's got to be twenty-one at least, isn't she? Come on now, you make me sound like some pervert."

"A pervert who got a *seventeen*-year-old drunk. Then dumped her when he found out she might be pregnant."

"She's pregnant?" Bose wiped his forehead.

"She thinks she is."

"It's not my responsibility. I thought——"

"It is your responsibility despite what you think. I didn't know what I would do with you tonight till a few minutes ago. Now I think you'll be happy to leave the country within the week."

"Is that a threat?"

"No, it's a promise. Bose, you made a fatal mistake. I read your dissertation tonight—or at least part of it. I thought I wouldn't have the objectivity to evaluate it, but that's not even a consideration, since you'll be leaving the country."

"What do you mean?"

"You plagiarized your main argument," said Web, extracting the paper from his briefcase.

"What?"

"You stole from a little-known government white paper. Don't pretend it isn't true. Is this title familiar? "Economic

Impacts of IBM Antitrust Suit in New York and Connecticut." I'll refresh your memory. It was written by Whittinger, Lydon, et al." Web spat the names out as if they were curses.

"The title sounds a little familiar, but I'm sure I didn't read it."

"Bose, don't bullshit me now. You didn't check to see who 'et al.' included. I did the basic research and wrote at least half that report for the Justice Department in 1980. Me. You stole from me."

Bose's eyes grew wide. He gritted his teeth like a cornered animal.

"Give that here!" shouted Bose, grabbing for the paper. When Web snatched it out of his reach, Bose kicked him in the shin. Web felt adrenalin seeping through his body like an electric shock. He drew back his arm, still in a cast, and let loose a blow that knocked the student to the floor and sent his granny glasses flying across the room.

"Don't mess with me, Bose. You can leave within the week—without a felony conviction following you back home. If you wait two weeks, I'll have you kicked out of UC Berkeley and your educational visa will be revoked unconditionally. If you wait any longer than that, charges will be filed. I know the law and I know the police. They don't take these things lightly. What'll it be, Bose?"

Bose grabbed his glasses and rubbed his chin. "It's not fair! You can't do that. You can't take everything away!"

"Yes, I can," said Web. He slipped the paper back into his briefcase and walked away, gently closing the door behind him.

28

The only obstacle that kept Mars from taking Alan home was a ream of forms that had to be completed in triplicate. She filled them out to spare him the ordeal of bureaucracy and was suddenly aware of how little she knew about the man who had shared her bed for half a year. She had no idea of his medical history, didn't know his next of kin, didn't even know whether to check "single," "divorced," or even "married." Alan kept his cards pretty close to the chest, always implying the details of his past rather than explicitly spelling them out.

Mars had heard of married men who suddenly walked out on their families. Never before had she seriously considered the possibility, but on reflection, he had never even mentioned any previous lovers. *Oh, well.* She hoped he was just being a gentleman. Mars checked off "single" and put the troubling thought aside in the part of her mind where a rapidly growing heap of Alan's inconsistencies resided. Why was he in Reno, when he said he was going to Oregon? Why did he take a part-time job with the cops no less (in her youth she would have said "the pigs") when he claimed to be a retired stockbroker?

Mars made a mental vow to ask him some of these questions, but only when he was better. She would avoid a confrontation now. Of course he was well enough to go home, but why nag him now, when he was weak? Maybe she was beginning to sense that the happy spin he put on his life was only a facade. Maybe she was delaying so she wouldn't discover the truth, but the facade made her happy. She was loathe to destroy it, much like a kid who pretends to believe in Santa Claus long after the ruse is revealed because of the wonderful gifts that even a phony Santa brings. Even if Alan did have a secret family hidden away somewhere or if the

IRS or the Mafia were chasing him, Mars didn't want to know. Why force the issue when he brought her so much happiness?

After one form too many, Mars determined that the hospital was primarily interested in seeing two things: first, that the bill would be paid and, second, that all the slots were completed regardless of accuracy. Vine County Employee Health Plan would pay the bill, so she focused her attention on completing the questionnaire with whatever popped into her mind. Next of kin? She put herself. Previous address? She wrote the only out-of-state address she had ever memorized: Spiegel, Chicago, IL 60609. *What the hell. It's none of their business and none of mine.*

She went into his semiprivate room. "Semi" meant that on the other side of a thick shower curtain lay a heavily sedated old man and his wife who sobbed nonstop for hours. When she wasn't praying in Italian, like now. Mars sat by Alan's side and tried to ignore the prayers.

"Alan, it's me, Mars." She gently touched his shoulder. His eyes opened slowly and then he grinned.

"Say, what's a nice girl like you doing in a place like this?" he quipped.

"They say you can come home, Alan. The doctor said you're recovering quite nicely and should be up and around in a couple of weeks."

He held his hands up in a gesture stolen from David Letterman. "What, and leave all this?"

Mars laughed. She knew he must be getting better. His sense of humor, however stale, was a sure sign of "the old Alan" that she loved. It had been touch and go for the first few days, but the doctors were constantly amazed at his will to recover. "A fighter," said the doctor. "If he doesn't fall off a cliff or get hit by a truck, he'll live to a hundred."

Mars drove Alan's Cabriolet, and an ambulance followed her the ninety miles back to Endocino. Alan might have ridden with her, but the doctor recommended the ambulance "just in case." Mars didn't quarrel, because the insurance company would pay for the ride. She kept an eye on the rearview mirror to make sure they were keeping up with her. Once when she swiveled her head around to look at them, she caught a glimpse of a fluorescent orange and green ski parka. *Never saw that before,* she thought. *Alan is a skier? Is there a girl on the side?* Heavy traffic cut off her reverie.

Once home, she treated Alan like a king. He took over her bed, and she brought the television in to keep him entertained, breaking her no-TV-in-the-bedroom rule. Besides the remote control, she'd given him a little bell to ring if he needed or wanted anything. She brought him any food he wanted, as long as it was low-fat, low-sodium Good to Heart frozen dinners, an imitation fat-free ice-cream-like product, or any of the other bland foods on the list that the hospital had provided.

She kept putting off asking the hard questions. Alan steered every conversation to upbeat and impersonal topics. She listened patiently each day as he reported what he had watched on "Donahue," "Oprah Winfrey," or "The Days of Our Lives." Besides, the doctor had left her with one standing order: *Don't upset him.*

After two days Mars reopened the bakery. Roslyn came in to help her set it up. Quickly the conversation turned to Alan.

"Why was he in Reno?" asked Roslyn while washing out the pastry mixing tub.

"Oh, you know, business I guess," replied Mars, eyeing her best friend warily.

"You don't know? He didn't tell you?" asked Roslyn in a semishriek, anxious for some hot gossip.

"He's very sick, Roslyn. I didn't ask," Mars said curtly.

"Mars, what do *you* think he was doing there?"

"Roslyn, I've started to ask him a million times and I always chicken out. I wish I knew."

"Sounds like another woman, Mars. Better face up to it now."

"Don't say it with such glee, Roslyn. I'm trying to hold together the one relationship I have. If it was another woman I don't want to find out. Maybe he had a fling. Yes, it entered my mind, but if she meant anything to him he would have told me by now." Mars dropped a fifty-pound bag of flour on the ground.

"You don't have to get so testy, Mars. I was just asking."

"I found a woman's ski jacket in his car. I asked him about it and he turned very pale for a moment. Then he said that a business contact left it in the car and he had to mail it back."

"Well, that's *plausible,*" said Roslyn, laying on the innuendo. "A *business contact.*"

"That's what I thought too, but then he burned it. Can you believe that? He's supposedly confined to bed and when I come home there's a fire in the backyard trash can and this horrible smell of burned feathers and stuff. I was going to stay with him at home all week, but if he's well enough to do that, he can take care of himself during the day."

"Did he say why he burned it?" asked Roslyn.

"He said it stank, but I didn't notice anything. He said he'd mail this 'business contact' a check."

Roslyn chuckled and touched her finger to her temple. "I would say that if he burned it, even if there once was another woman, he's blown her off for you. If he ever intended to see her again, don't you think he'd keep it for her?"

"Well, if he did cheat, then my belief in instant Karma is holding up."

"How do you figure?"

"His heart attack. That'll teach him to mess around on Mars Chittenden!" Her laughter was hollow. Mars wanted to believe that she had her man back in line, but in the back of her mind, she still had some doubts.

They worked to get the shop up and running. Roslyn finished cleaning out the pans, then turned her attention to the two little tables for customers.

"Look at this. You must have sped out of here in a hurry. Dirty coffee cups and last week's newspaper left on a table. Just like a ghost town!"

"Oh, shut up, Roz. I was worried. I did hurry out."

"You still recycle?"

"Of course. Put the papers up here, and I'll take them home later."

Roslyn set the papers on the counter, then carried the mold-filled dishes to the kitchen.

"Not up there! I just cleaned that counter," said Mars, picking up the newspaper. A photo on the front page caught her eye. "4 Students Slain on Spring Break," said the paper.

She glanced at the color photo of a group of college kids standing at the top of a ski slope. One of the girls looked familiar.

Not the girl herself; it was the distinctive geometric pattern on her ski jacket. *Funny.* Just like the jacket in Alan's car. *It must be a popular style this year,* she thought. Then she crumpled the paper and threw it into the trash.

Roslyn called out from the kitchen. "I thought you just said you recycled those!"

"I just don't have time. I'll keep it up again when we get the place in order but I don't want to look at a bunch of old newspapers."

"I saw that article about those kids in Tahoe," said Roslyn.

A wave of panic ran through Mars's body. "No, it was Colorado. I'm sure it was Colorado."

"Whatever. Yeah, that sounds right. One of those ski places." Roslyn turned her attention back to cleaning out the coffee cups.

Mars pushed the newspapers to the bottom of the bag, threw some coffee grounds on top of them, tied up the trash, and took it outside, although the bag was only half-full. It had to be Colorado, and if it wasn't, she didn't want to know about it.

29

Two days later and fifty miles south, Irwin Pearce made his third U-turn in a row on the heavily traveled Pacific Coast Highway, trying to act like he knew just where he was going. If he admitted being lost, his date would think he was stupid or a liar or both. He had to find mile marker 178, which seemed to be missing. He'd passed 179 and 177 twice.

"You're sure it's here? You've been here a lot, haven't

you?" asked Katrina Kennett, twenty-eight years old, blond, new to the typing pool, and in Irwin's opinion incredibly well proportioned.

He nodded. "I'm positive. I come here all the time, just not since last September. The mile marker must have gotten run over during the winter or something."

He slowed to a crawl on the two-lane highway, his eyes darting from the odometer to the road markers. If he didn't see 178 on this pass, he would stop anyway one mile after passing 177.

Katrina had entered Irwin's life three weeks earlier at a company party in San Francisco. The forty-two-year-old salesman, a divorcé, was drunkenly arguing with three co-workers about the benefits of legalizing nude beaches. They'd all read the same article in the *Chronicle* that morning. Although Irwin was theoretically in favor of nude beaches, he'd never actually *been* to one. The three older guys from the accounting department said it would promote promiscuity and make it impossible to take kids to the beach. Irwin lamely pressed the case that it was a matter of personal choice.

It was then that he saw Katrina, a golden-haired vision from heaven holding a rum and Coke. She stepped into the fray and forwarded a vociferous argument for free-thinking sunbathers everywhere to be able to enjoy lounging in public unclothed as was their natural right. The accounting guys were outgunned and soon shut up.

Later, Irwin continued his drunken discourse with Katrina in the mailroom, thanking his lucky stars that he had met *this* babe during *that* argument. Katrina said she'd never been to a nude beach, but Irwin assured her he went "all the time" and invited her to join him. To his astonishment she accepted his invitation. Since that night Irwin had been religiously checking weather reports waiting for the mercury to tip over 70 degrees.

Now, driving around on PCH like a fool, Irwin was blowing his big chance to see Katrina in the buff. He had gotten directions to the supposed nude beach from a high school friend who swore Irwin would have no problem finding the place, but there was no mile marker 178. When they got exactly one mile beyond marker 177, he stopped and pulled over.

"What about the No Parking signs?" Katrina bubbled.

"They never hassle beachers."

"They call them beachers?" she asked.

"Sure. That's what, uh, we call ourselves," he reported with a bit of swagger.

"That's so bitchin'. I hope we meet a lot of other beachers." She giggled.

Irwin was delighted. He hadn't gotten laid in seven months.

They unpacked the huge picnic basket from his trunk and stood by the edge of the road, looking in the direction where the ocean should be. A quarter-mile of thick forest on a steep slope separated them from the water.

"Need help with the basket?" she asked.

"Nah. I'll get it."

He followed her into the woods. The basket was awkward to hold and prevented him from using the trees as handholds. The ground was thick with a slippery carpet of pine needles. As he watched Katrina sliding from tree to tree, he visualized what she might look like naked. He wouldn't have long to wait.

"You sure this is the right way?" she asked, brushing golden locks out of her bright green eyes.

"Yeah. This is the trail," he answered, praying that there was at least sand at the bottom.

"Some trail," said Katrina, smirking. She was thirty feet in front of him, leaning on a stump, waiting for Irwin to catch up.

He felt quite unsafe traversing the slope with a picnic basket but had to impress Katrina. When she looked up at him, he tried to stand up straight as if he did this all the time.

"I'll catch up."

He took two steps and stumbled. The pine needles slid out from under his feet and Irwin landed flat on his face. The picnic basket flew out of his hands and fell down the hill, scattering twelve Amstel Lights and his ham and cheese sandwiches all over the hill.

Katrina laughed and caught a beer bottle under her foot. Something white on the ground next to the bottle caught her eye. She picked it up.

"Look at this—some sort of shell . . . no, it's a bone!" she said.

"Probably a coyote," replied Irwin, brushing himself off.

"There are no coyotes by the beach." Katrina dug deeper into the leaves. "Look, here are more bones! Cool!"

As he gathered the beer bottles, Irwin caught his hand on something sharp in the needles. He brushed them aside. What he saw startled him so that he dropped the picnic basket a second time. It was recognizably the top of a human skull, half-buried in the dirt. Irwin screamed and promptly forgot about persuading Katrina to undress.

Two hours later the site was swarming with police.

By the next day the police had positively matched the skull with a set of dental records.

Exactly fifty-three hours after unlucky Irwin Pearce had tripped in the woods, Maria de Rivera's phone rang. It was not the call she hoped to get.

Maria had just put a Budget Gourmet dinner in the microwave oven when she got the call. Since she lived alone, she ate almost nothing else; her time was consumed with the search, and it was too depressing to cook a regular meal just to eat it alone. The turkey and gravy with potatoes would sit forgotten for a week after the tragic news.

The officer who called initially asked Maria if she would be home for a visit from Detective Jannsen of the California Highway Patrol, who was handling the case. She demanded to know what it was regarding. The desk jockey placing the call wasn't permitted to tell, so she was on hold for several minutes until she was transferred to a person with enough authority to divulge the reason for a visit.

"We would rather have a representative visit you in person," said the detective.

"If it concerns me or my daughter, I want to know right now. I do not want to wait for some *hombre* at the end of his shift to come to my house," she said.

"They could be over quite soon."

"Just tell me. Just say the words." Maria was angry; she

did not want to wait even a moment, and she suspected the worst.

The detective on the other end of the line drew his breath.

"A body was found near the Pacific Coast Highway. It has been positively identified as Tanya de Rivera," he said.

"Dios mio." Maria covered the mouthpiece of the phone with her hand and wailed.

"Hello. Hello?" asked the detective.

"How are you so sure? How do you know it is my daughter?"

"Ms. de Rivera, maybe you should wait until the officers get there."

"You tell them to get here right away! I do not believe you have the right person. You people have made this mistake before. It's a mistake, I'm sure it's a mistake!"

"I'm sorry," said the officer.

"Damn well you should be sorry."

Maria slammed down the phone, then curled her hands into fists. Her knees became useless; she knelt down on the floor and rolled into a ball. *They can't have found her. She's got to be coming home. Damn the police anyway.*

Maria stood and moved listlessly to the empty table in the large, lonely kitchen and wept, holding her head in her hands. Her first thought, oddly, was of the pork chops and butter pecan ice cream in the deep freeze. Maria had planned to make her Tanya's favorite meal when she came home. Dozens of times during her search, when little glimmers of hope hinted that Tanya might be found, Maria had imagined making pork chops with cinnamon and apples, going over every detail so that it would be ready on the first night Tanya was back, but now Tanya was never coming home.

Detective Jannsen, a young light-haired officer, arrived within an hour, accompanied by a partner. Maria made him wait outside the door while she washed her face repeatedly. When she felt she must have washed away the tears, she allowed them in.

The detectives could tell from her expression that she already knew. They offered to leave her alone and come back later, but she wanted someone—anyone—with her, even unfamiliar officials. Jannsen offered to answer any questions.

Maria turned away from them as she spoke.

"How are you so sure it is Tanya? Mistakes have been made in the past, no?"

"Ms. de Rivera, we weren't sure right away, but we compared the body to her dental records. It's a definite match."

"Dental records? I have those here! It is impossible."

"You gave them to us in August, if you remember. I'm sorry, but there's no question." Jannsen looked at his partner. Next-of-kin visits were always the hardest to make.

Maria walked away from them and stared out the back window. "Is that all? Didn't you make fingerprints or anything like that?"

"Ms. de Rivera, perhaps you ought to sit down. We haven't told you how she was found. It might be quite disturbing."

"Just tell me. Do not condescend to me as if I am some child. I want to hear. I have to know that it is my daughter you found and not some mistake."

They told her how Tanya was abandoned in the woods.

Like an animal hit by a car, she thought. It brought tears to her eyes and a sick feeling to her stomach. She silently nodded as the policemen went through their paces.

They offered condolences.

They had forms emblazoned with the seal of the state of California for her to sign.

"What is this?" she asked.

Jannsen spoke plainly. "It's permission to keep the remains in case they're needed for a trial."

"Why must you keep her?" Maria was near shouting.

"They could be important evidence."

Maria rubbed her eyes. "Do I have to sign this? Is it compulsory?"

Jannsen looked at his partner, then at Maria. "Since no charges have been filed in your daughter's death, you are not required to sign. But if we were to develop a suspect . . . you never know."

Maria collapsed into the couch. *"Da me.* Give it to me,

please. I must consider this seriously—not to bury my daughter."

She tore the form off, then shoved the clipboard back at the officer.

"Mrs. de Rivera, take your time. I'm sorry."

"Please go."

"If you would like to speak to a psychological counselor, I can recommend several."

"No, I do not wish to. Please, just leave me alone."

The officers stepped outside and quietly closed the door behind them.

Maria tried calling her ex-husband. He wasn't home. She tried her mother; again, no answer. Then she looked up another phone number in her daybook and dialed.

Joyce Sloane had just gotten out of the shower when she answered the call.

"Hello, Joyce. Is your father home?" She spoke like an automaton, her voice devoid of emotion.

"He's just gone out for a walk but should be back soon," said Joyce. "Is this Maria?"

There was a long pause. "Yes. Would you please tell him I called?"

"Maria, is something wrong?" asked Joyce. This was not the resourceful, strong-willed woman she had met twice before. "Hello? Are you there?"

"Yes, I'm here. The police were here. My little daughter, my Tanya, she . . ."

Silence.

"Oh, no." Joyce understood instantly. "I'm sorry, Maria, I'm terribly sorry."

"She was just about your age . . . she would have graduated high school this spring . . ."

"Maria?"

"I told her not to go out alone. I should have known better. Why did I wait until so late to call?"

"Maria?"

"I should not burden you with this. I am sorry. Would you please ask your father to call me?"

"He's not here." Joyce could hear the instability in Maria's voice. She knew the woman shouldn't be alone. "Maria, is someone there with you?"

"No. I cannot reach my mother by telephone. She lives in Venezuela."

"Okay. How about a neighbor?"

"My neighbors are on vacation. I live on a rural road, Joyce. There aren't many people out here."

"How about Tico? There has to be someone in Tico that you know."

"Why are you asking this?"

"You shouldn't have to be alone. My father mentioned some sort of paramedic who runs a hotel?"

"Oh, Rowan. Yes, I suppose he would be in at his hotel."

"Okay. Give me his phone number, and I'll call him."

Maria gave Joyce the number to Peter's hotel. She dialed but got only an answering machine. She left a brief message, pleading with Rowan to ensure that Maria wasn't left alone. Then she called Maria back.

The phone rang fifteen times before there was an answer. It may have simply been a bad connection, but Maria sounded a million miles away.

"Maria, this is Joyce Sloane again."

"Oh, Joyce. I was just laying down a little bit."

"That's good. I'm going to come up there."

"You should not, I do not want to inconvenience you . . ."

"I want to. I should be there in a couple of hours. I just need directions on how to get to your house."

Maria gave Joyce the directions.

"I'll see you in a while. Do you need anything?" said Joyce.

"No, I'll be okay. Joyce?"

"Yes?"

"God bless you."

Joyce hung up the phone. In minutes she had changed into a dress. Then she raided the refrigerator, grabbing things she thought Maria might need: coffee, milk, bread, some canned food. She wrote her father a brief note, then left.

The Volvo still wobbled some from the accident but had been repaired pretty well. As the sun set over the ocean to her left, and the city lights came on, Joyce thought about what her father had said to her earlier in the week about obligation; but obligation wasn't what Joyce felt—it was a powerful instinct that she hadn't even known she possessed. Maria was falling apart, and something very serious might happen. Joyce didn't know what exactly to do, but she had responded to Maria's pain. She knew she had to help Maria if it was possible.

When she arrived, Peter Rowan answered the door.

"Hi, I'm Joyce Sloane," she said. "Is this the de Rivera residence?"

Rowan answered in a whisper. "Come on in. I'm Peter Rowan. Thanks for calling me. Maria was in bad shape, but she's resting now."

Joyce and Rowan played Trivial Pursuit in Maria's kitchen and answered the phone for her as inevitably her calls were returned. Rowan had brought with him an enormous tray of pastries that were laid out on the kitchen counter. After one round of the game, Joyce called home.

"Daddy-O? Did you get my note?" she asked.

"No. Where was it?"

"Right by the phone. It doesn't matter," she whispered. "Maria's daughter is dead."

"My God. Where are you?"

"I'm at Maria's. As soon as she called, I hit the road. I got here about an hour ago. She's okay, though, sleeping right now."

"Is anyone else with her?"

"A man named Peter Rowan is here, but her sister, who lives in Venezuela, won't be here till tomorrow morning. She can't track down her ex-husband."

"I'm leaving right now," he said.

"Okay. Daddy-O? Could you get my black dress?"

"Aren't all your dresses black?"

"Very funny. I mean the dressy one. I think we should stay till the funeral."

"I'll get it, Joyce."

"One more thing. Knock, don't ring the doorbell. It makes too much noise."

"Right."

Web arrived at the house to find a note on the door and let himself in. Joyce was asleep on the couch; Rowan had left. He quietly stepped up the stairs to see how Maria was. She was asleep, still dressed, laying on top of the covers. As he walked away from her room, he glanced into the second bedroom.

He realized he was looking into Tanya's room. It seemed like a room belonging to a historical figure that one might see in a museum; all it lacked was a velvet rope. Year-old high school photos and band posters were on the walls, no doubt where they were the night Tanya took her last bicycle ride. The desk had been dusted, but faint lines of dirt could be delineated around a spiral notebook opened to a half-completed mathematics problem. Her tennis racket and shoes leaned against the closet, ready to be picked up at a moment's notice.

Web tiptoed down the stairs and stretched out in a recliner chair across the room from Joyce. He watched his daughter sleep for a long time before drifting off himself.

He woke to the smell of coffee brewing. In the kitchen, he found Maria busily cleaning the kitchen, wearing a black dress.

"Good morning, Maria."

"Web." She hugged him. "Thank you for coming up here so soon."

"I'm glad to help. How are you?"

"What can I say? My sister's flight comes into Endocino airport at 11:00, and this morning I must go make funeral arrangements. My ex-husband will be here tonight. He's driving in from Nebraska."

"You never talked about him before," said Web, feeling the tiniest twinge of jealousy about the man.

"The less said about Claude, the better." She looked at the ground. "He was never satisfied just being a builder. He had scheme after scheme to get rich. I supported him for years as he put together pie-in-the-sky deals: He wanted to build a giant resort up here for yuppies, with a theme park and a golf course and whatever came into his head. Last I heard he has some wildcat oil drilling plan. If he meets you, he will try to sell you on it."

"Sorry I asked," said Web, embarrassed to have broached the subject.

"Don't be. You should know about him."

Web changed the subject. "Why don't I pick up your sister."

"That would be wonderful," said Maria.

"Is there anything else I can do?" Web asked.

"I have things under control, I suppose. Except could you do some shopping for me?"

"Absolutely."

"Here is a list I made. I can pay you . . ."

"I'll take care of it."

"Thank you, Web. I had a good talk with your daughter last night—what a lovely girl."

"Thank you."

As usual, Web felt unable to connect with the emotionally charged situation. He felt like an outsider looking in the window on a tragic scene while he was safely outside. He had little idea of what was expected of him or how to react.

Not so Joyce. She seemed intuitively to understand what was necessary: when to take charge, when to listen quietly, when to cheer Maria up with a funny story. Joyce sent Web on various errands, giving him concrete goals to accomplish. Between them they answered the door, accepted food, picked up people at the airport, met nearly everyone in Tico. They provided a buffer between Maria and the chaos in which she was immersed.

The funeral was two days later. The spring sun shone brightly, an odd counterpart to the somber occasion. Web had on a dark suit; Joyce wore the nicest of her many black dresses.

Tanya's funeral was one of the largest Web had ever attended. The Silber-Douglas mortuary in Tico had opened dividers between three rooms, merging them into one large hall that was packed to overflowing. Joyce became uneasy, surrounded by the large number of strange kids her age, quiet and unfamiliar with grief. She stayed close by Web's side.

Maria's touch was obvious in the beautiful eulogy delivered by a priest, which drew equally on Catholic themes and the day-to-day details of Tanya's life. The high school girls' choir sang, but not religious pieces—Maria wouldn't have it. Instead, they performed a medley of seven of Tanya's favorite songs, beginning with "That's What Friends Are

For." When they got to "Bridge Over Troubled Water," Joyce was in tears. Web gave her his handkerchief and stiffly put his arm around her shoulders.

On the way out of the funeral home, Web picked up two copies of the funeral director's business card, discreetly slipping them into his jacket pocket. In the crowd outside the funeral home, Maria busily accepted condolences from a long line of friends and relatives. Web stood a distance from her, as she was consoled by a vast parade of people, most of them unfamiliar to Web. During a brief break, he approached her.

"I'm terribly sorry, Maria," he said, frustrated at his inability to find the proper words.

"Thank you," she said, hugging him. "Thank you for everything you've done, Web. It means a lot. Will you call me soon?"

"We'll probably stay over tonight. Is there anything I can do?"

"Yes," she said, clenching her teeth. "I want you to help find whoever did this."

"I'll try."

Two teenage girls, eyes red with crying, stood in back of Web, waiting to talk to Maria.

"I'll call you," she said, then gently shook his hand.

Web hugged her. "Take care, Maria."

Web headed for the parking lot, where Joyce was. As he navigated the crowd, he bumped into someone familiar, but he couldn't quite connect the face with a name. The man had a strange air about him—youthful, but seemed older than his appearance. By the church steps, he turned around and noticed that the man was following him. Web had met quite a few people in Tico the previous week and assumed that the man must be local.

"Hi. I'm Web Sloane. I've forgotten your name."

"Clinton Bernard. You're so . . . civil! You've decided to help us out?" said the man in a voice too perfect to be real.

Suddenly Web stiffened. "Wait a second. You're that sleazebag from the TV show. I have nothing to say to you," said Web, turning away from the man.

"Hey, wait a minute. What are you doing up *here*, Sloane?

Is there something you're not telling us?" he asked, crowding Web closely.

"I've got nothing to say to you." Web forcefully pushed the reporter away.

"Did you see that? Did you see that?" Bernard yelled. An overweight TV technician jogged to the anchor's side.

"See what?" asked the out-of-breath technician.

"He hit me! That's assault. Try it again with witnesses, Sloane." Bernard braced himself for a blow. "Your dog bit my cameraman! I'll sue, you just wait!"

Web simply turned his back and walked to the parking lot, ignoring Bernard's curses.

Joyce sat in the car, looking melancholy.

"I wondered where you went, Daddy-O."

"I just wanted to talk to Maria."

"I didn't . . . I didn't know what to say to her today," said Joyce.

"I know what you mean."

Web looked at his watch.

"Joyce, it's getting awfully late. I thought we might stay up here another night instead of racing back to Berkeley," he said. "If that's okay with you."

"I guess so. I actually feel kind of bad." She folded her arms. "Dad, I was only ten when we had Vicki's funeral. I didn't understand it at all, but now . . ." Tears came to her eyes. "Now I know what you went through. I'm sorry, Dad."

Web climbed in the car next to her. "It's okay, it's okay."

"No, I'm such a brat. I feel terrible about the way I've behaved. I always made such a stink about it every time you went to look for Vicki, and . . ."

Web handed her a Kleenex. "Don't. It's all right now; it's all over. C'mon. Let's go to the hotel. Maybe you can take a nap."

"What about school?" she asked.

"You'll only miss a couple of classes tomorrow morning. What're your early classes?"

"Home room, study hall, then Driver's Ed."

"Drivers Ed.? You already have your license."

"It's a state requirement. I got my license in Washington, but I still have to take Drivers Ed. to graduate." She wiped her eyes, then forced a smile. "Part of the Mandatory Stupidity Plan."

"You can afford to miss one day of that."

"I can afford to miss a lifetime."

Web was barely in his hotel room when the phone rang. It was Maria.

"Web, I'm glad I found you." She whispered.

"Maria, are you okay?"

"Yes, considering. I have a house full of guests who are now all in bed for the night. I wanted to call you, though."

"What's up?"

"You tried to prepare me for the worst. I was angry with you then . . . but now Tanya's gone." She sobbed. "Now I want to find the person who did this to Tanya . . . and stop him."

"You should get some rest. It's been a long day."

"I will not rest until he's caught. Can you meet Peter and me at seven?"

"All right. Where? Here at the hotel?"

"Room 10."

When Web entered the hotel room that evening, Maria, Peter Rowan, and his companion Neil Dillon were already waiting for him. It was the room that several months earlier Web had helped set up as a command center. He had heard their voices when he was waiting in the hall, but they were suddenly silent as he entered and looked up at him oddly, as if he weren't a member of the club.

The chalkboards were filled with information from various runaway assistance organizations across the country, with notes on when they had been called and what they had said. All this effort had been useless now that they knew Tanya was dead.

"Hello, Maria," said Web, kissing her on the cheek. She wore a simple black pants suit, as if ready to get down to business.

"Hello, Web."

"I suppose we can begin," said Peter, slightly irritated.

"I guess so," said Web. He folded his arms.

Maria gave Web an odd glance. He attributed it to her exhaustion. There was a tense silence in the room.

"Why don't you tell him, Maria?" asked Rowan.

"I can't," she said.

Rowan spoke tersely. "Web, we've decided to turn everything over to the police. Let them handle it."

Maria looked away.

Web sensed a hidden agenda and answered cautiously. "There's a lot the police can't do! You know Block."

Rowan cut him off. "Yes, I know the sheriff. We buried the hatchet on this issue. He agreed to take all of our material."

"Maria, do you go along with this?" asked Web.

"I am not sure, but I think it is for the best."

Web stood up. "Vine County has limited resources. The murderer is probably still at large, and someone outside of official law enforcement can assist quite a bit by seeing the bigger picture." He turned to Rowan. "I thought you didn't trust Block."

Rowan lowered his voice with embarrassment. "Web, I have to give it to you straight. I met with him last week. He didn't ask me or Maria or Neil to stop working with him. He told me to keep our distance . . . from you."

The news came as a blow to Web. He sat back down at the table. "Why did he say that?"

"Well . . ." Rowan sighed. "He said you were interfering with police work. And it's not just him—he said there were cops in other jurisdictions who told the same story."

"Interfering? That's outrageous." Web could hear his heart pounding, anger leaping to life.

"Look—I'm just repeating what he told me. He said you were looking for the big conspiracy, trying to believe that every murder in California and Nevada and who knows where else is being committed by the same person. The police and FBI disagree and can't waste their time this way. He said you were chasing ghosts."

Web felt blood rushing to his head.

"Conspiracy theory? Ghosts? Let me tell you about ghosts. From a hundred missing person cases, I correctly identified three of them as probable kidnap or murder victims *before they were found!* Is that a conspiracy theory?"

"Web . . ." Maria tried to stop him but he shook off her grip.

"We're talking about an incredibly shrewd serial killer.

Someone who takes advantage of the infighting between police departments. Someone who is sharp enough to vary his methods simply to confound police investigations."

"Don't get me going. Block explained a much more plausible scenario to me," said Rowan, now standing as well. "He said it's not a single madman running loose. His explanation sounded good to me."

" 'Plausible scenarios' are easy to create. Somewhere out there right now this person is watching, biding his time. If it gets too hot, he'll leave the state, just to start over in a new part of the country, leaving a bloody wake of 'plausible scenarios' behind him. The time to act is now."

"How do you know that?" asked Rowan.

"Because he's copying a master. Some of my projections were accurate. Some of my suppositions were accurate, and every shred of evidence indicates that . . ."

Rowan cut him off. "I know, I know. That it's all one mad genius. I know why you want to see it that way. Block told me about what happened to your family. I don't think you're purposely interfering, but just struggling with your own demons. Your intentions are good," said Rowan, folding his arms tightly in front of himself.

"I don't have to listen to this. If it is one person—and I think it is—you're playing right into his hand."

Web stood up.

"Maria, should we go?"

Maria got up from the table, casting a backward glance at Peter and Neil. "I'll call you."

Web walked Maria to her car.

"I didn't know about Peter and the sheriff until tonight shortly before you came in. I'm sorry he had to put you through that."

"Maria, they don't know what they're dealing with."

"I don't know who to believe any more. To me, you seem right, but after hearing what Block said . . ." Maria was confused and tired.

"You should go home and get some rest. I'll keep up the search. There are many more leads to follow. We can't give up."

Maria went pale, as if ready to pass out.

"Hold me, Web."

He put his arms around her. Her head rested on his shoulder for a long time, and he just listened to her breathing and the beating of her heart.

She pulled away, tears on her cheeks. "Whatever you do, Web, don't give up. I need you. I need to know that you're still fighting for me, searching for this person, despite what Rowan or Block or anyone else says. You really care—you have the passion and drive that 'professionals' have lost."

"I will not give up, Maria. Believe in that."

"Good night, Web."

Web got out of her car. Maria started her car and drove away, toward her home full of relatives and food and grief. Walking back to his room, Web realized that he'd left his briefcase in the meeting room.

He went back to the room where he had left Peter and Neil Dillon. When he opened the door, he heard something drop to the table. Sheriff Block had joined them and defensively folded his arms on his chest.

Web stared the man down. "Block, you're blinding yourself. Your approach will only yield what you're already looking for."

The sheriff nodded. "I already know what you think of me, Sloane."

"Well, you can hope and pray this killer behaves like you want him to. Because that's the only way you'll catch him."

"Whatever," said the sheriff.

The three men stood up from the table as Web gathered his papers. They stared at him in silence.

"Don't forget your notebook," said Block, shoving a thick green binder across the table.

"Thanks."

Peter Rowan walked over to Web. "Thanks for everything you've done so far." Rowan extended his hand. "I'm sorry it had to come to this."

Web didn't shake. "Don't be."

Web left without saying good-bye. He put the notebook into his briefcase. He didn't remember taking it out, but it had been a long day.

That night he replayed the events of the day repeatedly in his mind. Something was out of place. Why did Block

consider him crazy? To whom had he spoken? The policeman in Sacramento? Reynolds of the FBI?

Nothing he had done justified such extreme treatment. In
the seventies, when half a dozen ad hoc committees assisted
in the search for Bundy, none of them had been so completely shut out of the loop.

Someone was making a concerted campaign to discredit
Web, but who? A thought flashed through his mind. Is
someone in law enforcement the killer? It had happened
before. Many serial killers were fascinated with police work.
It wouldn't be hard to imagine that a cop was behind
carnage. If the person had the right clout and credentials, he
could effectively aim the search in the wrong direction. Was
it Jack? Block? Someone in one of the multitude of other
tiny jurisdictions with whom he had spoken on the phone?
Web needed to see the official investigation records to find a
list of suspects, but he knew no one who would willingly
share such information with him. He would have to acquire
them, in the terms a spy might use, through "other channels."

30

At his next Ethics of Information class Web gave a presentation he usually reserved for professional seminars. Most of
those attending weren't ready for this advanced topic.
Although he spoke to a group of sixteen, he was really
targeting a smaller audience: one student. The lecture was
titled "The *Enigma* Enigma" and explored the moral ambi-
guities of "protected knowledge."

"The question of how to deal with ethical and moral
problems in the information age is not new. Just over fifty
years ago, a world leader allowed thousands of the citizens
of his nation to burn to death and tens of thousands of

homes be destroyed rather than reveal what hackers might call one 'bit' of information. He could have prevented widespread devastation with one phone call, but to this leader, protecting one single 'yes' or 'no,' an 'on' or an 'off,' was worth the deaths of thousands of his countrymen.

"In the spring of 1940 English Prime Minister Winston Churchill received intelligence that the city of Coventry was to be bombed by Nazi airplanes. The source was a high-level Nazi radio transmission that had been intercepted and decoded by English cryptographers. Churchill had little doubt about its authenticity.

"The intercepted message left Churchill with a moral dilemma that would have been unknown in simpler times. Should he warn the citizens of Coventry of the impending attack? If he did, thousands of lives could be saved. People could take refuge in bomb shelters, and fire fighters could be alerted. Churchill loved Coventry. He had family and friends living in the city. Its ancient cathedral was unique and irreplaceable.

"But any precautions taken in the city would reveal an important secret to the Nazis: Hitler would discover that England had the capacity to decode his communications. Unbeknownst to Hitler, England had obtained a sophisticated coding device used by the Nazis: the Enigma Machine. If Churchill sounded a warning, the Nazis would change their codes to ensure that future communications were secure. Churchill could no longer eavesdrop on Hitler and anticipate his battle plans. A vital channel of wartime information would be wiped out, and Churchill might not receive advance warning of the expected full-scale invasion of Britain."

"It was Churchill's legal and moral obligation as prime minister to evacuate Coventry. But he did not; he kept the intercepted message to himself. Churchill broke English law and let a horrible fate befall thousands of innocents; their blood was truly on his hands. If the public had discovered his neglect, Churchill might have been driven out of office or shot as a traitor, so easy would it have been to characterize him as a Nazi collaborator."

Web loved giving this lecture. It always created a heated

debate and alerted students to the notion that "greater good" cannot come without a cost, sometimes a terribly high cost. He spoke with dramatic flair, letting his voice fall down to a whisper so the students had to lean forward to hear him.

"Churchill later said it was the hardest decision he ever made. During that long, tragic night the prime minister prayed in a London bunker while he received report after report of the devastation. He was immediately faced with the ramifications of his decision. Thousands of lives were lost. The cathedral was damaged extensively.

"If Churchill *had* evacuated Coventry, we might be speaking German in this classroom today. Even with so great a justification, Churchill never overcame his remorse for Coventry's fate."

The students were silent. Web drank from a glass of water, then extracted several photos from a large envelope. They were images of Coventry on the night of the bombing: the cathedral surrounded by flames, its stained-glass window shattered; burned bodies on stretchers being moved by firemen; a British woman in a housedress, her mouth opened in a silent scream, a tow-headed toddler in pajamas dead in her arms. The students quietly passed the photos from desk to desk.

Web was interested only in the reaction of one skinny, long-haired kid. He watched as Renny McDonald, the computer hacker forced to take the class as punishment, looked at the pictures. The reaction was good. McDonald seemed to take the material seriously.

He talked for the rest of the hour about disinformation, moral ambiguity, and more technical issues, which in the context of the Coventry preface fascinated the students. At lecture's end he recovered his photos from the students and excused them. They marched out with stern faces, as if from a church service.

Web put his hand on Renny McDonald's shoulder as the student folded up the laptop computer on which he had been taking notes.

McDonald looked up. "Hey! Excellent lecture, Prof. Totally major."

Web smiled. "Renny, I wanted to talk to you about something," Web said.

"Is it about me keeping up? I've been doing okay, I think," said McDonald.

"Tell you the truth, you're doing better than anyone in the class. Can I buy you a beer?"

"No can do. I'm only eighteen. I'll take a Dr Pepper, though."

"All right."

At the student union, Web paid for a beer and a Dr Pepper and led Renny to an outside table away from other students, where they could talk without being overheard.

"So, what's hanging, Prof?"

"Renny, I want to tell you some things. They're going to sound outrageous—unbelievable."

"Fire away."

The student sucked on his soda as Web talked.

"The daughter of a friend of mine was murdered, her body left in the woods."

The boy set down his soda. He eyed Web cautiously. "Wow. I'm sorry."

Web raised his hand. "I just want you to listen for a bit. I think her murder is related to at least six and possibly as many as eleven murders and disappearances that have occurred over the last couple of years. I've been following related stories through the newspapers and a few contacts at law enforcement agencies. I predicted three missing girls would be found dead. They were."

"What is it? Some kind of psycho or somethin'?"

"Yes, something like that. I'm nearly certain that it's one person with recognizable habits and a criminal signature that is very distinctive. He will probably leave California, or even flee the country, very soon if he's not caught."

"Why are you telling me this?" asked Renny.

"I need your help. The FBI and Vine County sheriff's department have declared me a persona non grata. Even though I may be the best chance they have of catching this person."

"Why?"

"It's a long story, but they've decided my hunches were

luck, my insight paranoid, my predictions for this murder-er's future behavior wrong. But they don't know what they're dealing with. I do."

"Jeez, that's serious. What kind of help do you need from me?"

"Renny, I need to get into the FBI's computer system and see what they know."

"Jesus Christ. You know why they put me in your class, right?"

Web nodded somberly.

Renny rolled his head around on his neck, as if doing a stretching exercise. "You better give me that beer."

Web handed the beer to Renny. He put his hand to his temple. "You don't have to help me at all. It will not affect your grade if you don't. If you want to leave right now, you should."

Renny sipped on the beer and stared at Web. "How's it going to help you? I mean, what's the point?"

"I've tried to assess this killer's personality. I have a very good idea what he's like, and I've had success in predicting his behavior. But I don't know the specifics of his recent actions, or how far along the FBI is, or what connections they have made. More importantly, there are reasons to believe that someone who works in law enforcement may be . . . involved. I need to see the official records to find out." Web leaned forward. "It's a hunch. I've been right before, but I've also been wrong. If the killer works in law enforcement, the official records may point him out and stop him."

"You think this could, like, save a life?"

"It could save dozens, but it might be spitting in the wind."

McDonald squinted. Web could see a change in his posture, a change in attitude. The wheels were turning in the boy's mind. The Coventry lecture had done its work.

"I could get in big trouble."

"Renny, if we get caught, I'll take the rap. I'd also like to add something else to make it worth your while. No matter what happens, I'll recommend that the university remove the previous troubles from your records."

"That's not necessary," said the boy, grinning slightly.

"I'd be glad to," said Web.

"I didn't say I don't want you to. I said it isn't necessary to clean up my records. Those are two different things."

"It's been reversed already?"

"Let's just say my disciplinary file got . . . lost."

Web grinned. He was pleased that the boy was willing to confide in him, even if he so gleefully admitted having altered university records. He remembered a campaign joke that had followed Mayor Daley of Chicago all his life: He may be a crook, but he's *our* crook.

"About the FBI computer. Are you interested?" Web asked.

"Interested? Okay. You see, the FBI has two kinds of access. They either have a hardwire, in other words, a direct line that doesn't go through the phones. That's at their branches and stuff and is totally untappable. Their second main security attempt is automatic callback, and that's mostly for police stations and other people on the periphery of the loop." McDonald spoke in a different voice, rapidly spitting out the words. He was talking only about strategy; Web could see that he was already "on board."

"You think you can do it?" asked Web.

"Mm, depends, really. The auto-callback hack will only work if we're at a recognized node. Y'see, say you're Joe Local Cop. You want to get into Telnet FBI/SKID, right? You dial, put in a password, that kind of crap. It checks it against a list of who you should be, terminates, then calls you back. Asks you for the password again, and you're rolling."

Web followed the boy. "You have to call from a police station?"

"Bingo." Renny licked his lips.

"I have a phone number for Telnet/SKID . . ." said Web.

"Doesn't matter. The Telnet calls you back. So if you access initially from, like, your home, right? And like, you use Joe Local Cop's I.D., Telnet won't call you back at your home. It'll call Joe Local Cop back at the node in his station."

"I guess there's no way," said Web.

"I didn't say that. Just about every little jerkwater police station is on Telnet. It's in the name of having a complete system, right? But it also makes for a leaky system." The boy was on a roll.

"How do you know so much about it?"

"Well, number one, the specs for the sys are public info. I happen to know that *you* designed a significant portion of the database. FBI put out a bid in '88 to update the system, right? And they're government, so private companies have to be able to bid on the job. So let's say I got a copy of those specs somehow. You know, a guy says he's a computer contractor who does government work. He gets all kinds of interesting mail that way. And let's say this guy might have been on the system before they implemented the callback security." Renny referred to himself in third person as a way of denying responsibility.

"Do you think campus security is on the system?" asked Web, suddenly fascinated by the boy's description of the system.

"Everybody down to parking meter maids can be on it if they want to. That way some Washington suit says 'We have 54,000 police forces on the network,' even if three-quarters of them are a joke."

"I have a pass key to just about every building on campus. We could go in there at night . . ."

McDonald bit his lip and shook his head. "Bad idea. Nobody does work at night on those systems, or hardly anyone. They probably audit nighttime transmission a lot closer 'cause there's maybe ten or fewer lines active. During the day, we'd get lost in the shuffle a lot easier. I heard of one guy who got on a police system during the Fourth of July parade when hardly anybody was there. We need a parade or something."

"What about Saturday? It's a slow day on campus, and this weekend is Career Day. Chances are the security folks will be there rather than at the office." Web was beginning to think like a hacker.

McDonald let out a long, slow whistle. "Wow. You're talking for real. Jeez. You know this could mean jail. If we're caught. They jailed Robert Morris on his first offense. This would be my third."

Jail. The thought made Web cringe. "I understand if you don't want to do it. Don't let me pressure you."

The boy finished the beer in one big gulp. "I think it might be fun. It sounds like an interesting challenge. And if it saves a life . . ."

"You want to meet me here on Saturday?" Web asked.

"What the hell." He stood up to leave. "By the way, was that whole Coventry thing for my benefit?"

"Well, ah, it's a true story," said Web, unexpectedly caught in his own deceit.

"Yeah, I know. Enigma was what got me into the hacking and cracking game. I read about it when I was nine years old and got hooked; I always wanted to be one of those secret code breakers who saved the world. I guess this is my chance." The boy picked up his backpack and computer and disappeared into a throng of students.

Web sat at the table till the boy was a safe distance away, then got up and walked away in the opposite direction. He was beginning to feel like some kind of spy. He had already broken into a private home to get evidence; breaking into a computer was almost a step down.

The ashes he had stolen still languished in his office at home, untouched. First Joyce's pregnancy, then Tanya's funeral had taken up all his time. Now he had to find out how to analyze them. Web went to his office and called the funeral director in Tico.

"May I speak to Russell Haxby, please?"

"Speaking."

"My name is Web Sloane. I was at the funeral for Tanya de Rivera on Saturday. I first wanted to say that your service was beautiful."

Web thought flattery might get him off on the right foot.

"Thank you very much, Mr. Sloane." Haxby had a voice like a warm breeze, soothing and gentle. "It's not often that I get compliments in my field."

"That's actually not why I called. I have a question that no one can answer."

"Yes?"

"A relative was cremated. There was some talk that the

funeral home in Florida may have taken, uh, Grandma's gold teeth."

"Oh, my God. That horrible story again. I'm so sorry that had to happen to you, Mr. Sloane. Most homes belong to the National Association of Funeral Directors. You know the practice is strictly prohibited. But there are a few sad cases every year . . ."

"Well, I don't believe it's true, but my cousin is threatening a lawsuit. I was wondering if there is any way to test to see if the gold teeth are there in the ashes. I believe that the funeral director was honest." Web thought more flattery would be even more helpful.

"Why don't you just ask your cousin not to file suit? I would bet that his charges are groundless."

"I've tried that, but he's insistent. I think he's just misplacing his grief for Grandma. The proprietor of the funeral home seems like an upright small businessman and I don't want to drag him into court. Is there any way I could test the ashes to shut up my cousin . . . ?"

"Mr. Sloane? If I may level with you, lots of these cases are filed every year. Most of them, if not all, are without merit. We've been sued twice, the first time resulting in an exhumation. The second case was a cremation, like your late grandmother."

"And were you vindicated?"

"Of course we were, Mr. Sloane."

"Of course. How did you determine what had happened with the ashes?"

"Mr. Sloane, any good laboratory can do an analysis of gold content. We used two labs—our lab and the prosecution's lab, and both determined that we were innocent of wrongdoing."

"Oh, I see. Thank you so much for your time."

"Good-bye."

With one call to a friend at the chemistry department, Web located a laboratory that could do quantitative analysis. A test for gold would cost one hundred thirty dollars. Money well spent. On his way home he dropped off a Ziploc bag full of ash at the lab. They promised him results within a week. For purposes of the test, Web had to let them know that it was human remains. He was glad he didn't have to reveal whose.

Early Saturday morning Web went to the campus. He took a long walk past the central plaza where dozens of corporations and personnel recruiters had set up tables for Career Day. Military contractors, computer companies, engineering firms, and the armed forces were represented by shiny, expensive booths with video displays; smaller companies had card tables. All the recruiters wore suits or business dresses. Web searched through the maze of tables until he found what he was looking for: the UC Berkeley Recruiting section. Various Berkeley departments had their own tables, but buried deep inside was a stand occupied by five men in snazzy uniforms: Campus Security—Full-Time or Part-Time—Day or Night Hours PLUS PLUS PLUS Tuition Remission. Just what Web had hoped to see. Campus security was recruiting. They might not be tending the store too closely today.

In front of the military recruiters, several hundred students held placards and yelled chants, "DOD is death," "War machines have got to go," and similar sentiments. A large group of campus security stood nearby, keeping a watch on the demonstration. Web walked up to one of the students and discovered that they were protesting the proposed installation of a multimillion-dollar Department of Defense research facility on the campus. He thanked the student for his answers but refused to sign a petition calling for the resignation of three prominent professors who were accused of skimming millions of dollars from defense contracts. He was pleased that the protest tied up campus security forces.

He strolled back to his office taking a circuitous route. Web knew the main campus security office was staffed twenty-four hours a day, but there were three substations: one near the north end, one near the dorms, and one in the student union. The first two substations he visited were open for business and fully staffed. Then he walked to the student union. In front, a knot of street musicians played conga drums. He dropped a dollar into their hat, then entered the building. Activity in the bookstore was slow. An office door in a hallway that led to the bowling alley and photocopy center was marked Campus Security. The hours were listed: Monday through Friday, 8:00 A.M. to 6:00 P.M. He tried his master key on the door. It wouldn't even fit in. His pulse pounded in his forehead. "Damn."

He rushed across campus to his office. Renny McDonald sat on the floor in the hallway, immersed in his laptop computer. He wore a blue jumpsuit.

"Glad you could make it, Prof. Did you see *The Untouchables?*"

"Hi, Renny. *The Untouchables?* No, why?"

"There's this great line. Just before smashing down a speakeasy, Eliott Ness says 'Let's do some good.'"

"And then?" asked Web.

"And then Ness gets embarrassed by reporters because he breaks into the wrong place and there's no illegal liquor. I just watched it last night. It was great."

Web stared dumbfounded at the boy. "That's good?"

"Well, I liked it."

"I want to get my bearings," said Web.

"We should go for it before we get scared. Just march right in like we own the place."

"I checked the campus security offices. They're all open but one, and my key doesn't work in that one. We might have to consider a Plan B."

"I'm way ahead of you. Student union, right?" asked Renny, proving how much he knew.

"Yeah . . ."

"You can get in through the staff bathroom. I bet you could crawl through the ceiling."

"Are you sure?"

"Of course I'm not sure. It's worth a try though. Architecture school library has blueprints. I could have told you your key wouldn't fit. They rekeyed in '88. That was in the library, too."

"Let's go, then."

As they marched into the student union, Web directed the conversation to dull topics. He felt more like a spy than he ever had before. As they passed the street musicians, one of them made eye contact with Web and stared as he passed. It made Web uncomfortable.

Between the security office and the entrance of the eight-lane student bowling alley was a faculty rest room. Web fumbled with his master key, which wouldn't fit into the lock.

"Try the bathroom key, Prof," whispered McDonald.

Web laughed nervously and switched keys. *Of course.* The staff bathrooms all had the same key. He opened the door, then switched on a light. In the small room were two urinals and a stall.

Web whispered, "Security would be right back there." He pointed behind the urinals.

"You don't have to whisper. Here, I'll flip you to see who goes in." Renny flipped a coin into the air and yelled "Heads!"

The coin landed heads up.

"Looks like you're climbing, Prof."

"Do you think you could go first? I mean, with my arm and all . . ." Web held up his wrist, which was still in a cast.

Renny laughed. "Yeah. Why don't you take a closer look at my coin?"

Web picked it up. It was double heads.

"I didn't figure you'd want to go first anyway," said McDonald, with a smirk. "Okay. You hold the door to the bathroom closed. I'm going to climb into the ceiling. In a few minutes come around and knock on security's door. Bring my bag of tricks. I'll let you in." The boy climbed on top of the sink, then deftly shifted until he stood on top of one of the urinals. He pushed up a ceiling tile.

Web held the door closed. His knuckles were white with tension. The boy's feet disappeared up into the ceiling, then his hands reached back down and replaced the tile. The sound of the boy's feet banging in the ceiling echoed through the bathroom.

After the noise in the ceiling ceased, Web went into the hallway carrying McDonald's computer and backpack and paced up and down. He went into the bowling alley for a moment and watched a student bowl three strikes in a row to the cheers and shouts of his buddies. Then he went back into the hallway and tapped on the door to security.

There was no immediate answer. He knocked again.

McDonald's muffled voice came through the door. "Prof, is anyone out there?"

He waited till two girls passed him on their way to the bookstore. "Not right now."

"Okay. It's a double-key door. Can't get it open from inside. Come in through the ceiling."

Web's heart jumped a beat.

He returned to the faculty bathroom and slung the backpack over his shoulder. He lifted himself onto the sink, then perched his weight precariously between the sink and the urinal. Every noise seemed amplified.

Web pushed up a ceiling tile. He stowed the backpack and computer inside the ceiling, where he could get to them. He heard a click in the bathroom door and jumped to the ground. A tall man in a turban entered the rest room. Web nodded to the man, a stranger, and went into the toilet stall. He waited until he heard the urinal flush, the water in the sink run, and the door close. The man had left. Web stepped out of the stall.

The hole in the ceiling looked more obvious than ever. He wondered if the man had noticed. Then he climbed back to the top of the urinal and stuck his head into the dark ceiling crawl space. He latched his arm around a pipe. It was hard to pull himself up. He pushed his injured arm through the hole, then he braced his elbow in the space. As he dragged himself up, he knocked another ceiling tile out of place. Inside the crawl space, it took a moment for his eyes to adjust to the darkness.

He replaced the crooked tile, then started to put the other tile back into place when the door opened again.

It was a cleaning crew, a Hispanic man and woman pushing a large cart filled with cleaning supplies. He sat frozen as he watched them enter. Would they look up?

He had to move. He saw light shining through the ceiling ten feet ahead of him, where McDonald had presumably opened up a tile in the security office. He looked down into the bathroom. The cleaning people ran a vacuum cleaner and didn't seem to notice him. He crawled along the insulation till he got to the open tile.

"Renny!" he whispered.

No answer.

"Renny!"

He leaned his head out and saw the boy approach him.

"Hey, Prof. Hand me the stuff."

The boy stood on a desk and took the computer and backpack from Web.

"You hafta jump down. There's no support to hold on to," said McDonald.

Web jumped out of the hole in the ceiling, landing with a loud *thunk* onto the desk. He broke his fall with his good hand.

The room contained two desks, a reception counter, and a shelf full of forms—Burglary Report, Car Theft Report, etc. In the back corner of the room, a glass-paneled booth contained another desk equipped with a computer. The office was silent except for the eerie hum of the fluorescent light.

"I found the terminal, Prof. I don't think we'll have a big problem."

"Okay. Let's move fast," said Web. His palms were sweating.

They entered the glass booth. Web stood back as McDonald sat in the chair facing the terminal.

"Okay. Looks like we have basically a bread-and-butter AT hooked up to a standard-issue 9600-baud phone modem here. V.42 bis, MNP 5. Good stuff."

"That's good," said Web, not really listening.

McDonald reached around to the rear of the computer and flipped a switch. The monitor lit up and the computer hummed for a moment; then a message came onto the screen.

    BERKELEY CAMPUS POLICE REMOTE TERMINAL
    4211
    PLEASE ENTER USER ID:

Web groaned. "We can't even get into the terminal."

"Wait a sec," said McDonald.

McDonald quickly turned the machine off, then on again. He watched the screen closely.

"Mem test . . . BIOS power up . . . auto-exec bat," he announced.

Then he rapidly hit two keys, CNTRL and C, simultaneously.

"We hotwired in. I stopped the security program before it locked us out. Ancient trick; they don't have ROM security on here. We won't even show up on the user log."

McDonald caught Web's puzzled expression. "That's a good thing, Prof."

For all his years of computer training, Web had never illegally entered a system. Although he could make anything from a Cray down to a programmable calculator jump through hoops of fire, Web had never bypassed security arrangements; it had always been laid out for him. He marveled at Renny's encyclopedic knowledge of the weak links of computer security. It was like the difference between a safe maker and a safecracker. A safe maker has to know only one device, his own, whereas a safecracker has to be familiar with hundreds; the true expert is the safecracker.

After tapping the keyboard a moment, McDonald brought up a screen that would log them onto the FBI system.

"Okay, Prof, this is the hitch. We can get into the FBI's net, but we're going to need that entry code. You said you had it."

Web nervously fumbled with his wallet and showed a number to McDonald. "Here it is. I got it about two weeks ago at the FBI headquarters." He set the wallet down on the desk.

McDonald shook his head. "No, no. We don't need the phone number—that's in here automatically. I need a security code, the password."

"I thought you could . . ."

"I can't do miracles. Their system is open to lots of police stations, but you still need an entry code. Stand back for a minute."

Web got out of the way. McDonald pushed the chair out from the desk, laid down on the floor, and began pulling out the desk drawers, one by one.

"Nine out of ten dolts stick their passwords on the bottom of a drawer, thinking it's a great hiding place," said McDonald. He looked at the last drawer, then frowned. "I guess these folks are number ten."

"What about the other desks?" asked Web.

"It's worth a try."

Web went into the main office. He crawled under one of the two desks and pulled out drawers, one by one.

"Nothing here."

"Try the other one."

Web crawled under the second desk. After two drawers, he found a card.

"Something is printed on a sheet of paper."

"What's it say?"

"It's gibberish. KBX3FF8 is typed on a little sheet of paper, and handwritten it says EDWARD7."

"Bingo! You got it, Prof. That's why I always look there first."

Web pulled out a pen and copied the numbers down onto a scrap of paper. Just then, he heard the sound of a key being inserted into the door lock.

"Someone's coming!" said Web, but before he had the words out McDonald had already climbed on top of the desk and was pulling his feet through the ceiling.

Web exhaled and pushed the drawers of the desk shut. He could think of no reasonable excuse for being in there.

The door opened. He stood up, not knowing what to expect.

It was the janitorial staff. The man pushed in the cart of cleaning supplies and saw Web but did not react.

"Is okay? Good to clean now?" the man asked.

"No. Could you clean later?" said Web.

"We need to clean? Is okay?" said the man, obviously not understanding what Web had said. Web walked over to him.

"No. Not today. No clean today. No. Not necessary," he said, waving his hands in front of him while shaking his head, hoping to iron out any misunderstanding.

The man grinned. He was missing a front tooth. "Okay. No clean today, okay?"

"No. *Gracias,*" said Web, using the little Spanish he knew.

"Okay. Clean *mañana. Gracias.* Good-bye." The janitor pushed his cart back into the hall. Web leaned out the door. Nobody else was in the hall. He closed the door and went back toward the glassed-in portion of the room where he knocked on the ceiling.

"Coast is clear."

A panel of the ceiling moved and McDonald hopped down, landing on a desk.

"Good call, Prof. You handled that pretty darn well for a novice. Let's get moving."

"Yeah, okay." Web was shaken by the intrusion. *What if it had been someone from campus security?*

"Did you wedge the door open?" asked McDonald.

"No."

"Then we have to climb back through the ceiling again when we're done."

"Damn."

"Sit down, Prof. We'll be out of here real fast, I think."

"Okay."

McDonald took the slip of paper with the security numbers from Web, then tapped them into the computer. A few seconds later he sat back and watched.

"Okay. We're rolling. Let's see what happens."

An audible dial tone could be heard, then the series of beeps indicating a phone number being dialed. A moment later that noise was replaced by a high-pitched whine.

"It's dialing the host," said McDonald.

Web walked up to the front of the office to see if he had restored the desk to its original state. The sudden ringing of the telephone sounded like a jet taking off in the silent room. Web jumped.

"What's that?" he asked McDonald.

"It's just calling us back."

Web watched over McDonald's shoulder as the screen filled with numbers. The boy tapped a few keys.

```
BERKELEY 4211> telnet FBI.SKID /4211
Dialing . . .
CONNECT.
------------------------------------

       Federal Bureau of Investigation
   SKID Serial Killer Identification DataBase
              All Files Available
------------------------------------
```

AUTH CODE: EDWARD7
WELCOME BERKELEY 4211
USER LEVEL: FULL ACCESS READ-ONLY

"All right! We're in there! Full access!" said McDonald. "We can get at anything we want, we just can't change anything. So, Prof, what're we looking for?"

Web stood over McDonald's shoulder. "Search for three names: TANYA DE RIVERA, ANNABELL NORRIS, and KAREN SIMMONS. Then search for some place headings: TICO, CALIFORNIA; LAKE TAHOE, CALIFORNIA; and MOUNT DIABLO STATE PARK, CALIFORNIA." Web figured that would cover the major crimes he believed to be interrelated.

"Okay. I got SKID. What're we going to do with this info? Can't print it out on their printer. Can't really put it on their hard disk."

"Can we use a floppy? Look at it later?" asked Web.

"Yeah, yeah. Gimme my backpack."

McDonald reached into his bag and pulled out a plastic floppy disk, then jammed it into the machine.

"Okay. This'll take some time, depending on how much data there is. I'm going to route it to the floppy."

"Fine."

McDonald tapped some keys, and Web could see the drive humming; but then the screen went black.

"Is it okay?" asked Web.

"Yeah, yeah . . . It'll probably be a few minutes."

Web paced back and forth in the office. He realized that his fingerprints would be everywhere, if anyone ever suspected that he'd been in the office. While McDonald sat still, Web took out his shirttail and wiped off every surface that he had touched.

It was three o'clock. Career Day was nearing its conclusion; the stands would be coming down. If campus security was likely to show up, it probably would be within a half hour.

He went back into the room. McDonald had the chair leaning backward on two legs.

"It's doing fine, Prof."

"Okay."

The disk drive stopped humming. The screen lit up again.

"We're through here. It searched all six names. I'm going to hang up, okay?"

"Fine. Fine. Let's get going," said Web.

McDonald tapped a few more keys.

```
EXITING SYSTEM 16:04:44 P.M.
BERKELEY NODE 4211 ON-LINE 28 MINUTES
TOTAL CONNECT CHARGE: $462.00
.....
DISCONNECTED
```

"Think anyone will notice a four-hundred-dollar charge?" asked McDonald.

"Jesus!"

"Don't worry. They'll pay it. I bet they don't get the bill for months and by then nobody will think to check if the office was open."

"Let's police the area," said Web.

"Some pun," said McDonald.

Web scanned the entire room for anything out of place. It looked identical to when they had arrived.

"Let's go."

"Your disk, sir." McDonald handed Web the floppy disk.

"How do I read this?"

"It's just ASCII dumps. Any word processor will do."

"Cool." Web discovered that he was taking on the boy's language.

McDonald stood on the desk and removed the ceiling panel, then pulled himself up into the crawl space.

"Hand me the backpack and computer."

Web passed them up and watched McDonald disappear into the ceiling.

Web stood on the desk. The desk was much lower than the urinal; he couldn't quite pull himself up. The cast on his hand made it even more difficult.

"Renny!"

The boy looked down from the ceiling.

"Help me up!" said Web.

"Nothing for me to hold on to. You're pretty much on your own."

"Shit."

Web placed a chair on the desk, then stood on it. He easily pulled himself up into the ceiling but knew the chair would raise suspicion. Bracing his legs against a pipe, Web leaned down into the office. He reached the tip of the chair, lifted it up, and dropped it on the ground. It rolled away from the desk but remained upright.

"We have to straighten the chair," said Web.

"Leave it. Let's get out of here. They'll blame the cleaning crew."

They crawled back to the bathroom, jumped down, then let themselves out. The two regrouped in front of the student union.

"All right!" Renny held his hand over his head. Web puzzled for a moment, then gave an extremely slow high-five.

"Renny, I owe you one."

The boy grinned. "Yeah, well, you know, 'greater good!' "

"Right. How about dinner one night this week? Come out to the house?" asked Web.

"I'm always up for a home-cook. Name your day."

"How about tomorrow night?"

"Done. Take it easy, Prof. Lemme know if you catch your killer."

"Renny?"

"Yeah?"

"Could you please not mention that to anyone? I mean about the killer? Or what we did today?"

"My lips are sealed. Catch you in class next week, Intrepid!"

Web laughed. McDonald called him by the name of the spy who had masterminded the British code-breaking effort in World War II. He didn't feel that sharp, but he liked the compliment.

SKID contained information on virtually every unsolved murder in the United States. That night, on his home computer, Web perused the information stolen from the

FBI. First, he went over the Tahoe murders, with which he was least familiar. As Reynolds had told him, the FBI considered the crimes unrelated to any others, and the report contained a psychological characterization that Web felt was wrong. The file described the suspect as Disorganized Impulsive/Asocial. That meant the FBI believed they were dealing with a person who was out of control. This did not jibe with Web's analysis. He tapped a note onto the computer:

If out-of-control killer (impulsive/asocial), why are there no fingerprints? No hairs? Virtually no evidence of any sort whatsoever? Would an impulsive killer brush away footprints in snow?

The files regarding the bodies found in Tico and those found in Mount Diablo State Park contained nothing new to Web. Because of the length of time between the killer's visit and the discovery of the bodies, virtually no evidence was left to help characterize a suspect.

Even though he knew most details of Tanya de Rivera's case, he decided to examine the FBI file to see what they had listed. It contained familiar facts: date missing, the credit card charges, a list of friends and relatives, and the date and circumstances of the discovery of her body.

Something was wrong. In the computer system, information was listed by incident: For example, the murders in Tahoe were considered one incident, the bones in Tico another. Each time new facts were added, the date was listed at the front of the file. That way people using the system could skip along to files containing new information. But the report showing how computer equipment was purchased with Tanya's credit card had been updated eleven times. Yet, it contained no information beyond what Web and Maria had told the Vine County sheriff the first time they called.

For a wildly complex file, six or eight updates on the system would be a likely maximum. But eleven? On a record of a simple incident no more than two pages long?

Web compared the account in the computer to his own

files. At first glance, it seemed identical. Why had it been changed eleven times, then?

He printed out the report and compared it letter for letter with what he had told the sheriff.

The information had been subtly garbled. The serial number for the computer equipment, which could help find the person who used the credit card, had several transposed numbers. It should have read 2C55923A, but in the FBI computer it said 25CC932A. It could have been a typo; but the serial number for each of the other pieces of equipment was similarly jumbled.

Like the accountant who discovers a massive embezzlement from a seventy-five-cent error, Web methodically searched through all the other files for discrepancies. In almost every report, subtle differences could be detected. 6-5-90 became 5-6-90; a simple transposition, but a suspect who had been traced to an area on May 5th would be useless if the crime occurred on June 6th. A gray BMW convertible became a gray hardtop BMW. By three A.M., Web had uncovered thirty-six tiny errors, any one of which could be considered an innocent typo. Taken together, they pointed at a pattern of deceit.

But who? Someone in the FBI? A skilled hacker like Renny McDonald?

Web went through the files one by one. In every single report that had been altered, the most recent update had been made on "Terminal 02198." Web looked up the list of terminal numbers at the front of the file. 02198 was Vine County.

Vine County!

Web considered what he knew about Sheriff Block.

Block had actively fought against FBI participation in the case. Block had rejected the aid of the Tico committee, ridiculed Web's efforts, and actively stalled whenever any help was offered. It all fit together—perhaps too well—could Block be the one? Or was he being set up as a fall guy? Either way, it seemed the criminal had access to SKID.

Web made some notes:

Is Block killer? Or someone at his station?
1. Knows police procedure.

2. Able to commit crimes that leave little or no evidence.

3. Lives in area that is within one day's drive from the site of every murder and disappearance.

4. Possesses substantial physical strength.

5. Has access to all FBI records of investigation.

The prospect was terrifying to consider. Web looked at the maps he had marked up earlier. Every circle converged on Tico but also on nearby Endocino, a fact he had overlooked earlier since there had been no murders in Endocino.

But who could he tell? He couldn't call Reynolds at the FBI. They already thought Web was crazy and possibly dangerous. What would he say? *Hi, Jack. I just broke into your computer system and . . .* They would promptly throw him in jail and discredit him completely. He had to find out on his own.

If it was Block, he would aggressively move to cover up his tracks.

Web climbed in the attic and opened up a sealed metal box. Inside was a Colt .45 that he purchased after Vicki had disappeared. He hadn't fired it for more than a year, not since he'd left Washington State. He opened a box of shells and inspected them. There was no oxidation; the bullets were still usable. He loaded the gun, fastened the safety, and put it in his pocket. Then he put additional shells in his other pocket.

He climbed down from the attic. It was 5:00 A.M. Web scratched out a note to Joyce, jumped in his car, and sped toward Tico.

31

Mars was near exhaustion. For the three weeks since Alan had come home from the hospital, she had to be his nursemaid, his cook, and his gin-rummy partner. "He needs the rest," said the doctors. Every spare moment of Mars's time was consumed keeping him fed, bathed, and entertained.

Cabin fever was getting the best of both of them. For a week Alan had been well enough to get out of bed and roam around the house. She thought that would be an improvement over having him in her bed all day, but it was much worse. It meant only he followed her around the house. In the kitchen, he always had an opinion about her cooking; in the family room, he always wanted to change the channel of the television set.

Several small spats had erupted about little things— ridiculous things. Once, they got in a shouting match over which hand was better in poker—three of a kind or two pair. Another argument ensued when she screamed at him for entering the bathroom when she was in the tub. It was the only sanctuary in her home where she could get a moment's privacy, and she snapped at him when he walked in without knocking. He felt she overreacted, and the tension had evolved into a lovers' cold war.

In spite of it all, she still loved Alan. Mars believed their conflicts arose because they'd been crammed into close quarters for three weeks. She remembered what it was like before Alan came into her life: a depressing lack of adult conversation and, of course, sex.

Tonight Alan was gone. It was his first time out of the house. He was almost fully recovered from the heart attack and planned to go back to work the following week. He celebrated by taking Farrell to a movie. In spite of everything, her son had grown close to Alan. If not exactly a father figure, at least he was an adult male with whom Farrell could talk.

It was a perfect Saturday night to be home alone. She liked having a man around the house, but not twenty-four hours a day, seven days a week. She was glad, *delighted* actually, that he was well enough to go out with Farrell.

Mars took a long, leisurely bath and puttered around in a fluffy orange bathrobe, killing time, enjoying herself. At 8:30 she popped a bag of cheese popcorn in the microwave. Then she poured a big glass of wine and sat in front of the television, without intending to watch anything in particular. She just wanted to enjoy the luxury of mindlessly flipping through the channels, stopping at whatever amused her, reading her *People* magazine when she got bored.

She was deeply involved in an article about the Sexiest Older Man in America when an image on the television caught her eye. The sound was turned down, but what was shown was a charcoal portrait that reminded her of Alan. She dropped *People* and climbed to the floor to turn up the volume.

" 'Suspect at Large' will be back right after these important commercial messages."

She pulled the robe tight around her body. It wasn't a picture of Alan on the television, of course, just someone who looked a lot like him. *Wasn't it?* She remembered that once upon a time her sister Peggy had resembled Cher, the movie star, so much so that people would stop her on the street. But no longer; Mars teased her sister that Cher was Dorian Gray and Peggy was the aging painting.

The show came back on. The host interviewed a man in front of a hotel. *Oh, that must be Tico!* she thought, recognizing the hotel.

"And most astounding of all," said the host, "is the assertion that the unfortunate girls in northern California who have fallen prey to the monster who is now known as The Spring Break Murderer could be . . ."

The image jumped to Peter Rowan in midsentence.

"Theodore Bundy." Rowan looked pasty and tired in the glare of the television cameras. "Well, a copycat. That's what one guy says who has followed it since the beginning. He has these notebooks outlining a theory that the Spring Break Killer was the same criminal who was here in Tico. The real kicker is the sheriff saw a couple pages of his notes in which this guy says it could even be Bundy himself . . ."

If the producers hadn't edited him midsentence, Peter Rowan would have been heard to say, "but that's completely irrational. I don't believe it and certainly no one else does." But that wasn't how "Suspect at Large" operated. Rather than let Rowan qualify his remark, the TV show went back to their tacky studio where a panel of "experts" speculated on this theory.

Mars turned up the volume. Clinton Bernard's disembodied voice spoke in grave tones as various photos of Theodore Robert Bundy were superimposed on top of a police sketch that had been made of the Spring Break Murderer. Mars hardly heard a word of their wild speculation. All she could think of was how much the photos looked like Alan. The man who burned a ski jacket identical to the one a murdered girl wore. Her lover. Her housemate. The man who was watching a movie with her son.

She didn't hear the front door open.

She didn't hear Farrell yell, "Hi, Mom."

She didn't know that Alan stood in back of the couch until he shouted above the din of the television set.

"Hello, Mars."

She jumped up from the floor, then tried to place herself between Alan and the television. It was too late; he had seen her watching. He knew what she knew.

"Oh, God! You scared me!" she said, then backed up to the TV and turned it off.

"Interesting show." Alan didn't smile. He held his arms by his side. His fists slowly clenched.

"No, no, it's just mental junk food," she said, her voice trembling.

"What's the matter, Mars?" he said.

"Nothing. Nothing really. I didn't expect you back so soon."

"The movie was sold out. So we got a videotape," said Alan. A slight smirk crossed his face, then disappeared like the sun on a cloudy day.

"Good!" Her voice cracked and she forced a smile. "We can all watch it together." She didn't sound very convincing.

"Okey dokey." Alan sat on the couch. There was something vaguely threatening about him. Mars backed away and leaned on the television. She saw Farrell cross the room to the bathroom, a towel over his arm. She tried to catch his eye but failed.

"We have to talk, Mars," Alan said, lighting a Marlboro.

"They told you not to smoke!" she said.

"Don't tell me what to do, Mars. I'll be fine. I feel much stronger. Much better. One cigarette won't hurt."

"It's your life," she said.

"I wanted to talk to you about that TV show."

"What TV show?" she said.

"You know the one. I saw you watching. And I know what you are thinking. The circumstances and coincidences of fate look damning to me," he said, taking on a strangely clinical air. "You probably wonder why I was in Reno."

In spite of her several mental promises to ask him, Mars had never brought up that subject. She had assumed he had lied about going to Oregon and gone to Reno to get laid by whores or something. Roslyn had agreed, and she thought it was better left unmentioned. But now she imagined a much darker answer even than an affair.

"Why were you in Reno? I thought you were going north."

He stood up, waving the cigarette as he spoke. "In my capacity working for Sheriff Block, there is the . . . necessity of doing occasional covert work. Research. Like spying, but legal. I used to do occasional small jobs for the NSA and the CIA. Sometimes these things would be under such deep cover that even I didn't know where I was going until I was there."

"You were spying for a sheriff's department?" she asked, incredulously.

"Mars, I can't really talk about it. But it wasn't the sheriff alone. It was much bigger than that. And that's about all I can say."

"Is that what you did in New York? Not stocks and bonds, but spy stuff?"

"I can't really talk about it, Mars."

"You brought it up."

"I brought it up because of the campaign to discredit me. These things happen in the security community all the time." He looked far away. "I feel the Spring Break Murders were committed by the CIA. You saw that sketch on television. I believe, and this is based on knowledge I can't share, that they are trying to frame me to look like the entity responsible for what may have happened there." Alan spoke like a lawyer, as if he were describing someone else.

"The CIA?" she asked.

"They do more than you think. They could place me in that vicinity at that time, you know. And now this sketch. They may even have . . . drugged me, trying to kill me. But it only caused a heart attack. A little miscalculation. They don't know where I am and by circulating the picture they hope to catch me."

Mars didn't know what to think. She stared at Alan. It didn't feel true, but she had heard wilder stories that had some basis in truth. Mostly, she was scared.

"Alan, this is so outrageous, I don't know what to say."

His eyes darted quickly back and forth across the room.

"What's the matter, Mars?" he asked. "You look like you've seen a ghost."

"I don't know what to make of all this. You're telling me this, this story, but . . . is it true?"

He walked toward her.

"Alan . . ." Mars backed up, away from him, into the corner of the room. "Alan! Say it's true."

"It's true." His voice was flat.

He approached until he was a few inches in front of her. His eyes were flat and unexpressive, like a shark's. This was a side of him she had never seen.

"It's a question of who you trust. Do you trust me? Because then we can do business. If you don't trust me, if you don't for some reason believe me, then maybe we have a problem. The legal system can be bent and stretched into a mockery of truth. I have to know if you believe me. What is it, Mars? Do you trust me?"

"I . . ."

He grabbed her shoulder.

"I've lived here for almost eight months. By that time you get to know a person pretty well. I think you should know if you *trust* me or not? Isn't that a simple question? Can't a simple 'yes' come out? Or is it that you don't trust me? It's pretty fucking simple. What is it, Mars?" He spat the words out, his voice growing increasingly loud.

"Alan, you're scaring me."

"Oh. *I'm* scaring *you.*" He walked with a swagger. "I don't think you trust me, Mars. In a situation like this that could be a bad, bad problem for me."

"Alan . . ."

"Don't pretend it isn't true. I can see it in your face. I could be in a lot of trouble. These, these things . . . this Spring Break Murderer. He looks a lot like me, *doesn't he?*"

"I don't know," she said.

"Don't lie! Don't lie to me, Mars. I saw the sketch. He looks a lot like me. And even though I'm innocent of any crimes, even though I haven't ever done anything, I could be in trouble because of it, *couldn't I?*"

"Yes, I guess." Mars folded her arms in front of herself, as if for protection.

Alan stood up and paced back and forth, like a lawyer addressing a courtroom.

"You guess! You don't have any idea. I know how they work. They go looking for anyone they can hang a crime on and they put it there. If it's convenient they frame him. They don't care if he's innocent or guilty. That's how criminal justice works. It's totally unfair. If they think they can blame an innocent man for a crime, and they think they can prove it to a jury, they will!"

"But, Alan, you haven't done anything," she said in a cracked whisper.

"Of course I haven't! That's the whole point! What happens if you look at a bad picture, put there by the CIA, and even *you* think it looks like me? And you supposedly love me. Do you love me, Mars?"

"Alan?"

"I want you to get on your knees in front of me."

"Why are you doing this?" Tears came to Mars's eyes.

"Do it! If you love me, you will."

Mars slipped down to her knees in front of Alan. She shook with fear and tears ran down her face.

"Do you love me, Mars?" he asked.

"Yes, of course, Alan, of course."

"How much? Do you love me more than anyone else?"

"Alan . . ."

"Do you or don't you? Goddamit, I want an answer."

"Yes, I do," she said, trembling.

He walked across the room and yelled. "Well, then it's goddam high time to start acting like it! I could be in very bad trouble, by a fluke, by an accident of chance, a coincidence. I have to know who trusts me and who doesn't!"

He stormed out of the room. Mars grabbed the telephone and dialed Roslyn's phone number.

It rang twice. "Hello. This is Roslyn Tabor. I'm not in at the moment . . ."

She must be at the diner. Mars quickly dialed the number to the coffee shop where Roslyn worked. It rang several times. Finally, someone answered.

"Diner?"

"I need to speak to Roslyn right away," she said.

"I'm not sure she's here tonight. Just a minute, I'll take a look."

Mars could hear the hubbub of activity. Someone yelled Roslyn's name across the restaurant.

C'mon, get her, c'mon. Answer the phone, please answer the phone, she thought.

When she looked up, Alan had come back into the house. He yanked the telephone out of her hands. Then he ripped the wire out of the wall and threw the phone across the room.

"Goddamit! I knew you were lying! I can't trust you!"

"Alan . . ."

Alan stood between Mars and the kitchen, blocking the only exit out. She saw behind him that Farrell had emerged from the shower. Her son stood in the hallway, watching. The boy ran to the kitchen and grabbed a large knife.

"Farrell, no!" yelled Mars.

Alan whipped around. The boy faced him, a few feet away, the knife in his hand.

"Farrell, what are you doing?" he asked, in his best fatherly tone of voice.

"You leave my mother alone," said Farrell, keeping a firm grip on the carving knife.

Alan lowered his voice to a whisper. "Farrell, we're buddies. Your mother and I just had a little misunderstanding. Didn't I just take you to the movies?" He walked slowly toward the boy and spoke in a gentle, condescending tone. "Why are you treating me like this?"

Farrell tightened his grip on the knife. "I want you to leave my mother alone."

Alan spoke very softly, as if his feelings had been hurt. "I don't know what you plan to do with that knife, but I won't fight back. This is crazy! Don't you see how crazy this is? I'm your buddy, remember? Give me the knife. Let's not get in trouble." Alan shrugged his shoulders and relaxed his stance.

Farrell looked at Alan, then behind him at his mother, catching her eye, as if to ask what to do. Mars shook her head.

In that brief moment of inattention, Alan leaped forward like a cobra striking. He brutally slammed Farrell's arm and sent the knife flying across the kitchen. Then he grabbed the boy in a headlock.

"Don't!" shouted Mars.

Alan picked another knife from the drawer and held it to Farrell's throat. The boy's face contorted with terror.

"Alan, NO!" screamed Mars.

Alan raised his voice, shouting at Mars and into Farrell's ear. "I wanted to trust you. I wanted to, Mars, really I did. But it's apparent from the evidence assembled and from what I've seen tonight that is not a possibility that I can seriously consider any longer."

He backed Farrell into the living room, keeping his eyes on Mars.

"Give me a cigarette."

Mars reached into her purse and pulled out a Benson & Hedges.

"Put one hand behind your back. With the other, put it in my mouth. Do it!"

She put the cigarette into his mouth, then lit it. Alan puffed away, holding the cigarette between his lips.

"I loved you Mars, but I can see betrayal in your face. I have to leave now because you betrayed me. I don't want to hurt Farrell. I really don't. I need any cash you have. I need jewelry, anything I can sell quickly. I have to protect myself. I have to hit the road and I'm sure you'll help me."

She dumped her purse on the ground. Tears streamed down her face.

"This is the cash from the bakery today," she said. "There's about six hundred dollars in here."

"That's good. Put it in a bag. I need more. Don't you keep cash in the house? I thought you did."

"No, there's no money lying around."

"That's a lie!" Alan pulled the cigarette out of his mouth with the hand that held the knife. His other arm was wrapped tightly around Farrell's neck. He drew the lighted ember toward Farrell's cheek.

"Don't! Don't do that!" shouted Mars. Farrell was deathly white and crying.

"Where's the cash, Mars?" asked Alan.

"Um, um, there is the safe at the bakery. I think there's about four thousand dollars in there."

"I thought so. This is what happens if you lie any more." He pushed the cigarette into Farrell's cheek. The boy screamed.

"Stop it, stop it!" shrieked Mars.

Alan smirked at her. "Next time I might miss and hit his eye. So write down the combination."

She grabbed a magazine and a pen and wrote down four numbers.

"Good. I'm glad to see we're communicating." He dragged the boy backward toward the bedroom.

"Get the bag and put all your jewelry into it."

She followed him into the bedroom and dumped all of her jewelry, collected over years, into the paper bag. The last piece to go in the bag was the special Zuni necklace Alan had bought for her.

"That, too. Quit fucking around, Mars!"

She dropped it into the bag.

"Now let's go back to the kitchen."

He dragged Farrell backward down the hall. Mars followed two steps behind. Farrell never lost eye contact with her.

In the kitchen he reached into his back pocket and pulled out a pair of police handcuffs and threw them on the floor.

"Put your hands behind your back and put these on your hands."

"Why? Why, Alan?"

"I don't know if I can trust you any longer. So what if you call the police before I get to the bakery? Just do it. You said you loved me. I won't hurt you."

"What are you going to do?"

"I'm not going to do anything I don't have to. Now put on the handcuffs!"

Mars put her hands behind her back and clicked the cuffs over her wrists.

"Turn around."

She spun around. He reached forward and tightened the cuffs on her wrists until they cut off the circulation to her hands.

"Mars, I don't want to do this. I really don't."

Farrell coughed, then threw up. The vomit covered Alan's arm.

"Goddamit!" Alan pulled himself away from the boy, then with astounding force bashed his head, knocking him to the ground. With her hands behind her back, Mars kicked Alan in the crotch.

"You little shit." Alan picked up a glass blender from the counter and slammed it into Mars's face. She fell to the ground, blood gushing out of a wound across her cheekbone.

Then he kicked her son who lay prone on the floor.

"I really wish this weren't necessary." Alan opened the kitchen closet and took out a roll of packing tape. He sat on top of Farrell and taped his hands behind his back. He was very handy with the tape roll; it looked as if he had done this many times before. Very quickly he had completely incapacitated the boy, who lay helpless on the ground.

Mars reached for the knife.

Alan stomped her hand with the heel of his shoe.

"You made me do this, Mars."

He taped Mars as tightly as he had taped Farrell. Their knees were bound together so that neither could stand or move. Mother and son lay back to back on the kitchen floor. Mars watched helplessly.

He closed the door to the hall, then he closed all the windows in the room.

"I'm not going to kill you. Nobody will say I hurt you. I've never done anything like this before, but I've been betrayed horribly."

Alan lit a single candle and placed it at the end of the long hallway. Mars could see its flickering light.

Then he walked to the fireplace and turned the gas jet on. He returned to the kitchen and opened the oven. He twisted the knob. Then he started all four burners of the gas stove. There were no pilot lights. The jets made a tinny cacophony of hissing. Mars could smell the odorized natural gas.

"Good-bye, Mars."

He walked out of the room and slammed the door. She heard his car start and drive away.

Mars did something she had not done in years. She prayed. She and her son were immobile on the floor, back to back. Soon the gas cloud would reach the candle at the end of the hall and ignite.

She rolled over, so that she could see Farrell's face. The look in his eyes sent a shock wave of strength through her body. Mars struggled with the bonds but could not stand up or move her hands. The sickening sulfur smell grew increasingly strong. How long till it blew up? A minute? Ten minutes? A half hour? She didn't know.

Mars rolled over, then rolled over again. If she could reach the knife on the floor, maybe she could slit some of the tape on her hands. She slid the last several feet toward the knife, leaving a smear of blood where her face rubbed against the floor.

She touched the knife. It was flat on the ground. With her wrists she slid it against the bottom of a cupboard.

The gas was getting very thick. She was suddenly dizzy. *Please, God, please, oh please . . .*

She tilted the knife up. Then she rammed the packaging tape against the pointed end. The knife cut into the heel of her hand. But she didn't care. Her son would be killed. Her only son. She pushed the tape as hard as she could against the knife. Blood obscured the vision in her left eye. She ripped the tape free. With her left hand she cut the tape on her legs, then ripped it off her mouth. It pulled out a wad of hair.

"C'mon, Farrell!"

She quickly turned off the gas stove and oven, then lifted Farrell with all her strength, holding him in her arms, crying out as her broken hand bent unnaturally backward.

She took two steps toward the door. As she opened the latch, air rushed in. She heard a terrible whooshing sound. A ball of fire shot down the hallway from the candle. Suddenly flames engulfed her.

Glass flew out from the windows.

Mars dove to the ground, covering her son with her body. The world around her turned into an inferno. For a few seconds she heard nothing, felt nothing. Except her son. Propelled by instinct more than thought, she covered Farrell. Her only thought was *I will not let him die.*

Mars' hair was ablaze. If she hadn't been temporarily blinded she would have seen that dozens of glass shards were imbedded in her skin. She was covered with blood from the wounds.

She willed herself to stand up in the flames, protecting her son with her full body. Mars struggled out the door, dragging Farrell in front of her. She got several steps away from the house to the safety of the gravel driveway. In back of her the house was aflame, burning everywhere at once. But now Farrell was safe.

Mars dropped to the ground. The last thing she saw in the world was Farrell, helplessly bound with tape, staring pitifully back at her. But he was alive.

The explosion four miles behind him shook the VW Cabriolet. Theodore Robert Bundy glanced into the rear view mirror, satisfied to see the black smoke heaving into the air. He never gave another thought to Mars Chittenden or her son Farrell. Or to Roslyn Tabor, dead on the floor of her house a hundred yards from Mars's home. If he was lucky, the fire would obscure the fact that she had been smothered. Now he had to put to rest "Alan DeVries."

When he arrived at the Vine County sheriff's station, only the night dispatcher was on duty. The three deputies were cruising and no one else would come in until shift change at 6:00 A.M., barring a major incident. Bundy pressed his face against the window. A buzzer sounded in the door, and he walked in.

"Hi, Alan. I heard you're coming back on Monday! It's good to see you up and around," said Eunice, a forty-four-year-old ex-Texan. Vine County's first female cop, Eunice would still be on patrol if a stray bullet hadn't confined her to a wheelchair.

"Thanks, Eunice. How's it going around here?"

"Block's been saving up your work for when you get back. He's said a dozen times that he doesn't know what he'd do without you."

"Thanks! That's good for my job security."

"Sure enough. What're you doing in here so late?"

"Just wanted to see what awaited me on Monday. I guess I was just bored."

"Oh," she said.

"Can you let me back into the offices?"

"You know I can't, Alan. It's after hours, and you're not deputized."

"You're such a stickler, Eunice," he said with a grin.

"That's why they love me, Alan."

"Do you know where Block is?"

"Well, being as it's Saturday night, and it's nearly ten o'clock, he'll be at home for another hour till 'Twin Peaks' is over, then he'll be out drinking till dawn at The Forge. That's just a guess, based on the fact that Block has done that every Saturday night for the last six months."

"I didn't know he's a 'Twin Peaks' fan."

"A show about a small-time sheriff solving an inexplicable murder? Of course he is," she said, laughing.

"C'mon, you can let me into the offices. I promise I won't tell . . ."

He walked around to the back of her desk.

She looked up at him. Her face was stern.

"Alan, how long have you known me?"

"I don't know. Six months?" he said.

"More or less. In all that time have you seen me break a security rule?"

"No."

"Does that tell you something?" she asked.

"Well, I of course don't want to get you in trouble," he

said with a look of boyish resignation. Eunice winked at him, as if to say "we're friends but I still won't let you in."

Just then the phone rang. Eunice pushed a button on the board. As soon as the connection was made, the caller's address flashed onto the 911 system screen.

"Vine County Emergency," said Eunice.

The call could be heard over the loudspeaker.

"I'm calling to report a fire." Bundy recognized the voice. It was old Ed Ridenour, who had a vacation house only a few hundred feet from Mars Chittenden. He was rarely home; Bundy hadn't thought to check his house.

"What address, please?"

The line went dead. Eunice whipped around to see Bundy holding a severed phone wire. Before Eunice could speak, he wrapped the wire tightly around her neck. He pulled so hard that it knocked her wheelchair over backward. Bundy looked away from her bulging, purple face. Her expression was more of betrayal than pain.

Eunice eventually stopped struggling. Bundy felt her pulse. When he was satisfied that she was dead, he reached into her drawer and pulled out the keys to the main office. He knew the office file system like an old friend. It took only a few minutes to run every file about himself through the standard-issue paper shredder. Just to be sure, he ran the strips of paper through a second time so that only dust emerged.

He had one more stop before leaving town. He would have to pay Sheriff Block a visit at home. "Twin Peaks" would be on for another forty-five minutes.

32

The early morning haze combined with Web's lack of sleep made it difficult to locate Maria's house. Driving at a crawl, he finally spotted her mailbox surrounded by white and red roses and pulled into her gravel driveway. The Volvo lurched forward, spitting rocks to the side, the result of his hitting the brakes too hard. It was a few minutes past 6 A.M.

He walked across the lawn. When he reached the door, his feet were damp from the dew-covered grass. There was a long delay before she answered the door. Maria wore a velvet bathrobe and squinted at Web standing on her porch as if he were a tax collector.

"Web, why are you here?"

"I only have a minute. I want to give you some important documents. I think that Sheriff Block, or someone in his employ, may be involved in the murders."

She stood silent.

"Block? My God." She moved back into the house. "Come in."

Web walked into her hallway. Dozens of beautiful condolence cards covered the hall table, and every variety of flower filled the room. Web rubbed his hands together to warm them.

"Why do you believe this, Web?" she asked.

"It's a long story, Maria. Basically, someone at the Vine County sheriff's station is altering FBI records, trying to impede the investigation. If it's Block himself, I have to stop him. If it's someone else, I have to alert him right away."

Maria covered her eyes with her hand. *"Dios mio!* To think of all the things I told that man. Why right now, so early in the morning?"

"If it is the sheriff, I have to get to him while his guard is down."

She gently placed his hands between her own. The warmth felt good; she smelled like a scented bath. She looked into his eyes. "Do you think it is dangerous?"

"I don't know." Web saw Maria's worried reaction. "But I've taken precautions."

"Wait one moment before you go." Maria left the hall for a moment, then returned with a large travel mug of coffee.

"Coffee! You read my mind, Maria."

She set the mug on the hall table and met his eyes. Web leaned in and pressed his lips to hers. At first it was a simple good-bye peck, but then he pulled her close; Web felt desire flow into him like a volatile liquid.

"Web," she whispered. "You must come back."

Her words echoed in his ear for a moment before he answered. Web knew the dangers he faced; but he also knew he must do everything in his power to stay alive. "I will."

Web's tires screeched as he navigated the winding mountain road. As he neared Endocino, he suddenly plunged into a thick bank of fog, obscuring his vision of the winding road. Almost instantly the smell made him realize it was not fog at all; it was smoke coming from a forest fire. The flames were visible about a mile ahead of him, off to the left of the road. He turned on the A.M. news radio to see if there were any reports. There weren't.

As he drove through Endocino, the traffic signals were still flashing yellow; the town hadn't yet woken up. He passed a paperboy and a donut truck. When he got to the north side of the town, he opened his address book and a map. Block was only a couple of miles away.

He turned off the main road onto a heavily wooded lane with several widely spread out houses. He drove about fifty yards beyond Block's house, turned the car around, and parked.

He pulled out his gun and removed the safety. It was heavier than he remembered. The street was eerily calm.

After he walked past a clump of trees, Block's house could be seen. A '59 Corvette was on blocks in the lawn. The sheriff's Jeep Cherokee, caked with dried mud, was in the driveway. Block was definitely home.

Web walked around to the back of the house. He squatted

below one window, then another, peering in, hoping to ascertain Block's location. No lights were on inside the two exposed rooms. The other two were blocked by heavy curtains. He returned to the front of the house.

He positioned himself to one side of the front door. He took a deep breath, then shoved the door gently with his foot.

It swung open easily with a creak, unlocked and unlatched. Web peered into the living room, fully expecting to be shot. Magazines and newspapers were scattered across the floor. Several empty beer bottles were on the coffee table. The television was on, featuring the strangely happy faces of a religious program. But no one was in the room.

"Block?" yelled Web.

There was no answer. He held his gun at arm's length and took a few quiet steps, when something fell over in the kitchen, which was off to the right of the living room. He couldn't see into the room.

Web ducked behind furniture as he crossed the living room.

Another noise came from the kitchen. Web thrust his gun in first, then leaned in with his head. What he saw made him instantly put the gun down.

Block lay on the floor. A dark sticky pool of blood had formed around his head. Web ran over to him and knelt by his side.

"Sheriff," said Web. "Jesus!"

Block produced only a gurgling sound.

Then Web saw the bullet entry wound on the sheriff's jaw. Half of his cheek had been ripped away but he was still alive. Nearby on the floor lay Block's service revolver. Web grabbed a kitchen towel and formed it into a crude bandage to stop the flow of blood, pressing it against the wound in the upper orthodontia. When it was in place, he picked up the kitchen phone and dialed 911.

The phone rang a dozen times, then a shrill phone company circuit cut in. "We're sorry, your call cannot be completed as dialed." He dialed again and still got no answer.

Rowan is a paramedic, he remembered. He dialed 0.

"Operator, this is an emergency. I need to be connected

with Peter Rowan . . . No, I don't have the number. It's in Tico. 911 has been disconnected."

There was a long pause as the operator connected the call.

"Rowan, this is Web Sloane. I'm at Sheriff Block's house. He's bleeding badly. It looks like he tried to kill himself."

"Why didn't you call 911?" asked Rowan, groggy from being awakened.

"It's been disconnected. Something is up. Block's hurt bad. You need to get here with an ambulance as soon as possible."

"Is he breathing?" asked Rowan.

"Barely. He shot himself."

"Give me the address."

As soon as the address was out of his mouth, Rowan said, "I'm there," and hung up the phone.

Web adjusted the bandage. He hadn't taken a first aid class in a dozen years, but instinctively knew what to do. Block was breathing, all right, but made a horrible gurgling sound each time he inhaled.

"You'll be okay, Block, I've got an ambulance coming, you'll be okay."

Block opened his eyes for a brief moment and looked at Web, then closed them again.

"Come on, keep it together," Web pleaded.

Web ran to the bedroom and dragged out a feather comforter. *Always warm shock victims.* He returned to the kitchen and covered Block with the blanket, then knelt by him and waited. At least the man was still breathing.

Web heard the front door slam shut.

Is someone still here?

Web drew his gun.

"Who's there?"

He walked into the living room. Web turned off the television with his cast, holding the gun in his other hand.

He walked to the window and looked out. The morning was peaceful and silent; a neighbor's sprinkler had come on, but other than that the scene was unchanged from when he was outside.

He crept silently back to the bedroom. It was as he had left it. He went through the kitchen. Block had rolled over, but was still alive.

There was a door to the garage. He opened it slowly, standing to one side.

"Who's out there?"

He flipped on a light to reveal a workshop, some bicycles, and dozens of boxes filled with junk. There were a hundred places to hide in the garage. Web leaned back in, then closed and bolted the door.

He walked back to the living room and heard the door latch move. The door flew open.

"Freeze!" yelled Web, pointing the gun.

"Jesus God, Web, it's me!" shouted Peter Rowan.

"Get in here. Block looks bad."

Rowan ran across the room, carrying two first aid kits.

"I radioed for an ambulance on the way over here. They should be out right away."

Rowan took a look at Block, then let out a long, low whistle. "Who in the hell did this?"

"That's what I'd like to know," replied Web.

Rowan knelt next to the sheriff.

"He's bleeding pretty bad. This bandage probably saved his life. You put it on?"

"Yeah."

Rowan felt the man's pulse, then turned to Web.

"The blood is blocking his breathing. I need you to hold up his neck."

Web stuck his hands in the sticky brown puddle and lifted Block's head. Block's breathing sounded worse.

"There's an obstruction." Rowan reached his fingers into the man's mouth and pulled out a dish rag, dumping it on the floor. Block's breathing immediately became more regular.

"You're gonna be okay, you're gonna do fine," said Rowan.

After much wheezing and coughing, Block opened his eyes and spoke with great effort. He looked up at Rowan. "Never thought I'd be so glad to see your gay face, Rowan."

Rowan smiled. "Don't waste your breath. You'll be fine. An ambulance is coming."

Web whispered in Rowan's ear. "Will he survive?"

Rowan shrugged his shoulders solemnly. "I can't tell. He's lost a lot of blood, but the bullet seems to have missed the major arteries."

Web realized there wasn't a moment to lose and turned to Block. "Why did you . . ."

Block drew a deep breath. "I didn't," he gasped. "Was DeVries. Alan DeVries." He closed his eyes again. His breathing was forced and difficult, like someone blowing bubbles through a straw.

"Don't ask him any more questions," said Rowan.

Web and Rowan stayed by Block's side, holding him up so he could breathe for the three minutes till the ambulance came. When the medics arrived they lifted Block onto a stretcher and immediately put an oxygen mask on his face. Web and Rowan followed him out to the ambulance. Just before the door shut, Block with great effort lifted his arm and knocked the oxygen mask off.

"Catch DeVries" were his only words before the medic pushed the mask back onto his face. The ambulance doors slammed, leaving Web and Peter standing in the driveway. Several neighbors watched the commotion from the safety of their porches.

"Who the hell is Alan DeVries?" asked Web.

"I've never heard the name before."

The radio in Rowan's truck barked out reports of the fire emergency in the National Forest. He picked up the receiver and got a brief report.

"There's a huge blaze up near the forest. I should get up there," said Rowan.

"I'm going into town," said Web. "I want to see what happened at the police station that 911 has been disconnected."

Rowan stepped partway into his truck. "By the way, what were you doing up here?"

"Just one of my wild guesses, Rowan. It seemed to me that someone in Block's sheriff station was involved. And I think I was right."

"Maybe you do know a thing or two," said Rowan. "You probably saved Block's life."

"Now I have to find out who Alan DeVries is."

Web ran to his car and followed Rowan's truck into town. Rowan drove at top speed, lights flashing. When Rowan turned onto the National Forest road, Web waved and kept going straight to the sheriff's station. The parking lot of the sheriff station was completely packed with two state police vehicles, an ambulance, a county sheriff cruiser, and, strangely, half-a-dozen two-year-old Chevy Impalas: brown, beige, and blue. Web recognized them at once as FBI rides. A dozen men in suits were gathered in front of a green van. Either Web was right about someone at the sheriff's station being implicated or someone was holding an IBM sales convention awfully early in the morning.

33

Pushing aside a band of yellow tape marked POLICE LINE–DO NOT CROSS, Web crossed the parking lot to a green minivan where a knot of men in blue suits and one woman in a conservative business dress was gathered. He scanned the group for a familiar face and found none. Web stood a few feet away from the gathering and observed.

A young man with thick red hair and wire glasses broke off from the group and approached Web. "May I help you?" he asked.

"My name's Web Sloane. I think I may be able to answer many of your questions."

"One moment, Mr. Sloane," said the man. He returned to the group and spoke for several minutes to another of the agents who were gathered. Two more of the men and the woman joined their conversation. From their gestures, Web could see that they were discussing him. The group slowly spread out, as if after a football huddle, and positioned themselves in a line twenty feet wide. They kept a constant watch on him.

A tall dark-haired man, the eldest of the group and apparently the leader, looked back and forth at the agents stationed to his flanks. He held a coffee cup to his face but didn't drink from it. Web started to walk toward the man when he suddenly dropped the coffee cup.

At once the six agents drew guns from their coats. The man with the coffee cup did likewise.

"Put your hands over your head!" yelled the leader at the top of his lungs.

"But—"

"Do as I say motherfucker! Put 'em up slowly!" the man yelled. Web heard six guns being cocked and slowly lifted his hands high over his head.

The leader walked toward Web. "Keep 'em up!" The woman agent joined him. Then the man frisked him while the woman, inches away, held a handgun pointed at Web's head. The man started at Web's legs, hitting them hard with the palms of his hands. When he got to Web's wind breaker, he reached in and pulled out Web's handgun.

"Chen! Get this!" he yelled.

A Chinese-American man, who had been standing by the van, approached. He took Web's pistol from the leader's outstretched arms and placed it into a plastic Baggie.

"Lay on the ground facedown, cowboy, and put your hands behind your head."

Web did as requested, primarily because he knew that one wrong move and he'd be Swiss cheese.

He lowered himself to his knees and lay facedown on the ground. He felt the cold metal of handcuffs clamp over his good wrist then over his arm above the cast. He was frisked again—hands feeling every inch of his body. His keys were pulled out of his pocket and thrown on the ground, then one by one they pulled out each of his three pens.

"Stand up."

Web did as instructed. A crowd of townspeople had gathered outside the yellow tape and stared at the spectacle in the parking lot. Web felt naked before the world. It took incredible effort to keep from yelling at the men, *you fools, you fools.*

"I am Special Agent Carter Ellison of the Federal Bureau of Investigation." The man yelled, even though he stood inches from Web's ear. "You are now under arrest for theft of electronic information and obstruction of police work. You have the right to remain silent . . ."

Web didn't hear the rest of the Miranda warning. All he could think about was how they knew so soon what he had done.

"Do you understand those rights?" bellowed Ellison.

"Yes, sir."

"We would like to ask you some questions, Mr. Sloane. Would you like to wait until a lawyer is present?"

Web sighed. "Can I ask a question?"

"Yes, you may." The agent's expression didn't break.

"Is Jack Reynolds coming? If he is, I'd like to talk to him."

"I cannot say whether or not Special Agent Reynolds will be here. Can we ask you questions, or would you rather wait for a lawyer to be present?"

"Ask away," said Web. "I'm not concealing anything."

"Please sign this." Two men positioned themselves on either side of Web. One unfastened the handcuffs while the other held Web's forearms so tight he knew there would be a bruise.

Ellison put before him a copy of the Miranda warning and shoved a pen into his hand. Web affixed his signature, then two of the agents signed the form as witnesses. Immediately afterward, his hands were again handcuffed behind his head.

"Come this way," said Ellison.

With one agent in back and one in front, Web was led to a beige Impala. Ellison opened the back door and admitted Web, then walked around the car and sat on the other side. Another agent sat in the driver's seat.

"We're quite cozy here," said Web.

"I want to remind you that you've waived your right to have a lawyer present. Do you understand that?" said Ellison, as if reading from a prepared text.

"Yes, I do."

"Why did you break into the SKID system, Mr. Sloane?"

"I did it because I had to. Your people wouldn't listen to me, and I had to know what you knew." Web grimaced. "Could I put my hands in front of me? It's rather uncomfortable."

"No, you cannot. You realize that your illegal entry is a crime in and of itself. Your presence in Endocino makes you look even worse. I recommend you be completely frank with me in your answers. Now, why did you break into SKID?"

"I told you once. I am being completely frank with you. It seemed to me that . . ."

Ellison looked out of the window of the car. Web leaned

back. He could see a helicopter approaching. It landed about a hundred yards away in a shopping center parking lot.

"Wait here," said Ellison.

"I'm not going anyplace," said Web.

Ellison leaned forward to the agent in the front seat. "See that Mr. Sloane is properly tended to."

Ellison opened the door and got out of the car. As soon as he closed the door, Web heard a click. Childproof doors—to keep prisoners at bay in the back seat.

Web watched him cross the parking lot. The helicopter took off again almost as quickly as it had touched down. Ellison returned with Jack Reynolds at his side. Ellison was stern faced, but Reynolds was laughing. The two came to the car and opened the door.

"Fancy seeing you here, Sloane!" said Reynolds.

"Jack, what's going on?"

Reynolds turned to Ellison. "Take the cuffs off, Ellison," said Reynolds.

Ellison's bullying nature was instantly turned into blind obedience. It was obvious from his sudden change in behavior that Reynolds significantly outranked Ellison. He quickly and gently removed the handcuffs from Web's wrists.

"That's much better," said Web, stretching out his arms. "My hand went to sleep."

"Come with me, Web," said Reynolds.

The two walked across the parking lot a distance away from the other FBI men.

"You're no career criminal, Web. I want to help you out."

"Thanks."

"When I heard on Sunday night that SKID was hacked from the Berkeley campus, I had my doubts. When I saw what records were accessed I knew. It was you, Web, wasn't it?"

"There was no other way, Jack. I had to know."

"Now, what the *hell* were you doing hacking my computer?" asked Reynolds, cracking his knuckles.

"I had a hunch that our best suspect was probably working from the inside. It was worth the risk to find out. And I was goddam right, too. You may not know it, but about half the records had been altered by Vine County. The facts that I cross-checked were sabotaged."

"No one can enter that system," said Reynolds.

"Yeah, right. It took me all of ten minutes." Reynolds gave Web a dirty look. "Listen, Jack. All the records were changed in there—" Web pointed to the sheriff's station. "It looked like maybe Block was behind it. But he's a victim. It's someone named DeVries."

"How do you know that?" asked Reynolds.

"Block just told me," said Web ironically.

Reynolds ran his hand across his close cropped hair. "I don't know what goes on inside your mind, but you either have a hell of a knack for this kind of work or maybe you're psychic. I should arrest you until I cross-check Block's story."

Two agents rushed up to Reynolds.

The older one spoke. "Sir, we were just out to Block's home. His neighbors said he was taken away in an ambulance about an hour ago to Vine County General. There's blood on the kitchen floor and signs of a protracted struggle."

"This doesn't look good for you, Web," said Reynolds.

Web cut in. "Peter Rowan was the first paramedic there. He heard Block name DeVries. You can radio him to verify my story. He's out at the forest fire."

Reynolds barked at the agents. "Go to it. Radio this guy. Now!"

The two ran toward one of the Impalas.

"Sloane, I'm going to trust you're telling the truth, but this paramedic better goddam confirm your story." He glanced over at the other agents to ensure that no one could hear him. "As far as any of these agents know, I'm taking you into my custody. So shut up and follow me. Let's find out who this DeVries character is."

Web followed Reynolds into the station. Masking tape marked the spot where the dispatcher's body had been found.

"What's that?" asked Web.

"Whoever hit Block was probably here too. Eunice Ballard, the dispatcher, was found dead this morning. That's why they woke me up at 3 A.M. to come up here."

Four evidence specialists, in disposable white paper clean suits, were working their way through the police offices. The desks had been blocked off with color-coded tape. The red tape was marked EVIDENCE COLLECTION IN PROGRESS—DO NOT TOUCH, and the white tape was marked SAFE. The E-team moved slowly through, square foot by square foot, photographing every surface, taking with them every object that could conceivably be of value to the investigation.

One man took photos; another gathered evidence, initialed it, and stowed it in color-coded cellophane bags; one man supervised; and the fourth ran a special evidence gathering vacuum over each area to gather the microscopic hairs and fibers that might aid in an eventual trial.

"Hello, gentlemen!" yelled Reynolds over the roar of the vacuum.

The E-team stopped what they were doing. All but the vacuum operator stood up. Reynolds was obviously a commanding presence.

"What do you know about a man named DeVries?" yelled Reynolds.

The FBI men looked at one another. There was no indication that they recognized the name.

An older Vine County deputy leaned his head in from the front office. "DeVries is the nice computer guy who works here. Why?"

Web and Reynolds exchanged glances.

"Let's see everything you have on him."

"Sure. By the way, I'm Brent Lydon."

"Web Sloane."

They followed the man to a large filing cabinet in the front office marked Personnel. He flipped through the manila folders contained in the top drawer. He pulled out one marked DeVries, Alan. It was completely empty.

"Jeeze. We keep records on everybody who works here, but I don't know . . ."

Web spoke quietly. "He's taken his files and skipped. Are there any other records—especially photos or photo negatives?"

"There's one other place . . ." said Lydon. "Everyone has a photo I.D. A Xerox of the photo is . . ."

Lydon tenuously pulled out several file drawers, one after another. "Excuse me, I'm not quite familiar with this. Usually we have staff file these things, but under the circumstances, we told them not to come in today." He found the correct file and pulled it out.

Inside were high-contrast Xerox copies of identification photos, organized alphabetically.

"Let's see . . . here it is."

He extracted a grainy reproduction of an identification photo and handed it to Reynolds. The agent studied the image, disbelieving for a long moment.

"Well fuck me sideways," said Reynolds, staring at the photo. Web had never heard Reynolds use such an expression.

"What is it?" asked Web.

"Take a look for yourself."

Web examined the picture. It was a poor-quality reproduction, simply a Xerox of a photo. The man had a little gray hair, but the cool, insolent gaze staring out of the photo was that of Theodore Robert Bundy. He dropped it disbelieving on the desk.

"When was this photo taken?" asked Web.

"Date's stamped on the back," said the deputy.

Reynolds read the date. "November, 1990. Jesus Katy-Riste. That's a hell of a match."

The pose was a typical drivers-license-type image with a slightly forced smile. Bundy had never been distinctive looking: by changing his hair, growing a beard or mustache, or even hunching slightly he could alter his appearance radically. Yet the eyes never changed. This photograph had those hollow black eyes. Eyes you would never notice unless you were looking for them.

"You're thinking the same thing I am," said Web upon seeing Reynolds's frozen gaze.

"What is this? Some kind of sick joke?" asked Reynolds, holding the photo up to Lydon, the deputy. "Is this DeVries? Or did he swap his photo, too?"

"That's DeVries all right," said Lydon. "Why?"

"Goddamit to hell. What I wouldn't give to have come here twenty-four hours ago," said Reynolds.

"Me, too," said Web. "Slipped right through our fingers."

Reynolds cocked his head. "Web, I talked to Sheriff Block a couple weeks ago. He stole a glance at your notebooks."

"That sneaky shit! I never showed him my notes."

"I would have looked in those notebooks too, Web. When he told me you had notes about a Bundy clone, I said he should keep his distance from you. But I never expected to see this," said Reynolds, shaking the photo. "Whatever the hell is going on in your head, it's producing results. We have to make a deal."

Web bit his lip. "What kind of deal?"

"We forget about your little hacking expedition. You help us sort out the pieces of what's going on."

"That's what I asked you three weeks ago."

"Okay, I was an asshole, what do you want me to say? I'm sorry. What kind of notes do you have?"

"I have virtually everything you have, plus something much more valuable," said Web.

"What is that?"

"I've developed a fairly sophisticated model of how this person might behave. We may be able to anticipate his next move."

"Do we have a deal?"

"Sure," said Web, shaking Reynolds's hand.

"Can you meet us in the San Francisco office at 3:00 P.M. today?"

"It's a two-hour drive back!"

"You and I fly back. I'll get an agent to drive your car. We'll give you a car and driver upon our return. We have to move on this now, Web."

"The sooner, the better," said Web.

Reynolds smiled. "Let's get to that helicopter."

34

Web had awakened a sleeping giant. While the helicopter flew back to San Francisco, Reynolds and an assistant worked two secure cellular phones, tending to Web's every need. Everybody they talked to was "Special Agent" this or that. Web was tempted to say "isn't that special," but he liked having them on his side.

During the twenty-four-minute flight, an enormous amount of manpower was deployed. One agent was dispatched to Consolidated Chemical Analysis, the laboratory performing tests on the stolen ashes. Another agent in Sacramento was sent to the California Department of Motor Vehicles in Sacramento to speed up identification of license plate numbers that Web had mailed off weeks before—the convertibles that had visited O'Brien's 25-Hour Gas Station. Someone was sent to Maria de Rivera's home to recover Web's annotated SKID reports; and another would meet Web at the helipad to shuttle him to his home and office to gather his notes, then to the FBI meeting in San Francisco.

As the chopper approached a downtown San Francisco helipad, the three fastened their seat belts for landing and put down the telephones.

Web turned to Reynolds. He yelled over the roar of the helicopter.

"All these special agents doing all these errands at once. What the hell were they doing before?"

Reynolds arched an eyebrow. "Pursuing separate investigations. You know, the usual."

"For the last year?" yelled Web.

"Success doesn't usually come from leaps of faith, Sloane. It comes from boring old footwork."

Web pondered this as the helicopter set down on top of the building. They got out of the helicopter, jogged down a set of stairs, and stepped into an elevator.

"How much latitude does an individual have? What kind of footwork do they do?" asked Web.

"Procedures that are demonstrated to work. I can't have my people running off on wild goose chases."

"Your methodology—is it standardized? Published?" asked Web.

"Of course. That's how we work," said Reynolds.

The elevator let them out in the lobby.

"You've got to make some different assumptions from now on. This is a game of poker. And you can bet that this character has been looking at your hands from the first deal."

"Meaning what, Web?"

"This murderer had access to all your records and files. He has your playbook. And now, the closer you stick to business as usual, the more likely he will get away forever. Treat him like Ted Bundy."

"Look—you can't keep talking about Bundy. I agree, the photo looks awfully damned similar. But I'll be thrown out on my ass and the investigation stopped cold if I say we're looking for a ghost. For the time being, this is a copycat, okay?" Reynolds looked distressed, as if bracing himself for Web's next blow.

"I want you to try some highly unusual things. You see it as a criminal investigation; my view is that we should be treating this as war. My methods work. Yours don't."

"Name your plan."

As they stepped out of the elevator into the lobby of the building, the agent who had ridden with them on the plane waited patiently a few feet from Reynolds.

"Can we talk in private?" asked Web.

"Sure. Wait here for a bit, Clifford," said Reynolds. Then he turned to Web. "Let's take a hike."

They merged with a throng of pedestrians on the crowded San Francisco street. "No one can hear you out here. Inside, it's a different story," said Reynolds.

"Good. You have to bend some rules. Bundy or not, he has your number. He's seen your files. He knows what you've done in the past. He can guess what you'll do next. What this calls for is a little disinformation."

"Such as?" asked Reynolds.

"Number one, you can't let him know that Block survived. If he knows that, he'll know we're looking for him. We have to act as if Block is dead."

"You know I can't do that," said Reynolds.

"And our killer knows it too. If there is a funeral, and a press release says Block was found dead, our killer will let his guard down. I suggest that the press be told that Block was the killer and that he's been stopped," said Web.

"You're talking about a man who has family, friends! Are you suggesting we lie to all of them, too?"

"Yes, I am. I bet Block will go along with it. He'll be in the hospital for at least a month and he understands the urgency. Remember, he was a victim too."

"That would be a lot of trouble . . ." said Reynolds.

"But think of the edge it could give you if he thinks he's gotten away clean. You're talking about an extraordinary madman. The only way you can catch him is if we can get him to foul up. Now, what's more important? Propriety? Or stopping this killer?"

They stopped at the corner, then turned around and started walking back to the FBI building.

"Sloane, I'm going to play along with you, even though what you suggest is highly irregular. I don't know how I'm going to sell it, though."

"You'll find a way to make it fly."

"At this point I don't know what else to do."

"I'm not promising results. But if you don't follow this plan, I can almost guarantee failure."

They arrived back at the FBI building.

"You said I could have a car," said Web.

Reynolds walked past the building until he came to an Olds Cutlass parked in the loading zone. A man in a blue suit sat inside, reading the *San Francisco Chronicle*.

"Here's your ride."

They shook hands. Web got into the car. Reynolds walked around to the driver's window. "Have him back here by three o'clock. We've got a meeting."

"Yes, sir."

Web took a catnap while the agent drove him home. He picked up his notebooks, quickly washed his face and shaved, and then left a note for Joyce. On the drive back to the FBI building, Web talked with Jack Reynolds about his battle plan via secure cellular telephone. They arrived at the FBI building at 3:15, after the meeting had already started. It took only moments to give him a temporary I.D. badge, and he was whisked to a conference room on the top floor. When he walked into the room, several agents stood up.

"Gentlemen, this is Web Sloane," announced Reynolds. "He'll answer your questions."

Web looked across the room at a wall, where an overhead projector showed a list of vehicle registrations.

"Goddam! You already got those from the DMV? They told me four to six weeks."

Reynolds laughed. "Depends on who you know, Web. This is our resident DMV miracle worker, Susan Ng. What's the status of the plates?"

An older Chinese-American woman spoke up. "Based on credit card charges, we've produced reasonable alibis for all but four of the car owners. The remaining ones are a '72 Chevy registered in Los Angeles, a Utah plate we haven't been able yet to trace, an '87 Corvette, and an '84 VW Cabriolet, gray, purchased in Florida but registered in California."

Web thought for a moment. *The dock worker at Hardware Hypermarket had insisted over and over "BMW" but with his limited English could have easily confused it with "VW." And Bundy drove a VW. Of course!* "It's the VW," he announced.

"How do you know?" asked Ng.

"If he says he knows, he knows," said Reynolds. "Find out everything you can about that car. See if there are any charges from major gas companies on it. Check it for tickets."

"All fifty states?" asked Ng.

"All fifty."

She wrote down something and looked at Web Sloane. *Who is this man?*

Another agent interrupted. "The guy, DeVries. He drove a gray Cabriolet."

Web turned on his heel. "What else did you find out about DeVries?"

"What we have is very preliminary. DeVries never underwent the usual police background check. He only worked part-time and took his pay as an independent contractor," said the agent.

"Like a house painter?" asked Web.

"His job description was as computer consultant. I had to find out by asking deputies at the department since all his personnel records have disappeared. He probably took them. It's almost certain this DeVries was responsible for the SKID computer file sabotage. He was the only one at the station who could use it."

The agent flipped to another page of notes. "I got some interesting dope on the guy. He lived with a woman named Mars Chittenden—she ran the local bakery—and her son. The house where he lived was the point source of the forest fire near Endocino. Chittenden's dead. Her son is unconscious, in critical condition. It sounds to me like DeVries started the blaze."

"Who else knows what you just told us?" asked Web.

"Just myself, so far. I just got back from Endocino."

Web leaned over to Reynolds and whispered in his ear. Reynolds nodded, then closed the door. He flipped a switch on the wall, and an annoying buzzing sound permeated the room. Web recognized it as a white noise generator; it would muffle any efforts to eavesdrop or record the conversation in the room.

"I want you all to make some notes," said Web, addressing the group as if they were his students.

"Sheriff Block of Vine County sheriff's department is dead. He was the Spring Break Murderer and probably killed as many as seven others."

He walked up to the end of the table.

The agent who had given the report on DeVries raised his hand. "Mr. Sloane, what I've heard doesn't reflect . . ."

Reynolds cut him off. "Write down what Mr. Sloane says. Do I make myself understood, Walker?"

"Yes, sir."

Web continued. "In addition to those murders, Block also

started a fire that killed this Chittenden woman, her son, and . . . ," he paused, "as far as we can tell from the extensive damage, Alan DeVries himself died in the same fire."

Walker stood up. "This is patently wrong. Block is in critical condition at the hospital, and DeVries is at large."

Web smiled. "Yes, I know. Now, put your pencils down." The agents did as instructed.

"Agent Walker got ahead of me. Everything I've told you so far is indeed false. Block is still alive. DeVries is loose. That information is not to get out of this room. Everything I'm telling you now is for your ears only. No one without authorization can be informed of the truth. Anything you have indicating otherwise should be secured or destroyed."

Walker's face grew increasingly red. "Sir, I do not know who you are, but that's not how we do things around here!"

"Precisely," said Web. "As we speak, Block is being moved to a military hospital in Port Hueneme, California, two hundred miles south of here where he will receive excellent care, albeit under an assumed name. In a week or so, his funeral in Tico will make national headlines, especially since it will be announced that the Spring Break Murderer is Block and has been caught red-handed."

"The man calling himself Alan DeVries will believe that he's free and clear. He will become sloppy. His next move will be toward another college campus. My estimate is that he'll lay low for a period ranging from two to six weeks. Then, he'll become active again."

Web sat down. Reynolds took over the meeting.

"Memorize this face," said Reynolds. They put up a slide of the photo from Alan DeVries's photo I.D. card at the Vine County sheriff's station. A gasp came from the room as they saw the image.

"This is the man calling himself Alan DeVries. According to Mr. Sloane, he won't use that name any longer. And he will probably change his appearance. Next slide please."

It showed several computer-enhanced variations on the photo; one with a beard, one with glasses, one with long hair.

"When he's next seen, it's more likely he will look like one of these. One of these altered photos will be distributed to police departments and college campuses across the country. Our hot sheet will say that he's armed and dangerous and wanted for a string of violent drug killings."

"The press probably won't pick up on that story. We send out several drug-related tip sheets a month; a serial killer of this magnitude comes along only once or twice a century. This way, local enforcement can cooperate with us without the interference of the press and its inadvertent tipping off of the suspect. We're assigning the name Steve Talbot to this photo but alerting forces that he is likely using a pseudonym. The deception is not to leave this room. Is that understood?"

All around the table, the agents began grumbling. Walker stood up.

"This has never been done before!" he said.

Reynolds was ready for the objections. "The hell it hasn't. You worked on AbScam, right?"

"Yes, but . . ."

"AbScam was a sting operation. We lied, we spread disinformation, just to stop illegal campaign contributions. We've done stings to stop stock manipulation, bank fraud, and every white-collar crime in the book."

"But this isn't a white-collar crime," said Walker.

"Right, Walker. What's at stake is human lives. I think that's a lot stronger justification for a sting than any of our previous operations. Do I make myself understood?"

"Yes, sir." Walker sat back down. All around the room, the agents nodded in agreement. Reynolds had found his justification.

Web Sloane's meeting with the FBI lasted another six hours. By that time, he'd been running almost forty hours with only a nap, and even with a quart of Company coffee in his gut, his effectiveness was dwindling.

By the end of the meeting, their strategies had been laid out. Funerals would be held for Block and the Chittenden family; agents would surreptitiously photograph every person attending and make records of all license plates within half a mile of the funeral home. Reports of the "solved"

Spring Break Murders would be in newspapers and on television within twenty-four hours.

Hundreds of pages of new bogus records, supposedly "wrapping up" the case would be planted in the SKID computer system. Any time one of the files was accessed, a beeper would alert two separate agents, one in New York, one in San Francisco. Because the computer called back the user, no trace would be necessary. They nicknamed it the "Domino's Plan," because within thirty minutes an agent could be dispatched to any SKID terminal in the country. If the killer called the system again, it would take at least an hour to download the phony records.

The credit cards belonging to Chittenden and Block would be placed on a hot list. Any use of the cards would be reported to the FBI as soon as a verification of purchase was made.

An APB was put out for the pseudonymous Steve Talbot, who was listed as armed and dangerous. Additionally, FBI offices would be led to believe that "Talbot" was an accomplice to Block's crimes, with specific instructions not to share that with the press. The double layer of falsehood, first that the killer was Block and that "Talbot" was merely an accomplice, would hopefully ensure that the real killer wasn't put on guard. Reynolds could use the ruse to place one agent full-time in each of the locations where the murders had occurred: Tahoe, Sacramento, and the suburbs of San Francisco. Three agents would be stationed full-time in the Tico/Endocino area.

Web was interested in the plans the FBI had made, but he still doubted whether "business as usual" would do the trick. He addressed the group.

"I think that these strategies may lead us to this killer. But I also have doubts. This man is ruthless and extraordinarily cautious. At all the crime scenes, you know that no identifiable fibers and no fingerprints have yet been uncovered. I suspect that none will. Even though this man worked at a police station for the last five months, all records save one photo were destroyed. I would guess that his IQ is probably over 165; by that measurement he's smarter than me and very possibly smarter than anyone in the room. If he stays true to form, the first inkling he gets that a search is on will drive him to another state. So let's be sure there are no leaks."

The meeting broke up. Web gathered his papers as the agents filed out of the room. As soon as the door opened, a messenger stepped in and handed an oversized gray envelope to Reynolds.

"This is for you, Web," said Reynolds. "From what I can make out, it says something about your grandmother's gold teeth."

Web examined the cover letter of the report, skipping to the paragraph labeled Executive Summary of Results. *Traces of Ag (gold) residue consistent with the range of values to be expected from one to six gold human dental fillings were present in the sample, according to both chemical and electron microscopy scan procedures.*

Web knew what this meant: The ashes could not be Bundy. The man did not have gold fillings. He shoved the papers back into the envelope before Reynolds could see what they were.

"What is it, Web?" asked Reynolds.

"Remember when you said I was crazy?"

"Yeah."

"You said, 'Convince yourself that Bundy's dead.' I set out to do just that. Nothing I've seen proves conclusively that he was the one executed in Florida. There's no morgue photo, no witnesses who knew him personally. I got hold of his ashes."

Reynolds did a double take. "How?"

"I probably shouldn't tell a law-enforcement officer. But the upshot is—they're not his ashes. Whoever was cremated had gold teeth. Bundy didn't."

"Web, there are a million good reasons why that could happen. Maybe they cremate more than one person at a time."

"Jack, I know you don't buy it. I can't get more specific than to say it's a gut instinct. But my gut is smarter than most. Don't start up with me right now with reasons why not. Just do me one favor: get hold of Bundy's fingerprints. Attach them to the photo you're sending out."

"If I do that, they'll run me out of here on a rail, and next week you'll be buying hamburgers from me at McDonald's."

"Find a way. Even if I'm dead wrong, you're protected. Who could be mistakenly picked up for leaving Bundy's prints?"

Reynolds clenched his jaw. "I'll track down the prints—personally. But you didn't hear it from me," said Reynolds, looking at Web from the corner of his eye.

"Fine. I don't care how you do it, just as long as it's done."

Web left the room. Reynolds picked up his briefcase, switched off the lights, and walked down the hall to his office, wondering the whole time if he'd put a major investigation into the hands of a genius—or a lunatic.

Web entered his house, groggy from the long day and the nap he'd taken on the ride home.

Something was wrong.

He walked up the stairs. Joyce's bedroom door was open, but she wasn't in there. He walked back downstairs and inspected the kitchen and living room. Dirty dishes were in the sink—Joyce must have cooked dinner. Very odd. She almost always ate pizza or take-out when Web was gone. But there was a sink full of dirty dishes. Mud, the dog, guiltily looked up from the couch and sheepishly climbed off of it. But there was no sign of his daughter.

"Joyce!" yelled Web. "Hello!"

A voice called out from the front of the house. "I'm in here!"

He walked to the front hall. He hadn't noticed it before, but a motorcycle helmet was on the hall table. He saw a light coming from his office. He opened the door very slowly.

Joyce, seated in front of his personal computer, was giggling uproariously. He walked into the office.

"Joyce?"

He was startled to see a man seated to her side.

"Hey, Prof! Howzit hanging?"

It was Renny McDonald.

Joyce spun around, a mile-wide grin gracing her face.

"Daddy-O, you invited Renny to dinner and then stood him up!"

"Oh, my god. You're right. Hi, Renny."

"Long day, eh?" said McDonald.

"Understatement of the year," said Web.

Joyce rolled forward on the office chair. "Remember you said I could use the machine whenever I wanted? Well, after we ate, Renny was showing me how to send out college applications to twenty different schools. And now, we're in a game of Simulation City."

Web arched an eyebrow. "What?"

"It's just a game, Prof."

"Well, don't let me bother you two then. You didn't show her how to tap into the Pentagon or anything, Renny?"

"Well, we bombed Pittsburgh, but that's about it."

Web smiled. "Sorry I missed our dinner," then, with a sly smile, "dude."

"Hey, no problem, Prof. Joyce made macaroni and cheese, and lemme tell you, it was ten times better than what they serve at the dining halls."

"Good. I'm going to get something to eat. Take your time."

Renny grinned broadly. "By the way, Prof, I hope you get to run that CRAY lab. You're number one in the running."

He stared at the boy.

"You know—the DOD guy who ran it resigned, along with those other two. I have a hunch you might be at the top of the list."

"Renny, what are you talking about? I've had a long day."

"It's simple. Three professors resigned, right? You heard that. So there's a couple stray CRAY XMP computers left. I heard that maybe you're being seriously considered."

Joyce smiled. "Renny says you're getting the lab!"

"That sounds swell, but I haven't heard a word of it," said Web.

Renny grinned. "Well, let's say someone has a way to hear phone machine messages from the chancellor's office. And someone has heard the name Web Sloane quite a bit since the resignations." Renny grinned. "I won't say any more. But let's say they're revising their opinion about your Chancellor's Request lecture now that *everybody's* slagging on Department of Defense."

Web shook his head. "Whatever you say, Renny." Web

didn't believe it, but if the boy was right, the university needed someone with clean hands to take over the scandal-ridden, but state-of-the-art, information services department.

He walked slowly into the kitchen. He didn't know what had happened to Joyce, but he liked it. In the past two years, the mere mention to her of either "college" or "computers" meant that he would have a fight on his hands. Somehow, one night with Renny the Hacker had changed her mind.

After eating, Web drank a Scotch and soda and meandered into the living room, where he stretched out on the La-Z-Boy recliner. He meant to close his eyes just for a moment, but it was 11:30 when he awoke to the sound of a motorcycle engine roaring away. He got up to investigate the noise.

Joyce walked in through the front door.

Web rubbed his eyes.

"Joyce, you threw me for a loop. What's going on?"

"Oh, you know, just stuff," she said.

"I guess you hit it off with Renny?" Web asked.

She looked away. "He's okay, I guess. We talked about what he's doing in college."

"My class?" Web asked hopefully.

"He's in your class?"

"I didn't meet him at a horse race, you know," Web answered.

"No, we talked about, you know, what college is like. Not classes, but he just told me about some of the kids and . . ." Joyce covered her mouth and laughed.

"What's so funny?" asked Web.

"No, I shouldn't tell you. It was just a prank Renny played on his roommate. The dorms sound really funny."

"So maybe college isn't purgatory?"

"I mean, Renny makes it sound different from the way you talked about it. It's not all picking the right place, getting a degree, and getting a job."

Web nodded. "That's great, Joyce." Web bit his lip. "But there are some big issues we have to talk about first."

"Oh, I forgot to tell you," she said sheepishly.

"Tell me what?"

"I, um, started my period a couple days ago. I was just wound up I guess."

Web stared blankly. It was the best news he'd heard in a long time.

35

After a week of working with the FBI, Web recognized that there were three steps in an official investigation: first, call a meeting, then, have a meeting, and finally, schedule another meeting. After a day of interminable conferences he stopped by Reynolds's office.

"Jack, I've got to spend some time working at my real job. I've had every guest lecturer I can dredge up this week, and it seems like you're well on your way."

Reynolds stood up. "Good enough. Your help has been invaluable. You ever think of doing this professionally, Web?"

"I have a life, Jack. I don't want to chase down every two-bit killer and bank robber. I just want to stop this one man."

"What do you think our odds are?" asked Reynolds.

"Lousy." Web leaned forward. "But not zero. It's good that he believes the heat is off. He'll start feeling cocky. My guess is that he'll try to cover his tracks. And that's how we'll catch him."

"Where do you think we should we look?" asked Reynolds.

"Keep an eye on any forgers you know—guys who make passports or I.D. cards. Watch the DMV applications for new licenses. Get the list of stolen VW's—I think he'll change cars. I don't know what'll draw his fire, but he did a hell of a job trying to cover his tracks before. He may even try again to kill Block, if it gets out that he's alive."

"Or someone else who knows too much," said Reynolds.

"Yeah. I'd keep a couple extra agents in Tico and Endocino, especially around any acquaintances he had."

"You know they're already there."

Web left the building, wondering where Bundy would strike again. It was the old probability game; they could put men at all the most likely spots, but nothing was foolproof. Fools are too ingenious.

Web spent the rest of the afternoon trying to resuscitate his dying garden. The months of neglect had taken a depressing toll on his project; it was filled with weeds and aphids. He put on his kneepads, rolled his wheelbarrow out to the garden's edge and methodically went to work pulling weeds, inserting fertilizer sticks into the soil, and replacing brittle, dead rose bushes with new ones. The new bushes looked just like sticks to him; but this time, with water and care, he hoped they would bloom. To battle the aphids, he tried a new approach: The garden supply store sold him a quart box, "guaranteed to contain 1200 ladybugs." When he was finished with everything else, he released the colorful flying insects, who scattered among the plants. He silently wished them well in their hunt for plant-killing aphids.

Late that night Web was drawing up a list of probable spots where Bundy might turn up when there was a knock on his office door.

"Daddy-O? I got some brochures from colleges," said Joyce, beaming.

Web self-consciously covered up his papers.

"Good. Anything catch your eye?"

"There's one called North Coast College of the Arts."

Web nodded blankly. It took a moment to switch gears.

She continued. "A bunch of performance artists, like Hal Norton and that filmmaker Angela Phinlay, went there. They do all kinds of things—video, film, traditional art—and it sounded kind of cool."

"I've never heard of North Coast, Joyce," said Web, disapprovingly.

"Does that mean it's dirt? You can't possibly have heard of every college in the world, Daddy-O."

"You have to think of whether a school is accredited. Some of the newer colleges are almost worthless, Joyce."

Joyce pouted. "Of course. The only college I like, and you say 'no.' You still want me to be robo-girl." She made her voice sound like a robot. "Go to best school. Get good grades. Have an important career. Get ulcer. Die."

Web grimaced. "Okay, okay. Let's see it."

Web picked up the brochure. Instead of the typical photos of students walking through tree-covered paths carrying books, it was laid out in a frenetic, high-tech style. Glancing at the faculty list, he recognized a couple of familiar names. Larry Hanrahan used to be at University of Washington. A flake, but some thought he was a genius.

"If you really love the idea. What else do you know besides what's in this brochure?"

"Absolutely nothing at all. But they're having a kind of open house for high school seniors weekend after next. I called, and there's still room. Kind of check it out, you know?"

"Next weekend? I'm supposed to see Maria next weekend. Is it the only time they have an open house?"

Joyce folded her arms in front of her chest. "You were so hot and bothered to get me in college."

Web bit his lip. She had a point.

"You're right. What do you think about taking Maria with us?"

"That'd be cool. I'll call them right now."

"From now on, we'll look into any colleges you want. I'll try to give you the benefit of my knowledge—or in some cases, the benefit of my ignorance. And then you pick the one you want to go to."

"Yeah, right. What if I said Detroit Community College?"

"I'd say, 'fine.' But then you'd have to go to Detroit!"

"Hey, Jennifer's from Detroit."

"I didn't say anything bad about Detroit; I'm sure it's a very, very wonderful place to spend four years."

Joyce laughed. "Can I have your credit card?"

"Credit card?"

"I need to get some things if we're going to see a college."

Web obligingly handed over the plastic.

"Thanks, Daddy-O." She kissed him on the cheek and disappeared out the door.

36

Theodore Robert Bundy read the newspaper with glee. They
were trying to pin his crimes on that redneck Block. And
since Block was dead, they wouldn't check too closely.
Nothing could be better.

Once again, Bundy's "death" had given him new life. He
could now travel undetected. No one would look for him. As
far as anyone was concerned, Block was responsible for his
crimes. There would be no trial. There was only one more
thing to conceal.

The Cabriolet would undoubtedly raise red flags for any
policeman who stopped him. Never mind that it was now
bright red, thanks to a dozen cans of spray paint stolen from
Pep Boys Automotive. He needed to obscure the trail
further. New license plates would be a good start. Even
better if Bundy could kill off "Alan DeVries" at the same
time.

In a rotting industrial part of town he parked the car,
legally, in front of a large parking lot where dozens of
Greyhound buses were stored, like a herd of elephants
resting in the moonlight. Warehouses were spaced out, one
to a block. Much of the area was given over to storing trucks,
buses, road equipment, old signs, anything that was too
valuable to junk but didn't justify more careful storage in
covered garages. He had passed half a dozen station wagons
and mobile homes before stopping his car. In this forgotten
section of the city, people who lived in their automobiles
could rest without disturbance. There were virtually no
people here at night; no street lights; no traffic to speak of.
This would be an appropriate location for Alan's demise.

He pulled out his shoulder bag. Inside he placed the stun
gun, the handcuffs, some Vice-Grips, and a bottle of whiskey. Several old newspapers would conceal his tools in the

unlikely event that he passed another human being who was cognizant enough to understand what he might be doing. He threw the bag over his shoulder, then picked up a powerful flashlight and a leather wallet that he had shoplifted that morning from Nordstrom.

His footsteps echoed in the empty street. In the distance he heard a forlorn clinking and rattling. A hundred yards ahead of him a disheveled man pushed a shopping cart brimming with bottles and cans. As the figure grew closer, he could see that the man was talking to himself and was covered in dirt. Several pairs of socks covered his feet. He stopped the cart long enough to extract two Coke cans from a dumpster, then continued on his way. *The troll would never make a reliable witness. He can't even remember his own name, much less describe a passerby.*

He examined the license plates of cars that he passed. Most were twenty years old or older. Inside each car he could see one person or two, lonely, desperate people to whom a rusty automobile was home. Most did not even look out of their windows as he passed. He hoped to find a car containing a man about his own size and build. A man by himself.

He turned to a side street that dead-ended into a chain-link fence after fifty yards. Just before the fence sat a rusted AMC Pacer, which had once been bright green but was now the color of seaweed. The right rear panel had been smashed in. The license plate was from Nevada—far enough away to make for a couple week's delay in identification. The registration sticker wouldn't expire for several months. The prospect looked quite promising.

He walked around the car. A man, *by himself thank God,* dozed inside, his legs stretching from the backseat to the front seat. Bundy rapped on the window. There was no motion inside. He turned on the flashlight and illuminated the man's face. Good. He was white. Could be thirty, could be forty. He rapped on the window again.

The man inside stirred, then sat bolt upright. Bundy turned off the flashlight.

"Hello!" he yelled.

Startled, the man picked up a bottle.

"Who is it?" He drew up into himself.

"My name's Alan. I'm living down the street."

"Go away. This is my alley."

Bundy reached into his bag and pulled out the whiskey bottle.

"Some kids were hassling me out at my car on Seventeenth Street. I wondered if you'd be interested in sharing a bottle of Old Time." He flashed the light onto the fifth.

The man eyed him cautiously, then crawled to the front seat of the car and rolled down the window.

"You on the level?"

Bundy stepped up to the window. A stench like dead fish came wafting out from the car.

"You see, these kids were hassling me, a gang I think. I outran them but I don't want to go back to my car yet. I saw you . . ."

The man opened the door of the car. "Name's Winger. You can call me Ed though. I'm not usually living like this, you understand, but they've put radio signals all over my house so I have to come out here." He was about thirty-five and looked as if he hadn't bathed in a week. The left lens in his glasses was shattered and covered with tape.

Bundy smiled. Winger was crazy, but not as crazy as some he'd seen. He would fill the bill perfectly.

"Nice to meet you, Ed," said Bundy.

Winger got out and leaned against the hood of the car. "Nice of you to share some Old Time." He bounced his weight from foot to foot and held out his hand. "If you don't mind?"

"Sure. Glad for the company."

Winger took the bottle from Bundy and screwed off the lid. He lifted the liquor to his lips and took a long swig, then wiped off the neck of the bottle with his shirttail and handed the bottle back.

"Mm. That's fine. That's mighty fine, Mr.—"

"Alan." Bundy turned his back to Winger and pretended to sip from the bottle, leaving the cap on.

"Another sip?" asked Bundy, handing the bottle back.

"I don't mind if I do." Winger wiped off the neck again and leaned his head back, sucking down several ounces. He shivered when he took it away from his lips. "Thank you, sir. Gang hassled you, huh?"

"Yep. Beat me up real good."

"Where did you . . ." In midsentence the man's head slumped forward, and he fell to the ground. The eleven tablets of secobarbitol dissolved in the whiskey had done their job with great dispatch. Bundy turned Winger over, pulled out a motheaten, torn-up wallet from his back pocket, and examined its contents. Three newspaper clippings about UFOs, a Nevada driver's license, several photos, and a San Francisco library card. No parole card. *Good.*

Bundy opened the car and pulled out the man's sleeping bag and clothes, scattering them along the ground, then dumped out the contents of the glove compartment. There were several hundred matchbooks and dozens of newspapers, but nothing that would positively identify the man. He took the man's keys and opened the hatchback, which was stuffed beyond capacity with empty bottles and cans. He extracted the tire iron and stirred up the containers.

Satisfied that there was nothing to identify the owner, Bundy tossed the clothes, sleeping bag, and matchbook collection back into the car. He pulled out his own wallet and placed it into Winger's pocket. Earlier he had removed everything except for the driver's license, which identified him as Alan DeVries. Finally, using the Vise-Grips he removed the front and rear license plates and stuffed them into his bag. *If the registration had expired,* he thought, *I would have picked someone else. But better him than me.*

The drugs had accomplished their desired effect. Winger was incapacitated, unable to fight back. His breathing was heavy and labored. Bundy leaned over and brought the crowbar down on the man's head. It made a sound like a ripe melon hitting the pavement. Bundy looked away. The body twitched for a moment then stopped. A torrent of blood flowed out of the head wound and ran onto the ground.

Bundy rolled the man over onto his back. His eyes stared off into infinity. He felt the pulse. The man was dead. Now came the nasty part. He put on a pair of rubber gloves, then took the Vise-Grips out of his bag. With the crowbar, he pried open the corpse's mouth. An acidic burst of halitosis wafted into Bundy's face.

At his own trial Bundy had learned that bodies are often

identified by dental imprints. Eliminate the dental evidence and you slow or stop the identification process. Plant an I.D. on the corpse, and they'll likely assume the I.D. card belongs to the holder.

He looked down the alley to see if anyone was coming. Satisfied that he was alone, he tightened the Vice-Grip on one of the drifter's front teeth. He yanked up and away from the corpse. The Vise-Grip slipped off. He tightened the tool a notch and reapplied it to the tooth. Standing with one foot on either side of Winger's chest, he pulled up and away. Rather than coming off, the tooth split in two. This would be harder than he had anticipated.

Out of breath, he stood a step away from the corpse and evaluated the situation. It would take hours to pull out enough teeth to ensure a bad identification. That was too risky. The only option was to obliterate the teeth from the outside.

He brought the crowbar down on Winger's face again and again, pushing open the jaw with his foot to ensure that the impact would shatter the teeth. The crowbar stung in his hand after each blow. When he was satisfied that the corpse would be difficult or impossible to identify, he dropped the crowbar, grabbed his bag, and walked calmly back toward the main street. The trail leading to "Alan DeVries" would go cold right here. "Ed Winger" and the license plates should be good for another week. In that time, he could be anywhere in the country. Maybe he'd go to New Mexico this time. Lots of cute girls in New Mexico.

But first, he had one more task. The show "Suspect at Large" had found one person who didn't believe everything he read in the newspapers. He had to find out who that was and silence him forever.

In the dingy downtown hotel room he'd rented for twenty-two dollars, he leaned into the greasy mirror and checked his face. The goatee created an interesting effect; it accentuated his mouth, made it look smaller, and drew attention away from his eyes. The eyebrows, plucked into a point, gave him a slightly foreign look, like someone from Eastern Europe. With the shaver he moved the hairline back several inches, loosely matching the photo on Winger's license. Bundy was always amazed how a few subtle changes could radically transform his whole appearance. He winked at himself. *I could be a movie producer.* It took three calls to information to get the phone number in Los Angeles. The call was answered by a receptionist. Bundy held his nose.

"I'm putting through a call from Mr. Laughlin of Paramount Pictures for Mr. Clinton Bernard," he said in a nasal whine.

"Laughlin?" The secretary hesitated. "Is it important?"

Bundy spoke forcefully, yet retained the nasal tone. "Please tell him that Mr. Laughlin wants to speak to him regarding a motion picture deal."

"Just a moment." Bundy held his hand over the phone.

"Clinton Bernard's office," said another voice.

The only way to get through the bullshit was with more bullshit. He used the nasal voice again. "I'm putting through a call for Mr. Laughlin of MGM." *Did I say Paramount before? Oh well*, he thought.

"One moment."

"Clinton Bernard speaking." The velvety-smooth voice was proof that he had been connected with the right man.

Bundy switched to his normal voice. "Mr. Bernard? This is Roger Laughlin. I manage a movie rights acquisition fund at MGM and I wanted to ask you a few questions about one of your stories."

"You should really talk with the executive producer of the show, Mr. Laughlin."

Bundy spoke in a conspiratorial tone. "Mr. Bernard? Are you in a private office? Can I speak to you off the record?"

"Wait a sec. Let me turn off the speaker phone." Bernard was interested.

"We were hoping to attach you personally to the project, based on one of the stories from your show. There was some serious talk about putting you into the movie as the character who breaks the story. Ideally, buy the rights to *your* story. You of course spearhead most of the projects at 'Suspect at Large,' don't you?"

Bernard smelled money and lied. "Yes, of course, I'm on top of everything. You want to contract with *me* personally? Not the company?"

"Ideally, yes. It would be a win-win thing. The more

people we have to cut in, the less chance anything gets made. You know how the runaround is." Bundy instinctively mastered the bullshit doublespeak that would arouse Bernard's interest.

"Sure, sure. What story were you talking about?"

"Can you assure me confidentiality? I want to be able to say to the director, who, by the way, is very well known, that we have a lead on the competition."

"You have my word," said Bernard.

"It's the series of stories you did on those murders by that sheriff. A prominent actor is very interested. I can't tell you who, but his initials are M.G."

"Mel Gibson?"

"You didn't hear that from me. Do you think we could buy your version of the story directly?"

"What kind of figures are we talking about here?" asked Bernard.

"Well, let me tell you, if we went through your production company it'd cost us half a million at least, and that would scotch the whole deal. But if we went through you, maybe as much as a quarter million. If we could buy the rights without undue complications."

Bernard let out a low whistle. "I think we can do business, Mr. Laughlin. A quarter million will bend a lot of rules."

The old con man's trick. Get 'em to compromise their own principles for greed, and they'll do anything you ask. "Good. Now, to convince my money men that we've got a solid source, someone truly worth hiring, I need to see that you can really fill us in on the untold details. Mr. S., as I'd like to call the director, had some very specific questions. If you can answer them, I think we could meet within the week and start talking about numbers."

"Fire away."

Bundy asked lots of general questions about the murders —stuff he'd read in the paper. Bernard deftly answered questions about Tico, Endocino, and the various police forces who had worked on the case. Bundy directed the conversation carefully toward the only subject he was truly interested in.

"Now, on your show you mentioned that man who has this farfetched Bundy theory," said Bundy, trying to sound nonchalant. "I've already talked to him, you know, it's on the tip of my tongue . . ."

"Sloane! You mean Web Sloane! At UC Berkeley. He's a close personal friend," lied Bernard. "I think I can get his cooperation easily. I've met him dozens of times."

"No, that would dilute the payoff, I think. If you already interviewed him, then we don't have to buy his story separately. Now about when we can meet . . ."

Bundy had what he wanted. He quickly wrapped up the conversation and left a fake number in Los Angeles. It would be at least a week until Bernard told anyone, he figured. By the time Bernard found out that there was no Mr. Laughlin at MGM or Paramount or anywhere, it would be too late.

He hung up the phone and laughed. *Sloane.* The name rang a bell. Berkeley was only a short drive away. If this Sloane had assembled such a clear picture of what had happened earlier, he should be stopped. Then he could leave the state with a clean record and nothing behind him but a cold trail. If he learned anything at all in prison, it was that potential obstacles are best eliminated. He killed women because something inside him drove him to do so. Killing men was a different matter all together. He did so only when it was necessary to protect himself. But the judicious elimination of a few people could keep him free.

37

North Coast College of the Arts was located in what had once been a lumber town, halfway between San Francisco and the Oregon border. Web and Joyce left Berkeley at 7 A.M. and drove toward Maria's home near Tico, where they would have breakfast.

Joyce hadn't slept well. She spent the entire hour before they left changing clothes. Web watched with wry amusement as she changed into first a dress, then jeans, then another dress, before finally settling on a skirt and blouse combination that suited her. Considerable effort had been spent applying makeup, too; she rarely cared about things like that when she went to high school.

After they picked up Maria, Joyce turned off the news radio station and turned to her father.

"Daddy-O, I know you really want to see the college and everything, but would it be okay if you kind of stayed out of the way up there?"

"Maria and I weren't planning to follow you around or anything," he said.

"I know that, but I just want to be able to look at the college on my own. You know, see what I like and don't like. There will probably be some other kids there that I want to meet. Um, I want you to let me roam around on my own—like I was actually a real college student. Okay?"

Before Web could object, Maria caught his eye and gave him a slight nod.

"Okay, Joyce, no problem," said Web. "I just want to see Larry Hanrahan, and the only time we'll show up is for the parents' reception tomorrow night. You do the rest, okay?"

"Great, Daddy-O. Thanks a lot."

Maria and Joyce spent the rest of the trip passing fashion catalogues back and forth, commenting on the various dresses and skirts. Mysteriously, they seemed to grow closer with every new ensemble.

When they finally got to the campus, a conglomeration of postmodern buildings nestled in redwoods, Joyce seemed like a dog who had gone too long without a walk. She stared out the windows, drinking up the view of a place where she might spend four years of her life. At the gate, a guard gave them a map.

"Orientation weekend?" asked the guard. "Go over to the Norris Center, and they'll give you an information packet and directions for where to stay."

They drove to the building, and all three got out. A knot of high school students were lined up behind some folding tables stationed below a banner that said Welcome High School Seniors.

"Help you with your suitcase?" asked Web.

"No, I'll get it," she said, lugging the huge bag that contained enough clothes for six weeks. "Could you guys, you know . . ." Joyce pointed at the car.

"We'll just go then," said Web. Maria stood back.

"Okay. Bye, Dad. See you Sunday." Joyce gave her father a quick peck on the cheek and disappeared into the crowd, dragging the huge bag behind her.

"What was that all about?" Web asked Maria as they drove away.

"She is anxious to try her wings, Web. And I respect that. I think she must be pretty serious about this place. Weren't you that way at her age?"

"You're right. What can I say? My folks went nuts because I moved into the neighbor's garage for my last two years of high school."

Maria laughed. "You?"

"Hard to believe, isn't it."

"No, I don't think so. I can see there is a rebel in there somewhere, waiting to come out." she said.

As they drove off the campus, Web turned to Maria. "Hey! What do you say we tour one of those wineries up here? We can't check into the hotel until three anyway."

"Love to," said Maria.

Several other college parents attended the tour of the Bel Mar Vineyards. Web and Maria hung in the back of the group. At every step of the process, the ex-hippie wine maker who led the tour saw that samples of Bel Mar's wines were liberally distributed.

The wine began to make Web feel less inhibited, if not inebriated. When the group was led to the cavernous tunnels where the wine was aged, the lights went out for a moment. Web bumped into Maria. Standing behind her, he took the moment to slide his arms around her stomach. She didn't pull away; instead, she folded her arms on top of his. During the rest of the tour he heard almost nothing of what the guide said; he was aware only of her presence. In the narrow tunnels cluttered with bottles they kept brushing against one another, almost caresses.

At the end of the tour Web purchased two bottles of merlot, two wine glasses, and a corkscrew. Maria leaned her head against Web's shoulder on the drive back to the hotel.

The desk clerk, an older woman in a green dress, didn't look up from her Jude Deveraux novel until Web rang the bell.

"I have a reservation for Sloane."

The clerk pulled an index card out of a box.

"Two rooms, right?"

Web glanced at Maria. She gazed back, her large eyes half-shut. She mischievously shook her head so subtly it was almost imperceptible.

"One room," he said.

When they closed the door on the room overlooking the ocean, he was uncannily aware of the surroundings. He could hear the tiny hum of the electric clock and the ocean's roar equally well. He set a wine bottle down on the desk and savored the clink of glass on glass.

Maria stood frozen by the door, her arms curving loosely by her side, gazing toward Web. He took a tentative step toward her, then another. He put his arms around her. She closed her eyes, turning her face up to his. He gently brushed his lips to hers; they were warm and full.

Maria's arms slowly worked their way up Web's back, until they rested on his shoulders. Still standing, they kissed for a long time, slowly, deliberately, becoming acquainted with one another's rhythms.

After an eternity, he pulled back the bedclothes and laid her down gently on the sheets, then lay next to her. Without getting undressed they stayed there a long time, Web running his hands through her hair, touching her back, her neck, pressing against her warm body.

Maria leisurely unbuttoned his shirt, as if opening a long-awaited gift, kissing his neck, his chest, his stomach. Web gently drew down the top of her dress, inch by inch, concentrating on her skin, caressing the nape of her neck, kissing her throat, her breasts.

"Wait," she murmured. Slowly, catlike, she ambled to the dresser and opened the bottle of wine. Web admired her graceful, bare back as she filled two glasses. Her full breasts swayed slightly as she languidly walked back to the bed, carrying the two glasses of wine.

She set one glass down on the nightstand, then sat next to Web and extended the other toward his lips.

"To today," she said.

He took a sip of the wine, then took the glass from her hand and put it to her mouth.

"To us," he said.

She drew in a long sip of the merlot, then he set the glass down. He kissed her again and inhaled the savory combination of the wine and Maria's own ineffable scent. He wanted the moment to last forever.

Every action in slow motion, every advance deliberate, they made love for the rest of the afternoon, then fell deep asleep in one another's arms as the sun set over the Pacific.

38

Several pictures torn from *People* magazine were taped to the mirror in the old hotel room. Theodore Bundy studied them carefully. He had chosen a random selection of ordinary men near his own age: a photographer who had inadvertently snapped a picture of a plane crash, a fireman who had been hit by lightning seven times, a guy who owned a toy repair shop, and a scientist who claimed to have invented synthetic, calorie-free margarine. He would steal a detail from each photo to create a new identity.

His hair was red now, thanks to a nine-dollar bottle of Clairol. With a razor, he shaved back his hairline to match the bald spot in the fireman's photo. He plucked his eyebrows to match the photographer's, and chose from several pairs of glasses until he found the pair that most resembled those worn by the scientist. The glasses had been stolen from a Salvation Army store.

In the Florida State Prison he had learned this disguise technique from a con artist. *If you try to make yourself look "good," you'll be easily recognized. You see, you can conceal your looks, but you can't conceal your taste. The things someone remembers about a person are the details—such-*

and-such kind of hair or glasses or a particular kind of jacket.
You can radically alter your looks by just imitating random
people, whether or not you like they way they look.

His clothes came from a suitcase he'd pilfered from a tour
bus group staying in downtown San Francisco. It was his
favorite way to get clothes. He simply hung out in a hotel
bar, waited till a tour bus pulled up, and took a suitcase.
He'd done it dozens of times. This most recent acquisition
formerly belonged to an academic attending a New Literature convention at the hotel. The tweed jacket and khakis
made perfect camouflage for a college campus.

Knapsack or briefcase? he wondered. *Do I look like a*
professor or a graduate student? He examined himself in the
mirror holding first the briefcase, then the knapsack. The
knapsack looked better to his eye. He threw in several
books, his wallet, and the appropriate tool for his little
errand: a Saturday Night Special .38-caliber pistol, untrace-
able, purchased at a gun show. He'd learned about gun
shows in prison, too. Out of the hundred or so vendors at
any of them, it was pretty easy to find one who would skip
the seven-day waiting period. Especially if you said you were
a collector who lived out of town and didn't mind paying a
cash premium.

He hopped into the red Cabriolet and drove across town.
Although he'd never been there, UC Berkeley brought on a
wave of pleasant memories. *There's something about a*
college campus! Healthy, good-looking kids of every race,
color, and description, the smartest and most beautiful in
the world, turned loose in a protected world. Well, at least
they believed it was protected. Bundy instantly felt younger
as he mixed in with the throngs of students whom he
imagined were rushing from one intellectual high to another.

It didn't take long to find Web Sloane's office. Exam
results were posted on the door, listed by social security
number to ensure anonymity. A handwritten note read "I
will not be here for Friday or Monday office hours. If you
have an appointment, please reschedule. Sloane." He tried
the door. It was locked. He pulled out a credit card and
slipped it in between the door and the frame, but it wouldn't
budge. He'd have to get in by a ruse.

Bundy wandered down the hall until he came to an open door.

"Hello?" he said, affecting a slight accent, that didn't really come from anywhere, like the supposed British dialects spoken in old Hollywood movies.

An elderly professor in a beard pushed open the door.

"May I help you?"

"Hi. My name's Vance Britten. I was wondering if Dr. Sloane was around."

"Out of town, I think, for the weekend," said the scowling professor, who had thick cataracts in his eyes, like a day-old trout.

Bundy forced a smile. "I'm an old friend of his, and I was hoping to leave him some books that I think would interest him. Could you possibly let me into his office?"

"I don't know you, Mr. Britten," said the man. "Maybe you could just leave the books here, and I'll give them to Mr. Sloane upon his return."

"That'd be fine, but I'd rather surprise him with them on his desk. It'll only take a minute."

The old man grumbled, "all right then." He pushed himself up from the desk with a cane and trudged down the hall, Bundy following close behind.

"Thank you ever so much for helping me out. Webster will appreciate the surprise."

The old man raised an eyebrow. "Webster, eh? I never heard anyone call him that before."

"Old school joke," said Bundy.

The man opened Web's office door. Bundy was immediately confronted with an oversize photo of himself posted on the bulletin board. It was the booking photo from Florida. The shock caused him to lose his bearings for a moment. The professor tapped his cane on the ground.

"Well, put the books down. I have things to do," said the old man.

"Okay." Bundy pulled the two paperbacks out of the bag and set them down on the desk. He stepped back to the doorway and leaned against the door frame.

"Thanks for helping me out, Mr., what is it?"

"It's *Doctor* McCloud. Are you through?"

"Yes."

The old man slowly returned to his office. Bundy walked the other direction down the hall, waited till he heard the professor's door close, then returned to Sloane's office, opening it immediately. He had unlatched the lock while leaning against the door. Easy trick. If you can get someone to open a door for you once, you can open it yourself later.

Without turning on the office light, Bundy rummaged through Sloane's files and notebooks. Within minutes he recognized that Sloane knew too much. Some of the photos on the board were damned familiar. There was the girl from Tico. The girl from Vallejo. And—*Jesus Christ*—Sloane had a photo booth picture of the bum he'd rolled in Sacramento. The transient whose driver's license Bundy carried for months—Alan DeVries.

That meant that Sloane might know everything. He must be stopped.

He flipped through the pages on the desk. *Here's Sloane's home address. Here's his phone number. Here's a photo— who's this, a daughter?* He stuck a photo of Web and Joyce into his backpack. Then he lifted the entire Rolodex. *Might come in useful.*

He heard footsteps coming down the hall and froze in position. The person stopped outside the door and knocked. Bundy ducked behind the desk. A moment later an envelope was shoved through the mail slot, and the footsteps walked away.

Bundy picked up the envelope. Just a flyer from the university. He turned his attention back to Sloane's desk.

Under the Rolodex were some notes scratched onto a yellow pad.

Hotel—SeaView Inn, Sat/Sun, 18th & 19th, ½ block east of PCH on Oceanside Drive, Bel Mar

That would mean Sloane's in Bel Mar right now. Bel Mar was the perfect place to accomplish what needed to be done. It was out in the middle of nowhere, halfway to Oregon. *Nobody will be looking for me or my car in Bel Mar. And I can get out of state before the body's cold.*

He quietly slipped out of Sloane's office and headed back across campus toward his car.

Something held him back. He didn't want to leave the campus just yet. *So many wonderful sights. So many beautiful people. Over there are some girls playing tennis. The other way is a young couple just gazing skyward, laying on the grass.*

I'll just have a beer at the stu U, he thought. *Then, I'll hit the road.*

The Michelobs hit the spot; icy cold and mildly intoxicating. He felt the cares of the world slip out of him. He sat by a sunny window in the student union and gazed at the students coming and going. By the time he'd finished his third beer, the room became quite crowded. Every table was filled.

He stared at two girls across the room who held hands in the line. *Lesbians,* he thought. Thoughts of their sexual habits filled his mind as he gazed toward them. *Look at her—beautiful girl, tall, good-looking, could have any man she wants, and she's with a tub of lard in jeans and a dirty T-shirt.* His reverie was broken off.

"Excuse me?"

He looked up. Directly in front of him was a mousy girl with long, brown hair, seven pairs of earrings and chopsticks in her hair. She held a tray of food and had a bag of books slung over her shoulder.

"Yes?" he asked.

"Do you mind if I sit down here?"

He set the beer down on the table. "Go right ahead. Please, I'd love it if you joined me."

She dropped the books and put the tray on the table.

"I wouldn't bother you, except it's so full," she said, taking a seat directly opposite him.

"No, I'm pleased to have the company. Ed Winger," he said, extending his hand.

"Amanda Dell," she replied, smiling. "God! I just finished my last exam, and I think I aced it!" she said.

"What class?"

"Unconditional Positive Regard." She adjusted her huge glasses. "It's a psychology course. Really difficult."

Bundy immediately drew her into a conversation about psychology. It was ridiculously easy to get her to chat. It was criminal how ready she was to share a couple drinks with him. *Exams, you know. I just need to unwind. Tomorrow I fly to San Diego.* And it was fatal that she accepted his offer of a ride home. Within three hours her body was dumped in the state forest. Her remains would never be found.

The sun had set when he drove through Tico and Endocino. Once he was on the other side, it took two hours to get to Bel Mar. He checked into the Whispering Pines Motel, eight rooms by the side of the road, a trucker's stopover that had been built in the fifties. After a shower and a six-pack of Anchor Steam, he passed out on the bed.

39

The Parents and Relatives Reception was a low-key affair with wine, cheese, and lots of North Coast staff pressing the flesh in the lobby of the school theater. The arts college was only seven years old. It had been established with a grant from Parker Lazlo, the animation and theme park tycoon, and needed to double its enrollment or risk depleting the fifty-million-dollar bequest very rapidly.

Web and Maria arrived promptly at 7:30 P.M., hoping to meet some of the faculty and then quickly leave for a late dinner out. Web spent a long time chatting with Larry Hanrahan, who bored him with tales of a million-dollar media laboratory that specialized in interactive instruction. At around 8:30 he finally spotted Joyce, who was talking to two other kids, a boy and a girl, both of whom looked like Bohemians ordered from central casting—long hair, leather everything, earrings, and tattoos. Joyce had dressed up, too: She had on a black beret and her favorite black skirt and blouse. Web always wondered why she loved black so much.

Web nodded to Maria, who was talking with a dance professor wearing a spandex skirt. Maria broke away to join Web, and the two walked over to Joyce.

Maria whispered to Web. "That's Angela Phinlay, the one who was in the papers over the NEA controversy."

Web glanced back at the spike-haired woman. "The one who did the ballet about whale killing where they filled a swimming pool with blood?"

Maria smiled. "Sh. That's the one. I never would have picked her out. She said none of the students get to do that kind of avant garde work; she stresses fundamentals and discipline. Seems very nice."

As they approached, Joyce caught Web's eye and self-consciously held her plastic wine glass down by her waist.

"Hi, Dad," said Joyce, trying not to scowl.

"Hello, Joyce. How's it going so far?"

"Good, really good." She set the wine glass down on the nearest available table. She leaned toward her father and whispered. "I thought you said you wouldn't hang around a lot."

"Oh, come on. This is the parents' reception. I promise we'll leave you alone soon enough."

She turned the charm on again. "Dad, Maria, this is Eldridge and Elaine Hill. I just met them this afternoon. They do a science fiction comic book together."

"You're students here?" asked Web.

The boy spoke first. "No, we're only—"

The girl finished his sentence, "seventeen, but we thought we'd look up here at—"

The boy picked up where she left off. "North Coast since it's the coolest school in the country."

Maria stepped in. "What kind of comic book? For a school paper or something, perhaps?"

Eldridge looked at her. "It's for Marvel Comics, and Elaine writes them—"

"And he illustrates them. It's called CyberEvolution, and—" said Elaine, turning to Eldridge.

"It's not a school thing," finished the boy.

Joyce smiled proudly, as if it were her own accomplishment. "They're real comic books—everybody reads them. It's the hot thing now. I didn't know they were my age."

Elaine spoke. "Nice meeting you, Mr. Sloane. We want to—"

"Go meet one of the professors here. Bye."

The twins walked across the lobby.

"They get paid thirty thousand dollars per comic, Daddy-O, and they still want to go to college. Can you believe it?"

"That's wonderful," said Maria.

Joyce leaned against an hors d'oeuvres table.

"I think I really want to come here. But I was hoping to just meet some more students by myself." She added, "It would mean a lot to me."

Web didn't catch her drift. "Hey! If you'd like, you and your friends can come to dinner with Maria and me. We're going to a place called Chez Bel Mar; it's fancy and right on the water."

"Chez Bel Mar? It sounds like where Lucy and Ricky would go for a big date or something, kind of old-fashioned."

"It's supposed to be very nice," said Web.

"Dad, that's very sweet and everything but I was just hoping to meet some of the students, *by myself,* you know?"

"All right, then pass up Chez Bel Mar. I hope you're not embarrassed by me or anything," he added, smiling.

"It's not that. I promise, Daddy-O. Okay?"

Web got it. "Okay. Come on, Maria. Let's go."

Joyce escorted them to the door of the theater, watched till they were gone, then made a beeline for the Hill twins.

"I can sure tell when I'm not wanted around," said Web.

"I don't blame her, really. How would you like her tagging along at a research conference?"

"It's just odd feeling like a fifth wheel to my own daughter."

He impulsively kissed her on the neck.

"What do you say to dinner?"

"I'm famished."

Bundy woke up in a sweat, hungry, dehydrated, and sore. He had turned on the gas heater before lying down, and now the room felt like a sauna. He checked the clock. It was quarter after nine. He thought that he should get going; if he waited much longer he would have to stall another day before eliminating Sloane. By that time the professor might be back on his way to Berkeley.

He dialed the SeaView Inn.

"Web Sloane, please," he said to the receptionist.

"One moment."

The room phone produced an electric buzzing sound, as is heard on older telephone circuits. It rang four times, and then the desk clerk picked up.

"I'm sorry, Mr. Sloane is not in. May I take a message?"

Bundy lowered his voice, trying to sound like a working-class stiff. "I'm confirming a pizza delivery order. I think some kids placed it as a prank. They gave me room 505. Is that right?"

The desk clerk laughed. "Mr. Sloane's in 8B. There is no room 505 at the SeaView. It must have been a prank. We're only one floor."

"Hey! Thanks for saving me a trip. These college kids drive me crazy."

"I know what you mean. Especially this weekend," said the clerk.

"Bye."

Bundy wrote down the room number. 8B. That's all he wanted. The ruse had worked.

Bundy wet down his hair, then drove to the SeaView Inn. It was a pseudorustic vacation spot with lots of exposed timbers, overlooking the Pacific Ocean. There were two buildings, and guests entered directly from the parking lot to their rooms.

He quickly found the back building. 8B was on the west end. No cars in the lot. He parked.

He sat in the front seat and opened the breach of the handgun. It was full. He wrapped a towel around the barrel as a makeshift silencer and draped a jacket over his arm. He would look like any guest.

He knocked on the door. There was no reply, so he knocked again.

He walked around the building to a porch that overlooked the Pacific ocean. It was easy to climb up. Sliding-glass doors opened onto a deck where guests could have coffee or tea and watch the sunset. He looked around the porch. No one was in sight. He turned around and tried the sliding-glass door.

It slid open.

The sheets from the queen-size bed were pushed to the floor. An empty wine bottle and two glasses lay on the bedside table. He looked around the room. Nothing extraordinary: an open suitcase, some change on the dresser, a few books.

He set down the handgun and knapsack and flipped through Sloane's suitcase to see if there was anything useful.

He happened upon a form letter addressed to Joyce Sloane. It described the events scheduled for the North Coast College Get Acquainted Weekend. Underlined was "Parents Reception—5/19, 7:30 to 10:00 P.M."

That was tonight. Sloane wouldn't be back for an hour at least. If he waited for the man and finished him off here in the hotel room, someone was sure to remember the red Cabriolet. Better to draw him out. But how?

He looked through the rest of the packet underneath the form letter.

Handwritten on the back of a brochure was: *Joyce staying in Lazlo Dorm.*

That would do it. Joyce must be the girl in the photo. *It will be messy to fight with the Sloane guy. Easier to get to the daughter. Find out what she knows, use her to get him. Then pump him for information before killing him. Much better plan.*

He pocketed the brochure, picked up his backpack, and exited through the front door. *Why draw attention to myself by going out the back? It's a hotel. No one will notice.*

Bundy guzzled the last few drops of a warm bottle of Anchor Steam and tossed the bottle into the backseat, where it landed with a clink on top of several other empties. Sitting in the parking lot of the four-story Lazlo Dormitory Complex he gazed hungrily up at the lighted windows. Shadows moving across the lighted windows formed shapes like paper dolls blowing in the wind. Looking through binoculars he determined that the lower two floors were for boys; the upper floors for girls. *To protect their precious daughters,* he thought.

Security in the lobby. Probably an elevator with a key. Two floors of boys to get past. Sneak in the back? Nah. Too dangerous. Walk in the front door. Much better. Much classier. He got out of the car, put on his gas company jacket, and pulled a toolbox from the trunk. *Something not quite right.* He grinned as he attached a yellow ribbon in a fancy bow to the toolbox. *The piece de resistance. Hell, who wouldn't trust a patriotic guy?* Bundy stuffed the rest of the stolen ribbon into his pocket.

He looked at his reflection in the side mirror. Eyes as red as blood. He put two drops of Visine in each eye, blew his nose, and headed for the lobby.

"May I help you?" asked the student watchman sitting in the lobby. He was at most twenty years old. He sat behind an office desk by the door, reading the classic film textbook by Novros, *Shapes and Motion.*

Bundy mumbled, "Gas leak. Might be a main. Gotta check it out."

The boy set down his book. "I didn't hear about that. Is there any danger of explosion?"

"Can't tell just yet. Probably not a big danger," said Bundy. "But if there is I'll tell yah."

"Can I see some I.D.?"

Bundy pulled the homeless man's driver's license from his wallet and pushed it in front of the boy's nose.

"You're really from the gas company?"

"Hey! I don't leave home at ten at night for my health."

"I have to call to make sure."

"Suit yourself. I'm on the clock, though. Weekend rate, golden time. One-forty-five an hour. I could be done in fifteen minutes. But you can call whoever you want. I need the money." He moved to a couch and sat down, as if for a long rest, all the while keeping a close watch on the boy.

"Who should I call?" asked the boy.

"Hey! You're the one who wanted to call. I don't care."

The boy grimaced. "Okay. You need the elevator?"

"Yeah."

The boy turned a key, and the elevator door opened. Bundy stepped in. When the doors shut, he rolled his eyes. *People just love a man in uniform.* He pushed 4.

The doors opened. A huge sign drawn with Tempra paints proclaimed Welcome Future North Coasters, with frills and flowers around the border. Music and laughter seeped into the empty hallway from behind doors. He picked one at random and knocked.

A girl's voice yelled, "Is that you, Toni? Just a second!"

The door opened wide. Behind it stood a nineteen-year-old redhead, wearing only a Mickey Mouse tank top and panties. Seeing Bundy, she quickly hid herself behind the door. Bundy's heart raced as he caught a glimpse of her full breast peeking out from her shirt. *Keep it together, don't blow it, don't fuck this up.*

"Gee, I thought it was someone else," said the girl, peeking out from behind the door.

"Gas leak. I gotta check for a gas leak," said Bundy. His hand shook.

"Hold on a sec." She started to close the door. He put his foot in, blocking it.

With his whole weight, Bundy forced the door open. He dropped his toolbox. In seconds, one hand was on her mouth, the other pawing her body. He kicked the door shut behind him.

Digging his fingers into her cheek, he held tight onto her mouth as he tore off the girl's underpants. Tears of terror ran down her cheeks, and she whimpered under his grip.

He pressed her head against his chest as he clumsily unzipped his pants. He dropped his underwear to his ankles and forced the girl down on the bed.

Something is wrong. He looked down. His flaccid member stubbornly refused to budge. He massaged it with his hand, but to no avail. He tried rubbing against the girl, but still nothing. Her tears flowed uncontrollably.

"You bitch," he yelled. Bundy stuffed the end of the sheet into her mouth and pushed her head facedown against the bed. "Quiet! Just shut up!"

Pinning her down with one arm, he opened the toolbox and extracted a large pipe wrench with the other. She continued to squirm.

He hefted the tool over his head and brought it down. The girl writhed in agony; instead of crashing into her head it landed with a thud on her neck. He was sickened by the sound of the bone cracking under the force of the iron.

Frantically, the girl kicked him.

In a rage he brought the wrench down again. This time it landed squarely on the back of her skull, splitting the skin open on the crown of her head where her part had been. Blood and hair sprayed onto a Jim Morrison poster gracing the wall behind her bed.

The girl's body convulsed violently. Bundy was nauseated by the sight and brought the tool down again and again, losing himself in a ballet of repetitive motion. A coroner would determine later that he had hit her more than forty times, mostly after her death. It would be almost a footnote to the other more reprehensible posthumous indignities she suffered.

Self-control snapped back into his mind, like waking up suddenly after a nightmare. *What the fuck is this?* he thought. He looked at the girl's mutilated body on the thin economical student bed. She had Calvin & Hobbes sheets, *no doubt brought here from the pathetic smarmy happy family somewhere in Bumfuck, Iowa.* He tugged on the girl's feet, still warm, stretching her out faceup on the bed. Then he covered her with a sheet, as if she were asleep. The only telltale sign was the blood-covered Doors poster. He ripped it off the wall and stuffed it under the bed. *Gotta find the Sloane girl. Can't lose track of the primary objective.* He hunted through the desk for a student directory.

Toni Warrell bounded up the four flights of stairs up to her dorm room. She was supposed to study for a comparative literature test with her roommate, Beth. Toni was late because she played three sets of tennis instead of two, winning all of them against a cute boy from the studio arts department.

She was looking forward to telling Beth about the tennis but, more importantly, about the invitation she'd finagled to visit the boy's parents down in Marin County. The rumor was that they were wealthy entertainment people, and she was scared and delighted about the prospect of visiting. She would never get to go.

In Beth's dorm room, there was a knock. Bundy stepped cautiously into the tiny closet. The door opened.

"Beth?" asked Toni, tentatively.

The door creeked open.

"Beth, wake up!" The lights flicked on and off repeatedly. "You'll never believe who got invited to Marin County! Hell-OHHH-hooo!" She sang the last words. The lights flicked on and off again, then Bundy saw the girl walk toward the bed. She had long dark hair, tied in a ponytail. She wore a Nike sweat suit and carried a tennis racket, which she threw on the ground. He was filled with tension; like a third-grader who needs to go to the bathroom, he bounced slightly from foot to foot.

"Beth?" said Toni.

She shook the blankets.

"Come on, Beth, this isn't funny."

The girl lifted her hand suddenly from the bed. The sheet was damp to the touch. A deep burgundy stain spread from the neck of Hobbes the cartoon tiger all the way down to the foot of his good friend Calvin.

Toni peeled back the blanket and screamed. Blood was everywhere. Her roommate, Beth, was dead, her head twisted to the side like a broken mannequin.

Bundy sprang from the closet. Toni's scream was cut short when he pushed her head down onto the bed.

Toni could not breathe, much less scream. She tasted something warm, salty, and fat, like uncooked bacon. Her mouth was pressed against the open wound where her roommate's head had been smashed open like an overripe melon. Bundy's fingers clawed the back of her scalp, the full force of his weight pressing down. She felt her sweatshirt being lifted up from behind, then a shock jolted her into unconsciousness.

Bundy quietly closed the door. Then he stared at the young girls face down on the bed, one dead, one unconscious. To his surprise, an exquisite sensation began to fill his loins. A smirk moved across his face. *Two girls at once. That's the ticket.* He didn't consider that one was dead.

Bundy yanked the sweaty tennis shoes off of the unconscious Toni, then pulled off her bright sweatpants and threw them across the room. He rolled her to the floor like so much baggage, then yanked the Calvin & Hobbes sheet off the bed and studied the dead Beth. Her face was annihilated; but her body was largely untouched. Bundy covered her face with a pillow.

On the floor, Toni began to move. He flicked on the stun gun again and touched it twice to the back of her neck. She groaned and fell back into unconsciousness.

He lifted her onto the bed, on top of her roommate, putting her facedown on top of the gory corpse. Breathing hard, he dropped his pants to his ankles and mounted her.

Toni struggled up from the murky stupor, like swimming from the bottom of a pool, never quite able to reach the surface. She felt horrible pain in her lower back; something was violating her.

With firm resolution, she tried to break through to consciousness; she finally forced herself awake. The pain had subsided somewhat. When she opened her bleary eyes, she saw Beth's mutilated face. A hulking figure was still grunting away on her back, but she did not feel the pain of penetration. Then she realized: *He's raping her dead body beneath me.* Toni screamed.

Her scream was cut short by several lengths of yellow ribbon digging into her neck, restricting precious air, and the pain of a second violation. This intrusion was more personal, more horrible; he was doing the sex act she never would allow her boyfriend even to suggest: *the dirty thing.* If air were available, she would have cried out when he bit off her earlobe; if she could will herself to die, she would have before he flipped her over and sank his teeth into her breast. The last thing she saw before succumbing was the face of the murderer, her own flesh hanging from his mouth, blood covering his cheeks. Death was in his eyes.

Bundy withdrew and felt himself dizzy from the complete loss of control he associated with sex and death, especially when they were simultaneous. *Gotta clean up, Jesus fucking Christ.*

He threw a pillow under her head to catch the blood and dragged her to the closet. Then he stood silent, waiting to hear if there was any reaction. There wasn't. He threw a sheet over Beth's mutilated body and stuffed the bloodied clothes under the bed.

Breathing heavily, he wiped off his face with a towel.

Some blood was on the jacket. He wiped it off as best he could. When it dried, it could be mistaken for a rust mark.

Still breathing hard, he rummaged through the girl's desk until he found what he was looking for: Get Acquainted Weekend Directory, a mimeographed sheet with phone numbers and temporary dorm assignments. He folded the paper and slipped it into his pocket.

Momentarily he caught a glimpse of himself in the mirror. *I look fucking crazy!* he thought. *Can't go running around like that!* To regain his composure, he executed a deep-breathing exercise that he learned in a college psychology class. *Still got a long night ahead. Can't get frazzled.* He counted backward from fifty, and by the end, just as promised, he felt *relaxing warmth spreading through every cell in his body.* He pulled out the bottle of Visine and squirted a few more drops in his eyes, staring at himself until the red disappeared. Then he reached into his toolbox and extracted a lab coat. *That'll cover the goddam stain.*

Joyce was in her dorm room with the Hill twins, looking over the comic books that they had drawn. When they heard a scream, all three looked up, surprised. The scream suddenly stopped and they laughed.

"Seems like a pretty wild dorm, doesn't it?" Joyce asked. "So different from high school."

"Yeah, yeah," said the twins, more interested in Joyce's reaction to their work than a wild party down the hall.

It was astounding to her that kids her age had already been doing professional work for three years. She never before had been interested in comics, but somehow the twins made them seem fascinating. There was a knock at the door.

"Just a minute!" she yelled.

She opened the door a crack.

"Joyce Sloane please."

She opened the door the rest of the way. Outside was a man who looked like a medical technician—sort of. He had on a lab coat, but she noticed a jumpsuit underneath. He seemed to have a bad complexion or something, but she couldn't put her finger on it.

"I'm Joyce. May I help you?"

"Your father's been in a car accident," said Ted Bundy.

"Oh, my God." Joyce put her hand to her mouth. "Is he okay?"

"You better come down and see him. He's at the hospital."

Joyce went pale. She turned to the twins. "You guys, I have to go."

"What is it?" asked Elaine.

"My dad. I have to go right now. Are you going to be at the good-bye brunch tomorrow?"

"Yeah, I think so." said Eldridge.

"See you there," said Elaine. The two picked up their comic books and left the room.

"Wait a sec," Joyce said to Bundy. "I have to get my purse."

"It's very urgent," said Bundy, shifting on his feet.

"Okay." Joyce grabbed her purse and left. She followed the man, who walked quickly.

"What happened?" she asked.

"A drunk driver hit him. He should be okay, but he asked for you. I think he needs a blood infusion," said Bundy.

"Transfusion?" asked Joyce.

"Yes, a transfusion."

She followed him out. He left through a back fire exit, rather than taking the elevator.

"Hey, where are we going?" she asked.

"I have a hospital vehicle back in back. I'm going to take you there."

They ran down the metal stairway, footsteps echoing in the corridor. Joyce's thoughts were with her father: *Is he hurt?*

When they got outside, Joyce noticed the medical worker looked left and right, as if crossing a street. *Or to see if we're alone.* He briskly walked toward the parking lot.

She slowed her pace, letting the man get a few steps ahead of her. Something seemed wrong. Besides the weird jumpsuit, he wore dirty tennis shoes. She looked around to see if anyone else was nearby. A knot of students chatted on the steps of a nearby dorm.

"Hey! Could I see some I.D.?" she asked.

"I'll show it to you as soon as we get to the vehicle. Your father is very sick," said Bundy.

"I want to see something right now or I'm not coming with you."

Bundy reached into the lab coat he wore and pulled out a wallet.

"Here you go. Hospital I.D."

Joyce was ten feet away; too far to see the wallet. She cautiously walked toward the man.

"Let me see."

When she was next to him, Bundy suddenly pulled out the gun and pressed it into her ribs.

"You'll do what I say right now. Or I'll shoot. Do you understand?"

Joyce put up her hands.

"Put your hands down," hissed Bundy.

She slowly lowered them. "Who are you?" she asked.

"Wouldn't you like to know?" He chortled. "Now, wave at those kids over there. Do it!"

She waved to the students on the steps. They were within shouting distance but may as well have been a hundred miles away. They waved back, then entered the building, oblivious to her plight, leaving her alone in the night.

"Now, I'm going to put my arm around your stomach. The gun will be pointed at your heart. If you run or scream, I'll shoot."

Joyce felt the breath go out of her body as his sinewy arm grappled around her waist. His fingernails dug into her flesh. His breath smelled of cigarette smoke, beer, and halitosis.

"Keep on walking. Don't look around," said Bundy.

He led her to a parking lot. It was well lit. Bundy opened the trunk of his car.

"Turn around," he said, grabbing her shoulder and spinning her.

"Why are you doing this?" she asked, crying.

"Shut the fuck up. What is it with kids today? Doesn't anyone listen?"

He twisted her arms up behind her back and slipped a blood-stained pair of handcuffs over her wrists.

Joyce screamed. She kicked backward with her shoe, just like her father had taught her, and ran as Bundy loosened his grip.

"Help!" she yelled. Bundy ran across the parking lot and tackled her, driving her face to the ground. He pulled her head up by the hair.

"Why did you do that?" he spat. "I told you not to run."

He slapped his hand over her mouth and lifted her from the ground. No one came running to help; there was no one anywhere near.

He lifted her cuffed arms so high she thought they would break. His hand tightened on her mouth, his fingers cutting into her lips. *This is it,* she thought. She opened her mouth and bit his finger.

"Ow!" he yelled. "You bitch."

Joyce felt his fist connect with her temple. Then blackness enveloped her.

When she came to, she was facedown in the backseat of the car. She tasted blood. She looked down at the seat. It wasn't her own blood. *Oh, my God.* She knew the attacker wasn't just a rapist. It had happened to her sister. It could happen to her.

She thought about what her father had told her time and time again. *Stall. If you're ever in a kidnap or rape situation, throw every possible obstacle in the way of the attacker. Never, ever hope that cooperating will help you.*

She looked out the window at the pavement speeding by. They seemed to be in a rural section of the Pacific Coast Highway. Joyce tried to formulate a plan for escape. Lights were up ahead; it was just a gas station. As she sped by, she could see people filling up their cars, oblivious to her fate. They were quickly in the dark again.

As they came around a bend, a neon light caught her eye. It was in red and blue script and took a moment to register. *Chez Bel Mar.* Her heart jumped to her throat. Her father and Maria were there right now. *If only there was some way . . .* She made a plan.

A gag was in her mouth. She tried talking in spite of it, letting out animalistic grunts.

"What is it?" yelled Bundy, leaning over the backseat.

"Mmph gohn thow uhp."

"What?" he screamed.

"Umm goan thow uhp," Joyce repeated, making a gagging sound.

"Throw up? Don't puke in here. Jesus Christ."

He pulled to the side of the road.

"Don't move. I'll open the door and you can puke out there." He got out of the driver's door and walked around to the passenger side to let her out.

Joyce leaned forward. She couldn't reach the passenger door handle; but she was able to lean her head on the door lock. Bundy inserted his key, but couldn't unlock the door. Joyce pressed her chin as hard as possible against the lock.

"Get off that, you bitch!" he yelled. Joyce didn't move. He ran back to the driver's side of the car. In the time it took him to get around, Joyce scooted into the front seat and slammed her left foot on the driver's side lock. Then she pushed her right knee into the horn. It blasted out with deafening loudness. The man pounded on the window and yelled, but the horn drowned out what he was saying.

Joyce pressed her foot down hard on the lock and kept an eye on the man. The parking brake between the two front seats dug hard into her spine; it hurt, but she knew if she moved he would get in. With her handcuffed hand, she pressed hard on the button of the parking brake. She had no leverage, but finally forced the button down with sheer force. The brake snapped down, and the car rolled forward on the slight incline, halfway into the highway before stopping. The man walked back to the passenger side and tried the lock again, but Joyce had the latch secured with her forehead before he could get the key in the lock.

She kept her knee on the horn, but instead of holding it down solidly, she began pressing a distress call. Three short blasts, three long blasts, then three short blasts of the horn. Dot dot dot. Dash dash dash. Dot dot dot. Maybe someone would recognize it. It was all she could think of.

It seemed to make no difference; three cars passed without stopping. The man positioned himself by the passenger door window, pounding on the glass with a stick. The window shattered; but the safety glass stayed in the frame. It would undoubtedly soon give way. Then she would again be trapped.

Half a mile further down Pacific Coast Highway, Web Sloane and Maria de Rivera walked slowly across the Chez Bel Mar parking lot toward his car. They were full of mussels and white wine; the night air felt good after the somewhat stuffy but beautiful restaurant. Web wrapped his arm around Maria's waist; she fit herself snugly underneath.

They casually sauntered to his car. He opened the passenger door of the Volvo and stood between Maria and the seat.

"Maria, I've really enjoyed myself tonight," said Web. He leaned in toward her and pressed his lips against hers. She tasted like lipstick, candy, and perfume; he held the kiss until a distant noise interrupted them. Maria pulled away.

"Do you hear that?" she asked.

"Sounds like a boat in trouble," replied Web. "That's Morse code for SOS—a distress call."

Maria cocked back her head and listened. "Too high pitched for a boat or a foghorn. Maybe just some kids."

The intermittent pattern stopped, and for a moment the horn blew steadily, then stopped, echoing against the hills.

"Strange," said Web. They climbed into the car and drove out of the parking lot.

"There it is again," said Maria.

Web put down the window. The car horn was growing louder: They were getting closer to the source. Then it ceased again. Web rolled up the window.

As they rounded a curve in the road, his headlights flickered across a car stalled in the opposite lane. The driver stood in back, pushing the trunk lid down. Several suitcases were dumped on the road in back of the car.

"That must be it," said Web.

As they drove away from the site, Web saw the man struggling with the trunk lid. It was dark, and he was watching through the rearview mirror, but it looked an awful lot like something or someone was in the trunk, pushing the lid back up. *Why is he closing the trunk when his suitcases are spread out on the road?* thought Web. His hunter's mind wrenched control of his psyche: Something sinister was occurring. His pulse raced.

"Maria, I want to get a better look at that."

"You can't make a U-turn here," said Maria. "Someone could come around one of those bends and smash into us."

"I'll turn around further up."

He pushed the car as fast as it would go. It was another mile before the hairpin curves straightened out. Web pulled onto the berm, scanned for traffic both ways, and turned back toward the scene of the accident.

He went around the bend preceding the spot where he had seen the car and immediately stomped on the brakes. Three suitcases were directly in his path, and a trunk blocked the opposite side of the road.

"Look at that. The jerk just left all this junk in the road. Someone could get killed."

Web pulled over to the berm.

He got out of his car and kicked the three suitcases to the side of the road. A few feet ahead, shattered glass flickered in his headlights. He walked up to it and pushed it to the side of the road with his foot.

His attention was diverted to a brown object in the grass next to the road. Web picked it up.

It was a purse. Joyce's purse.

Web's heart jumped a beat, and he ran back to the car. *Someone in the trunk. Convertible.*

He jumped in and screeched onto the road.

"What is it, Web?" asked Maria.

"Maria, I'm going to drop you off back at the restaurant when we pass it. Go inside and call the police."

"What are you going to do?"

"I'm going to follow the car. Joyce is in it."

Web skidded to a stop at the end of the driveway in front of the Chez Bel Mar.

"Run," he rasped. "We don't have much time."

She jumped out and slammed the door. Before it closed, Web was already back on the road.

He pushed the car over seventy miles an hour, as fast as the winding roads would permit. Three miles south of the restaurant he got stuck behind a lumber truck doing thirty. The tight curves blocked his view beyond the truck. Do Not Pass signs were positioned every quarter mile.

He veered out into the opposite lane and looked for an

opportunity to pass. The road straightened out for a mere fifty yards.

Web held his breath and gunned the engine. The slight incline made it hard to pass the truck; as soon as he was even with the cab a pair of headlights popped out from around the curve.

Web turned on his brights and pressed the accelerator down as hard as it would go.

He wedged himself in front of the truck. The station wagon in the opposite lane honked its horn and skidded over into the breakdown lane. Web didn't care. He sped away.

The road twisted and disappeared into darkness in front of him. His high beams illuminated the pine trees that closed in on the road like mourners leaning over a grave. There was no sign of the Cabriolet further up the road, merely a black void.

Web opened the window hoping to hear another engine roaring. He was going seventy-five miles an hour. Web had to drive into the opposing lane to make the hairpin curves, the wheels whining against the pavement.

If he went this way there are no towns and no turnoffs for thirty or forty miles, he thought. *I just need to go faster.*

Web saw headlights belonging to an oncoming truck. He decelerated to fifty; the sign for the curve said 25 MPH. Pulling the wheel hard to the left, his car hit a patch of gravel as the truck passed and the rear wheels slid out of control. The back bumper of his car scraped the truck's rear fender. Web's car whipped around furiously. He stepped on the brakes, spinning out of control before he stopped across both lanes, pointed toward the curb.

The truck, by now a quarter mile down the road, pulled over and stopped. Web drove to the curb, got out, and inspected the damage.

The back bumper was bent out in a hook shape away from the car, a jagged edge of the metal dragging against the ground.

He opened the trunk and pulled out the crowbar, which he then wedged into the exposed edge of the bumper. He pulled up on it with all his strength. The bumper moved up a fraction of an inch, then the crowbar slipped out and he lost his balance. He tried again, this time using the crowbar as a lever, and forced the bumper up a mere inch off the road.

The trucker ran toward him, yelling out.

If I wait for him, it'll be several minutes at least before I can leave. Maybe he'll call the police on me. That would be the best possible outcome.

He leaped back into the car and continued driving. When he drove through curves, the hanging bumper raked the ground with a shrill metallic squeal like fingernails on a chalkboard. He looked in his left mirror. Sparks flew behind him from the bumper.

He concentrated as hard as possible, trying to overcome the effects of the wine he'd drunk at dinner. *Joyce was up there.*

The terrain gradually changed as he went further south. The road slithered along a path that traversed bluffs overlooking the ocean. Periodically the tree cover broke, and the black ocean below opened up. At one such spot, a long, wide curve gave him a view a half-mile ahead across a cove. *There.* He caught a glimpse of taillights disappearing into the woods on the other side of the inlet. *That must be the car.*

Web pushed the car to its limit. He tried turning out the lights for a moment, hoping to conceal himself, but could not see ten feet ahead of himself on the overcast night.

As the road turned back into the hills, he could occasionally witness the flicker of the red taillights through the trees. He kept the high beams on. There was little traffic coming in the opposite direction; only an occasional car or truck.

His lights suddenly became palpable; he could make out the edges of the high beams. *Fog. Dammit. But if I'm in fog, so is he.* Thirty seconds later, though, the fog cleared. Within a minute, another lumber truck blocked him. The road was too convoluted to easily pass it. *If I can't pass, then he couldn't pass. Was that fog back there? Or dust?*

He slammed on the brakes and executed a U-turn. Back at the spot where he had seen the dust was a faded sign painted on logs: Sun Holiday Campground. The sign was riddled with shotgun blasts. Spray-painted on the bottom of the sign was: CLOSED, FOR SALE, 22 ACRES, 916-555-7842.

He got stuck behind the truck and turned up this road. Web turned off the high beams and drove up the washed-out road using only his parking lights. The bumper caught on several spots on the rough trail. He forced it through.

The trees cleared away, and Web saw the lights of the car, which was now parked. He stopped the car, picked up the crowbar, and got out.

Web walked ten feet off the dirt road into the woods toward the car. No one was in the car. He crawled forty feet from the woods to the red Cabriolet. As he neared, he could see that the color red came from a hack spray paint job. *Gray Cabriolet*. This was the car. He opened the passenger door. Bits of glass fell out of the window. Web looked in the back seat and saw the large blood stain. *Trunk*. He crawled over to the driver's side and yanked on a latch. A dull click indicated the trunk had opened.

Web crawled around to the back of the car and opened the trunk. Empty.

He slammed the trunk and stood up to look around. When he heard a loud crack, he instinctively ducked. Two more cracks. Someone was firing at him. He could only tell that it came from the general direction of the cabins further in the woods.

"Who's there?" a voice echoed from the same direction.

"Sloane." Web felt any deception would be pointless. The unseen opponent had a gun.

"The Web Sloane," said the stranger. "Walk away from the car. Keep your hands where I can see them." *That voice—where had he heard it before?* Web knelt behind the car.

Another shot rang out.

"You just don't listen, Sloane. We're playing Simon Says. I didn't ask you to hide behind the car. I asked you to come out where I can see you."

He heard a cry that was abruptly cut off. Web didn't budge. He lifted a stick and threw it a short distance. It made the leaves crackle when it landed, then another shot rang out.

"Sloane. I know everything you know. You're very clever."

Web crouched down behind the bumper.

"Daddy, I'm up here."

But we're not the only two up here.

Joyce. He really did have Joyce with him.

Then he knew where he had heard the voice before. *That one played saxophone.* A cold deadly feeling filled Web from head to toe.

Web slowly stood up and raised his hands. He heard footsteps crashing toward him through the clearing. Bundy emerged, one hand on the gun. With the other he dragged Joyce backward by a pair of handcuffs. Her clothes were torn and smeared with blood. Her bare feet were cut from walking on the stones.

Bundy stood before him.

Theodore Robert Bundy, in the flesh.

Web shook with emotion. Bundy, who should be dead. Bundy, who left his daughter Vicki naked to die in the woods like an animal. Now the man stood before Web. The living incarnation of everything that he despised, the cause of unmeasurable suffering in Web's life. And Bundy had the upper hand.

"Mr. Sloane," he said with a smug grin. "You really have caused me considerable trouble. There are times when a person must, for various reasons, do something that is against his nature. I'm not usually like this."

Web stared. Nothing in the world could stop him from attacking except fear for the safety of his Joyce.

Bundy yanked on the handcuffs, causing Joyce to fall.

"Get up," Bundy said. In the moment of distraction, Web inched closer to Bundy.

"Why did you do this?" spat Web.

"Do what? I don't need to justify anything. I just want you to answer every question I ask you. And I think you will."

Web adjusted his weight on his feet and crept six inches closer to the man.

"First," said Bundy, "how much do you know?"

"About what?" asked Web.

"About me. About Alan DeVries. About Ted Bundy. How did you find out? And who else knows?"

He yanked on the handcuffs. Joyce stood up and faced her father. There were scratches on her stomach from the gravel.

Anger overcame Web, and without thinking he smashed his cast into Bundy's outstretched arm.

The gun went off. Web fell to the ground. He looked at his hand. A bullet had torn through his wrist. Blood oozed out of the cast. A spasm shook through his arm and slowly crept up to his shoulder. He tried to block out the pain, but it felt as if his whole arm had swelled to ten times its size.

Bundy yelled. "Okay, smart guy. If I don't like your answers, I fire the gun again." Bundy obscenely stuffed the barrel of the gun into Joyce's mouth, until she gagged. Web grabbed the hole in his cast, but the blood slowly leeched out. Pain crept through his body like a nest of poisonous spiders. Web knew one thing: Bundy never left any witnesses. The time to act was now.

Suddenly anger overcame Web and a power he had never known surged through him—here was his personal nemesis. He would beat him or die trying.

Web pretended to stumble. He groaned and fell to the ground, grabbing his hand. The crowbar was inches away. He snatched it with his good arm, turned, and pounced on Bundy.

Bundy pulled the trigger. Joyce screamed. But there was only an empty click. Web had counted the shots off carefully. Six. The gun was empty.

Web pounded the crowbar directly across Bundy's forearm, knocking the empty weapon across the dirt. Bundy howled, then turned and ran into the woods. Web ran after him. He yelled back at his daughter.

"Get away, Joyce! Now!"

It was so dark Web could only navigate by the sound of Bundy's feet ahead of him. Web felt dizzy from loss of blood. Sharp twigs clawed his face as he blindly ran through the woods.

All at once, he emerged from the trees and the moon burst through the clouds, making the world visible again. A thin strip of tall grass separated him from the edge of the universe. The vast Pacific stretched out five hundred feet below. He looked to the left, then to the right. Bundy was nowhere to be seen.

Web carefully took several steps, staying a couple feet away from the edge, when he was violently knocked to the ground.

Bundy's knee smashed into his back, and he felt his head forced repeatedly into the ground, an elbow smashing into his skull. He could feel the consciousness receding. *This is what he did to Vicki. If I die, he'll get to Joyce.*

Anger rushed into him like an elixir. He heaved himself up, taking Bundy backward with him. He smashed the cast into Bundy's nose. Blood gushed out of his assailant's nostrils. Bundy drew his hands to his face and emitted a feral cry. Web leaped onto him, knocking him to the ground.

Web's foot pinned Bundy's arm to the ground; now his knee was on the man's chest. He forced Bundy's neck under the cast and pressed with brutish force. Bundy's face bulged and began to turn purple. Web grunted and pushed tighter on Bundy's neck, determined to end the killer's reign of terror right then and there. A single word kept flashing through his mind: *Die! Die! Die!*

But then he heard a voice.

"Don't, Dad! You can't. Stop it!"

Joyce stood behind him, tears streaming down her face. The horror he saw there brought him back to himself. He had nearly killed a man with his bare hands in front of his daughter. Gradually he made a connection with the passionate world that she represented and loosened his grip enough to let Bundy breathe.

Bundy wheezed and drew in his breath.

"Where's the keys?" Web asked.

Bundy spat out blood, then answered. "Right pocket. Don't kill me. Please don't kill me."

"Get them."

Web held his cast on the man's throat and kept his knee on his chest. Bundy reached up to his pocket and produced a set of keys, then tossed them toward Joyce.

Joyce knelt down. With her hands behind her back, she lifted up the key ring. She shuffled through the keys until one fit the lock. It took a long moment to unlock the first cuff, then she brought her hands in front of her, and unlocked the other. Deep bruises on her wrists showed where they had been fastened. The bruises made something in Web snap.

"You son of a bitch," he said. Web flipped Bundy to his stomach, then shoved his bloodied face into the ground.

"Give me the handcuffs, Joyce." Web moved around so that he held Bundy's neck with the cast and took the cuffs in his good hand. He pulled Bundy's face up by the hair.

"Put your hands behind your back," ordered Web. Bundy put one hand behind him, and Web fastened the metal to the wrist. Then Web drew himself up, keeping his arm around Bundy's neck, and his good hand on the cuffs. Bundy lifted himself slowly, appearing to cooperate.

Web grabbed his other hand, and just as he was about to fasten the second cuff, Bundy spun around and flung the loose handcuff into Web's face. The swinging metal cut a deep gash above Web's eye. In an uncontrollable rage Bundy threw himself on Web and encircled his neck with the chain from the handcuffs, drawing them back hard.

"You'll never stop me," hissed Bundy. "No one can stop me." Bundy lifted the cuffs up high, across Web's throat, pulling his head backward to an inhuman position.

Web sucked for air, but none came in. The chain across his neck dug into his flesh, deeper and deeper, unstoppable. The world began to go black. Web's eye caught Joyce. *Can't die, can't die, CAN'T die, MUST NOT DIE.* He whipped back his head, smashing it into Bundy's face. Bundy lost his grip.

Web spun around and cracked Bundy's jaw with the cast.

A rock slipped out from Bundy's foot, and he tumbled to the ground.

Bundy stood and tried to regain his balance, putting up an arm for someone to help him up. As Web extended a hand, Bundy grabbed hold and yanked with all his might.

Bundy's fingernails dug into Web's arm as they stood precariously on the cliff's edge. Web lashed out and pounded onto Bundy's shoulders.

Suddenly, Bundy was gone.

Web looked on as the events played in front of him like a bad dream.

It seemed to take hours for Bundy to fall backward, reaching out. He flailed his feet for something to stand on, but nothing was there. He performed the dance on air of the condemned.

Bundy's arms flapped helplessly, and he looked as if he were underwater, his mouth formed into a perfect circle, eyes darting from Web to Joyce then back to Web again, as he slipped away into the void.

The man grew smaller and smaller. Halfway down to the ocean, Bundy bounced against a protruding rock like a rag doll and ricocheted out toward the sea. Web would never forget the terrible cracking sound that was Bundy's spine snapping in two like a schoolchild's pencil. And he kept falling.

The scream receded until it was cut short by the sounds of tree branches cracking and then the dull thud as the body slammed into the rocks at the bottom.

Then, all they could hear was the roar of the ocean pounding against the rocks.

"Dad! Daddy-O!"

Web embraced his daughter. "Joyce."

He wrapped his coat around her and they walked together through the woods back to the car, back to safety, back to the world. Web felt his step grow lighter. The crickets chirped frenetically, as if in relief.

40

Web collapsed from blood loss shortly after flagging down a passing truck; Joyce waited by his side until the ambulance came. Father and daughter rode to the Bel Mar hospital together.

When Web woke up the next morning in a hospital room, it took a few moments for his eyes to focus. He looked down; his right arm was immobilized in a new cast that ran to his shoulder. He felt slightly stoned from painkillers.

Maria de Rivera stood in front of him; next to her stood Jack Reynolds. Web strained to talk; a feeding tube running through his nose and down his throat made his voice sound slightly alien.

"Where's Joyce?" he asked.

Maria sat by his side. "She's resting now. She was treated for shock and had some bruises and cuts, but the doctors say she will be fine."

Reynolds stepped forward. "She told us some of what happened. She says you killed a man last night."

"Not just a man, Reynolds. You know damn well I killed Ted Bundy," Web said.

"Our men found his prints all over the place. But they've gone over every square inch of the site and haven't found a body."

Web sat up until the tube yanked at his nose. The pain killers were wearing off. A steady throbbing was growing in his left hand.

"What?" he yelled. "Take me out there. I'll show you where he died. I want to see the body. I have to know that he's dead."

Maria stroked his hair with her hand, trying to make him lie back down. "Relax, Web. You are badly hurt. You cannot go out there."

"I can and I will," said Web, then groaned as a sharp pulse of pain shot through his hand. He grimaced. "Take me out there, Jack."

"Web, why don't you just tell me where it is. I'll show you a map," said Reynolds.

"It was night. I don't know the location well. I have to go with you."

Reynolds slipped out and returned with the attending surgeon.

The balding, red-haired doctor leaned over the bed and spoke in soft, quiet tones. "Mr. Sloane, it would be disadvantageous to your recovery to leave the hospital. Perhaps you should tell Agent Reynolds where to look. He'll go."

Web gritted his teeth and forced out the words. "What would you do with me if the hospital was on fire?" he asked.

"We're in no danger here, Mr. Sloane. You ought to . . ."

"What would you do?" repeated Web.

The surgeon looked to Reynolds, who nodded his head.

"We would put you on a stretcher or in a wheelchair and remove you to another hospital."

"Get me a wheelchair then."

The surgeon rolled his eyes and drew Maria and Reynolds to another part of the room.

"This is highly irregular. He's under my care, and I can't advocate this frivolous transportation," said the surgeon.

"He is very strong-willed. If there is any way to move him, I suggest we do it," said Maria. "I am sure he will not take 'no.'"

"You people are crazy," said the surgeon.

"If you don't believe he's serious, look over there." Reynolds pointed at Web, who was choking and spitting while he pulled the feeding tube out through his nose.

"Jesus Christ!" said the doctor.

Reynolds put his hand on the doctor's shoulder. "Can it be done?" asked Reynolds.

"Yes, it can."

"Then let's do it."

Web signed several malpractice waivers and within the hour was carried out of the hospital on a stretcher.

The ambulance was crowded. Web rested on a stretcher wrapped in blankets. Next to him was Maria de Rivera, and next to her sat Jack Reynolds. A paramedic monitored the patient during the trip.

By the time they got to the Sun Holiday Campground, a light rain was falling. Evidence vans, FBI cars, and state police cruisers were parked at the entrance to the campground. A flatbed truck with a winch and crane was parked just inside the campground. Reynolds climbed to the front of the ambulance and flashed his I.D. card at the flunky who was supposed to keep gawkers out.

Bright yellow tape labeled POLICE LINE demarcated the area where two cars were parked: Web's Volvo and the red Volkswagen Cabriolet. Five men were busily erecting a tarp over the whole parking lot to keep the rain from tarnishing any evidence.

The ambulance came to a stop.

Web opened his eyes. "We're here."

"Yes," said Reynolds. The agent opened the backdoor of the ambulance. "You can tell us where to look."

"Stop dicking around, Jack. I'm going with you."

* * *

Web looked like a disabled Ottoman potentate: Two FBI agents carried his wheelchair through the woods, and a third held an umbrella over his head. Parading behind were Jack Reynolds, Maria de Rivera, and several evidence specialists, one of whom took photos every ten feet or so. The disgruntled paramedic brought up the rear.

"Straight ahead," said Web. "We went into the woods there." He pointed to the thick brush.

The procession passed silently through the woods, emerging at the cliff's edge.

"To the right. Further down. Right about here. This is where it happened."

"What happened, Web? What was it?" asked Reynolds.

"I pushed him over the cliff."

Reynolds spoke into a walkie-talkie. "Point to base, point to base. We need that chopper now. In four minutes I'll shoot a flare. Tell them to hover and wait for further instructions. Over."

"Ten-four," came the reply.

"You can go back to the ambulance if you want," said Reynolds.

"I'll stay," said Web.

The paramedic threw up his hands.

Maria stood by Web, holding an umbrella over both of their heads.

A few minutes later, Reynolds fired a brilliant orange flare into the air. Almost immediately, a Huey police chopper emblazoned with the FBI logo roared overhead. Reynolds spoke into the walkie-talkie.

"Sky One, can you see us? Over." asked Reynolds.

"Ten-four. What're we looking for? Over."

"A man's body should be on the rocks directly below us. Over."

"Ten-four. We're reconnoitering the area now. Over." came the radio reply.

The helicopter made several passes, swooping over the assembled crowd, creating a tremendous roar and blowing leaves and dust. On its third pass, an excited voice came over the radio.

"Visual contact with body. Near the inside of the cliff, prone, looks like white Caucasian male. Over."

"You got a climber and a winch in there, right, Sky One? Over." asked Reynolds.

"Ten-four. Sending climber down now. Over."

Web watched with great fascination as two cables were lowered out of the hovering whirlybird. One rope held a stretcher; from the other hung a man dressed from head to toe in black. The ropes extended down below the cliff's edge. Web couldn't see where they were going but heard the radio reports.

"This is Special Agent Geiss. I've made contact. Victim is DOA. Fastening to stretcher. Over."

There was a long pause as the gathered group waited breathlessly. Then another transmission came.

"You can haul it up. Careful—some local gusts down here. Over."

Reynolds spoke into his radio. "Put it down up here. Over."

The helicopter drew in a cable, straining at the additional weight. All at once, the dangling cargo came into view. A man's body laid out on a stretcher. The stretcher turned frenetically in the wind and chopper wash. As it spun around and grew nearer, Web could make out details. The corpse was bent over, one arm contorted into an unnatural position, the face covered with blood.

The chopper pulled up and deposited the cargo twenty-five yards from the gathered group. The black cable detached itself from the stretcher and slithered back into the chopper, which roared away.

Web heaved himself out of the wheelchair.

"No!" yelled the paramedic.

"Out of my way," said Web, pushing the man aside.

Web hobbled over to the spot where the body rested. In the short walk a million thoughts crowded for Web's attention. He thought of Vicki. His beautiful daughter. She might have been a doctor by now if Bundy hadn't cut her down in the prime of life. He remembered the way that Bundy had confessed to his heinous crimes, trying to buy himself time, without remorse for his victims or compassion for their families. *That one played saxophone.*

Web thought of Joyce. Resting in a hospital now. But if Bundy hadn't been stopped, Joyce too would have been senselessly slain. As he struggled across the tall grass, his eye caught Maria's. A strong woman, a good woman, a woman who had done nothing to deserve the untimely loss of a daughter. How many more grieving families would there have been if not for Bundy's complete destruction? He had to see for himself. He had to know that Bundy was dead.

The agents gathered around the corpse cleared a path for Web and watched him cautiously. He dropped to his knees by the body's side and stared into the face.

There was no doubt: It was Bundy. The corpse's complexion was pale green from blood loss, and rigor mortis had twisted the arms into an unnatural pose. A loose handcuff dangled from one wrist. Bundy's sharklike eyes stared angrily at the world, cold and evil in death as in life. Even though the body was cold, Web impulsively grabbed a wrist to feel for a pulse. He had to be absolutely certain.

"You can't touch him," yelled Reynolds.

"I've earned it," said Web.

Reynolds backed off.

The arm was rock hard. There was no pulse; not a trace of life left in the body. Web dropped the wrist. A smile worked its way across his face.

He slowly stood up. Ted Bundy was finally dead.

For a moment, the pain of his injuries disappeared. Web felt rejuvenated; he could see a new future opening itself ahead of him, like the sun emerging from behind clouds.

Web embraced Maria. For the first time in fourteen years, he finally felt peace of mind.

By the time they got him back to the hospital, a dozen news crews were stationed strategically by the door. They yelled questions at Web as he was rolled back to his hospital room, but he completely ignored them. Once they were inside, Web, Maria, and Joyce closed the door to his room.

"Daddy-O, did you see all those news crews?"

"Yeah. So what?"

"You wanna talk to them?" asked Joyce.

"Joyce, go to the nurse's station and ask if I can meet them in here. Tell her that tomorrow morning at 8:00 A.M. I'll talk to every single one of them at once—with one provision."

"Yes?"

"Under no circumstances whatsoever will I talk to Clinton Bernard or anyone from 'Suspect at Large.'"

Web, Maria, and Joyce all laughed. Nothing would annoy Clinton Bernard more than the knowledge that every news station in the country had the most sensational crime story of the decade—and he didn't.

Epilogue

September 22, 1991

Dear Joyce,

You'll have to excuse my sloppy writing—I still haven't regained full use of my right hand and have another operation (my third) just before Christmas that they "promise" will fix everything up.

I hope that you're taking time out to study during your first semester at college (ha ha). Since you haven't written or called very much, I assume you're having the time of your life.

The months of hearings with the FBI, police, and Congress finally seem to be drawing to a close. One result is that I've been named to head an official citizen advisory group—a job that will pay your college tuition plus some. I won't bore you with the details, since you had to suffer through the hearings all summer, but I've gotten enough frequent-flier miles from trips to Washington, D.C., and Florida that we should be able to go to Europe this summer for free.

Jack Reynolds and I buried the hatchet over eighteen holes of the worst golf I think any two human beings could possibly play. If I hadn't blabbed so much during our game, I might have played better than a 112 and Jack wouldn't have swiped my brilliant new teaching assistant.

Renny McDonald's going to work his way through college testing computer security systems for the FBI. He's as happy as a drunk in a distillery, since his whole job will be to try to break into their computer systems *(with their permission, of course) to expose security problems. I wish he'd work with me, of course, but you can't make a kid like that spend his life Xeroxing exams.*

Just like the kid said, when the Berkeley Department of Defense contract talks turned into the huge skimming controversy, they needed someone untainted who was still qualified to head up the new artificial intelligence project—and, according to the rumor circuit, guess what name tops the list?? Renny heard about it six months early, of course, but I prefer the "aboveboard" method.

You may wonder how come the cookies I've put in this package aren't burned to a crisp as usual. The truth is, I'm as bad a cook as ever, but it wasn't me who made them. Maria gets the credit. She and I have decided to get married this coming spring. We were wondering if you'd be so kind as to be the maid of honor at the wedding. I hope you'll say yes.

Love,
Daddy-O

P.S. Flowers are FINALLY blooming, and all over the yard! You should see them. Roses, chrysanthemums, daffodils, spread out randomly through the whole lawn, wherever Mud decided to bury them.

ONLY ONE YOUNG POLICEWOMAN STANDS
BETWEEN A MAD KILLER AND YOUR

DYING
BREATH

A Novel Of Terror By
JON A. HARRALD

Simon Proctor has come across the
country to put down his bloody roots in
the peaceful suburb of Stoneham. He
won't leave until he's claimed his prey
and fulfilled his vile, deadly needs.
Marianne Byrne, a brilliant young
policewoman, is piecing together the
clues following her instincts into a living
nightmare. Simon Proctor is about to
take her on a terrifying journey into the
heart of human evil...

POCKET
BOOKS

Available from Pocket Books